Tom Holt was born in 1961, a sullen, podgy child, much given to brooding on the Infinite. He studied at Westminster School, Wadham College, Oxford, and the College of Law. He produced his first book, *Poems by Tom Holt*, at the age of thirteen, and was immediately hailed as an infant prodigy, to his horror. At Oxford, Holt discovered bar billiards and at once changed from poetry to comic fiction, beginning with two sequels to E.F. Benson's Lucia series, and continuing with his own distinctive brand of comic fantasy. He has also written an historical novel set in the fifth century BC, *The Walled Orchard*, and has collaborated with Steve Nallon on *I, Margaret*, the (unauthorised) biography of Margaret Thatcher.

Somewhat thinner and more cheerful than in his youth, Tom Holt is now married and lives in Chard, Somerset, just downwind of the meat-canning factory.

WISH YOU WERE HERE

Tom Holt

ORBIT

An *Orbit* Book

First published in Great Britain by Orbit 1998
This edition published by Orbit 1999

Copyright © Tom Holt 1998

A CIP catalogue record for this book
is available from the British Library.

ISBN 1 85723 687 4

Typeset by Solidus (Bristol) Limited
Printed and bound in Great Britain by Clays Ltd, St Ives plc

Orbit
A Division of
Little, Brown and Company (UK)
Brettenham House
Lancaster Place
London WC2E 7EN

For John and Mary Creasey
and Joe Bethancourt:
Sweet Charioteers.

CHAPTER ONE

'Yes, sir,' said the tiresome old man, leaning back in his rocking chair, 'that there's Lake Chicopee right enough. Ain't no other lake like it in all of Iowa.'

Below them, the lake lounged motionless in the late morning sun like a well-fed cat in a window-seat. Because it's surrounded on all four sides by the crests of the Chicopee Hills, the wind seldom ruffles its surface, making it one giant mirror. Accordingly, unless you look closely, you don't actually see a lake; just a ring of ingrowing mountains and stalagmite pine trees surrounding an oval of blue. That, perhaps, was what the old man was referring to; or maybe he had something else in mind.

'Thanks,' muttered the motorist, glancing sideways at his watch. 'So to get to Oskaloosa we just follow this road until it brings us out on the . . .'

'They do say,' the tiresome old man continued, lighting his corn-cob pipe and blowing smoke in the motorist's face, 'that this here lake's haunted.'

The motorist coughed pointedly. In New York, blowing tobacco smoke in someone's face would get you arrested for assault with a deadly weapon. 'Is that so?' he said, trying his best to load each syllable with patent lack of interest. 'If I just follow this road as far as . . .'

'By an ole Injun spirit,' the tiresome old man said, 'name of Okeewana or some such. Now I lived in these parts all my life and I never seen her, but who's to say, huh? Who's to say?'

A scowl swept across the motorist's face like an empty polythene bag windblown across an empty car park. 'Who indeed? Look, I don't want to seem rude, but . . .'

'They do say –' The tiresome old man leaned forward, giving the motorist a unique opportunity to study at first hand the effects on tooth enamel of sixty years of chewing tobacco and industrial-grade bourbon whiskey – 'that if you're lucky and meet that ole spirit and jump in the lake after her, she'll grant you anything you truly wish fer.'

'Look—'

'And if you're *really* lucky,' he added, with an evil grin, 'you drown first.'

When the motorist's car had disappeared over the skyline – going the wrong way, but some folks just won't stop to listen – the tiresome old man smiled indulgently, shook himself like a wet cat and turned into a beautiful young girl. Then she stood up, disappeared the rocking chair, the quaintly tumbledown timberframe house and the white picket fence, and ran down to the shores of the lake. Duty done; time for a swim.

However long it was that she'd been here – it seemed like for ever, which is no time at all – in all that time she'd never grown tired of swimming in the lake. Sometimes she would be an otter, floating on her back or scudding like a sleek brown torpedo a few inches under the roof of the water, letting the bubbles stream after her like a dragon's tail. At other times she'd be a trout or a duck, occasionally a human; it all depended on the weather and the time of year, the mood she was in, whether she was working or off duty. There were all manner of delightful things to be in a lake; and that was only on this side of the surface. Underneath the reflection, on the mirror's flip-side, the possibilities were, of course, infinite.

Today, it was her fancy to be a water-beetle. Having first scanned air and water for unfriendly birds and fish, she took a deep breath, drew down her mind into the tiny parameters of beetlehood and found herself balancing on legs thinner than her own eyelashes, standing on the surface of the water. It was a tricksy metamorphosis – the difficulty being how to get any purchase on the meniscus of the lake, rather like ice-skating with a single six-inch nail strapped point downwards on each foot instead of a nice wide blade – but the exhilarating effect of being able to scamper over the surface of an element that usually prided itself on always getting the last word generally made up for the time expended in mastering the art. As soon as that first, inevitable wave of shape-changer's panic had died away she began to feel the sheer bliss of unlimited choice, with nothing to interfere with her pleasure except a very slight breeze setting up a few trivial ripples, and the occasional wolf-whistle from the male water-beetles hanging round a belly-up dead fish a few yards further out. This, she reflected, is the life.

Her mind, or at least the tediously sentient part of it, was on the point of floating away when her insect vision caught sight of a human shape making its way down the southern slope of the encircling hills. A customer. Damn.

With a faint buzz she opened her wing-case, spread her wings and sawed up off the surface of the water, making a noise like a tiny Japanese motorcycle engine.

She wasn't the only one to have noticed the new-comer. On the opposite side of the lake, high up in the branches of a tall pine tree, Talks to Squirrels shaded his eyes with his hand and did some complicated mental arithmetic.

Range: seven hundred and fifty yards. Windspeed: five, maybe seven miles per hour. Allowance for thermal currents rising off the warm surface of the lake: well, his best guess would have to do, so say five degrees. In which case, let x equal the coefficient of drag . . .

With an ease that mere quartz could never hope to achieve, his mind sifted the numbers, made the corrections, compensated for the effect of air-pressure on an irregularly knapped obsidian arrowhead spinning anti-clockwise against the wind on a sunny day and gave him the precise angle and the exactly quantified weight of draw on the bowstring that would have allowed him, if he was still alive, which he wasn't, goddamnit, to stick an arrow smack bang in the middle of the intruder's eye-brows. In his mind's eye he could see the spiralling flash of the arrow's fletchings against the blue sky, the pear-shaped curve of its descent, and (short pause, while his mind's eye changed lenses) the look of dumb incredulity on the sucker's face as he realised he'd suddenly and unexpectedly been taken dead. Hah! I'd have had you, you bastard, except for a technicality.

Remember the furious indignation you used to feel when you were young and the teacher kept you in after school for something you hadn't actually done? Quite. Think how much worse it must be to be kept in after life.

And it *hadn't* been his fault, damnit; because they'd

started it, with their treaties and railroads and forked-tongue promises. Fair enough, he hadn't exactly loathed every minute he'd spent in the armed struggle for his nation's liberty; but so what? How can it be wrong to enjoy doing well a job that has to be done? A skilled woodworker making a fine job of a difficult piece of carpentry is allowed to feel good about it; so why not a warrior? Hadn't been any of this fuss before *they* arrived. Great Spirits, but what wouldn't he give for just one more shot. Just one.

He sighed, and the world of the living would have heard the wind softly mussing the branches of the tree. While he'd been calculating and pondering on his wrongs, the scumbag had moved. Range now seven hundred and twenty yards, windspeed now dropping, let y be the effect of the archer's paradox. Ah, shit, it just isn't *fair* . . .

If only he hadn't fallen in the goddamn lake.

The beetle had landed.

It shook itself and studied the newcomer. Was he, it wondered, the observant type, the sort of man who'd notice a timberframe house with picket fence, stoop and rocking chair and realise that it hadn't been there a moment ago? Probably not; a dreamer, if ever it had seen one. Quite liable to fall in the lake of his own accord, simply by not looking where he's going.

Still, duty called. A heartbeat later, he tasted the bitterness of tobacco in the back of his throat, breathed out a thin plume of smoke through his nose and set the chair rocking.

'Howdy,' he said.

The young man looked up. For an instant the tiresome old man wondered if perhaps he'd underestimated the lad, because there was just a tiny flicker of puzzlement in his eyes as he looked up and saw the house for the first time. But if his subconscious mind had noticed anything, it kept it to itself. The young man blinked, said, 'Hello,' in an unfamiliar accent, and turned back to stare at the lake.

Unfamiliar? No, it was just that the tiresome old man hadn't heard it for a very long time. A Britisher, by the Spirits; a direct descendant, maybe, of the dim-witted clowns who'd passed this way three hundred years or so since.

Hum. Unlikely to be a direct descendant of that lot. Where they'd gone, people don't have descendants. A relative, maybe. Sixteenth cousin thirty-two times removed, something like that. A collector's piece, at any rate.

'Mighty fine view of the lake you get from here,' the tiresome old man observed. A blue cloud rose over his head and hung there for a moment.

'Yes.'

'They do say,' continued the tiresome old man, 'that this here lake's haunted.'

'I know.'

'Haunted by an ole— you do?'

The young man nodded. 'That's why I'm here,' he said.

'Gosh darn,' muttered the old man, taken aback. For technical reasons too complicated to explain, he knew he wasn't dreaming; but to get a mark who'd actually come here on purpose – hell, if he was inclined to be paranoid he'd be looking for a trap of some sort. 'Yup,' he continued lamely, 'the ole Injun spirit of Lake Chicopee . . .'

'Okeewana,' the young man recited, 'Daughter of the West Wind. If you throw yourself in the lake, she grants you your heart's desire.' He made a peculiar noise with surplus breath and his teeth, which the old man recognised as a sigh of rapture. God *damn*it! 'I saved up for two years to come here,' he added. 'In the Post Office. You know, I still can't believe I'm actually here.'

I know the feeling, the old man said to himself. I can't believe you're actually here either. Still; the thing to bear in mind when dealing with mortals is never to give them an even break. 'Where you from, son?' he asked, and blew a smoke-ring.

'Brierley Hill,' the lad replied. He couldn't be more than twenty-five; tall, unfinished-looking, the sort of man who doesn't look like he's dried properly until he's about forty. Looking at him, the old man felt an overwhelming urge to fold him up and put him neatly away. Somehow, he made the world look untidy. 'That's near Birmingham,' the lad went on. 'England.'

'Is that so?' Birmingham? After my time. Tentatively, he probed the youth's mind for an image of the place; the result was strange, to say the least. Hell, whatever will they think of next? 'Well, you sure's tarnation a long way from home here, bud. Is she like you figured she'd be?'

'No.' The lad shook his head. 'It's better. It's really – you know, amazing. All that water and stuff.'

So what did you expect to find in a lake? Porridge? 'And you reckon you know all 'bout ole Okeewana,' he continued, feeling ever so slightly as if he was advising his grandmother to bore a small hole in the pointed end, taking care not to crack the shell. 'They do say . . .'

'It's been my ambition, like,' the boy went on. 'Ever since I was twelve. I got this book out of the library, *Myths And Legends Of Many Lands*. All in there, it was.' He paused, and seemed to be bracing himself as if to confess some dreadful sin. 'I like all that stuff, mythology and things.'

'You do, huh?'

He nodded. 'I think it's great. I think I like the Aztecs best, but you can fly here direct from Birmingham and anyway, I can't speak Spanish. Plus the exchange rate's better. My mum works in a travel agent's.'

The old man frowned. Following the kid's train of thought was a bit like trying to find the end of a rainbow with your eyes shut. 'They do say,' he persevered, 'that if you was to jump in this here lake . . .'

He paused. He could feel vibes.

Talks To Squirrels! Put that thing down, for pity's sake, before you injure somebody.

Hell, 'Kee, I'm only practising. All I can do these days, practise. You should know that, better than me.

Cut it out, Squirrels, before I cut it out for you. And maybe later, if you're good—

Huh. You always say that.

Actually, I've got a good feeling about this one. And if it does come off, you can have first crack at him. Promise. Honest Injun.

'Kee, that wasn't funny the first time you said it.

The youth was looking at him curiously, as if he could hear echoes of the unspoken words. The old man pulled himself together.

'Sorry, kid,' he said, rallying gamely. 'Reckon I was miles away. When you been living here long as me, you get so's you think you hear things that ain't there, if you know what I mean. And just now, darn it if I wasn't sure as I could hear that ole spirit calling to me . . .'

Thanks to his unique insight into what goes on under the surface of lakes, the old man actually did know the look on a fish's face just before it takes the baited hook; a sort of stupid, greedy, well-bugger-me-there's-lunch-just-hanging-there sort of a grin that generally tends to dissipate any sympathy you might have for the fish. Just such a look was spreading over the lad's face, swiftly and indelibly as blackcurrant squash on a white rug. *Yessir, got me a sucker*, rejoiced the old man's soul, as it slowly began to turn the reel.

And lay off the Tom Sawyer stuff, will you, 'Kee? You're about as convincing as a five-dollar Rolex Oyster, and you're giving me a pain.

'Really?' the kid was saying. 'You can actually, like, *hear* her? That's *unreal.*'

'Hey, son, you can hear her for yourself if you just mosey on down to the edge of the water.'

There are some fish so gullible you don't need to bait the hook. They're the ones who look up at the three-sixty-degree sky and say to themselves, *Hey, wonder what it must be like up there, and wouldn't it be just great to find out if only I could find some way out of all this boring old water.* They're the ones who say, a fraction of a second before the gaff cracks them on the head, that it's one small tail-flip for a fish but a giant splosh for fishkind.

'Wow!' said the kid. 'You know, I might just do that.'

With a big silly grin all over his face, he set off down the hill. The old man watched him go, sighed a little, and shook himself.

'Yes,' said the editor, leaning back in his chair and loosening his tie. 'That's one hell of a story.'

'I know.'

The editor swivelled his chair round and scrolled back through the text on the screen. Occasionally he paused to nod his head, grin and catch his breath.

'One hell of a story,' he repeated.

'Yes.'

'I particularly liked,' the editor said, 'the way you link

it all up at the end. Must have taken some doing.'

'Not really.'

'Ah.' The editor rubbed his chin. Something; not a worry, not even a niggle, as such. On the other hand, the *Tribune*'s circulation was up four per cent and the *Globe* had run rings round him with the Hudson Bay radiation leak scare. Something like this could change all that. Overnight.

'I really liked the bit where you link that guy the President's hairdresser's uncle was at high school with to the car smash where that ecology activist's arm got broken, which has never been conclusively proved not to be a bungled CIA hit attempt.' He chewed his lower lip thoughtfully. 'That had, you know, overtones. Could mean absolutely *anything*.'

'Thank you.'

The editor grinned. 'And that bit about the leading US company supplying components to the Brazilian company that supplies components to the French company that made all the filing cabinet divider cards used by Sadam Hussein during the Gulf War. Masterly. No other word for it. Their stock's gonna go through the floor when this hits the stands.' He frowned, and made a mental note to call his broker.

'Yeah. It's a pretty damn good story.'

'Good?' The editor gestured vaguely. 'It makes Woodward and Bernstein look like a couple of old guys doing a gardening column.' He frowned. 'Just one thing,' he added. 'You couldn't work in anything about Kennedy, could you? Only we haven't had a good JFK conspiracy story for . . .'

'Three weeks.'

'OK, OK,' grumbled the editor. 'Three weeks is a long time in journalism.' He flicked through the story again.

'Here,' he said, pointing. 'In this bit where you link Mark Twain with the rise of the Hitler Youth. Couldn't you kinda just squeeze it a bit and—?'

'No.'

'No?' The editor pulled a little face. 'Fair enough, I guess it's your baby. All right, how about here? The part where you claim the guy who's doing all the Senegal famine relief stuff is really Klaus von Mordwerk, the Butcher of Chartres. If you just . . .'

'No.'

'Huh? Pity. Because, you know that bit where you say his birth certificate says he was born in 1957 but it's all a fake because really he was kidnapped by aliens who whizzed him round the galaxy at seven times the speed of light, so he only looks forty years old even though really he's ninety-seven; if you were to imply that the same aliens were the ones who snatched Kennedy—'

'No.'

The editor shrugged. 'You know best,' he said. 'It's just I hate to see an opportunity going to—'

'That's the follow-up. For next week.'

'Ah.'

'I suggest you put Chlopeki on it. She needs the experience.'

The editor nodded, and reached for a cigar. He was just about to light it when it was taken from his hand, snapped neatly in two and dropped in the bin. 'Sorry,' the editor said sheepishly. 'I forgot.'

'Don't.'

'Which reminds me,' the editor added. 'That bit where you attributed Rasputin's madness to passive smoking while he was a novice in Kiev. Do you think we could work that up into a major feature? Only, we haven't had a passive smoking scare for, oh . . .'

'Two days.'

'Right. Yeah, well, we could call it a follow-up. You know; *write your congressman NOW!!!* kinda thing . . .'

A shrug. 'You can if you like. Look, I'm really glad you liked the story, but I haven't got time right now. I'll catch up with you when I get back, OK?'

'Back?' The editor looked up. 'You off somewhere?'

'Yes.' Linda Lachuk nodded. 'Iowa. Looks like something big.'

'Another one? Hey.'

'No.' Linda allowed herself a thin smile. 'That one you got there's just a bit of fun. The Iowa thing is *big*. See you.'

The editor opened his mouth and closed it again. 'Hey,' he said, 'bigger than this? What's the story?'

Linda shrugged. 'You'll see.'

'Just a little hint?'

'Let's see, then.' Linda sat down on the corner of the editor's desk. 'We've got a secret nuke installation that's causing ecological havoc, maybe even bending the fabric of the space/time continuum, and it's all tied in with the clandestine arms scandal, which means . . .'

'Huh? What clandestine arms scandal?'

'This one,' Linda replied. 'The big question will be, did the President know about the existence of the second-generation tapes? And then, when we bring in the women's health issues, not to mention the cute little furry animals angle . . .'

The editor's face slumped into a stunned grin, so that he looked like a lemming version of Cortes gazing with a wild surmise at the Grand Canyon. 'There's a cute little furry animals angle?' he breathed.

'There's always a cute little furry animals angle,' Linda replied casually. 'If not express, then implied. You just gotta look for it, is all.'

Which was true, the editor admitted, as he recalled Linda's own stunningly innovative slant on the farm subsidies story. Who else, he asked himself, would have dreamed of leading with a full-page close-up of the cutest little mouse you ever saw, under the screamer: CONDEMNED TO DIE!! ('*If secret plans now being rushed through Congress are allowed to go ahead, millions of cute furry mice like Wilbert will be ruthlessly exterminated as callous farmers sadistically prepare grain silos for expected megabuck bumper harvests . . .*') He closed his eyes, and grinned. 'Way to go, Linda,' he said. 'I can hardly wait.'

Linda nodded and stood up; and the editor reflected, not for the first time, that for one person to be so incredibly successful, so stunningly beautiful, so completely integrated and at one with her lifestyle, wasn't perhaps the way it was supposed to be with human beings. Maybe, he surmised, she's got this really awful-looking painting in her attic. Or maybe not. If she had, she'd have made a story out of it long since.

With an ethnic rights angle to it, probably. Not to mention the cute little furry animals.

Ninety feet above the surface of the lake, the duck air-braked, banked sharply and turned.

Because a part of its mind, unused even after all this time to lightning-fast changes of body, was still being a tiresome old man with a corn-cob pipe, the duck made its way slowly down the sky, taking care not to pull a wing muscle or dislocate an arthritic joint. The rest of its mind used the response-time lag to assess the situation and demand to know, one last time, where the catch was. Too easy, it screamed. Nobody, not even a goddamn Brit, is this daffy. It's got to be a set-up or something.

Got to be.

But, the duck reflected as it lowered its undercarriage and aquaplaned a silvery gash through a reflected mountain, if there's a catch, buggered if I can see it. Not that I'm in any position to pontificate right now, what with being a duck and all. Stupider creatures than ducks are hard to find, if you leave out the sort of life-form you can comfortably fit on a microscope slide.

Having gathered its wings in tidily to its sides and preened them with its bill, it turned to face the shore and settled itself down to watch. Any minute now, there was going to be a loud splash.

Four. Three. Two. One.

Splash!

When the kid stopped flying through the air and touched down on the water, he fell through the reflection of a rocky outcrop on the south-western crest of the hills, smashing it into thousands of tiny shards of image. As he struggled to keep his head above water, each shard was further fragmented, making the surface of the lake a mosaic of tiny bits of hillside, each one perfectly mirrored but no longer making up a whole recognisable anything. When the kid finally realised that the swimming techniques he'd learned in the municipal swimming baths of the West Midlands didn't seem to work in the admittedly unusual waters of Lake Chicopee, the reflection healed up over his head with surprising speed. Four and a half seconds after the first splash, the ripples had stopped and the mirror was unbroken once more.

You get seven years for breaking conventional mirrors. That's a conditional discharge and an apology from the judge compared to the penalty for disturbing this one.

Glug. A last few air bubbles floated up and burst.

The duck put its head down, and dived.

★

Oh God, Wesley Higgins said to himself as the water filled his lungs, *I'm drowning.*

Entirely against his will, he breathed in water through his nose. It felt –

Good. Odd, that. Hell, it felt *healthy.* Fresh, clean water and plenty of exercise. Just what the doctor ordered.

Hang about. I'm not drowning. I'm bloody well floating. I'm floating on top of the water.

Surely not; but it felt like floating. Mind you, the water in his lungs felt like air, so who was he to judge? Every scrap of logic remaining in his oxygen-starved brain yelled at him that this was Death; if not the real thing, then an introductory free sample designed to encourage him to sign on for the full course of treatment. *No way he could still be alive.*

And yet here he was. Floating on his back, like a damn Poohstick. And alive too, by every indication he could monitor. For a start, don't drowned people float face down, just a few inches under the surface? He'd read somewhere – at school, probably – that they do.

He opened his eyes and saw the sky, oval-encircled by a rampart of hills and a fuzzy ring of trees. All perfectly normal, except –

Except that they were all back to front, turned through a hundred and eighty degrees, mirror-fashion. For two pins, he could make himself believe that his body, the long, embarrassing thing he'd shuffled around in all these years, really was bobbing along upside down on the surface of the lake. And here he was, floating serenely on the underside and staring at the sky. And breathing the water.

Query: was the water safe to breathe in these parts, or should he have brought along an aqualung full of Perrier?

Did they even have Perrier in Heaven?

Who said anything about Heaven?

The voice seemed to come from inside his head. Maybe, he reflected, this was how it started for Joan of Arc. One day she'd been relaxing in a nice pine-scented bath, just like I'm doing now, and suddenly there were voices in there between her ears; quiet, whispering little voices just like this one, saying wasn't it a scandal, all those English people coming over here buying weekend cottages and second homes, forcing property prices up, writing books about how comical the locals are, it's high time somebody did something about it. And the next thing she knew, of course, there she was tied to this big hunk of wood and some grinning bastard was waving a burning torch at her and saying, Now then, this may hurt a little. With hindsight, she'd have done better to buy a Sony Walkman and drown the buggers out till they went away.

Joan of Who?

Arc. It's a place. In France.

Excuse me, but I think you're wrong there. Because according to what you've got in your memory banks, it's either a segment of a circle or a big boat full of animals. No, hang on, I tell a lie. Here we are, Joan of Arc. Hey, going on what you've got in here about her, she doesn't seem like a terribly nice person.

'She was a *saint*, damnit,' Wesley said aloud. 'And who the hell are you, anyway?'

Would it help if I came out of your ear? No offence, but it's not exactly a welcoming environment, not unless you happen to be a bee.

Something went *pfzzzz!* in his ear, and a moment later he caught sight of a round, beady black eye, on a level with his own. It seemed to be inset in a pointed, furry head with a sort of Disney-cuddly face and whiskers. He looked at it. It looked at him.

'Hi,' it said. 'I'm an otter.'

First voices in his head, now talking animals; spiffing. Dying and going to Heaven would have been nice. Dying and going to hell – decidedly lower down on his list of preferences, but still well within the scope of his expectations. Dying and going to *The Wind In The Willows* struck him as insult added to injury, with ice, lemon and a sprig of mint.

'I expect you're wondering,' the otter said, 'what's going on.'

Wesley would have nodded; but as far as he could tell he was playing fast and loose with the laws of physics just by being there, lying on top of water he'd drowned in not two minutes earlier. The slightest movement on his part might draw attention to the fact that by rights he should be under the surface, not on top of it.

'Yes,' he said.

The otter dived, resurfaced, flipped over onto its back and drew alongside him, like a launch beside a tanker. 'I'm not surprised,' it said. 'This must all seem rather strange to you. In fact, you're probably thinking you must be dreaming or mad or something. All perfectly normal.'

If, half an hour earlier, someone had told Wesley that later on that day he'd find comfort and reassurance in something an otter had told him, he'd have been sceptical, hard to convince. Only goes to show what a difference thirty short minutes can make. 'Normal?' he whispered. 'What—?'

The otter waggled its wee forepaws. 'This,' it said, 'is Lake Chicopee. Remember? The place you've come all that way just to see?'

'How d'you know that?'

'You told me. And you recall what happens when you jump in Lake Chicopee when the water's still?'

'You drown.'

'Oh no you don't,' the otter contradicted cheerfully. 'If you were drowning you'd be saying things like *glblblblblbbbbb* right now, take it from me. When you jump in Lake Chicopee, your heart's deepest wish comes true.' The otter made a face which, on a human physiognomy, would be a smirk. 'And so it has.'

It crossed Wesley's mind that if his subconscious deepest wish was to be floating on a lake talking to an otter, maybe drowning was too good for him, but he decided not to say it out loud on diplomatic grounds. 'It has?' he said.

'You bet. Your deepest wish,' the otter continued, 'is to find release from this mundane, commonplace world by bursting into some wild, fantastic adventure in a magical realm where anything is possible. Am I right or am I right?'

Wesley considered for a moment. 'Well . . .'

'Oh come on,' the otter said briskly. 'I was in your mind, remember. I can see the interior of your home. A bedsit over a chemist's shop, right?'

'Well,' Wesley replied dubiously, 'yes, I suppose—'

'We open the door,' the otter went on. 'Directly in front of us on the wall is a map of Middle-Earth, framed. You know your way round it better than you know the centre of Birmingham.'

'Actually, that's not difficult. They haven't got a one-way system in Middle-Earth.'

'To our left,' the otter continued, 'is the bookshelf, covering the whole wall. And what do we find? Tolkien. C.S. Lewis. The complete works of Anne McCaffrey.

Yards of the stuff, enough dreams to float the Graf Zeppelin. To our right, ignoring the unmade bed and the rather disgusting mound of used laundry, we have the mantelpiece, which is covered in skilfully painted lead figurines representing elves, dwarves, orcs, wizards, heroes, disturbed-looking young women with big swords and hormone imbalances, trolls, giants, self-propelled trees, dragons – they come in three sections, and the wings can be displayed in the open or folded position – and God only knows what else. Melt that lot down and you could re-roof the Vatican.'

'No! I mean, you lay off my collection. Taken me years . . .'

'Ever since you were twelve,' the otter agreed. 'Have I proved my point, or shall we take a peek inside your wardrobe?'

'All right,' Wesley snapped. 'You can make fun all you like. I still don't see what that's got to do with lying on my back in a bloody lake talking to an otter.'

'You don't?' Amusement permeated the otter's voice like the writing in a stick of rock. 'Then you're being deliberately dim, friend. Oh, I didn't mention the life-size handcrafted Franklin Mint replica of Excalibur, on which you still owe nine instalments. Late at night you draw the curtains, take it down off the wall and do feints and little slashes with it. There's a great big hole in the wardrobe door you're hoping the landlord won't notice, though from what I saw of him while I was inside your head, he's not the sort of guy who's going to be fooled by chewing gum and shoe polish.'

Wesley thought hard. Excalibur. 'You're the Lady of the Lake?' he hazarded. 'But I thought—'

'This is a lake,' the otter replied. 'The rest's just a matter of morphology and capital letters. Principle's the same, I guess. What it all boils down to is, you're a very sad kid who's never grown out of fairy stories. Yes?'

Despite the various disadvantages he was obviously under, Wesley couldn't let that pass without rebuttal. 'No I'm not,' he replied. 'There's nothing wrong with me. I've got a car. I've got a responsible job in a building society.' He remembered something which struck him as being of great evidential value. 'I've got a personal pension plan,' he added triumphantly. 'With the Norwich Union.'

The otter looked at him. 'Bully for you,' it said. 'Do you want your heart's desire or not? Because if you'd rather go back to your bedsit and your spavined Metro and your screen in Mortgage Processing, you've only to say the word. And you'll prove my point, while you're at it.'

'Yes, please,' said Wesley 'It may not be much, but it's what I am. And I'm not a loony, like you're trying to make out I am. And,' he added savagely, 'I don't talk to otters. Let me out of here.'

The otter looked at him gravely with deep black eyes. 'No,' it said.

Before he could argue further, the otter grabbed him by the scruff of the neck and started to tow him towards the shore. He struggled and tried to kick, but the water around him was thick and unbelievably heavy, like mercury, and he found that he wasn't strong enough to move it out of the way. Another thing; there were no ripples on this water as he moved through it, unwillingly and backwards. He simply slid through reflected mountains and trees, as if he was the image and they were real. He felt as if the lake was the screen and he was a movie being projected onto it. It wasn't the happiest of sensations.

'All right,' he said. 'Will you slow down, please?'

The otter, which had been cracking on at a fair rate, decelerated. 'Is that better?' it asked. 'If you're going to be sick, please don't throw up on the mountains, they stain as soon as look at them. We're nearly there, anyway.'

'Are we?'

'Nearly.'

Calvin Dieb parked his car at the side of the road under a tall fir tree, pulled his binoculars out of the glove box, and turned to look at the lake.

Lake Chicopee, Iowa; several thousand acres of the most enchanting, mouth-wateringly promising real estate he'd seen in the course of a long and vigorous legal career. It seemed to call to him; in the sighing of the trees, the soft plashing of the waters, the sound-kaleidoscope of birdsong. 'Develop me!' it was saying. 'Make me pay!'

Right opposite where he was standing, they'd have the shopping mall; and next to that, the drive-ins. On this slope, where he was standing, the first phase of residential, with its unrivalled view of the health complex below, phase two on the left, phase three on the right, and a big fluorescent plastic M dead ahead. If they decided to keep the water, the M would reflect nicely, especially at night.

It had taken God, he reflected, seven days to make this. His clients would take seven years, but they'd do a *proper* job. Not that he was knocking God; the guy hadn't had the advantages. For a start, He hadn't had the benefit of top-flight legal advice from Hernan Piranha and Cal Dieb. All in all, it was a miracle the roof hadn't fallen in yet.

But that's what lawyers are for; to put the Real in realty. He scanned the lake and caught sight of something moving on the surface of the water. A fingertip adjustment to his executive Zeiss binoculars revealed it to be just an otter, furrowing the water and pulling runs in the reflections like unravelling knitting. Dieb frowned. He'd heard horror stories of dream deals crashing head-long to the ground, their wing-wax melted by the presence on-site of one miserable rare bird or endangered frog. Only last month, he'd been talking to a guy at a seminar who'd nearly lost a deal because of Lexington's Vole; except that the guy had had the foresight to fly in ten crates of heather-buzzards from Colombia and have them turned loose one dark night when the protesters were too cold to keep a proper watch. The buzzards had scarfed up the voles inside a month; and, since the birds were even more protected than the wee rodents, there was nothing anybody could do. Then, when the food supply was exhausted, the buzzards had moved on, leaving the site clear for the diggers to roll. Best of all, the feathered pests had taken residence on a neighbouring development site owned by clients of a rival law firm, and put them out of business. It put a whole new slant on the term legal eagles.

Wonder what eats otters? Something must. He murmured a few words into his pocket dictaphone. Wolves? Bears? Giant turtles? Were otters a big deal anyway? Probably worth checking while he was here. He took his phone from his belt.

'Cindi? Is Jack there? Thanks. Jack, otters. Yeah. Look, I'm at the Lustmord Corporation site and it's ankle deep in goddamn otters. Can we waste the buggers or—? We can? Good work, Jack. Ciao.' He snapped the phone shut and put it away; another crisis averted, another five hundred bucks on the bill. It was turning into a good day.

But, he reflected as he swung the binoculars round, just because otters weren't going to be a problem, it didn't necessarily follow that there weren't a whole load of other furry saboteurs out there all poised and ready to pounce. Now sure, he could wait for the report; but then he'd be getting the data at the same time as the clients, which wasn't his style. Far better to be able to turn to Frank Lustmord at their next meeting and say, 'Oh, and by the way, Frank, you'll be pleased to hear we've got the Van Sittaert's Rat situation nicely in hand.' And Frank would look worried and say, 'I didn't know we had a Van Sittaert's Rat situation, Cal,' and then he could say, 'This time next week you won't, Frank'; and that'd be worth another ten grand, possibly even a step closer to getting Lustmord's corporate acquisition business. Worth a little mud on the trouser leg, particularly since he was doing it on Frank's time.

He returned to the car, pulled on a pair of thousand-dollar gumboots and started off down the slope towards the lake. It wasn't easy going underfoot; bits of the hill tended to break off under his heel, roll down and go splash in the lake. He tried not to watch them; heights made him nervous, and if he were to fall and injure himself horribly, he wasn't quite sure who would be the appropriate person to sue. A fine fool he'd look, a man in his position, ending up all hideously mangled and not a cent in damages to show for it. Above all, he didn't want to fall in the lake, because he couldn't swim. Well, why should he? Never, in twenty years in the legal profession, had he found occasion to include in any of his bills the entry: *To swimming, pursuant to your instructions* .... *$1,000.00* – so why bother with it? If any swimming ever needed doing, he could hire some guy. From an agency or something.

He felt a stone break loose under his left foot, listened as it bounced and clattered down the hill and heard the splash as it hit the water.

Trouble is, there isn't always an agency handy when you need one.

Perhaps, he decided, quickly, it would be a good idea to stay exactly where he was until he'd had a chance to collate relevant data, assess the position as regards short, medium and long term eventualities, formulate a plan of action and only then implement it. He did so. Then he started to yell for help.

'Howdy, mister,' said a voice behind him. 'Fine day again. What you hollerin' fer?'

'I need help,' he replied, not turning round. 'I'm stuck.'

'Don't look stuck to me,' said the voice. 'What's the matter? Put yer foot in a bear-trap or something?'

Being rooted to the spot, he couldn't turn and look at whoever it was, but the voice alone was enough to rough out a picture in his mind. It was one of those folkloric, old-fashioned All-American voices that go hand in glove with the expression 'old-timer'. It wasn't a section of American society he was familiar with. Presumably they did go to law sometimes – all Americans go to law sooner or later – but they never walked into his office, quite possibly because they couldn't afford to talk to his receptionist, let alone him. He assumed they consulted check-shirted, chaw-chewing, four-wheel-drive-driving, stoop-sitting, harmonica-playing, sandpaper-chinned lawyers with offices over lumber mills in towns with quaintly evocative names; the sort who still use embossed letterhead. On the other hand, their legendary woodcraft and oneness with the environment probably made them experts in the field of getting people off dangerous hill-sides. In any event, it was a fair bet that the concept of money as a reward for services had permeated this far by now.

'Get me off this goddamn hillside,' he said, 'and I'll give you twenty bucks.'

Behind him he could hear a wheezy cackle, like a bad telephone connection in a high wind. 'Say, mister, why don't you just walk back up the hill and save the twenty bucks?'

'I can't. I'm stuck.'

More cackling. 'You mean you're too darn scared.'

'Yes. Look, get me out of this and I'll make it fifty bucks.'

'You got it.'

As fingers like steel rods gripped his arm and wrenched him up the slope, he was already wondering whether he might not have been too generous in his offer. Twenty bucks cash and a Piranha & Dieb gift voucher, fifty dollars off the divorce of your choice, might have done just as well.

'You OK now?'

He opened his eyes. Below him, the lake sparkled. The otter, still ploughing its way through the water, was nearly to the shore. A few mallard pitched out near the western edge, shattering a mirror mountain.

'I think so,' he said. 'Jesus, I was scared there for a minute. It's a long way down.'

'Sure is, mister. I recollect you saying something about fifty dollars.'

Why am I not surprised? 'That's right,' he said, turning round. 'Will you take a cheque? Only I haven't . . .'

He stopped. Facing him was no grizzled old wood-whittler, as traditionally portrayed in the movies by Slim Pickens; instead, he was staring at a beautiful young girl, with straight black hair, skin the colour of peanut butter and the lissome grace of a top-flight defence attorney squirming his way past the prosecution's key forensic evidence.

'No cheques,' said the vision of loveliness, her full lips slightly parted. 'Strictly cash.'

Whereupon she put her foot in the middle of his chest and pushed him back down the hill.

CHAPTER TWO

'Sorry?'

'I said,' Wesley repeated, 'are we nearly there yet?'

'What? Oh, yes, right.' The otter nodded a couple of times. 'I was miles away,' it added. 'Look, here we are. You can wade from here.'

Whereupon it let go of Wesley's collar. After a few panic-stricken kicks he managed to get his feet onto something solid, and stood up, to find himself still waist-deep in water. Straight ahead of him was the lake shore. He waded towards it, and the water seemed to drift away from him as if it was some heavy, swirling gas. He wasn't at all wet. His knees hurt, and he had pins and needles in his feet.

'Hurry up,' the otter called.

There was something odd about its voice. Up till now, it had been a sort of falsetto squeak, the way you'd expect an otter to sound if you'd been brought up on cartoons. Now there was a rather more human tone in it; feminine, even.

'I'm coming as fast as I can,' he shouted back. 'My feet have gone to sleep.'

'Probably got bored waiting for the rest of you. I haven't got all day, you know.'

As Wesley limped up out of the water, a human figure appeared from behind a rock. The sight of it stopped him in his tracks.

Facing him was no sleek-furred water-mammal; instead, he was staring at a beautiful young girl, with straight black hair, skin the colour of peanut butter and the lissome grace of an elf-maid at a Broadway audition. Wesley, who had always tended to regard young women with the mixture of admiration and apprehension that a dedicated trainspotter might feel at the sight of a perfectly restored vintage steam locomotive coming straight at him down a tunnel at seventy miles an hour, wasn't entirely happy at the substitution. Somehow, he knew he'd be better able to cope with talking otters than girls; especially pretty girls.

'Welcome to your heart's desire,' said the pretty girl.

In the circumstances, Wesley took it quite well. It wasn't the usual sort of thing that girls, pretty or otherwise, tended to say to him. Even short, circular girls with complexions like the skin on cold custard tended to talk to him as if he was something they'd just trodden in. To be welcomed to his heart's desire by something out of one of the better-class mail order catalogues was something entirely new. It was as if, a second or so before the train hit him, he'd realised that it was a 1930s' Castle class Swindon-built double-chamber locomotive in fully authentic GWR livery, still retaining its original glass oil-valves.

'Oh,' said Wesley, beetroot-coloured from collar to hairline. 'You mean . . .'

'Get real,' the girl replied (normality has been restored; we apologise for any inconvenience). 'I mean, we're now on the other side of Lake Chicopee. You understand what that means?'

'No.'

The girl sighed. 'Fine. Then I'll tell you.' She sat down on the rock, pushing her hair back over her shoulders in a way that made Wesley want to climb a tree and hide in a hornets' nest till she'd gone away. 'I'm not sure how observant you are, but did you notice something about the lake? How perfectly it reflects everything around it?'

'Sure,' Wesley replied, truthfully as a newspaper. 'What about it?'

The girl swung her head, so that her hair swayed. 'The surface of the lake's a sort of mirror-fronted door, like the ones you get in shops and bathrooms. That's rather a confusing way of putting it, but you'll get the general idea later on. There's the side you come from; let's call that topside. We've come through that and now we're on the flipside. It's an exact mirror image of topside, except that here the rules are different.'

'What rules?'

The girl shrugged, doing things to parts of her anatomy that Wesley really didn't want to know about just then. 'Any rules you like, that's the whole point. On Flipside, the world's the way you want it to be.'

'Oh.'

'Or rather,' the girl went on, 'it's the way you *think* you want it to be. You made a wish when you jumped in the lake. Right?'

Wesley nodded.

'What you wished for, you got.' She smiled, rather unpleasantly. 'Whether you like it or not. Go forth and enjoy.' She yawned, putting one hand over her mouth and the other behind her head. 'You get the bill later.'

'The *bill*—?'

'Of course the bill. You think I run this place as a public service? Yes,' she added, looking at him, 'probably you do. I don't suppose such concepts as overheads and maintenance and repair mean an awful lot to you. Remind me later on and I'll let you see last year's accounts.'

Her tone of voice made Wesley feel he ought to apologise, though he wasn't sure what it was he'd done wrong. The least he could do, he reflected, was try and show a little enthusiasm. The fact that he didn't really believe that any of this was actually happening was neither here nor there; even if it was only a dream, he reckoned that he stood a far better chance of waking up if he didn't antagonise anybody until he was safely back under his own duvet, with Old Mister Sun beaming in at him through the mildewed curtains. 'I'm sure you're right,' he therefore said, 'and I didn't mean any offence, honestly. It's just I didn't realise . . . I mean, I spent all my savings on the air fare, so if there's going to be a bill to pay, maybe we'd better call it a day now.'

The girl grinned at him, making him wonder exactly what she was. A few moments before, she'd been an otter. Before that, if his intuition was correct, she'd been an old man with a pipe. Now, with that grin on her face, she looked just like a wolf.

'I wouldn't worry about that,' she said. 'I don't render the sort of bill that money can pay.' She paused for effect, and then continued, 'After all, if it was money I was after, I wouldn't need to bother. Money's easy.'

Wesley blinked. He didn't know precisely how many adjectives there are in the English language – a hundred thousand? Quarter of a million? Five million? – but there were a hell of a lot, and virtually any of them seemed more appropriate than easy when applied to money. 'Gosh,' he said. 'You reckon?'

'Yes,' the girl replied; and it started to snow banknotes. Before Wesley had time to move, he was up to his shins in crisp, new thousand-dollar bills. He didn't need to hold one up to the light to see that they were genuine; somehow it went without saying. He took about a second and a half to recover from the shock; then he started grabbing with both hands.

'If it was just a matter of money,' the girl went on, as a sudden gust of wind blew a heavy drift of thousand-dollar bills straight into Wesley's face, 'my job would be a doddle. If giving you your heart's desire was as simple as sending you home with enough of those things to fill a large container lorry, believe me, I'd be absolutely delighted. Trouble is,' she said, with a sigh that made all the money vanish as suddenly as it had come, 'it isn't. Money wouldn't solve a thing. You'd just be a rich fuck-up instead of a poor one.'

'You know what they say,' Wesley muttered, his hands still tightly clenched on what was now nothing but empty air. 'A change is as good as a rest. I'm prepared to give it a go if you are.'

'That's terribly sweet of you,' the girl replied, vaporising a thousand-dollar bill that had somehow managed to get lodged down the back of Wesley's neck, 'but it'd only make me lazy. No, I know what you really want, and I intend to see that you get it.'

Wesley made a little whimpering noise and sat down on the ground. He wasn't sure he understood this dream. If his heart's desire wasn't the gorgeous girl and it wasn't all that wonderful money, what in hell was it? Later, he resolved, he and his heart were going to have a serious talk about the meaning of the word *priorities*.

'All right,' he said. 'You've told me what it isn't. Now tell me what it is.' A disturbing thought crossed his mind. 'Hey,' he said, 'if this turns out to be one of those time-share presentation things and the free gift's really only a radio alarm clock, I'm not going to be happy.'

'Be happy. It's not that.'

'Then what is—'

'*Look!*'

Linda sat back in her seat, waved away the offer of a drink, and gazed out of the window at the clouds below.

Iowa.

She frowned. Deplorable but true; she knew only two things about Iowa. One, that it was big, dull and agricultural. Two, it was reputedly the birthplace of James T. Kirk.

Briefly she considered these two nuggets of wisdom and came to the conclusion that there wasn't a story angle in either of them. A pity; because, like Pythagoras, Linda lived her life by and for angles, and accordingly straight lines bothered her, in the same way as a vacuum is reckoned to bother Nature. As far as she was concerned, if you can't crack it open and pick news out of it, there's not much point in it being there. By those criteria, they might as well dig up Iowa and use it to line window-boxes in New York.

Nevertheless; by some divine mistake the Story to end all Stories was happening in Iowa. To be precise, at a place called Lake Chicopee, a little-known beauty spot situated in the exact geometric epicentre of nowhere.

She wrinkled her exquisite nose. As far as she could make out, there were Strange Happenings at Lake Chicopee. Mostly, it was people disappearing; but there were also uncanny sights and noises, weird manifestations, things appearing, disappearing and changing shape, things going bump in the night. She switched on her laptop and waited for the lights to stop flickering.

Seven people, five males and two females, all of them from out of state, had last been seen or heard of setting out to walk to the lake. No bodies, possessions, footprints or bloodstains had come to light, though for some reason the police department adamantly refused to drag the lake. Among the manifestations there was a long, low ship that appeared and disappeared, strange whispering voices in the woods, unexplained lights and animals and birds that were supposed to have changed their shape in clear view of what passed in Iowa for reliable witnesses.

Yes. Well.

Those, then, were the raw materials:

- Lake
- Remote
- People disappearing
- Boat appears and disappears
- Funny lights
- Cute furry animals changing shape

As the great silver bird sliced its cloud-splitting way like a light-sabre through wedding cake, Linda typed the ingredients in and read the list back two or three times, occasionally changing the order and flipping across to the readership profile database. Then she took a deep breath, flexed her shapely fingers, and set to work.

When a cook cooks, he gathers the ingredients before him and makes them into something. He doesn't wait for them to march into the pot and semaphore a message to the cooker to switch itself on. He doesn't agonise over whether the carrots really belong in the sauce or whether the parsnips are true. He goes to it with a container, a source of heat and a big sharp knife.

She paused, scrolled back and noticed an omission, which she rectified by typing in:

• Native Americans

– which was likely enough; and in any case, the casserole needed them. She had to have Native Americans or there wouldn't be an R to go with the C, the A and the P:

• Conspiracy
• Racism
• Animals
• Politics

Put 'em together and what do they spell? News.

Weird things happening in a remote spot = secret Government scientific research. Funny lights and things mutating = nukes. People disappearing – see above. A *ship* that appeared and disappeared; on a *lake—*

She furrowed her brows, bit her lip and let her mind off the leash.

Sherlock Holmes' law, as amended to fit the require-ments of journalism. Once you have eliminated the unnewsworthy, whatever remains, however improbable, *will* be the truth . . .

Yes!

Submarines. Secret Government nuclear submarines. Neo-fascist CIA warmongers were covertly stockpiling Armageddon submersibles in America's heartland, not giving a damn about the catastrophic effects on the cute furry environment and the cute furry Native Americans, cold-bloodedly jeopardising world peace with the intention of . . .

Of?

Yes, murmured her internal devil's advocate. Why would anybody go to all that trouble? Not, of course, that a motive is essential; people will believe that the Government will do anything, provided they can be made to appear to be covering it up. On the other hand, there's nothing quite like a good solid motive for building a story that'll keep going for a week. Leave it all shrouded in enigmatic over-tones and by Day Three you'll find yourself sandwiched in between the film reviews and the crossword.

Motive?

Linda clicked her tongue, reproaching herself for her lack of vision.

Obviously, they were doing it secretly because they were planning to give the submarines as clandestine military aid to a sinister foreign power.

Right.
Database; SFP/LIST.
Crossreference; readership profile database.

Only a fool would choose an SFP that'd offend half the readership. Merge; and—

'Oh,' she said aloud.

She looked at the screen. She raised an eyebrow. On the other hand, it must be right, or it wouldn't be on the screen. After all if you can't trust the database, what can you trust?

• Vatican City

OK, clandestine military aid to the Vatican. Saint

Petergate. Pausing for a moment to speculate as to why the paper had so few readers among the Irish, Italian and Hispanic communities (bad business; must do something about that), she filled in the bare facts with some mental colour.

Vatican? Well, it was beginning to make sense. Most people knew next to nothing – she knew next to nothing – about the recently elected Pope Shane III, formerly Cardinal Archbishop of Adelaide. On the other hand, very little real hard news ever seemed to come out of Australia; and it stands to reason that any country that goes out of its way to be obscure and secretive must be up to something. She tapped a few keys, and the screen read:

• Australia — State Department backing — ultimate aim world domination.

Which was much more like it. After all, nobody ever claimed that Australians were a minority of any sort, so she could say whatever the hell she liked about them and nobody'd be in the least offended.

She sighed contentedly and looked out over the clouds again, consolidating the progress so far in her mind. In unspoilt idyllic environmentally sensitive Lake Chicopee, renegade CIA elements are funding a massive program of clandestine nuclear submarine building, with the sinister intention of funnelling Armageddon technology through the Vatican to the warmongers of the shadowy, secretive Australian ruling junta. Psychotic antipodean death squads with corks round their hats are systematically wiping out anybody who happens to stumble across this terrible secret, including the once flourishing Native American population, who stand by helpless as their proud cultural heritage is ground into dust under the jackbooted paw of the kangaroo. Meanwhile, your tax dollars are going to help fund the greatest threat to world peace since Genghis Khan.

She smiled, saved the file and closed her eyes. As she drifted into sleep it crossed her mind that one day the world might of its own accord produce enough genuine organically grown news to satisfy the needs of the global media, in which case she wouldn't have to do this sort of thing any more. Which would be a pity; but that day, if it ever came, wouldn't be in her lifetime. They'd just have to start up more newspapers and more TV channels and more radio stations, just to redress the balance.

Having bounced off a couple of rocks and a tree-root or two, Calvin Dieb came to rest in a tangle of briars.

Once he'd realised he wasn't dead a number of thoughts crossed his mind, all of them to do with money.

First; he'd been crazy to offer fifty bucks to someone to get him off the hillside, because in the event he'd been able to roll down it with only superficial scratches and bruises to show for it.

Second; in the time he'd taken to roll down the slope, he could have earned, at his usual charging rate of two thousand dollars an hour, eighteen dollars and forty cents.

Third; he would willingly pay the cash equivalent of ten hours of his time to anybody who would show him where that goddamn lunatic female had gotten to, and provide him with a large, sharp knife.

He stood up. Because of his involvement with the briar patch, this entailed a certain amount of ripping of his five-thousand-dollar trousers, but he was (a) past caring and (b) so heavily insured that he was in danger of becoming a gravitational anomaly and attracting his own meteorite belt. Someone else was going to pay – heavily – for this whole episode in any case, so the hell with details.

Thoughts of money always inspire strong emotions in lawyers, and this particular train of thought aroused in Calvin Dieb a flashback of anger of the intensity usually reserved for rival law firms who filched his richer, more gullible clients. As he gained his feet and sent out search parties for his breath, his anger started to cool; or rather to temper, becoming harder and more capable of keeping an edge. Forget the sharp knife, he muttered to himself, and bring me a writ. And, more to the point, bring me someone I can sue.

After all, he told himself, as he removed a length of bramble from around his ankle, kill a guy and there's an end to it. Sue him and you can do to him in this life what the devils in Hell will do to him in the next, only rather more thoroughly. They didn't phase out trial by combat because it was too cruel; quite the reverse.

But all that could wait. In the morning, he'd have a team of investigators down here to get him the name, address and financial details of the crazy broad who'd pushed him, and in the afternoon he'd send in the cops and the process servers. Right now, he wanted to get back to his office, where iodine would heal his wounds and foreclosing on some poor bastard would salve his mind. He looked up at the gradient he had to climb, took a deep breath and reached in his pocket for his car keys.

His car keys . . .

Psychiatrists say that the fundamental subconscious anxiety that all men suffer from, and which underlies all their actions, is a morbid fear of castration. Wrong. Unzip any man's mind and you'll find, right down there in the dark, terrifying place where the soul never goes, a primeval dread of losing his car keys. Just think how many times a day you instinctively reach in your pocket or pat your hip, just to know they're still there. Upon Calvin Dieb, already thorn-ripped, humiliated and physically and mentally out of pocket some tens of thousands of dollars, there descended the horrifying realisation that he had been gelded of his keys and that his car, the external expression of everything he was, now sat useless and undrivable in the lay-by above.

Shit!

He stood for some ninety seconds, tracing by eye the path of his fall from the crest of the slope, where he'd encountered that goddamn female, down here to the very shore of the lake. Anywhere along that line his keys could have fallen out. It could take him hours – tens of thousands of dollars – to find them in all this scrub and undergrowth. On the other hand, it would take him at least nine thousand dollars to walk to the nearest town, another thousand or so to wait for a car or a helicopter to come out from the city and pick him up, not to mention all the pain and suffering involved in walking too far in boots as expensive as those he was wearing. It's an odd fact, but an undeniable one, that once you start paying four-figure sums for footwear you tend to end up with magnificently hand-stitched instruments of torture that reduce the backs of your heels to raw flesh if you do more than hobble from your car to the elevator; part of the price you have to pay for being rich, he'd always rationalised. As it happened, he had in the trunk of the car a pair of worn-out old sneakers, $4.99 from K-Mart, that were the nearest thing a mortal could ever experience to floating on a cloud. If he only had his keys, he could go back up there and put them on. If only . . .

OK. Forget the writ. Forget even the three fingers of

single malt and the hot tub that had started to figure prominently in his subconscious thoughts. What I really want now, more than anything in the whole world, is to find my goddamn keys—

Just as the thought crossed his mind, he tripped over a briar-root, fell heavily, tumbled down a steep incline, hit a boulder and rolled off a rocky ledge into the still, calm waters of the lake.

A second or two later, an otter slid into the water and began swimming out towards him.

'Look!'

So Wesley looked. But there wasn't anything to see—

Except, in the far distance, a ship. No, the *reflection* of a ship, an upside-down mirror image of a dragon-prowed, clinker-built, square-sailed fifty-oar longship, a black pinewood killer swan with brightly painted round shields all along its sides in the manner of a Hawaiian flower wreath.

'Bet you never knew,' the female was saying, 'that the Vikings got this far. Well, they did. Two generations after Eric the Red reached Newfoundland, this lot—' she waved vaguely at the mirror-ship. 'This lot, fifty fearless explorers led by Thorfinn Piglet and Einar Bluetooth, sailed down the coast until they blundered into the mouth of the St Lawrence river, which they rather liked the look of. So they pottered down that, past Quebec, into Lake Ontario, where they ran into a little problem known to you and me as the Niagara Falls. Now we both know that there's no way on earth to get a ship by there; but they didn't, so they took it to bits, plank by plank and nail by nail and little-widgetty-thing-that's-always-left-over-once-you've-put-everything-else-back by little-widgetty-thing-that's-always-left-over-once-you've-put-everything-else-back, and they carried it down into Lake Erie, where they put it together again and went on their way; past Cleveland and Toledo, except they weren't called that then, of course; past Detroit, across Lake St Clair and down the St Clair river into Lake Huron.' The girl paused. 'Are you taking any of this in, by the way? I mean, you do know where all these places are?'

'What? Oh, yes,' Wesley lied. 'Course I do.'

'That's all right, then. I'd hate the awesome scope of their achievement to be wasted on you just because you think Lake Erie's in Cumbria. Anyway, off they go across Lake Huron, all the way round the fair state of Michigan, passing through the Mackmac straits into another whopping great big lake which happens also to be called Michigan, either through coincidence or a stunning lack of imagination. So there they are, skirting Lake Michigan, and they see Green Bay. They're sick and tired of Lake Michigan by now, so they hang a right and toddle down the Bay, down the Fox river, sometimes carrying that damn boat more often than it carries them because of all the falls and rapids and so on; then they bear right again and get lost in lots of itty bitty rivers, the sort that make a country look like it's got varicose veins. Just as they're starting to feel depressed, they trip over the Wisconsin river and follow that; and when it merges with the Mississippi, they follow that; and when they're bored with the Mississippi, they branch off down our very own local-river-made-good, the North Squash; and one quick taking-to-bits-and-putting-back-together-again later – they're really good at that by now, by the way; they can take that boat to bits and put it back blindfold and wearing two pairs of gloves – here they are in Lake Chicopee, bright-eyed, bushy-tailed and eager for whatever new nugget of happenstance Fate chooses to bestow on them.' The girl paused and gazed at the two-dimensional longship under the shadow of her palm, so that Wesley couldn't see her expression. 'In about five minutes,' she continued, 'they're due to hit the one submerged rock in the whole lake, sink and drown. Pity, really.'

Wesley stared at her. 'Why?' he demanded.

The girl shrugged. 'They felt like it. Not the sinking part, of course, the rest of it; they felt like going for a run out, and one of them had this boat, so why not? I think the captain muttered something about wanting to travel courageously where nobody had been yet. Some people are like that.'

'Yes, all right,' Wesley interrupted. 'I can understand that. But what I mean is, after that really incredible journey, why've they got to go and get drowned *here*, of all places? I mean, it's so flat. I mean calm,' he added, before the girl had a chance to point out that lakes are usually flat, which is what stops them falling off the edges of hills and turning into rivers. 'I mean, how the hell could anybody drown in *that*?'

'You nearly managed it,' the girl pointed out.

'Yes, but I'm not – I mean, *I* couldn't have sailed all the way up those rivers and down those lakes.' He stared at the reflection as it slid, noiselessly majestic, over the upside-down mountains. 'Isn't there something we can do to warn them?' he asked. 'Or are they, like, sort of *ghosts* . . .' He shivered a little as a pair of landing ducks splashed straight through the ship, sending bits of it rippling in all directions. 'I mean, is that why we can only see the reflection and not the actual boat?'

The girl watched the reflection slowly take shape again and shook her head. 'Not quite,' she replied. 'In about four minutes they'll hit the rock and come on down this side. Then we'll be able to see them.'

'But they'll be *dead*.'

The girl shrugged. 'You some sort of bigot?' she asked. 'I'll have you know, some of my best friends are dead. Wouldn't want my daughter to marry one,' she admitted, 'but that's not prejudice. It's just, think of all the problems their kids'd face, at school and so on.'

A light-bulb, no more than forty watts but still bright enough to see by, lit up in Wesley's brain. 'Just a moment,' he said. 'When they fall in the lake, you grant them their heart's desire, yes?'

The girl beamed. 'So you *have* been listening!' she cried, clapping her hands together. 'Oh, that's so encouraging. Yes, I certainly do.'

'By drowning them in a lake?'

'Yes.' The girl shrugged again. 'It's like I told you. They get their heart's desire, but it's up to me exactly what form it takes. Now, what these clowns really wanted was to go on an awfully big adventure. Ah,' she added, as the sound of wood splintering on rock echoed around the amphitheatre of mountains and lake. 'Party time!'

The reflection dissipated into another clutch of ripples, out of the centre of which a longship rose, submarine-fashion. Apart from a few wisps of pondweed draped round the top of the mast and a very upset-looking trout thrashing about on the deck, it seemed none the worse for its recent misfortune. The girl stood up and waved.

'Over here!' she shouted.

The ship changed course, until the dragon's head was facing them square-on. The oars started to move, keeping metronome time and sending out great sunbursts of ripples each time the blades hit the water. Wesley could hear wood groaning and rope creaking; he could feel the enormous amount of physical effort it took to propel the great heavy thing just a few yards across the water. It must be, he felt, like pushing a lorry that's run out of petrol.

All the way from Newfoundland, up rivers and down lakes, oarstroke by oarstroke. He felt sick, and his back started to hurt.

'Excuse me.' The voice was coming from the ship. 'Excuse me, please, young lady, but on the right way for Duluth are we being?'

'Duluth?' The girl shook her head. 'No, sorry, you're well out of your way here. About seven hundred miles, give or take a bit.'

'Bother!'

'To get to Duluth,' the girl went on, 'you want to head back to the Mississippi, right back up the way you came as far as Lake Huron; then stick to the north coast round into Lake Superior, carry on hugging the north coast and head west till you come to the pointy bit, you can't miss it. You took the wrong turning.'

'Silly old us,' the Viking shouted back, shaking his helmeted head. 'Joshing us the fellows will be when we are to home returning. Nevertheless the funny side visible is. Thank.'

'You're welcome.'

The ship swung round – Wesley could hear the cracking of joints as arms wrenched in their sockets with the effort – and headed back up the lake, the way it had come. Then it hit the rock again and sank.

'Why Duluth?' Wesley asked, after a long silence.

'Hadn't ever been there, I guess,' the girl replied. 'That's explorers for you. Marvellous people, Heaven only knows where the world would be without them. Actually, it was a cousin of Thorfinn Piglet who was the first man ever to set foot on the North Pole.'

'Gosh!'

The girl nodded. 'Bjorn the Stupid, his name was,' she said. 'He had to walk the last three hundred miles, all on his own. Hell of a journey.'

'He died too, presumably.'

'Oh no.' The girl shook her head. 'Lost quite a few fingers and toes and things through frostbite, but he made it home alive to the Viking colony at Brattahlid. Not all in one piece, but the majority of him.'

For some reason, that made Wesley feel a whole lot better. 'Well, then,' he said. 'So why do the books say it was Scott, or Amundsen, or whoever? I'd have thought—'

'Oh, he never *told* anybody,' the girl replied. 'Too embarrassed. You see, he was supposed to be heading in the other direction. But he got lost, went north instead of east. He'd only set out to deliver a load of timber a few miles up the coast. When they asked him why it'd taken him so long and what'd happened to his appendages, he made up some story about being set upon by polar bears. Nobody believed him, of course. They all assumed he'd got plastered and fallen off his boat into the ice-cold water.'

Wesley didn't say anything for a very long time. He didn't like this dream very much, he decided; it was too depressing, and unlike all his other horrible dreams, which usually involved him standing up in front of a crowded Wembley Stadium with no trousers on, it was just close enough to reality to be thoroughly unpleasant. He sent a memo to his inner brain saying, *Wake up now, please*, but nothing happened.

'There's a point to all this, isn't there?' he said at last. 'I mean, there's a moral or motto or whatever you call it.'

'Correct.' Without taking her eyes off the lake, the girl nodded. 'I suppose you could call it the vanity of human wishes, except that's a bit trite. Anyway, that's a sort of introductory session. Passive learning. All the rest of it's a bit more hands-on, or do I mean interactive? What I'm trying to say is, instead of just sitting there on your bottom and listening, you actually get to do things and have adventures. Isn't that fun?'

Wesley thought about it for a moment. 'No,' he said.

'You don't mean No,' the girl replied cheerfully. 'What you really mean, though you probably don't realise it, is Yes. Trust me, I know about these things.'

Wesley allowed his slump to melt into a crouch. 'Does interactive mean you're going to drown me too?' he asked. 'Or will you let me off with just losing all my fingers and toes?'

The girl smiled. Whether it was a nice smile or not, Wesley couldn't tell. 'Whether you get to keep your fingers,' she said, 'depends rather a lot on whether you pull them out. Come on.'

On the far western shore of the lake, under the shade of a tall pine tree, sat a border guard, waiting for her eggs to hatch.

Throughout the history of conflict, ever since the first primitive humanoid picked up a ploughshare and realised that, with the help of a forge and a big hammer, he could turn it into a moderately efficient sword, every army ever raised has sooner or later taken on the basic diamond-shape form of organisation. At the apex, the uppermost point, you have the top one per cent who make up your élite forces; the guys who swing through windows on ropes and hold off vastly superior numbers while swigging vodka martinis. In the middle come the squaddies, foot-sloggers and cannon-fodder; people of all shapes, sizes and qualities who complain a lot, do as they're told, make of it the best they can and die from time to time, even when the cameras are looking the other way. And, at the reverse apex, the whole thing dwindles away to the bottom one per cent; the incurably hopeless, incompetent and disaffected, neither useful nor ornamental. It's this section of the military community that gets ordered to stand in front of things and guard them. Wherever there's a mountain or tall building that might get stolen, or a lake or river that might burn down, there you'll find a little wooden kennel with a pointy roof, and in it a nerk with a gun, called a sentry.

In this instance, Jemima. So highly was she thought of by the rest of the Lake Chicopee Defence Force that they hadn't actually told her she was in it. It took an atypically bright young lieutenant in the Household Frogs to notice that whenever anything moved within ten yards of Jemima's eggs, be it a moose, a squadron of armoured cars or a falling leaf, Jemima started making a horrible noise which lasted until the thing went away again. All that remained was to move Jemima's nest thirty yards or so to the right, until it was within spitting distance of the border gate, and that was one more loophole effectively plugged, relieving a proper soldier of a boring job and leaving him free to perform the vital function of bashing the butt of his rifle on the ground every time his sergeant yelled, 'Hut!'

There were five of these vulnerable points – known as 'gates' for convenience, though they were more complex than that; think of them as ill-fitting lavatory windows round the back of the cinema of Time and Space, through which the recklessly brave can sometimes climb in to watch the film for free – and each one had a sentry. Because of the peculiar physics of Lake Chicopee, there was no knowing what lay on the other side of each gate at any given moment, or (more to the point) who or what might be trying to get through it. Hence the need for sentries, who had to be fearless, vigilant, not easily bored and, above all, expendable.

Jemima had just completed twelve hours sitting on her eggs facing north–south, and was performing the delicate manoeuvre of turning east–west, when a tiny movement caught her eye. No human, no featherless biped of any description, would have noticed it; nor would the latest state-of-the-art monitoring device, for there was no displacement of air, no microsubtle temperature change, no physical transfer of mass to get in the way of an infra-red beam. In fact, it wasn't so much a movement as a minutely small editing of reality, whereby a few motes of dust stopped being in one place and found themselves in another.

'Ark!' said Jemima. 'Ark ark ark ark ARK ARK ARK!'

'Oh for crying out loud, it's that bloody duck again,' said Cap'n Hat, bravest and boldest of the transdimensional smugglers of Lake Chicopee. 'I thought I told someone to deal with it the last time.'

His henchmen exchanged guilty looks. 'Sorry, Chief,' muttered Squab, Hat's stubble-chinned, eyepatched bo'sun. 'Slipped me mind. Here, I'll shoot the bugger if you—'

'Please don't,' Hat said wearily. 'Quacking ducks are bad enough without gunshots as well. Besides, you'd only miss.'

'No I wouldn't, Chief. I been practising.'

'Squab, my dear old mate, you couldn't hit a large building if you were inside it. Now shut up and let me think.'

Given the amount of noise the duck was making it was inevitable that somebody would come soon, if only to wring its neck. Caught as he was, in the open, in broad daylight, with two handcarts laden down with Flipside plunder that he'd really rather not jettison if he could help it, he was left with a meagre choice of three options; hang concealment and make a run for it, stand and fight it out, or try and find something to hide under. Dismissing the first two options, for he was essentially a realist, he ducked under an ivy leaf and gestured to his men to follow suit.

'Wassat damn racket?' yelled the distant voice of an owl.

'Just that duck again,' replied an equally distant frog. 'Prob'ly seen its own shadow or somethin'.'

'Take a squad an' have a look anyhow,' ordered the owl. 'Just in case.'

Swearing fluently under his breath, Hat peered round the edge of the leaf until he located the frog-squad. Typically, they were directly between him and the gate, which put paid to making a run for it. As for fighting; instinctively he reached for his pistol and thumbed back the hammer, but he knew as he did so that he was hopelessly outnumbered. Indeed, bearing in mind the calibre of the forces at his disposal, he was theoretically outnumbered even when there was nobody there at all.

'Nobody move,' he hissed.

'But, Chief—'

'Shuttup, Twist.'

'Chief, I need a pee. Would it be all right if I just crept very quietly over to those bushes and—?'

Hat was tempted; after all, when Twist crept unobtrusively he was about as hard to spot as an earthquake in central San Francisco. That meant he'd be pounced on and instantly nabbed by the patrol, thereby causing a diversion under cover of which—

'I said be quiet. Should've gone before you came out.

Cross your legs and try not to think about it.'

The smugglers of Lake Chicopee, who make their living by scarfing up props and scenery from the infinite variety of Flipside, sneaking them Topside and selling them, are probably the most extraordinary parasites in the Universe. They're also, of course, a dangerous pest, since many of the commodities they bring across aren't supposed to exist on the obverse side of the lake; dragons and thunderbirds, magic rings, cloaks of invisibility, bottomless purses, seven-league boots and radio alarm-clocks that actually go off when they're supposed to. The damage they do in Reality is mirrored (of course) Down Under. Many's the time a long-lost prince has turned up to draw a sword from a stone only to find that someone's beaten him to it; and by the time he discovers it's missing, the sword has already been sold off a barrow in some street market, making a bemused Japanese tourist the rightful king of all Albion. In other words, the equilibrium is upset. Ripples get into the reflections.

The smugglers are not, therefore, terribly popular; hence the Defence Force, the sentries and the armed duck.

'Chief.'

'Shut *up*, Twist.'

'Yes, but, Chief—'

'Tie a bloody knot in it and be *quiet*!'

'I was only going to ask,' said Twist, 'why we don't just slip away through that tunnel.'

'Because, you stupid oaf – what tunnel?'

'That tunnel, Chief.'

And Twist pointed. Sure enough, there was a tunnel. It looked like the entrance to a mine (except that there was no way it could be, because it led directly under the lake; start digging into the floor there, and you'd break through and fall down out of the sky).

Hat stared at it. 'Where the hell did that come from?' he demanded.

'Dunno, Chief. Funny I never noticed it before.'

'You and me both.' Hat rubbed his chin. He had no idea how long he'd been around this lake; vaguely he recollected a time when a little trickle of water had come down the side of the mountain with a sheaf of estate agents' particulars in its current, taken one look at the bone-dry valley below and said, 'Yes!' In all that time, he'd never seen any tunnels or mineshafts or underground railways of rustic construction. What the—?

On the other hand, the frogs were closing in fast.

'This way,' said Hat.

CHAPTER THREE

CALVIN DIEB: INTERNAL MEMORANDUM
From: *subconscious mind & memory archives*
To: *awareness control centre*
Message: *Please remember that you can't swim*

Thank you, Dieb muttered under what little remained of
his breath, I hadn't forgotten. Instead of wasting my time
telling me things I already know, tell me some way I can
get out of . . .

The rest of Calvin Dieb's breath, by far the majority,
was floating on the top of the lake in bubble form.
Another stream of bubbles headed towards it on an intercept course.

*Sorry, can't help you on that score. Query whether you
could sue your school for negligence/breach of contract in that
they failed to teach you to swim when you were ten. Query
also joining the estates of your deceased parents as co-
defendants.*

He was just drafting a scathing reply when something

nudged his ear. Without actually ceasing to drown, he put drowning on hold for a moment or so. It was, he saw, an otter.

'Hello,' said the otter. 'Bears.'

'What?'

'And wolves, if they can catch us. But bears, mostly.'

'Bears? What about goddamn bears? And how come you can—?'

The otter flipped over and floated on its back. 'You were speculating earlier,' it said, 'about what sort of animals eat otters.'

'I – How did you *know*—?'

'Mind you,' the otter went on, paddling languidly with its back paws, like a small furry paddlesteamer, 'that wouldn't be much use to you, would it? Bears'd be even harder to get rid of than otters. Can't think offhand of anything on this continent that eats bears.'

'Look, I'm really sorry, I didn't mean . . .'

'Except,' added the otter, looking him in the eye, 'humans. I believe barbecued bear steak with onions is considered a delicacy in these parts.'

'No. I mean yes. I mean, do you want it to be?'

The otter shrugged. 'Don't make no never-mind to me,' it said. 'I'm not a bear. Not at the moment, anyhow. Welcome to Lake Chicopee, by the way.'

INTERNAL MEMORANDUM. *Hey, we're floating. Didn't know we could do that. How are we doing that? Hell, I thought you knew.*

'Thank you,' Dieb replied.

'You're welcome,' said the otter. 'Have a nice day now, d'you hear?'

Whereupon it rolled over, ducked its head under the water and vanished. Immediately, Dieb started drowning again.

'Hey!' he yelled. 'You in the fur! Come back!'

No reply –

– Except, just as he'd assumed he'd gone under for the last time, there he was floating again. Or at least, he was lying on his back on top of the water, staring up at a blue sky –

– A blue sky with trees and mountains in it. Having given the situation some thought, Dieb came to the conclusion that lying very still was probably the most sensible course of action. Lying on water wasn't something he'd ever tried before, and he wasn't sure he knew the rules. Maybe it was the same basic technique as walking on water. Which can't be all that difficult, at that. If God and crane-flies can do it, so could he.

'Hello again.'

This time, the otter was on the other side of him. It too was lying on its back, nibbling at a fish clutched between its front paws. The fish, Dieb noticed, was still vaguely alive.

'I meant to ask earlier,' the otter said. 'When you were drowning just now, did your entire life flash past you, the way it's supposed to? Sorry if that's a rather personal question, but I'm interested. I meet a lot of drowning people, you see, and about half of them say, "Yes, it does," and the other half say, "No, it doesn't," and I'd really love to do some serious research here. I mean, do you only get a memory flashback if you've lived a really happy life, or the other way round, or doesn't that come into it at all? What about you, for instance?'

Status report: *you're lying on your back in the water, talking to an otter. Why are you doing this?*

'I don't know,' Dieb replied. 'I mean, no, my life didn't flash before my eyes. And it's been a very happy life, I guess.' His face clouded for a moment as he said the words; and his brain's credit control department raised a query along the lines of *Why are you lying when you're not getting paid for it?* 'I guess,' he repeated. 'Yes, I'm sure. I mean, look at me. I'm the senior partner of one of the best goddamn law firms in the state. Annually, after tax, I take home—'

Suddenly, the fish between the otter's paws lashed out frantically with its tail, shot up into the air and crashed into the lake with a *plop!* and a shower of fine spray. The otter lifted its head and watched the ripples with the air of a park keeper watching people walking on the grass.

'Damn,' it said. 'I was just getting to the tasty bit.'

'It was still alive, for Christ's sake!' As he spoke, Dieb wondered at his own passion. Hell, it was just a fish. Now it was a partially eaten fish, still gamely swimming. Under normal circumstances, his instincts would have been to try and interest it in substantial personal injury litigation, but for some reason all he could think was: *Why bother? Why make a run for it when effectively it's dead already?*

'I might ask you the same question,' the otter replied. '*What?*'

'Look at you.' The otter obeyed its own suggestion. 'Forty-nine years old, grossly overweight. Severe – I mean *severe* – stress-related disorders, badly aggravated by chronic alcohol and tobacco habits, virtually a suicide diet, no exercise ever; you're about five years overdue for the Great Meathook as it is, and you're exhibiting all the self-preservation instincts of a dishonoured samurai. But when you feel yourself drowning, you thrash about. Why bother?'

Calvin Dieb scowled. 'Ah, cut it out,' he growled. 'I get that all the time from the quacks, and I'm still here, aren't I?' A horrible thought struck him, precisely at the same moment as an unexpected wave splashed water into his face. 'I *am* still here, aren't I? Shit, did I die? Is this some sort of goddamn afterlife or something?'

The otter twitched its nose at him. 'Welcome to Lake Chicopee,' it replied, as if answering the question.

'Huh?'

'It's a moot point,' the otter went on. 'I won't bore you with the equations, so let's just say it's – what's that phrase you lawyers use when somebody asks you a question and you don't know the answer? Let's just say it's a grey area. On the one paw, you're definitely taking time out from your usual continuum. Your watch, for instance, won't work. Time doesn't work, come to that; it just doesn't seem to pass here, is all. Hey, that must be hell for you; I could ask you for all sorts of complicated legal advice and you couldn't charge me a cent.'

'Hey . . .'

'On the other paw,' the otter continued, 'don't try collecting on your life policies, because you can't, 'cos you're still alive.' It made a tiny hacking noise, presumably analogous to laughter. 'You're stuffed, Dieb, you know that? You can't earn money, and you can't collect for being dead. Since your only purpose in existing is to accumulate dollars, what the hell is the point in you?'

'Shuttup!'

At once, the otter flipped and dived. A surge of panic swept through Dieb like on a bad day on Wall Street, and he began to feel desperately heavy, as if he'd just stepped out of a twentieth-storey window. The water was just starting to get into his mouth when the otter popped up again, just by his left ear.

'But we digress,' it said, and at once Dieb was floating again. 'This is Lake Chicopee. You know the old legend?'

'Get me *out* of here!'

'The old legend,' the otter said, ignoring him, 'has it that if you make a wish and jump in this here lake, you get your heart's desire. Good, huh?'

'Fine. My heart's desire is to get out of—'

'Wrong.'

'I beg your pardon?'

'Wrong,' the otter repeated. 'Your heart's desire, as at 11:04 and sixteen-point-two seconds, which is the precise moment you hit the water, was to find your car keys.' That tiny hacking noise again. 'Your wish is my command, buster. You ready?'

'*Hey!*'

'Then here,' said the otter, 'we go.'

'That's it?'

'Sure is, miss.' The cab driver pressed a button, and the window on Linda's side wound down with an electric purr. 'Kinda pretty, ain't it?'

'Hm?' Linda shrugged, as if he'd asked her to perform some abstruse mathematical calculation. 'Yeah, sure. What do I owe you?'

'Call it thirty bucks, miss.'

'I'll need a receipt.'

'Huh?'

Linda frowned. 'It's what we call a piece of paper with the cost of the ride written on it.' She sniffed. 'They do use writing around here, don't they? Or do you muddle through with body language and smoke signals?'

'Just a second,' the cab driver said. 'I'll write it on the back of one of my cards. There, that do you?'

She nodded, took the card and put it away. 'Say, mister,' she said, 'you wouldn't happen to have seen any submarines in these parts at all?'

'Submarines.' The driver looked thoughtful. 'Can't say

as I have. What with the lake being so far from the sea, and all. Course, I could be mistaken,' he added fair-mindedly. 'Don't reckon I'd necessarily know one if I saw one.'

'Quite.' Linda sighed. 'All right, then, how about Australians?'

'Australians?'

'That's right. People from Australia. Seen any?'

'Can't say as I . . . '

'Forget it.' Linda opened the door, threw out her bag and slammed the door shut behind her. 'Don't wait,' she added. 'When I'm ready to leave I'll ring through on my mobile.' She hesitated, as a disturbing thought occurred to her. 'Mobiles do work in these mountains, don't they? I mean, you can get a signal?'

'Can't say as . . . '

'It's all right,' Linda growled. 'If necessary, I'll walk. Don't let me keep you.'

The driver looked at her, smiled a thin little smile and drove away, much to Linda's relief. He reminded her a bit too much of her father, who had driven the station cab at Parsimony, Utah until they closed the station (not, mercifully, before she'd had a chance to use it to get the hell out of Parsimony, Utah and that whole goddamn way of life) and the resonances unsettled her. One of her dad's favourite apothegms was that you can take a girl out of Utah but you can't take Utah out of the girl; and it was remarks of that sort that tended to undermine her belief in language as a viable means of communication.

God, she muttered to herself, I *hate* the countryside. It's so . . .

Well. Quite.

Still, if there's a story in it somewhere, then it had to be tolerated; humoured, even. Even if it meant having to walk on grass and cross rivers and shelter under trees and all that crap. Feeling more than a little resentful, she hefted her bag onto her shoulder and set off towards the lake.

Whereupon the tiresome old man, who had been watching her through the eyes of an eagle circling a long way up above her head, pottered out of a sudden and unexpected timber shack and said, 'Howdy.'

Linda turned and looked at him, assessing him in his capacities as (a) threat, (b) informant and (c) eyesore. No to (a), yes to (c); she resolved to investigate (b) further.

'Hello,' she said, switching on her smile at the mains. 'You live around here?'

The old man nodded. 'Sure do,' he said. 'Been livin' here all my life. You come to look at the lake?'

Linda nodded. 'It's very . . .' She remembered the technical term the cab driver had used. 'Kinda pretty,' she parroted.

It seemed that she'd said the right thing, because the old man smiled, revealing a set of teeth that reminded her of baked beans swimming in mustard. 'You said it, miss,' he replied, and wheezed; a general purpose combination laugh/cough. 'Kinda pretty all right. Though,' he added, after a tiny pause, 'they do say this here lake is haunted.'

Linda stepped up the smile by an amp or so. 'Really,' she cooed. 'How fascinating. You don't say.'

'That's right,' the old man said, doing something disgusting with his tongue. 'By the ghost of an ole Injun sperrit, name of Okeewana or some such. By Jiminy, miss, the tales I could tell you 'bout that ole—'

'Submarines.'

The old man hesitated, like a jammed machine. 'Beg pardon, miss?'

'Have you seen any submarines, by any chance? You know, ships that suddenly appear from out of the water and then—'

'You mean like that one?' He pointed.

Linda swivelled round like a small boy on an office chair and saw a *thing*; something that looked for all the world like a wood-carving of a dragon's head, just breaking the surface of the water, surrounded by ripples swarming like disturbed bees.

'A periscope!' Linda breathed.

'Keep lookin'.'

The thing rose steadily up out of the water, followed a moment later by what was unmistakably a mast, and then by a whole ship; broad-beamed, clinker-built, bristling with oars like a squashed-flat centipede. Brightly painted round shields encircled its bows, and a few disgusted-looking fish flapped wearily on the planks of the deck.

'Right,' said Linda contentedly. 'Thought so.'

Cursing fluently, Talks To Squirrels loosed his last arrow, following it with his eye all the way from his bowstring to the newcomer's heart. Bang on the money, as always; enough to make a man weep. He'd just put six consecutive arrows into a space the size of a playing-card at a range of a hundred and seventy-five yards, and the bugger hadn't even noticed. The irony, the cruel, savage, merciless irony of it was that when he'd been alive he'd been hard put to it to hit a sleeping bison at five paces.

Where the hell were they all coming from? Three of the sons of bitches, all in one morning; and he'd come out with just two dozen arrows and a small flint knife. The question was, if he sprinted back Flipside for more arrows and his business tomahawk, would the scumbags still be here when he returned, or would he come running back, armed to the teeth, only to find they'd moved on? Whereas if he stayed here, at least he could pelt them with insubstantial rocks and batter them around the head with non-existent tree-branches. It was a difficult choice to make. Or rather, it wasn't, since he wouldn't be able to stir so much as a hair on their heads even if he had a battery of cannon and a Gatling gun at his disposal. Quit kidding yourself, Talks.

Gloomily he shoved his bow back into its buckskin case, sat down on top of a disused anthill, wrapped his hands round his chin and sulked. When he'd made his wish, all those years ago, to be able to carry on fighting the paleface until the sun went out and the moon fell from the sky and the mountains slid down into the lake and were swallowed up, he hadn't pictured it working out quite like this. Admittedly, if you worked on the basis of mortal wounds delivered and direct hits inflicted, at the last count he had eighty-six thousand, four hundred and ninety-seven notches on his bowhandle; not bad going for a brave who used to be known as Trips Over Own Feet While Running Away. The figures were, however, deceptive, not least because of the duplication factor. At least twenty-seven thousand of those notches were multiple hits on the driver of the mail truck. He'd also killed old Mr Tomacek, who drove the garbage truck along the valley road once a week, sixteen thousand and eight times, and Mrs Bernstein from Owl Farm nine thousand, six hundred and twenty-four times. The first time he'd shot Mrs Bernstein, she'd been six; she was now a sprightly eighty-seven, and showing no inclination whatsoever to fall over and die, leaving Talks With Squirrels to draw the demoralising conclusion that shooting the buggers was actually good for them.

'Still,' said a small bird above his head, 'it keeps you out of mischief.'

'Get lost, you,' Talks replied without looking up. 'Since it's all your fault, I'd be obliged if you'd keep your witty remarks to yourself.'

'My fault?' The bird flapped its tiny wings, caught a gnat in mid-air and returned to its perch. 'Here we go again. I'm sorry, but I can't see the point in going through all that again. I only came by to say that if you want to nip home for more arrows, they'll still be here when you get back.'

'Can't be bothered.'

The bird twittered cheerfully. 'Oh no you don't, Talks. Till the sun goes out and the moon falls out of the sky, remember? I don't recall anything about only when you feel in the mood.'

'But it's so pointless,' Talks growled wretchedly. 'I mean, what exactly does it *achieve*? Ninety-four times I've crushed young Duane Flint's head with a rock, and he's never had so much as a bad cold in his life.'

'At least you've learned something,' the bird replied. 'Pointless. Doesn't achieve anything. Out of the mouths of babes and dead Indians, huh?'

Talks shook his insubstantial head. 'Don't give me that,' he snarled. 'It's only pointless and doesn't achieve anything when they don't fall over when you kill them. Let me have one real shot – just one – and then we'll see . . .'

'Oh, you,' said the bird indulgently. 'At least you're consistent, I'll give you that. Consistent as five hundred generations of lemmings, but consistent nonetheless. Good shooting.'

'Ah, piss off.'

Wearily the ghost dragged itself to its feet and trudged away, mingling with the dappled shadows on the forest floor until it wasn't there any more. The bird watched him go, then shook itself, swung her legs over the tree-branch and dropped lightly to the ground. Shading her eyes with the palm of her hand, she gazed across the valley to where she was talking to Linda Lachuk; another customer, three in one day. She wasn't sure she liked these sudden flurries of new business; she was spreading herself pretty thin as it was. How people who *couldn't* be in two places at once ever managed to cope, she had no idea.

Time she wasn't here. Time she was –

– An otter, floating on its back in the middle of Lake Chicopee alongside a resolutely not-drowning lawyer.

'Here we go,' she said.

'How?' the lawyer replied. 'I can't swim, remember.'

'Then,' said the otter, 'maybe we should hitch a ride. Tell you what, the next ship that passes this way, we'll flag it down.'

'Oh, very—' Calvin Dieb didn't finish his sentence, because just then a Viking warship rose up out of the water next to him. It was probably at this point that the skeleton crew who'd been doggedly manning the key positions in his sanity got up from their seats, switched off the lights, locked up and went home. At any rate, he found himself lifting his right arm out of the water and waggling his thumb furiously.

'Hello,' said a voice from the ship. 'How can I of assistance be?'

'You, um, going anywhere near dry land?' Dieb heard himself say. 'Only I could really use a lift right now if you are.'

'Dry land,' the voice repeated, as if confronted with a disturbing new concept. 'Near dry land we may be passing. To be aboard welcome.'

'Well,' muttered the otter in his ear, 'what're you waiting for?'

Dieb reviewed the options available to him, the way he'd been taught in law school. Something they don't teach you in law school, although maybe they should, is that climbing aboard mysterious Viking longships that suddenly materialise in the middle of mirror-calm mountain lakes is, at best, something of a gamble.

Quite where they'd fit it into the syllabus is anybody's guess. Probably they'd have to shoehorn it in between second-year conveyancing and industrial tribunals procedure. It ought to be in there somewhere, all the same.

'Can one of you guys throw me a rope?' Dieb yelled.

'Certainly we can. Here a rerp is to you coming.'

'Ouch. I mean, thanks.'

'Now then, Thorvald, Oddleif, if to pull upon the rerp so kind you would be.'

Not long afterwards, Dieb was lying on the deck, panting like one of the fish he'd seen there when the ship first emerged, and wondering what he'd gotten himself into. Round him stood a ring of the most ferocious-looking warriors you'd ever hope to see outside of the more flamboyant parts of Los Angeles. Some of them were lacking an eye, others a selection of teeth or fingers. All of them had patches of smooth, shiny pink skin on their arms, legs and faces that bore witness to a time when they'd nearly come second out of two in a hand-to-hand combat with sharp weapons. If someone had told Dieb at that moment that the ship's hold was stuffed full of customised Harley-Davidsons, he wouldn't have been in the least surprised.

'How are you feeling?' asked a particularly serrated giant with a horned helmet and only one eye. 'Perhaps of warm milk a cup good would do you.'

'The water at this year time,' added an even larger Viking, 'cold is being. A chill you might be getting.'

'Scerns there are,' pointed out a third. 'Freshly today baked by Little Olaf.'

'Scerns?'

'Scerns, with yam and clooted cream,' the first Viking explained. 'Little Olaf, it is his mother's recipe.'

For the first time, Dieb realised that the second Viking, the one with arms like legs and only three teeth, was wearing a blue-and-white-striped pinafore. 'Little Olaf,' said the first Viking, 'is the cerk.'

'Ah.'

'Also there are dernuts.'

'Right.'

'And pastries Danske.'

'Great.' Dieb swallowed hard. 'I'd just love some, er, dernuts and a pastry Danske with my, ah, warm milk.'

Little Olaf departed, grinning, while the other Vikings produced a barrel for him to sit on, a blanket for his knees and a huge plump cushion with a rabbit embroidered on it.

'Hey, guys,' he said, trying to manufacture a smile that didn't look like a Jack Nicholson crazed grin. 'This is really, um, really decent of you. Thanks.'

'You're welcome. Ah. Here Little Olaf with the milk is.'

Dieb took the cup, doing his best not to notice that it was formed from a human skull, the eyesockets and ear funnels of which were filled with gold and massive uncut gemstones that traced a runic inscription which undoubtedly translated as *World's Best Cook*.

'While it warm is, be drinking.'

'Yeah, right.' He took a deep breath and drank. Yuk! Warm milk!

'And here, behold the dernuts.'

Still recovering from the milk, he glanced down and

beheld the dernuts, still faintly glistening with oil. It made him nostalgic for the lake.

Which reminded him. What had become of that goddamn chatty otter? If he'd managed to show it a clean pair of handstitched heels, he was at least that much ahead of the game.

'It's not that easy,' said a seagull perched on the rigging just above his head. 'Oh, and before you think to ask, they can't hear me.'

Dieb groaned, prompting a worried enquiry from Little Olaf about the quality of the dernuts. He made a conscious effort not to look up.

'Now then,' said the first Viking, who appeared to be some sort of leader. 'You are to where going?'

'Um,' Dieb replied. 'Actually, if it's no trouble for you guys, maybe you could drop me off at the shore. Anywhere round here'll do.'

For some reason, this seemed to disturb the Viking; he looked away and fidgeted with his bears' teeth necklace for a moment before answering. 'Clerse to the shore go we cannot,' he said. 'For fear the ship aground to be running. This very sad is, that help you we cannot.'

'Oh. Well, never . . .'

'As hosts in our duty failed you we have,' the Viking went on. 'Never in Valhall honour shall we have, if before as hosts our duty we our lives put. Scorn us will Thor. Upon us spit will the Valkyries. But our ship aground to run . . .'

'Hey guys,' said Dieb, nervously, 'please. Doesn't have to be here. Anywhere that's convenient for you will me do just fine.'

The Viking narrowed his eyes ferociously, until he put Dieb firmly in mind of Clint Eastwood trying to stare down a tax inspector. 'Saying that you sure you aren't our feelings just not to be hurting?' he said.

'Huh? I mean, quite. Yes. I mean no.'

Suddenly the Viking smiled, flashing two rows of teeth like badly weathered tombstones. 'Then fine that shall be,' he said, standing up. 'Maybe now below you to go would like, sleep to be getting. Arriving at Duluth, calling you we shall.'

'*Duluth?*'

Immediately the Viking's face subsided into a look of utter self-reproach, so rearranging the scars that you could have played noughts and crosses in them. 'Right I was, and out of your way too far Duluth,' he exclaimed, jumping to his feet. 'Ashore at once to be putting you, and the ship aground to be running matter not at all will. Thorvald!'

'No,' Dieb said imploringly, 'please! Duluth'll be just great, I can charter a plane or something – I mean, Duluth's actually where I was headed anyhow. So that's great. Really.'

'Sure?'

'Positive. Word of honour. My, these really are mighty good, um, dernuts. Haven't had dernuts this good since I was a kid.'

The Viking sat down again, beaming like a lighthouse. 'Then to take with you in a bag of paper more shall you have. Olaf I shall instruct freshly them to bake.'

'Great.' The bridge of Dieb's mind sent a frenzied message down to Engineering: *Quick, for Christ's sake, fabricate some enthusiasm. How? We ain't got the recipe. Then improvise, dammit.* 'Looking forward to it. Yum!'

'And now to be excusing me,' the Viking said, standing up again. 'The ship to be running I must.' He wandered away, turning occasionally to smile and wave. Eventually, Dieb was left alone with his blanket, his cushions, several remaining pastries and the seagull.

'Duluth,' muttered the seagull. 'Wonder what's at Duluth?'

'I'm gonna find out, aren't I?' Dieb replied irritably. 'You know, this is costing me *thousands*—'

'No you won't,' the seagull said, preening its wing feathers. 'Ship's gonna hit a rock any minute. If I were you, I'd go up the rounded end.'

'Hit a rock?'

The seagull nodded. 'And sink. With all hands. That's a nautical expression meaning all these folks are gonna die. Not you, though.'

Dieb's jaw dropped, and for a moment – the first since he embraced the art of advocacy – he was fresh out of words. 'Die?' he repeated.

'Drown. Glug glug. Davy Jones' locker. But like I said, you make it, so where's the problem?' The seagull opened its beak wide, as if yawning. 'Means you can't sue them for anything, true, but what the hell, they haven't got that sort of money anyhow.'

Dieb opened and closed his mouth several times, like a fish drowning in air. 'But can't we warn them, for God's sake? Tell 'em to steer the boat to one side?'

'Compassion, Mr Dieb?' The seagull regarded him for a while, standing on one leg. 'That's a word for feeling sorry for people, in case you've never come across it before. No, can't warn them. Against the rules.'

'But . . .' Dieb looked around; at the blanket, the cushions, the home-made doughnuts, the gold-and-gemstone-encrusted skull . . . . 'But they *rescued* me,' he said feebly. 'I *owe* them.'

'Nah.' The seagull shook its head. 'Moral obligation only. Nothing on paper. And besides, if they're all dead, who's to know?'

'But . . .'

The seagull spread its wings. 'Anyhow,' it said, 'this isn't getting your car-keys found, is it? Now remember; get up as near to the stern as you can without attracting attention, or else one of 'em might follow you – to ask how you're doing, offer you another doughnut, that sort of thing – and that'd be no good. The sucker might survive along with you.'

'But that'd be great. I thought you said—'

'Maybe I didn't explain properly. If any of these guys makes it, you don't get to find your keys. You'll have to stay here and drown too. Think about it. Pity there's always got to be a loser, but hey, that's litigation.' The seagull spread its wings and flew away before Dieb could answer.

He stood up. He looked once again at the blanket, the cushion, the home-made doughnuts, the skull. If any of these guys made it, he wouldn't. Then he looked over the side at the still, wet water, and remembered what it had been like being in that stuff, that fluid, alien element that makes no allowances. And on the bridge of his mind, the captain turned in his swivel chair and muttered, *Hell, we didn't ask to get involved in this. And the suckers'd have drowned anyway. Not as if them drowning's our fault.*

Which was true.

Picking up the blanket, and stuffing doughnuts in his pockets for later, he set off for the rounded end.

Janice DeWeese climbed over the brow of the ridge, her feet hurting like something the Spanish Inquisition saved for people it really didn't like, and looked down at a big, mirror-still lake.

'Hey!' she muttered. Her map, once she'd wrestled it out of her pocket and turned it the right way up, told her that this Lake Chicopee –

– Which was supposed to be over *there*. This was supposed to be a valley, not a lake. There should be a stream running through it, and a disused powder mill, and a small wooden hut put there by the Forestry Department for muggers and rapists to rest up in between jobs.

She'd come the wrong way.

Wearily she dropped herself on a fallen tree, cleaned her glasses on her sleeve and smoothed the map out again. Right; over there, the Squash river, so that was north. Over there, the tall pointy mountain with trees up to its neck, so that was west. Accordingly . . .

Accordingly, she was going to have to turn round and go back the way she'd come, seven miles of overgrown paths and savage inclines, if she wanted to get to Broken Heart by nightfall. Or, if she had the sense she was born with, she could go down to the lake and up the other side to join the road, which would take her to Claremont, the Greyhound bus and civilisation; and the hell with Broken Heart, pop. 361. She was faced with a long, long walk whichever way she went, and this lousy backpack wasn't getting any lighter. Some vacation, huh?

But, she reflected, as she scrabbled in her pockets for life-giving chocolate, this is the sort of vacation you get to go on when you're, to take an example entirely at random, twenty-eight, short and dumpy with a face like a prune. Vacations involving swimming-pools, long cool drinks, hot sun and slinky black evening dresses tend to happen to other sorts of people.

At least it had been something to talk about at the office, for a day or two. Something she could have talked about, if somebody had actually asked her. If somebody had asked her where she was going for her vacation, she'd have answered in a light, devil-may-care tone of voice that oh, she was backpacking across Iowa again this year. *Backpacking* across *Iowa?* Sure; don't you just love the freedom, the big open spaces? You can really be *yourself*. Oh yes, on my own, naturally; wouldn't be any point otherwise. If anybody had asked her, she could have been great. And if she ever got home again (could a person die of sore feet?) then she'd have some really spellbinding stories to tell, if anybody ever asked her.

The hell with it. She could go crawling round the moon on her hands and knees and nobody'd ever know. Last year, for instance; last year, she'd spent her entire savings on an overland expedition down the Nile, by boat, Jeep and camel. She'd slept under desert stars, huddled in her government-surplus sleeping bag while sandstorms howled, basted in red-hot winds and walked silent-footed through the dead cities of Ancient Egypt; she might as well have stayed in Pittsburgh, because (owing to a freak succession of cancellations) the expedition consisted of her and two seventy-year-old Egyptian guides who spoke no English, and when she got back to the office, sun-bleached and crispy-thin, Mr Marcowitz had said it was just as well she was back, the R304Es were all down again, they were knee-deep in pink PZ23s and could she take a look at the Xerox machine? Come five o'clock that first day back, she was into the chocolate again and hard put to it to remember anything about Egypt at all.

She dragged herself back onto her feet, speculating as she did so what the world would have looked like if she, not Chris Columbus, had discovered America. Easy; flat, with a big drop at the edges. Back the way she'd come, or on past the lake up to the road? The lake; why not? At least it'd be a different set of ankle-breaking trails and tendon-sapping gradients.

As she trudged, the phrase 'holiday romance' bounced about in her mind like a small child in a collection of Oriental porcelain. That, as far as she could tell, is what vacations meant to the rest of the girls in the office; see bedroom ceilings the length and breadth of the USA. Quite probably some of them could write a learned text-book on the different types of light-fittings used across America. Not Janice DeWeese, though; all she got to see was mountains and lakes and rivers and deserts and sun-rises and sunsets and fallen-down old buildings. Oh, she had often sighed as she gazed out across some breath-taking panorama someplace, to be an egg; because at least an egg gets laid *once* . . .

Me, though, I just look like one. Maybe, if I'd saved all that money I've frittered away on seeing the goddamn world and spent it on some really drastic cosmetic surgery; well, then I'd look like an egg with Sharon Stone's nose. Fact is, either you got it or you ain't; and I . . .

I get to see lots of countryside. Lewis and Clarke, and Jan DeWeese; to boldly go where no one with any sense has gone before. If I had any sense, I'd jump in this goddamn lake right now and do myself a favour. Oh, if only I didn't have a face like a prune. If only I was—

So musing, she stuck her foot in a tree-root.

Splash.

'Hang on,' Wesley grumbled. 'There's something in my shoe.'

'That'd be your foot, surely.'

'As well as my foot.'

'Never mind. We're nearly there now.'

Wesley laughed, although the sound he produced had as much to do with amusement as an oven has to do with efficient ice-cream production. 'I think you said that before,' he sighed.

'I did. This time, it's true.'

This time, it was a squirrel saying it. On the previous occasions the words had been spoken by a beautiful girl, a whitetail deer, a wild turkey, a brown bear, a pheasant, an elm tree and a derelict 1974 Chevy. This perpetual flitting from shape to shape was beginning to get on Wesley's nerves, and he said as much.

'Bigot.'

'Oh come on,' Wesley replied, stopping where he was and sitting down on a rock. 'It's hardly fair, is it? I mean, how am I supposed to have a sensible conversation with you when I don't even know what you are?'

'Don't see the problem myself. And do you mind not sitting on me when I'm talking to you?'

Wesley looked down. 'Oh, you're that now, are you? What was wrong with the squirrel?'

'Heights. And besides, we're here now.'

'Are we?' Wesley lifted his head and looked around him. It wasn't an enlightening experience; this patch of forest looked just like the patch they'd traipsed through an hour ago. He could even still see the lake below them through the trees. In fact, the lake didn't seem to have moved at all. Wesley voiced this suspicion.

'Well, it wouldn't, would it? Be reasonable.'

'Does you being a rock now have anything to do with us having arrived?'

'Yes,' replied the rock. 'Hey, you're beginning to get the hang of this.'

'OK,' Wesley said. 'Why, now that we're here, are you a rock?'

'Because bears don't eat rocks.'

'Bears? What bears?'

'Hey. I'm in no position to point them out for you, being a rock and all, but if you stay there you'll see them soon enough.'

'Oh, for God's—' Wesley jumped up, swivelled his head two or three times, then looked up at the tree above him.

'Bears can climb trees,' said the rock. 'Rather better than you can.'

'Thanks a lot. What can't they do?'

'Oh, all sorts of things. For a start, they can't play musical instruments.'

'Apart from not play musical instruments.'

'Well,' said the rock pleasantly. 'I never yet heard of a bear who could pull a magic tomahawk from a tree and use it to defend himself with.'

'Neither can I.'

'Huh!' replied the rock scornfully. 'That's what you think. Why don't you give it a try? After all, this is supposed to be a learning experience.'

'Because,' Wesley said, 'there isn't one. Not in this tree, anyway.'

'What?' That's what a puzzled rock sounds like, folks. Now you know. 'How do you mean, there isn't one?'

'I mean there isn't one. Come on, I thought rocks were what they make silicon chips out of.'

'But there ought to be . . .' The rock fell silent. 'Oh. Sorry about this.' The rock vanished, and was replaced by the beautiful girl. Wesley took one look at the expression on her face and decided there were probably more ferocious things in the forest than bears, after all.

'Talks!' the girl shouted. 'Yes, you, Talks To Squirrels! Put it back!'

There was a *tchock!* noise directly above Wesley's head. He glanced up, and suddenly there was this sort of axe thing sticking in the tree, or rather hanging loosely from the bark. It had a stone blade and the haft was perhaps eighteen inches long and decorated with two threadbare eagle's feathers. It'd terrify the life out of you if you happened to be a small twig.

Wesley looked at it glumly. 'Magic tomahawk?' he asked.

'Magic tomahawk,' the girl replied, vanishing.

He reached up and managed to catch it before it fell out of the tree. 'Magic,' he asked, 'in what sense?'

'Give it a top hat and you'll never want for rabbits.'

Wesley was just about to pass an observation on the appropriate timing of comic remarks when the bears arrived. There were seven of them, and the smallest would just about have squeezed into a Ford Fiesta if you took the seats out first.

'If I were you,' muttered the rock, 'I'd run away.'

CHAPTER FOUR

Someone with rather less self-confidence might have found it just a trifle disconcerting.

Not Linda Lachuk. She had postulated submarines, as being journalistically right, and here submarines were. Naturally, if she ordained submarines, submarines would be provided. To have expected anything else would have been like Christ taking a hip-flask to the wedding at Cana.

'Ahoy there!' she shouted.

The ship turned obediently, like a good dog, and sliced a deep cut through the lake top towards her. An otter popped its head up above the surface, took a good look and vanished again, leaving a circle of ripples like a cup-mark on a newly french-polished table.

'Good morning, miss,' someone shouted from behind the dragon prow. 'And how you can we be herlping?'

Linda caught her breath. That was no American voice, booming out to her across the meniscus of one of Uncle Sam's most secret military installations. That high, nasal, sing-song quality – instinctively she sent a search-and-correlate memo to the librarians of her memory, ordering them to pull the file on *Crocodile Dundee*.

An Australian . . . .

Actually, he didn't sound all that much like Paul Hogan; but there were other similarities, too striking to ignore. The blond hair. The leather jerkin. The necklace of wild beast's fangs. The big knife strapped to his mid-riff.

Probably, she rationalised, it's some kind of regional accent. Adelaide, or one of those places.

'Hi,' she yelled back. 'Are you Australian?'

'Your pardon begging?'

'Are – you – *Australian*?'

She scowled. Perfectly simple question; but by the looks of it, either he didn't understand or he was playing dumb. He shrugged his huge shoulders and plastered some kind of dumb friendly smile across his face. She tried again.

'From Australia,' she shouted slowly. 'Down under. Um. Oz.'

'Oz?'

'Yeah.'

'Ah!' The man nodded, with such overpowering friendliness that she half expected him to vanish and reappear a moment later with a rubber ball in his mouth. 'From Oseberg. Yes, from there am I. Presently.'

'Right. Now then—'

'My name,' he went on, 'is Lief the Lemming. To be helping you, in what manner?'

Linda breathed in. 'Your subm—'

The rest of her sentence was drowned out by a horrible noise, as the ship seemed to trip over something. It shuddered, from carved wooden periscope to pointed duck's tail thing at the other end. From below the deck came muffled cries of 'Excuse me, please,' 'Drat,' and, 'To be sinking, the ship!' They sounded surprised; but Linda wasn't.

They were being silenced.

Typical CIA trick. She should perhaps have thought about that, before she blew their cover with the direct accusation of Australianness. Still, couldn't be helped now. At least she'd be able to get some good shots of the boat sinking. Quickly she felt in her bag for her camera –

– And remembered. Damnit, no batteries in the misbegotten thing. Of all the rotten luck.

'Hey!' she shouted. 'Excuse me!'

Lief the Lemming froze in the act of lowering the ship's only lifeboat, and turned to look at her. 'Excuse me, please?'

Linda smiled. 'You wouldn't happen to have any batteries, would you? For my camera. Just plain old LR13s, if you can spare me a couple.'

'Batteries?'

'Yeah. You know,' Linda replied crossly. 'Power cells. C'mon, you gotta have some on that tub of yours. Or does everything in Australia run on clockwork?'

'Excusing me please a moment.' Lief left the lifeboat dangling six feet or so above the water and ducked down under the deck. From where she stood, Linda could hear a muffled conference but no distinguishable words. This was so *frustrating*—

'Little Bjorn,' said Lief, popping his head up above the level of the deck, 'speculating is batteries to mean instances of battery or common asserlt. To which truthfully answering, on a voyage long, tempers to be occasionally fraying but rarely in fisticuffs resulting, rather to be out of our systems got by exercise healthy and good and much of deck footberl playing. And now to excuse me, the ship . . .'

Linda folded her arms grimly. 'Quit fooling around, will you?' she growled, and the severe expression on her face made her look like an angel who's just been given a dodgy cheque. 'Don't act dumb with me. I want those batteries now, mister. The people have a right to—'

But at that moment the ship suddenly capsized, hit the reflection of itself in the still water and vanished into a bubble and an empty-bath gurgle, leaving Linda standing on the shore breathing hard through her nose.

Yes. Well. She'd see about that. Sooner or later, people were going to learn that the more you tried to put Linda Lachuk off the story, the harder she came back. OK, so it would have been nice to have gotten real live-action pictures of the sub going down; staged re-creations for the camera are all very well, but they lack that intangible spontaneity that you only get when there are actual people genuinely dying for real. Still, it wasn't the end of the world. There'd be other chances; and at the very least, she'd seen a palpably real submarine and spoken to a palpably real Australian. If they thought she was just going to shrug her shoulders and meekly walk away, they had a surprise coming.

She picked up her bag, shrugged her shoulders and started to walk (unmeekly) away. She had gone maybe ten yards when something warm and wet pressed against her ankle. She stopped.

It wasn't a wholly unfamiliar experience; but where she came from, something warm and wet rubbing against one's ankle usually turned out to be one of the guys from the sports page crawling back to his desk after lunch. She looked down.

It was an otter. It was long and sleek and cute, like a

performing bratwurst, and in its mouth it held a packet of four LR13 batteries.

'Why, you little—' Linda stooped and lunged for it with both hands, but it slipped through her fingers and waddled jauntily into the lake. A moment later, as soon as she'd dumped her bag and kicked off her shoes, Linda dived after it.

The last thought to cross her mind before the water closed over her head was, *God, I really want this story!*

'Chief!'

'What now?'

'Where are we, Chief?'

'If I knew that, Twist, we'd be somewhere else by now. Shut up, there's a good lad.'

After half an hour in the tunnel it had occurred to all the smugglers, even the ones with oatmeal for brains, that something was wrong. A tunnel where a tunnel had no business being. A tunnel that hadn't been there before. A tunnel leading where?

'Chief!'

'So help me, Twist, just as soon as there's enough room I'm going to wring your bloody—'

'Light, Chief. Straight ahead. Can you see it?'

'Damnit, yes!'

'It's the sort of white twinkly stuff, there, just a bit to the left of where I'm—'

'Thank you, Twist, I have seen daylight before. Like when you're standing sideways on and I look through your ear.'

'Chief?'

'Forget it. Get a move on, will you? Let's get out of here, for pity's sake.'

A few anxious moments later Captain Hat scrambled

out of a hole in the ground, looked round to make sure the coast was clear and hauled himself to his feet. His knees hurt; or, to be more accurate, his knees hurt most.

'OK, lads,' he called back down the tunnel, 'it's all right. Come on out, we're—'

He froze, and in consequence was butted in the rear by a procession of crawling, mole-like smugglers. He didn't seem to notice them.

'—Right back where we started,' he concluded quietly. 'Goddamnit, we've come round in a bloody circle.' He rubbed his eyes, opened them and looked again. 'Hey,' he murmured, 'that's crazy. Could've sworn we went in a straight line. Anyway, no sign of the frogs. Hurry up, people, we don't want to be standing out in the open like a lot of garden gnomes. Is that the lot? OK, let's move.'

They moved. Around them, the undergrowth popped and crackled, for all the world as if it was sniggering at them. They began to feel uncomfortable.

'No,' said Hat at last, as they passed the same tree for the fifth time. 'I refuse to believe we're lost. There's got to be some simple reason.' He peered through the branches of the trees at the lake, no more than a couple of hundred yards away as the crow, having fallen off its perch, slithers. Put him two hundred yards from Lake Chicopee and Hat would know where he was with his eyes shut, his ears stopped up, his nose and mouth blocked with clay and his hands and feet encased in concrete. All right, he'd be dead within a minute, but at least he'd know exactly where he was. He could easily picture himself losing his way on the back of his hand, but not here.

But . . .

'North-west,' he muttered. 'We haven't tried north-west yet. Come on, you lot.'

'Chief.'

Hat closed his eyes again. Give me strength, he prayed; not very much of it, just as much as it takes to throttle Mr Snedge will do just splendidly. 'Well, Snedge?' he said sweetly. 'And what can I do for you?'

'Isn't that them Vikings over there, Chief? You know, the ones whose boat keeps sinking?'

Hat followed the line indicated by Snedge's grubby finger, and saw eight or nine bedraggled figures squelching up out of the lake below them. He recognised them all, though he wasn't sure what they thought they were doing on land. It was a big day for surprises, evidently.

'What I thought was, Chief, maybe we could ask them.'

Hat shook his head. 'Don't think so,' he replied.

'Oh. Why not?'

'Don't think we're terribly popular with them, Snedge. Not since we nicked their lifeboat.'

'Oh.'

Hat narrowed his eyes. 'Mind you,' he said, 'usually they drown. This time, apparently, they haven't.'

'Well, then. Maybe they wouldn't mind us asking.'

'They're still sopping wet, Snedge,' Hat replied thoughtfully. 'I mean, they didn't row their way to shore all nice and dry. I expect that when the time came and they started abandoning ship and they went to find the lifeboat, they still went through that good old where-is-it-I-don't-know-who-saw-it-last? routine.' He looked up at an unfamiliar tree – he'd known all the trees round this lake since they were seeds, and this wasn't one of them – and sniffed. 'Mind you,' he said, 'they do seem to know where they're going.'

'Yeah.'

'Which is more than we do.'

'Yup.'

'OK.' Hat stood up. 'Let's follow them,' he said.

'Somewhere around here, I guess,' said Calvin Dieb, pointing at the rocky slope that fell away into the water. 'I think. To be honest with you, this whole place looks the same to me.'

The Vikings nodded, and started to look. They turned over stones, they prised apart tangled knots of bramble, they combed grass. While they were at it, Dieb looked up into the branches of the tree above him, and saw a squirrel.

'Bad move,' it said.

Dieb scowled. 'Sez who, tree-rat?' he snarled. 'Look, I saved these guys from drowning. They were all scheduled to die, and I saved them. Told them to get down the rounded end of the boat, and they did. Isn't that something?'

'Bad move,' the squirrel repeated.

'And,' Dieb went on, 'to show their gratitude, they've agreed to help me find my keys. Mutually beneficial, I call it. So what's so bad about that?'

'On the other paw,' sighed the squirrel, 'it's exactly what you're supposed to have done. Don't worry about the arrows. Be seeing you.'

'What arrows?' Dieb demanded, as two feet of straight, obsidian-tipped pine flicked past him and buried its nose in a tree. 'Oh, those arrows. Hey,' he yelled up into the branches, 'you didn't explain why I shouldn't worry about them. I'm sure there's a perfectly good reason, but . . .'

He didn't continue the sentence, because he'd seen something. Fifty yards or so away, the Vikings who'd been looking for his car-keys had suddenly fallen over. There were arrows sticking out of them. In fact, there were arrows everywhere, and sticking out of everybody except him. He dropped to his knees and put his hands over his head, whimpering. Something like a moustache brushed the little finger of his left hand. It was a moment or so before he realised it must have been the fletchings on an arrow-shaft, missing him by—

And then the trees echoed to a series of shrieks and whoops, as strange, savage buckskinned men poured out of every patch of cover large enough to hide a pheasant. They were after the Vikings; Dieb didn't look, but what he heard convinced him that they made a thorough job of it. There were shouts and screams, and from time to time heavy, dull bashing noises, the sort of sound an overweight lawyer with a morbid imagination might connect in his mind with a not-too-sharp flint axe mashing a man's skull. Distantly, in a remote part of his mind where he simply didn't care, he wondered whether it would hurt terribly much, and came to the conclusion that by the time it started hurting he'd be past feeling it. *But don't quote me on that,* added that remote part of his brain, remembering that it was part of a lawyer. *Hey,* it added, just before Dieb located it and yanked it off line, *why don't you call the cops?*

And then there was silence, except for distant low-voiced conversation in a strange language. What, he wondered, were they saying to each other, as they collected up their arrows and wiped their axes on the grass? Although he couldn't make out the words, it sounded like any conversation between people who spend a lot of their time working together. Hey, looks like this weather's set in for the rest of the week. Saw your sister's boy the other day; he's grown, hasn't he? You think the Redskins gonna make it to the Superbowl this year?

And then he thought he could hear words he could understand—

That bloody squirrel again—

'Yo, Talks.'

'Much obliged.'

'You're welcome, Talks.'

'Where'd this lot come from, then? I thought you said . . .'

'It's this clown I'm taking round. Not the English kid or the journalist or the droopy girl, the lawyer. Didn't do what he was told.'

'Ah.'

'I said to him, Don't try and warn them. So of course he did. Guessed he would. That sort always have to know best.'

Dieb cringed. *All his fault!* He recognised the feeling that flooded his body as if it was a leaky submarine; it was that oh-shit sensation he used to get as a young lawyer when he realised he'd failed to meet a time limit, missed out some procedural step, lost the deeds, whatever. Partly it was straightforward pain, as if his mind had been burnt and was still raw and seeping; mostly, though, it was a great gush of rage building up pressure inside him, searching for an outlet. When he'd been a young lawyer he'd hated everybody he could think of; his boss, for giving him work he wasn't fit to do; his secretary, for not reminding him; his colleagues, for not warning him; the client, for getting him into this mess in the first place. And God, of course. When he'd been a young lawyer, Calvin Dieb had sworn a lot at God. Now that he was a middle-aged lawyer, used to having the buck screeching to a halt at his feet every day of the week, he didn't hate anybody in particular (even now, he didn't hate the Vikings, or the Indians, or even the squirrel). He just hated. And, of course, he got even. Usually he got even first; if he had a philosophy of life, it was huddled round the concept of pre-emptive revenge.

It was very quiet now; either they'd gone away, or they were all standing round him in a circle, waiting for him to open his eyes. He opened them. As far as he could judge, he was on his own.

'Hello?' he heard himself call out – Jesus, how stupid! No harm seemed to come of it, however. No more arrows, no more howling warriors, not even a chatty squirrel. It occurred to him that maybe he should go and see if any of the Vikings was still alive. If so, he could use the phone in his car to call for help, if only he could get into his car, which he couldn't, not without the keys. Unforceable locks, unsmashable glass, an alarm that boiled your eyes in your head at forty paces; it was one of the reasons he'd gone for that particular model, the security. If only, if only he could get back inside it and raise the windows and deadlock the doors and call the National Guard and the Air Force on the phone, then everything would be all right.

If only he could find . . .

Survivors. There had to be survivors. With every muscle, tendon and nerve in his body clenched – except for victim photographs usable in evidence, he couldn't stand the sight of blood – he tiptoed down towards the lakeside—

(Oh God, what if they've scalped them? He didn't actually know what scalping really involved, but he was prepared to wager relevant money that it was truly horrible.)

And found it empty. Not a corpse. Not an arrow, or a tomahawk, or a splatter of blood. The whole scene was cleaner and tidier than a Swiss operating theatre.

A wave of relief and a surge of panic raced simultaneously through his mind, turning it into a jacuzzi of conflicting emotions. Maybe it hadn't happened, and nobody had been killed; in which case, he'd hallucinated it all, and he was going mad, and they'd lock him up in the funny farm and debar him from practising as a lawyer, and then the bank would foreclose on the house and his wife would be put out on the street—

Hang on, he remembered, I haven't got a wife. And the house is paid for, at least the town house is, and the apartment in Des Moines. The farm and the ski lodge weren't, but as far as he was concerned they could have those and welcome, what with interest rates and negative equity and all. Shit, he muttered to himself, I'm having an anxiety attack here and it's not even my anxiety. Get a *grip*, for Chrissakes.

All I have to do is find my keys, and I'm out of here.

'Try looking under that rock,' suggested a beaver, poking its dear little head up out of the water. 'No, not that one, the flat one to your left. I expect you're quite comfortable with the undersides of flat stones, in your line of work.'

Dieb winced, as if someone had carelessly stubbed out a cigarette in his eye. 'It's you again, isn't it? Goddamnit, why can't you just leave me alone?'

'Be like that. Only trying to help.'

'I am not lifting up that rock.'

'Don't, then.'

'Ah, shit.' He bent over, got his fingers under the edge of the rock and heaved.

'Hi.'

He stared, for maybe a fifteenth of a second; then he let go of the rock, but too late.

Peering up at him, his hair tousled, his glasses misted,

his beard full of earwigs, was his partner, Hernan Piranha.

The biggest bear, a mountain of fur and muscle with a claw salad and teeth garnish, turned its head and stared at him.

'Er,' said Wesley, and dropped the tomahawk on his foot.

''Scuse me,' said the bear.

A sharp blow on the toe can be excruciatingly painful, and the agony deprived Wesley of the power of speech; no great loss, in the circumstances, since there was absolutely nothing he could think of to say to a huge bear in any case. He refrained from screaming, and as far as he was concerned that was his lot.

''Scuse me,' repeated the bear, in a deep, reverberating growl, 'but could we possibly borrow your axe thing?'

'M?'

'You see,' the bear continued, 'we forgot the tin opener. At least,' it added, turning its head just far enough to be able to give the bear to its right a vicious look, 'one of us forgot the tin opener, the same way she'd forget her own head if it wasn't tied to her shoulders with her neck, though that's an arrangement that might well be subject to review.'

'M?'

'Ignore him,' said the female bear. 'Have you got it? I asked, just before we left. Yes of course, he said, d'you think I'm thick or something. And then when we get here it's I thought you had it. Well—'

'I bloody never!'

'That's right, shout. That's your answer to everything, shouting.'

'Tin opener?' Wesley enquired.

The male bear nodded. 'For the picnic things. The corned beef and the potted shrimps and the crab paste. And some pillock,' he added, looking left this time, 'managed to snap off the little rings on forty-seven cans of beer, though God only knows how he managed it. I mean, forty-seven!'

'Picnic things?'

'That's right. And if you could possibly hurry it up, that'd be really great, because the rest of them are due along any minute now.'

'Every bear that ever there was,' confirmed the female bear.

'And if there's nothing for them to eat except bread and butter and orange squash, life might get a bit hectic, if you see what I mean.'

''S all your fault,' the female bear sniffed. 'This'd never have happened if we'd gone to Weymouth like I said.'

'Nobody wanted to go to bloody Weymouth 'cept you,' the male bear snapped, 'so shut your noise. You can see what I've got to put up with,' he added, as Wesley backed away another step and got a low branch in the small of his back for his pains. 'So if you could just see your way . . .'

Pulling himself together like a zombie jigsaw, Wesley picked up the tomahawk and held it at arm's length. 'Please,' he said, 'help yourself. Keep it if you like.'

'Can I really? Thanks.' The bear lumbered forwards, took the axe gently, as if carrying a captured crane-fly to the window, and waddled back to where a massive wicker basket was lying on the ground, being unpacked by the other bears. One of them, who had been trying in vain to bite through a tin of salmon, grabbed the tomahawk and drew the sharp tip of the top horn of the blade round the lid of the tin. ''Scuse paws,' it said, and then levered the severed lid back delicately with one clawtip. 'Hey, salmon,' it said. 'Always it's bloody salmon. What's wrong with pilchards?'

'In the other basket, stupid.'

'Ruddy marvellous picnic this is turning out to be.'

'Oh, go climb a tree,' snarled the she-bear. 'Some people,' she sniffed, turning to Wesley as if expecting agreement, 'are never satisfied.'

'Ah, but bear's claws must exceed his paws, or what's a Heaven for?'

'Your father's off again,' sighed the she-bear. 'Who rattled his cage, then?'

'Excuse me,' said Wesley.

'Yes?'

'Excuse me,' he repeated, 'but I thought the picnic was for teddy bears.'

The bears looked at each other. 'What was that he said?' one of them asked.

'Teddy bears,' the male bear replied. 'I think he means that lot that go around on scooters wearing long thin trousers and big jackets.'

'Not our lot, then.'

'Actually,' interrupted the bear who was someone's father, 'I think he means soft, cuddly toys made in the shape of bears.'

'Don't start, Dad, please. You know it upsets the kids.'

Wesley bit his lip, rather harder than he'd intended. 'In fact,' he said, 'that's what I did mean. There's a song, you see . . .'

This time, the bears looked at Wesley. 'Come off it,' said the salmon-hater, 'that's silly. How could a lot of cuddly toys have a picnic?'

Wesley decided not to reply to that; instead, he

watched the bears ripping open tins with the tomahawk. Despite the fact that they didn't have thumbs, which is supposed to make handling things like axes extremely difficult, they were getting through them at an impressive rate. There were also two enormous brown bears, who were digging a hole.

'Excuse me,' Wesley heard himself say, 'but what's the hole for?'

'To bury the litter, of course,' replied the she-bear who'd wanted to go to Weymouth. 'We're green, we are.'

'Speak for yourself.'

'I heard that.'

Sure enough, the two bears stopped scrabbling with their tennis-racquet paws and started shovelling the empty cans into the hole they'd made, swearing occasionally as a ragged tin edge snagged a glove-leather-soft paw-pad. It was at that moment that Wesley forced himself to admit that this was really happening, and it wasn't some bizarre sport of his imagination; because however weird and disturbed he might be, there was no way that he was capable of imagining *this*. Even his odder acquaintances, the ones who regularly chatted to angels or acted as franchisees for Martian Equitable Life, might get embarrassed and remember distant appointments if he started telling them about this.

'Thanks.'

The first bear, the one he'd lent the tomahawk to, was talking to him. He turned his head and smeared a bewildered smile on the front of it.

'Sorry?' he said.

'Thanks,' the bear repeated. 'For the loan of your axe. Did the job a treat. Would you like a pickled walnut?'

'I, er – yes, that'd be great. Fine.'

The bear reached out a treelike arm and put

something small, black and shrivelled delicately into his hand. It looked like something a nine-year-old head-hunter might have brought home from school. He shuddered and said thank you nicely.

'Saving it for later?'

'Yes,' Wesley replied. 'Much later. I'll, er, appreciate it more then.'

'Suit yourself,' said the bear equably. 'Well, we'd better be getting along. See you around.'

'Will you? I mean, yes, right. Cheers for now, then.'

The bears waved their paws, turned and wandered off into the forest, until their lumbering backs merged into the dappled shadows. When Wesley was sure they'd gone, he opened his hand, looked at the strange black fossilised thing clutched in it, and threw it away. A squirrel ran down the side of the tree over his head, pounced on the reject walnut and ate it quickly.

'Waste not, want not,' it said with its mouth full. 'Sure you don't want some?'

'Very sure indeed.'

'Your loss.' The squirrel twitched its nose and spat something out. 'Well, maybe not,' it added. 'Anyway, how are you liking it?'

Wesley made a peculiar noise. '*Liking* it,' he repeated. 'Oh for God's—'

'You mean you aren't? That's a pity. Particularly since you saved up and everything. Hell, for that money you could have gone to Disneyland. I would've,' the squirrel added wistfully. 'Of course, *I* haven't had a holiday in, oh, twenty thousand years.'

'This is a holiday?'

'Supposed to be, yes.'

'A holiday!' Wesley burst out. 'So far I've nearly drowned, I've witnessed a shipwreck and I've been set upon by seven enormous bears. If that's meant to be a holiday, what the hell do you think I do the rest of the year?'

'I wouldn't call it being set upon, exactly,' the squirrel pointed out. 'As I recall, they gave you a walnut.'

'Set upon,' Wesley affirmed. 'By seven enormous bears. Look, is there a point to all this, because if so I'd like it if we could get to it now, please, so I can go home.'

'We're getting there,' the squirrel replied. 'I mean, we're past stage one, the suspension of disbelief.'

'Oh, I've suspended my disbelief all right. Lynched it, in fact. Now can I please—?'

'Not yet,' said the squirrel firmly. 'Boy, you ain't seen nothing yet.'

Funny bugger, Old Mister Instinct. At school, Janice DeWeese had been a keen swimmer. (See that rubber-capped, goggle-faced egg shape chugging up and down the school swimming bath, lacking a salt-caked smoke-stack but otherwise a dead ringer for the ship in the poem? That's her.) The human otter, they'd called her, to her face. And yet, when she got her head up out of the water and realised what was going on, she found she was doing the doggy-paddle; not very well, either. The thing that had somehow got into her mouth was either a newt or a small fish. The backpack wasn't helping, either.

In her defence, she could have argued that this wasn't the sort of water she was used to. Swimming-pool water, like tap-water, sea-water and pretty well any kind of water apart from the stuff you find in Lake Chicopee, flows. Push it aside, and it goes away. In other words, it's liquid. This stuff was more like runny aspic. You'd be hard put to drown in it, in the same way that it's hard to drown on a stone floor; but it wasn't much good for swimming in. It wasn't particularly – what was the word she was groping for? – wet.

'Gnurrgh!' she said.

'It's an acquired taste,' said a voice by her ear.

'Gnargh?'

'Not,' the voice added, 'that I'd go out of my way to acquire it, if I were you. There's things living in it that aren't house-trained.' The otter shrugged. 'Texture's not all that hot, either. You wouldn't want to irrigate your tender young seedlings with it, for fear of squashing them flat.'

'You're an otter!'

'Yes.' The otter twitched its nose. 'So?'

'But . . .'

'Look, if you've got a problem with that, I'm terribly sorry. But it's turning out to be a long day and I've got a lot on my plate right now, so if you could just accept the fact that you're talking to an otter, it'll save a whole lot of time.'

'But . . .'

'Ah, don't be like that. The others were all right about it, so why should you be any different?'

'Others?'

'Whoops, me and my big mouth. You can see I'm tired, can't you? Look, any minute now you're going to see this Viking longship, okay?'

'What?'

'Longship. They're called that because . . .' The otter shrugged again. 'Because they aren't short, I guess. That's beside the point. There'll be this ship, OK? Oh *bugger*, here it comes now. The thing I want you to remember is, don't worry if they drown, all right? I dunno, goddamn lousy tight schedules . . .'

The otter dived, leaving a string of bubbles like three

dots at the end of a sentence. Janice realised that she'd stopped swimming, panicked and thrashed out with all available limbs. This at least did have some effect on the water around her; it made her go downwards. She was just about to have a go at underwater screaming when she heard something so unusual that she forgot all about drowning and bobbed back up to the surface again.

It was a wolf-whistle.

'Grrnyahgh!' she said, finally getting rid of the fish, newt or water beetle. At the periphery of her vision she could see something that looked vaguely like a ship. She craned her neck and looked round; and as she did so, she heard voices.

'Thorgrim! I am telling you how many times that not to be doing! Disrespectful it and sexist is!'

'Splut?' Janice murmured, puzzled.

'Apology,' said another voice. 'Ernly, away carried I was. It a long time been has. And loveliness such!'

'Ah!' agreed the first voice. 'Agreement. But the whistling not, to be so kind.'

Jan kicked feebly against the jellied water. She couldn't remember having banged her head, but maybe the bang on the head was affecting her memory. 'Hey!' she shouted.

'Hello, gorgeous one,' replied the second voice. 'Often here are you coming? In this damp water all alone a nice girl doing what is?'

'That, Thorgrim, not much better is. A line that is so old whiskers on it there are . . .'

'Help!' Janice yelled. 'Somebody get me outa here!'

'To be saving you a privilege, entrancing one. If a little patience—'

'You, Skaldulf, too presumptuous are,' interrupted a third voice. 'You saving her who was it said it should be?

On this ship others beside yourself—'

'First I was seeing her, of a lady dog offensive off-spring!'

'My bones breaking sticks and stones may be, of a crow the excrement! And out of the way to be getting—'

'My dead body over, of a dog the breath! And your feet putting—'

Janice trod water, wondering what in all hell was going on. She could see the ship clearly now; a big wooden row-boat, with painted lids on the sides. The decks were lined with men, who were *looking* at her.

'Straws we could I suppose be drawing,' someone was saying. 'Straws here I happen to have, by some chance . . .'

'With your straws perhaps aware you are what you might do, Bjarni Oddleifsen. Now, my way out of.'

'The contrary, serpent—'

'*The ship, where it is heading!*'

There was a crash, as of stone on timber. There was a gurgling, like the water draining out of God's bath. There were complicated refined curses, and glugging noises. And then there was silence, except for the slight lapping of the water as the ripples were ironed away.

'Ah, shit!' Janice said.

CHAPTER FIVE

'Hiya, Calvin,' said Hernan Piranha.

Usually, Calvin Dieb could recover his composure so quickly that you'd never notice that he'd lost it. If a Greek god were to descend from the heavens and prove to him that without knowing it he'd murdered his father and married his mother, by the time the god had finished speaking, Calvin would have adjusted to the fact and be ready to explain precisely why killing your dad and marrying your mom was probably the brightest thing you could do if you really wanted to cut your tax bills. On this occasion, however, he stood with his mouth open, looking very much like a two-legged, expensively suited goldfish.

'Hi, Hernan,' he eventually replied.

There was, of course, a lot of subtext going on here. Inevitably, their spectacularly successful partnership was built on a solid foundation of implicit mutual mistrust. If, at the start of the office day, Calvin said, 'Good morning,' Hernan would spend the next hour and a half trying to work out exactly what Cal had meant by good. If Hernan said to Calvin, 'No, you drive,' Calvin would make damn sure he wiped any fingerprints off the steering wheel before getting out of the car. They were both, after all, Americans and lawyers. On finding Hernan under a flat stone in the middle of all this utter weirdness, therefore, he didn't ask himself, *What's Hernan doing under that stone?* but *What's Hernan up to under that stone?* And although paranoia was thrusting daggers of panic into his heart, it sure was comforting to see him, in a life-threatening sort of a way.

'Bet you're surprised to see me here, kid,' said Hernan.

'No, not particularly. Why?'

– And that was another thing; seventeen years Hernan Piranha had been calling him 'kid', and only last week he'd found out that the sonofabitch was actually three weeks younger than he was. At the time, he'd merely requisitioned another propane torch and barrelful of six-inch nails for the customised Hell he'd been designing for Hernan since the first day they'd met. Here and now, he felt a more immediate response was called for. Like calling him 'gramps' or something equally mordant.

'Because I don't usually hide under rocks in picturesque valleys is why, Cal. Or hadn't you noticed?'

Calvin smiled warmly. 'Jesus, Hernan, you know I'd never question your judgement on anything. If hiding under rocks is the right thing for you just now, then go for it.' He turned up the smile a volt or so, in his mind imagining those extra volts added to an already plentiful supply going up into the seat of Hernan's trousers from the electrodes of Old Sparky. 'I know you never do anything without a darned good reason,' he added. 'Oh, did Niedermeyers call back about that railroad thing?'

Herman shook his head, not even bothering with an old ploy like that. For the first six years of their association, Calvin had managed to keep Hernan permanently twitching by asking him throwaway questions about entirely non-existent cases. The way in which Hernan ignored the question convinced Calvin of one thing, at least; this was his partner, in person, and not just some jerk from an agency made up to look like him.

But Piranha, damn him, was grinning all over his overfed-Chinese-god face. 'Admit it, Cal,' he said, 'you're just burning up inside to know what I'm doing here. But you're such a stubborn old cuss, you'll never ask in a million years. Am I right?'

'You go ahead and tell me, if it'll make you feel better. You know, it often does help to talk about these things.'

'Yeah. Well—'

'And you know, Hernan,' Dieb pressed on ruthlessly, 'that whatever happens, I'll always be here for you. Whatever happens.'

'Sure, Cal,' Piranha replied, eyes twinkling. 'With a knife up one sleeve and a sharpened stick behind your back, you old coyote. But it so happens that today, *I'm* here for *you*.'

'That's good to know, Hernan.'

'Because,' Hernan continued, holding up something small and shiny, 'I know you want these.'

The car keys, goddamnit! For a split second Calvin Dieb lost his cool, and grabbed. By the time his hand had moved the eighteen inches separating his fingertips from the keys, they'd vanished. Not that Hernan had perceptibly moved; his hand just wasn't there any more.

'Perhaps it'd help,' he said, 'if you thought of me as Jacob Marley.'

Thirty-two feet per second per second; eventually the

penny dropped. When it did, Calvin Dieb took a step back, crossed his arms and said, 'Actually, I preferred you when you were an otter.'

Piranha shook his head, and turned into a beautiful young girl with hair the colour of freshly laid Tarmac. 'Took you long enough,' she said. 'I thought you lawyers were supposed to be smarter than that.'

'I was humouring you,' Dieb replied as best he could. 'Can I have my keys now, please?'

The girl shook her head, so that her hair swung. 'Nope,' she said, sitting down on a rock and crossing her knees. 'Here, come and sit beside me.' She patted the rock beside her and smiled a dazzling smile.

'You can forget that, by the way,' Dieb said, doing so. 'Now that I've seen you as Hernan, there's no way it's going to work. So, you're gonna Scrooge me, are you? Well, you're welcome to try, but as your legal adviser I have to tell you, you're wasting your time.'

'Not my time,' replied the girl sweetly. 'Yours. Your time, which costs two thousand dollars an hour. If I were you, Mr Dieb, I'd co-operate.'

Dieb shrugged. 'OK,' he said, 'I'll co-operate. What've I got to do?'

'Find your car keys,' the girl said. 'That's all. A smart guy like you ought to be able to manage something simple like that. Hey, do you know that talking to you in your office for *one second* costs fifty-five cents? I mean, what can you possibly tell me in one second that's worth as much as a pint of milk or a game of pinball?'

'Easy,' Dieb replied wearily. 'In one second I can tell you Yes, or No. My yes or no could make you a fortune or save you millions. More to the point, whoever you are, what can *you* do in a second that's worth – oh shit, no, I didn't mean that—'

'Oh yes you did.'

'No, please, forget I—'

You could have skewered chunks of barbecued lamb on the look in the girl's eyes. 'One second, Mister Dieb? You wanna see what I can do in one second?'

'No,' Dieb replied with uncharacteristic honesty.

'Tough. You ready? *Now* . . .'

One second later, Calvin Dieb opened his eyes, to find himself surrounded by bears.

Funny what a few hours can do to a man. Earlier that morning, if you'd offered him a choice of being surrounded by bears or having lunch with his ex-wife, he'd have chosen the bears so fast you'd scarcely have seen his lips move. Now, however, he'd have welcomed Thelma with open arms. For one thing, she'd scare off the bears.

Jesus, he made a mental note, but they're *big* fuckers. And how come they've got such big, sharp teeth? All his life, Calvin Dieb had lumped bears together with cashmere scarves and English tea and detective stories where the little old lady solves the mystery before the cops have even taken their hats off, all falling into the category of soft, cuddly things that you can only afford if you're hard and mean, really. Hard, mean bears were something entirely outside his experience; and something told him that these were seven hard, mean bears.

Hungry, too, by the look of them.

'Help?' he suggested, looking round for the girl. But she wasn't there. For all he knew, she was one of these goddamn wild animals. Not that the thought was comforting; rather, the reverse.

'There now,' he muttered. 'Good bears.'

The second largest bear growled at him; a low,

rumbling noise like some horrible machine. Its eyes were small, circular and hostile, and it was paying him full attention. Inside its head, he could almost hear the wheels turning as it asked itself the only question it knew: *Food/notfood?*

There were six more like that. Great.

'However,' said a squirrel on a branch above his head, 'they do eat otters, so that's all right. If you had an otter problem, you'd be real glad to see these guys.'

'HELP!'

'Don't shout,' cooed the squirrel, 'it excites them. Movement, too. Now, I bet you're wondering how seven hungry bears are going to help you find your car keys.'

Having been advised to stay still and quiet, Calvin Dieb neither nodded nor spoke. Instead he concentrated on emitting inedibility vibes.

'Well,' continued the squirrel, 'here's the deal. There's an old Iroquois legend that a warrior who kills a bear in single combat and eats its heart raw gains great wisdom. If you had great wisdom, you might be able to find your keys. Well, what're you waiting for?'

The third largest bear straightened its back and rose up on its hind paws, rumbling ominously. One swat of its front paw would turn Calvin's head into bonemeal and jam. It opened its mouth and licked its lips.

'I know,' said the squirrel. 'You're waiting for me to let you have the magic tomahawk. Coming through!'

Something fell at Calvin's feet; or, to be precise, something fell on Calvin's big toe, just exactly where he had the bunion. It speaks volumes for his self-control that, instead of screaming and leaping in the air, he merely said, 'Eek!' in a muted whisper and stayed put. Meanwhile, the largest bear of all put its ears back and growled.

Calvin had a very unpleasant feeling that it was saying grace.

'The tomahawk, dummy,' the squirrel was yelling at him. 'C'mon, for Pete's sake, it's magic, you won't really have to do *anything* and there'll be bits of delicatessen-style thin-sliced bear all over the place. Ah, come *on*!'

The biggest bear's shoulder muscles tensed; and here it comes . . .

But it didn't. Instead, there was a shrill, ear-splitting yodel that turned Calvin's blood to yoghurt, and something crashed through the trees on the end of a long rope. The something turned out to be a tall, slim, striking-looking woman with fiery red hair, a severe black pinstripe suit with massively padded shoulders and a skirt that came up to her chin, and eyes of cold blue flame. As soon as her feet touched the ground she whirled round, kicked high in a manner that would have made Bruce Lee's eyes water, slammed the megabear in what Calvin assumed was its nuts, punched out the two bears to its left and right with knife-hand blows that sounded like pistol shots, swooped to gather up the tomahawk with her left hand, threw it spinning through the air and caught it backhanded with her right, jumped and landed in a perfect axefighter's stance, threatening not just the cowering bears but the whole world.

'Hi, Thelma,' Calvin squeaked.

'You're pathetic, Cal,' his ex-wife replied, not looking at him. She was staring down the bears so ferociously that at any moment you'd expect them to melt into little pools of tallow. 'God, you haven't changed one bit.'

'That's right, Thelma. You chase away those goddamn bears and I'll be as pathetic as you like.'

'Hah!' By the time the echo of her shout died away, even the biggest of the bears had lumbered away, moving at lightning speed despite its obvious agony. The squirrel, meanwhile, had retired to the very top of the tree and was hiding behind a thick branch.

'Way to go, Thelma,' Calvin sighed, pulling himself up from the heap into which he had subsided. 'How's life in Chicago, anyway?'

'Hell of a lot better since I dumped you,' Thelma replied, tossing the tomahawk up and catching it again. 'Shit, Calvin, I've been tracking that big fucker for *hours*. Trust you to mess it all up for me.'

'Sorry, Thelma. Don't let me keep you.'

'I don't suppose you happened to notice which way it went. Or were you too busy pissing your pants?'

'I made the time, Thel. It went that way, up the slope and left by that fallen tree.'

Thelma nodded, stooped to pull the strap of her shoe back over her heel, flicked a blood-red lipstick round her mouth and stalked off up the slope. 'You know what, Cal?' she threw back over her shoulder. 'You always did lack that killer instinct. That's why you'll always be nothing.'

'Very true. Be seeing you.'

'I hope not, Cal.'

A moment later, she was gone. Calvin gazed after her with a mixture of horror and respect in his eyes, as the squirrel tentatively made its way down the branch.

'There,' Calvin said reverently, 'goes the best damn divorce attorney in the state of Illinois.'

'Hey.'

'Which is a big state, but not nearly big enough. Sorry, you were saying?'

'The bear,' said the squirrel. 'Actually, it went down the slope and into those bushes.'

Calvin nodded. 'I know,' he replied. 'But hell, what harm did it ever do me?'

*

'Admit it, Chief,' said Mr Snedge. 'We're lost.'

Captain Hat didn't answer. Instead, he sat down on the ground, took off the flamboyant, ostrich-feather-trimmed hat that was his trademark, and spun it slowly round his finger, as his eyes strayed out over the silver waters of the lake. They were about two hundred yards away, and they'd been trying to reach them for four hours.

'This,' he said eventually, 'is silly.'

'You bet, Chief. The lads and me, we were just saying . . .'

'Maybe,' Hat mused, 'we're going about this the wrong way. Maybe we should stay here and let the damn lake come to us.'

They sat in silence for ninety seconds; after which time, Mr Squab cleared his throat and said, 'Hasn't moved yet, Chief.'

Hat shrugged. 'Maybe it's shy or something. Everybody close their eyes, quit staring at it.'

They shut their eyes. Seventy seconds later, they opened them again.

'OK,' said Hat, 'at least we tried it, so we can eliminate that as a possibility. Any other suggestions?'

Just then, something large and heavy crashed past them, bulldozing a straight path through a briar patch. A moment or so later, something else followed it, leaving behind the impression of ferocious energy, short skirts and flaming red hair.

'Hey, Chief,' said Mr Snedge. 'What was that?'

'I think,' Hat replied, his chin rested on his hands, 'it was a huge bear being chased by an attractive older woman with some kind of axe.'

'Not an axe, chief. A tomahawk.'

'Really?' Hat sighed, without looking round. 'How come you're so sure?'

'I nicked it from her, Chief.'

Captain Hat closed his eyes. 'Snedge,' he muttered, 'I wish you'd stop doing that. One of these days it's going to get someone really pissed off with us, you know?'

'Sorry, Chief.'

Hat shrugged. 'Yeah, well. Neat piece of work, though. You sure she didn't notice?'

'They never do.'

'Pass it over, then, and let's have a look at it.'

A simple tomahawk it proved to be; knapped flint and pine and elk sinew, nothing more. Hat looked at it for a while, then closed his eyes, tossed it up in the air and caught it.

'Yo, Chief, where'd you learn to do that?'

Hat shook his head. 'No need,' he replied. 'It's one of those magic things. Hell, a snake could juggle with these babies and still catch them.'

'Magic, huh?' Squab didn't sound impressed, exactly. 'What's those curious symbols incised on the handle mean?'

'Symbols? Hey, he's right, let's see. *Made in USA by union labor.* CAUTION *Read safety warnings in manual before use.* Well, I guess that's another little mystery cleared up. Shall we try going up the trail instead of down it this time, or did we try that already?'

'We tried it, Chief.'

'Nuts.' Hat lay back, tipped the brim of his hat down over his eyes and folded his hands behind his head. 'Let's stay here, then. Perhaps if we stay here long enough, the universe'll get bored and go pick on someone its own size.'

'Chief.'

'What?'

'It can't do that, Chief, on account of nobody's the same size as the universe. That's called Einstein.'

'I stand corrected, Mr Squab. Let's just stay here anyway.'

Far away, a bird sang. An otter slipped into the water, strewing bubbles. A bear roared, either in rage or in terror.

'Chief.'

'Yeah?'

'Wasn't it Einstein who directed *Battleship Potemkin*?'

'That was Eisenstein, Snedge.'

'I thought Eisenstein was US chief of staff in World War Two.'

'I don't think so, Snedge. He was a Russian.'

'Hey! You mean like a spy or something?'

'You're thinking of Eisenhower, Snedge.'

'Ah, right. You mean the relativity guy.'

'That's him, Snedge. The very same.'

A plane flew overhead, very high. Just before it was due to pass directly over the lake, it changed course slightly and flew round it. They always did. Nobody, not the pilots, not flight control, ever knew why. In the distance, a longship sank.

'Chief.'

'Oh, cut it out, will you? I was just getting comfortable.'

'Chief,' insisted Mr Squab, 'there's someone coming.'

Immediately Hat was on his feet, hat on, right hand on the butt of his pistol. 'Damnit,' he hissed, 'we're right out in the open, too.'

'It's them Injuns again, Chief.'

'You mustn't call them that any more, Snedge, they don't . . . Where?'

'Coming over the ridge, look. Hey, you remember the time we stole their . . .'

'*Hide!*'

'No, Chief, we stole their canoe, remember? Don't think they had any hides.'

'I mean conceal yourself, you dummy.'

'Sorry Chief.'

Linda Lachuk stopped in her tracks, turned round and looked. Nobody there. Odd; she could have sworn she was being followed.

She shrugged and carried on walking, just as the ninth consecutive arrow from Talks With Squirrels' bow hit her smack between the shoulder blades. It was archery of a kind that would have left Robin Hood weeping with jealous rage; nine hits within a half-inch circle at seventy-five yards. For the record, she'd also trodden right on the dead centre of the fragile platform of branches covering the deep pit full of sharpened stakes, put her feet in the tripwires of four noose-and-bent-sapling beartraps and strolled through a direct frontal assault by Talks' entire war party without even blinking an eye. If she'd only known what kind of footage she was missing, she'd have died of frustration.

Just as she was beginning to feel that a nice sit-down and a cup of coffee would be really helpful, she caught sight of a building, fifty yards or so away under the shadow of a stand of tall pines. She stopped, turned off the path and sauntered up to the front door. It wasn't locked.

'Hello?' she called out. 'Press. Anyone home?'

The place seemed deserted, but the occupants couldn't be too far away; there was a roaring fire in the grate, and the red check tablecloth was laid for a meal.

There were cute little wooden bowls, with cute wooden cups and spoons. A cute cottage loaf and an old-fashioned wood-handled breadknife sat on a cute wooden platter in the middle of the table. A big copper kettle hung on a hook in front of the fire.

Ah, said Linda to herself, a Tea Shoppe. Probably out back they keep the postcards, souvenir mugs and expensive home-made fudge. She sat down on one of the cute wooden chairs – oddly enough, there was only one she could sit on; the other two were too big and too small respectively; rural inbreeding, probably – and looked round for a waitress.

A moment later, one appeared. She was tall, slim, dark and beautiful, with hair like a black waterfall. 'Hiya,' she said. 'What'll it be?'

'Coffee.'

'Sorry,' the girl said. 'No coffee. All we got is milk.'

'Milk, then,' Linda replied. 'Is there anything to eat? A triple pastrami on rye with alfalfa sprouts and blue cheese relish, and . . .'

The girl shook her head. 'There's porridge,' she said.

'Porridge?'

'It's mighty fine porridge,' the girl said with a smile. 'Best in all of Iowa. With cream and honey.'

'Porridge, then,' Linda sighed. 'Oh, and while you're here, I don't suppose you know anything about the submarine base, do you?'

The girl chewed the end of her pencil. 'You mean the secret nuclear submarine base in the lake? The one that's a joint venture between the CIA, the Pope and the Australians?'

Linda nodded, unable to speak. For a split second, she even forgot her resentment about there being no pastrami.

'Sure,' the girl replied. 'Just wait there till I fetch your order, and I'll tell you all about it.'

She swayed gracefuly away, leaving Linda looking as if she'd just been trapped in amber. *Yes!* The CIA, the Vatican *and* the Ozzies, with alfalfa sprouts, blue cheese relish *and* a fennel salad. Good menu they got here, she muttered to herself, except for the food.

Her daydream froze-framed, and splintered into fragments as she looked at the open doorway and felt the muscles of her stomach tighten into a hard knot.

In the doorway stood three bears.

'All right,' said the squirrel, 'we're here now.'

Wesley, who had been trudging along looking where he was going, stopped and surveyed.

'We came *here*?' he demanded. 'On *purpose*?'

The squirrel's tail quivered; body language for, *Yes, I know*. And it wasn't a prepossessing spot; all that picturesque scenery, all that awesome majesty of nature, the trees, the scree-covered hillsides, the silvery cascade of the waterfall – and here they were, at a garbage dump.

'But not,' the squirrel pointed out, 'just any old trash-heap. Look carefully.'

Wesley sniffed, his manner reminiscent of the food-taster to a psychotic Roman emperor who's just slapped an extra denarius on beer and ciggies. 'Must I?' he queried. 'Squirrel, this place smells like where I live. I don't *want* to look carefully.'

'Look carefully.'

'Oh, all right.' With his toe, Wesley tentatively nudged a parting into the overgrowth of nettles and briars. 'Like I thought,' he called back over his shoulder, 'it's nothing but a load of old – *oh my God!*'

'Impressive, huh?'

'But—' Wesley turned his head slowly. 'This hillside,' he said, slowly and nervously. 'It's not all—?'

The squirrel nodded. 'The whole hillside, as far as the eye can see. Just one huge great pile of bones. I'm telling you, if you were a dog with a weak heart, you'd be dead meat by now.'

'Er . . .' Wesley knelt down, uncomfortably aware of creakings and snappings underfoot. 'Might I ask what sort of . . . ?'

'It's all right, they're not human bones,' the squirrel replied. 'Just look at the size of them, for a start.'

Wesley peered closer. They were, indeed, *huge*; enormous ribcages and tibiae and femurs. And skulls too, of course. As soon as he saw them, he knew what the bones were.

'Buffalo,' he said.

'Bison,' the squirrel corrected him. 'Look around you, and you're looking at all that remains of roughly a billion bison. Hey, you're into making model kits; if you like, I'll get you some glue and you can piece a few of 'em back together again.'

'Shuttup!' Wesley felt the shudders coming on, but there was nothing he could do about it. 'Did you say . . . ?'

'A billion's maybe overdoing it, I couldn't resist the assonance. Well over ten million, though. Must be pretty close to eleven million. Can your mind conceive of eleven million of *anything*?'

'No,' Wesley answered without hesitation. 'Anything over four hundred is basically just lots.' He took a deep breath and managed to slow his shivering down a little. 'What is this place, Buffalo Bill's skip?'

'Hell, no,' the squirrel replied. 'Bill Cody and his type only helped sweep up the very last knockings. There used to be *lots* of bison in these parts at one time.'

'OK.' Wesley folded his arms and looked resolutely away. 'So what happened?'

'Before Buffalo Bill—'Wesley glanced up into the tree; the squirrel had vanished, and the voice was coming from immediately behind him. 'Before the red man, even, there were an awful lot of buffs around here. They had it good, too; no natural predators, plenty of suitable food and clean water, amenable climate – the living was easy if you stood six feet at the withers and weighed a ton and a half. In fact, it got so easy that the buffs found they had time for other things besides mere survival and reproduction.'

'Huh?'

'Music,' said the buffalo behind him. 'Poetry. Philosophy. The arts. And, shortly after that, the sciences too. Ten thousand years ago, these babies were highly civilised. Sophisticated, enquiring minds. Sensitive souls capable of savouring the beautiful and strange. Impeccable table manners.'

'Table manners?'

'Never spoke with their mouths full. Digested everything in the proper order. Table manners can get really sophisticated when you've got two stomachs.'

Wesley frowned. 'All right,' he said, 'point taken. So what happened to them?'

'Bit slow on the uptake today, aren't you?' replied the buffalo, pawing absently at the crust of the bonehill. 'They wiped each other out, is what. Par for the course, when a species gets so far above itself that it's got time on its hands. Remind you of anyone?'

'Um.'

'Actually,' the buffalo went on, swishing its tail, 'our lot at least had the common sense to use an ultimate weapon that didn't blow up the planet. As I recall, it was a highly selective synthetic virus that only affected the American bison. Wiped out ninety-nine per cent of the population in just under forty-eight hours.'

Wesley swallowed the nasty-tasting stuff that was creeping up inside his throat. 'And the other one per cent?' he asked.

'Oh, they'd made plans. Before the war started, they got the other bison to dig them nice deep bunkers, usually underneath lakes where the virus couldn't get through. Water filtered it out, you see. Then, when all the others were dead and the virus had died out along with them, up they came and got on with the job of rebuilding the breeding stock.' The buffalo sighed. 'It was sort of arse-about-face Darwinism, if you like. Survival of the most devious. The idea was that the genetic matrix of a bunch of creatures who could cheerfully send the rest of their species to their deaths must be pretty hot stuff; so if they could wipe out the rest of the species until only they were left to breed from, pretty soon they'd have a race of genetically perfect Superbastards; you know, the sort who not only inherit the Earth but duck out of paying the inheritance tax. Can you follow that line of reasoning? It has a sort of ghastly logic, don't you think?'

Wesley nodded. 'Where I come from,' he said, 'we call it government policy. The needs of the many outweighing the needs of the few. Sorry, you were saying.'

'Quite,' the buffalo replied. 'The misrepresentation of the people, and all that. In our case, though, the whole scheme blew a fuse at the last minute.'

'Really?'

'Really,' the buffalo confirmed. 'What actually happened was that immediately after the war started, just before the bunker hatches were due to be sealed, the cleaners who'd been ordered to spruce the place up a bit

before the superbison moved in – you know, give it a last
going-over with the Hoover, air the beds and so on –
changed the locks and refused to come out. The superbison all died of the plague, and as a result the dumb
beasts Bill Cody's boys polished off were all descended
from a bunch of cleaners and carpet-shampooers;
marvellously gifted at keeping the prairies neat and tidy,
not much cop when it came to outwitting the white man
and his stick that spoke thunder. I suppose you could say
it served them right. After all, survival of the most house-
proud; it's not exactly a manifesto for a brave new world,
is it?'

Wesley shrugged. 'It was a pity, all the same,' he
answered. 'I mean, they couldn't exactly help the mess
their ancestors made.'

'Sure.' The buffalo sounded unsympathetic. 'And if
the egg you had poached for breakfast this morning had
been allowed to hatch, maybe it'd have gone on to write
Beethoven's symphonies. I wouldn't lose much sleep
over it, though, if I were you. In the final analysis, what
tastes better on toast, a symphony or a poached egg?'

Wesley shifted his weight off his left leg, which had
gone to sleep. 'Is there any point in you telling me this,'
he asked, 'or is it just to make me feel rotten about being
human?'

The buffalo snickered into its beard. 'This is just the
setting,' it replied. 'The adventure'll be along in a
minute.'

'The adventure? What adventure?'

'Ah.'

'So you're the little bastard who's been sitting in my
chair,' snarled the Daddy bear. 'Muriel, hold her arms.'

Linda rose to her feet like a firework from a milk

bottle. As she did so, she heard the chair go *snap!* under her. 'Now just a minute,' she said.

'My chair!' yelped the bear. 'Look what the bitch's done to my chair! Goddamn thing isn't even paid for yet, and she's gone and bust it.'

Linda looked down, gulped and turned back, trying to fumble her face muscles into a smile. 'It's OK,' she croaked, 'really. The paper'll pay for any damage. Look, I'll give you my card, and . . .'

'Like hell you will. Junior, run and get the big hammer.'

Many years ago, when she was nothing but a cub reporter with a spiral-back notebook and a dream as big as Mongolia, Linda had been sent on a course. The title was *Handling Awkward Confrontations*, and the idea was to train the young newshound how to blarney her way past the fact that she'd been caught taking pictures of the secret military installation, resting her elbows for a one-fifteenth second exposure on the big sign saying *Photography Punishable By Death* while wearing a T-shirt of the local military dictator dressed in horns, cloven hooves and a frock. At the time, Linda had been rather more interested in following up a potential story about corrupt coursework-grading practices at that particular summer school, and she'd missed quite a few useful hints. Short-sighted of her, in retrospect (although in the end it had made a fine story).

There were, however, three magic words that usually worked in these situations. She tried them.

'I'm a journalist,' she said, and held her breath.

Daddy bear's brow furrowed. 'A what?'

'Journalist,' Linda repeated, in that patient voice grown-ups use when teaching backward children to read. 'I write things for the newspapers.'

'Newspapers?'

Before Linda could say anything, Mummy bear leaned forward and whispered something in her partner's ear.

'Oh, right,' he said. 'That stuff. And you write the words, do you?'

Linda allowed herself to relax ever so slightly. 'That's right,' she said.

'Ah. Actually, I've often wondered, maybe you can tell me this. Why do they bother printing words all over the stuff when all you ever use it for is wiping your—?'

'Hey!' Linda objected.

Hard-bitten, cynical newshound that she was, Linda Lachuk still had a small, battered compartment in her soul labelled *Dreams – Handle With Care*. About the only thing in that compartment that hadn't been reduced to glass dust years ago was the quaint notion that whenever a story of hers got printed in a newspaper, people would actually read it and take it seriously. Although, generally speaking, she wouldn't give you the pickings of a piranha's teeth (you collect) for any matter of principle that wasn't good for two thousand words and a photo spread, all it took was somebody speaking blasphemously about the media to make her as ideologically ferocious as, say—

A she-bear defending her cubs? Well, why not?

The bear stared at her down its long snout. 'You say something?' it demanded.

'I said, Hey,' Linda replied. 'Want to make something of it, fuzzball?'

'Don't you call my husband a fuzzball.'

'Go on, Dad, eat her.'

The bear growled. 'Yeah,' he said. 'I want to make something of it.'

'Right now?'

'Right now.'

'Then perhaps,' Linda said, slowly taking off her jacket and rolling up her sleeves, 'you'd care to step outside.'

The bear frowned. 'But you're a girl,' it objected.

Linda nodded. 'Yeah,' she said. 'I'm the girl whose gonna shove your dumb face down your dumb neck, you fleabag. Now, you wanna step outside or not?'

The bear opened its mouth. 'You bet.'

'Me, too. Oh please, Mum, can I step outside, too? Oh, go on.'

'Let's all step outside,' snarled the she-bear. 'Nobody calls my husband a fleabag and gets away with it.'

Linda nodded. In her eyes flickered the light of battle. The three bears looked at each other, and their eyes said, *Right*.

'Go on, then,' grunted the bear.

'No, after you,' Linda replied, dipping her head in a disdainful bow. She stood up, crossed to the door and held it open for them.

'Right,' said the bear.

'Right.'

'Right.'

'Right.'

The three bears stalked outside, breathing heavily through their snouts; whereupon Linda slammed the door behind them, shot the bolts, dragged up a chair and wedged it under the handle and sprinted for the stairs. By the time the Daddy bear had smashed down the door, Linda had one leg over the sill of the bathroom window, and was calculating approximately how hard she'd hit the tin roof of the scullery ten feet below.

The answer was: quite hard, but not nearly as hard as,

for example, three angry bears. She rolled down the roof, landed awkwardly on her right hip, swore, picked herself up and ran. Mummy bear reached the open window just as Linda disappeared into the trees, and although she threw several articles of crockery and footwear after her, she missed.

Some considerable time later Linda caught her foot in a low trailing bramble, measured her length on the ground and lay still. When her head came back on line she got up on her hands and knees and listened for sounds of pursuit. Silence, except for soft forest murmurs and the welly-booted tap-dancing of her own heart. Shaken them off. Phew.

'Damn,' Linda said aloud. OK, it was good to have escaped from the bears, but that didn't alter the fact that she'd been *that* close to getting a full eyewitness statement from that waitress which sounded set fair to link the CIA, the Pope and the Australians to this submarine thing.

If she was half a journalist, she'd go back.

Yes, reasoned the better part of her valour, and if you do go back, fairly soon you *will* be half a journalist; the bottom half, probably, all chewed and covered in scratch marks. And to die without having filed the story – what a terrible, terrible waste that would be. Once she'd filed the story – well, once they'd printed the story and she'd won a hatful of awards and done her acceptance speeches – then all the bears in the Universe could come and eat her with English mustard and hack sauce for all she cared. Until then, she was the guardian of a Sacred Trust.

To cover the story . . .

Bring 'em back alive . . .

And me too, please, added discretion's better part, which had been kibbutzing on this train of thought. *If that's all right with the rest of me, that is.*

The hell with it. There would be other witnesses. All she had to do was find them.

Pulling her shirt collar up round her ears – it was turning cold, and she'd left her jacket behind – she set off to do just that.

CHAPTER SIX

'I should've taken that job,' muttered Four Calling Birds, the second in command of the war band. 'Maybe then I'd have had a cigar store of my own by now.' He flopped down on a tree-stump, hauled off his left moccasin and evicted a small stone.

Talks To Squirrels, who was just as weary and footsore as his first officer but felt the need to set an example, scowled at him. 'Selling tobacco,' he sneered. 'Fine trade for a brave.'

'Look,' Four Calling Birds replied, 'if I had, I'd have killed a hell of a lot more palefaces by now than you have, and that's no lie. Why do we bother, Talks? It's a waste of—'

'Shut up!' Talks To Squirrels dropped to his haunches and hauled his comrade down out of sight, signalling to the rest of the band with his other hand to do likewise. 'Something's coming.'

'So what? Worse case scenario is, we'll fail to kill it or it'll fail to kill us. We're ghosts, for crying out loud.'

It turned out to be a large shaggy bear, lumbering on all fours. 'Only me,' it said, in a feminine voice. 'It's been one of those days, so I thought I'd take a break and see how things were going.'

'Same as usual,' Talks replied, getting up and brushing leaf-mould from his knees. 'Scragging the Vikings was fun, but apart from that it's been dismal.'

The bear shrugged. 'You're welcome,' she said. 'And in any case, next time it's their turn to massacre you. Your unique cultural heritage snuffed out by brutish foreign adventurers, all that jazz. Oh come on, Talks, don't make faces. You know it's only fair.'

'Takes me all my time not to burst out giggling,' Four Calling Birds said. 'Those Vikings couldn't massacre their way out of a paper bag.'

'True,' admitted the bear. 'But the punters don't know that.'

Talks To Squirrels shook his head. 'It's dishonourable,' he muttered, 'having to hold still while a load of amateurs massacre you. My mother didn't raise me to be cut down by incompetents.'

'She didn't? What a very narrow-minded woman she must have been.' The bear sniffed, and licked its paws. 'You know the rules, Talks. If you don't want to play you shouldn't have joined.'

Talks With Squirrels made a get-lost gesture with his hand and changed the subject. 'Awful busy all of a sudden,' he observed. 'How many of them are there?'

'Four,' the bear sighed. 'Simultaneously. Takes it out of a person, I'm here to tell you. Still, they've all done the Vikings, and three of 'em have done the bears. I always reckon that once you've got the bears out of the way, the rest's pretty well plain sailing. Still, if it keeps up like this I'm going to have to think seriously about taking someone on.'

'Really?' Three French Hens, the band's master-at-arms, looked up sharply. 'You mean, like an apprentice or something?'

The bear nodded. 'Just someone to answer the phone, make the coffee, do the ottering, nothing too taxing. Why? Interested?'

'Sure,' said Three French Hens. 'Beats this dead-end job,' he replied, ignoring the look on his CO's face. '*My* mother didn't raise *me* to hang around for centuries after my death haunting no duckpond. Come to think of it,' he added, 'my mother didn't raise me, period, I was found in a basket and brought up by wolves. But you know what I mean.'

'Fine.' Talks To Squirrels threw his hands up in the air melodramatically. 'Get lost, the whole lot of you, leave it all to me to do. Don't reckon anybody'd notice if you did, at that.'

The bear extended a footstool-sized paw and patted him gently on the shoulder. 'Don't be like that, Talks,' it said. 'You're doing a fine job, really. And who knows, this time round or maybe the next, you might just strike it lucky and get sent Home. Well,' it added, as Talks expressed his cynicism by way of a vulgar noise, 'you never know. One of these days we'll complete the Cycle and you'll get exorcised. See if you don't.'

Talks shook his head. 'Going round and round and round and getting nowhere,' he grunted. 'Sounds just right for an Exorcise Cycle to me.'

The bear removed its paw. 'Save it for the customers, Talks,' it sighed. 'And cling on like grim death to the day job. By seeing you, guys.'

The braves waved as the bear lumbered away. The band relaxed. Some of them lit a fire. Two Turtledoves and Five Gold Rings started to fix dinner. In the distance, the mountains stirred in their sleep.

'It's all very well her saying that,' Talks growled. 'But we've been through this – hell, I don't know how many times, and we're still here, damnit. All I can figure is, we must be doing something wrong.'

'Just worked that out, have you?' Four Calling Birds replied. 'With a response time that quick, maybe you should go work for IBM. Hey, anybody seen my toma-hawk? I thought I left it under this tree.'

'Can't leave anything for a second round here,' Talks sighed. 'I'm telling you, if ever I get my hands on those no-good smugglers—'

'They'd go right through them,' Two Turtledoves interrupted. 'Forget it. We aren't scheduled to do the bears for a while anyhow.'

'Yes, but it's my—'

'Get another one from the Stores,' snapped Talks To Squirrels. 'Great Spirit, have you got nothing better to worry about than a goddamn stone axe?'

'No.'

Talks To Squirrels pulled a sad face. 'To be honest with you, neither have I. Probably explains why I'm depressed. Come on, let's go shoot some motorists. Mr Paliachiewski's due along any minute now with the bread van. Two squirrels' tails for the man who can shoot out his tyres in five shots.'

He set off up the hill. Behind him, the war band exchanged glances.

'Might as well,' Four Calling Birds admitted. 'It's not as if we're snowed under with more exciting things to do.'

''S'pose not. Hey, Birds, you got any idea where he gets the squirrel tails from? Being a ghost and all?'

'Mail order,' Four Calling Birds replied. 'And they're synthetic fur fabric, made in Indonesia.'

'Hey, that's amazing,' said Two Turtledoves, impressed. 'Where's Indonesia?'

Four Calling Birds furrowed his brow, until his eyebrows collided like furry trucks. 'Somewhere south-west of Chicago, I think. Out that way somewhere.'

'Oh. I thought that was Indiana.'

'No, he's the guy who swings in and out of old ruins on a rope, wearing a hat. They call him that because he comes from Indonesia.'

'Ah,' said Two Turtledoves. 'I see.'

'Knowledge is power, Doves.'

'You bet, Birds. Last one up the hill gets an Iroquois haircut.'

'Well?' Wesley demanded.

'Sorry about this,' replied the bison, tight-lipped. 'Slight technical hitch, by the looks of it. Honestly, you can't leave anything these days except it's nailed down.'

Wesley raised one eyebrow, Mister Spock fashion. 'Excuse me,' he said, enjoying himself, 'but are you trying to tell me someone's *stolen* the adventure?'

'Not the adventure itself,' the bison replied, turning over a rock with its snout. 'Just one of the props, is all. Unfortunately, it just so happens it's one of the important ones. Goddamnit,' it added.

A thin, soft wind flicked over them, mussing up Wesley's hair and ruffling the fur on the bison's shoulders backwards, against the pile. Tiny ripples moved on the surface of the lake, frosting the glass of the mirror. The bison snuffed at the ground with its broad nostrils, then pawed dolefully with its front left hoof.

'Bugger,' it said.

Wesley got up from the bison skull he'd been sitting on. 'Fair enough,' he said, 'I suppose that means we'll have to miss out this adventure. Never mind, eh?'

'Oh no you don't,' grunted the bison. 'You'll have this adventure, and like it. And if you don't have it now, it'll be put in front of you every day until you do, so be told.'

'You sound just like my . . .'

'Ah,' said the bison, 'here we are. Now, I want you to imagine that sticking in this rock here, there's a sword.'

'*Imagine . . . !*'

'Yes, damnit,' replied the bison, annoyed. 'Come on, for God's sake, you're the one who lives in a world of fantasy and imagination, peopled by strange gods and the weird offspring of the subconscious. Imagining a sword ought to be a piece of cake.'

'That's not the point. Sure, I *can* imagine swords. I just can't see why I should have to. Like, I can sleep on the beach under a black dustbin liner, but that doesn't mean I'm satisfied when I get off the plane and find they haven't built the hotel yet.'

'Imagine,' repeated the bison, 'there's a sword in this here stone. Big shiny job, OK?'

'With a bejewelled hilt?'

'Naturally.'

'Runes?'

The bison considered for a moment. 'Probably not,' it replied. 'Wrong tradition. Make it sigils instead.'

'OK, I've got the sigils. Are the quillons straight or curved?'

'The whats?'

'Quillons. The arms of the crossguard, which I think ought to curve inwards, like a coathanger.'

The bison shrugged; no small undertaking, for a creature whose shoulders are higher than its head. 'Whatever's right,' it said. 'Far be it from me—'

'And the pommel,' Wesley went on, looking into space.

'Is the pommel disc-shaped, in the French style, or more of a semicircle with the flat edge facing the quillons, owing more to the Scandinavian—?'

'I think you're getting the hang of this,' said the bison, breaking out the emergency supplies of self-restraint. 'Now then, this sword—'

'Hang on, we haven't discussed the ricasso profile yet.'

'Take hold of the hilt,' growled the bison ominously, 'in your left hand. Above it, place your right. You there yet?'

'I think so. It'd help if you'd specified it was a two-hander. I'm having to do some pretty substantial revisions as I go along here. For example, the fifteenth-century Swiss zweyhander . . .'

'Both hands on the hilt,' snarled the bison. 'Ready? Now pull.'

'I can't.'

The bison looked up. 'You what?'

'I can't,' Wesley repeated. 'It's stuck in this rock.'

'Oh for fuck's— Imagine it isn't.'

'But it is. Rusted in solid. These finely tempered Solingen steels, they rust as soon as look at them. You'd need a gallon of WD-40 and a jackhammer to get the ruddy thing out.'

A bemused expression flitted over the bison's face, as if it had been God saying *Let there be light* and having the Void reply *Only if you've got fifty pence for the meter*. 'All right,' it said, slowly and patiently, 'imagine a gallon of WD-40 and a jackhammer.'

'WD-40. Jackhammer. OK.'

There was silence for a moment, disturbed only by the bison breathing loudly through its nose and Wesley making bda-bda-bda noises under his breath. When the bison felt it couldn't really take much more of the sound effects, it lifted its head and said, 'How's it coming along?'

'Not good, I'm afraid,' Wesley replied. 'You see, the rust's really taken hold here. We've got to be a bit careful if we don't want the bloody point to snap off.'

'I see.'

'Of course,' Wesley continued, rubbing his chin, 'we could try heating the rock with a propane torch until it's really hot and then splashing water on it. That'd crack the rock, and then maybe we could sort of ease the sword free.'

'Good idea,' sighed the bison. 'Why don't you try that, then?'

'Ah,' Wesley replied, 'but then you'd run the risk of taking all the temper off the sword itself and ruining it. You've got to be a bit careful with heat around best-quality steel, you know.'

The bison shut its eyes tightly, until the muscles of its eyelids hurt. 'Look,' it said. 'If you can get this sword, this *entirely imaginary* sword, out of that rock, that'll make you rightful king of all Albion. Doesn't matter if you snap off the tip or spoil the frigging temper, when you're king you can have the royal swordsmiths make you a new one. All you have to do . . .'

'But that's silly,' Wesley retorted. 'If it's an imaginary sword, how will anybody know I've actually done it?'

The bison made a small noise, in which bewilderment and rage were mixed in the same proportions as gin and vermouth in a dry martini. 'Look,' it whimpered furiously, 'they'll trust you, OK? You'll be their goddamn king, it wouldn't even occur to them you might be lying. I thought you were dead keen on royalty where you come from.'

'We are,' Wesley replied. 'At least, some of us are. My

mum is. But where I come from, there's a bit more to being royal than pulling imaginary swords out of chunks of masonry. If it was as easy as all that, the whole system'd fall to the ground.'

'All right,' said the bison wearily. 'You wait there. Don't move. Don't even breathe. I'll be right back.'

'Where are you going?' Wesley cried.

'To get you a real sword, of course. Because you're so damn literal-minded you won't do the adventure unless there's an actual sword. Which means I've got to go traipsing all the way down to the Stores, fill in a pink requisition slip, a blue confirmation slip, a green—'

'Hang on,' Wesley shouted. 'I've nearly got this one free now. I felt it move just now.'

'—Authorisation docket, a mauve receipt, a blue confirmation slip for the mauve receipt, an orange cashier's voucher, a—'

'That's got it, here we – Oh my God!' Wesley stood for a moment, a huge double-handed sword with curved quillons and a disc pommel wobbling in his hand; then he remembered that swords of this style weighed anything up to twenty pounds, and dropped it with a clang.

'Told you it was a piece of cake,' said the bison smugly. 'Hey, you forgot the sigils.'

'Um.' Wesley stared at the sword as if it was a cat he'd just run over. 'Hey, does this mean I'm rightful king of Albion?'

'Yup.'

'Wow.'

'All hail,' said the bison, in a bored monotone. 'Long live the king. May the king reign for ever. You realise you've spoilt this whole adventure for me now.'

'Hey, I'm sorry. I was just . . .'

'Gallon of WD-40 and a jackhammer,' the bison went

on. 'Never heard the like in all my born days.'

Wesley cupped his hands to his cheeks. 'Hey,' he whispered, 'you realise what I just did? I *materialised* that sword, just by imagining it. One moment there was just this rock, the next . . .'

'Missed a trick though, didn't you? I mean, any sensible person would have imagined a sword he was actually capable of lifting; but not you, oh no. You had to go and dream up something that weighs half a ton. All I can say is, look out Albion.'

'Yes, but . . .'

'Well then,' the bison muttered, as it started to walk away. 'If I were you, I'd get straight on with imagining a block and tackle and a fork-lift truck. I'd get a wiggle on as well, before the goblins show up.'

'Goblins?'

'You bet. You don't suppose you were issued with that thing just so as you could open sixteen-gauge steel envelopes, do you?'

'You never said anything about goblins.'

'Didn't want to alarm you. Not then, at any rate. Right now, I'd just love to see a little pool of yellow liquid form at the bottom of your trouser leg. You see, I belong to the school of thought that holds that blind gibbering terror brings out the best in people.'

'You—!' Wesley wobbled, as fear melted the bones in his legs. 'Get me out of here, for Christ's sake.'

'But I thought you wanted excitement, adventure and a chance to do heroic deeds.'

'Eeekl!' There was a scuffling noise just inside the wood, like feet scrabbling on loose stones, or whatever. Wesley swung round, desperately looking for the best direction to run in. While doing so, he noticed the other goblins.

'They have you surrounded,' said the bison placidly. 'Just to make sure you don't pass up this once-in-a-lifetime opportunity of doing heroic deeds. Actually, the phrase *once in a lifetime* may be a trifle unfortunate in this context, so let's say *unique opportunity*. Don't want to strike the wrong note, after all.'

Goblins was what they unmistakably were; no risk of confusing them with fluffy kittens or social workers. Each of them was about four feet high and the same wide, with shoulders like American footballers and wicked pointy teeth sticking out of the corners of their green-lipped mouths. The knuckles of the hands they weren't holding their scimitars in trailed on the ground. They all had big noses and little round, red eyes.

'Wesley, goblins,' said the bison. 'Goblins, Wesley.'

The goblins advanced, moving as fast and as erratically as spiders. As Wesley stooped to where the sword was lying, a particularly chunky and red-eyed specimen darted towards him, brandishing a scimitar –

– Which he dropped, as he backed away screaming, his hands over his eyes. Wesley squirted another long jet of WD-40 at him, just to make sure, and spun round on his heel to confront the goblins who were sneaking up behind him. They shrieked out the first few notes of their blood-curdling war-cry, but got no further than 'Eeeeee!' before the sound was drowned out by a staccato pounding, thudding noise that made the ground shake. Four goblins went down like sacks of potatoes; the others ran away, very fast.

'My,' murmured the bison, as Wesley peered round over the sights of the Uzi in his hands, 'you've really taken to this conjuring-stuff-up-out-of-thin-air business like the proverbial duck to water. Do you mind not pointing that thing at me, by the way?'

'Sorry,' Wesley mumbled, staring at the slaughtered goblins. 'Fuck it, bison, I *killed* them. Oh God . . .'

'Wouldn't worry about it if I were you,' the bison replied, nibbling at a thistle. 'They'll be right as rain in an hour or so. Hungry, of course, but that's their look-out. I guess having to miss the occasional meal is something you learn to live with if your staple diet is people.'

Wesley shuddered from his toenails to his scalp. At some stage, the Uzi had vanished again, although the shiny golden spent cases still glittered on the ground at his feet. The WD-40 and the jackhammer had gone, too, but the sword was still there. 'You bastard,' Wesley said, with feeling. 'You—'

'Whether or not that counts as a glorious deed,' the bison continued serenely, 'is rather a moot point. I think I'll have to look it up and get back to you on that one. I must say, though, it shows initiative, not to mention a pragmatic streak I must confess I hadn't expected of you. You've gone up in my estimation a bit, young Wesley. You'd best change your trousers, though.'

Wesley gave the bison a long, hard look but didn't say anything. What he was thinking ran too deep for words, except for a few short, vulgar ones mostly beginning with B.

The bison shook itself and became the lovely girl again. 'Come on,' she said. 'I'd pencilled in this time for a coffee break, but we're running a bit behind schedule. This way.'

Janice swore.

Around here somewhere, there must be a telephone. You'd have thought that, wouldn't you? A civilised country like America. In your dreams.

Not, she told herself as she sat down and fished a

small boulder out of her boot heel, that there was any
great rush, being realistic about it. If the people from the
ship had all drowned (as she feared was the case) then
they'd still be just as drowned even if she didn't make it
to a phone booth before nightfall. More drowned, even.
So why should she break her neck scrambling down
semi-vertical deer trails and break her back scrambling
up the other side? Pointless . . .

Hang on, she muttered to herself as she struggled with
a recalcitrant bootlace, just a cotton-picking minute. For
a girl who's just witnessed a major tragedy – Ship Sinks
In Lake, Fifty Feared Drowned – she ought to be going
through all kinds of ghastly mental trauma, with a side
order of guilt and choice of emotional damage from the
trolley. And here she was, sitting grumpily on a rock
cussing out a bootlace.

Delayed shock? The anaesthetic effect? Probably.
Truth was, however, that all she really felt was rather silly.
Did those strange men really steer their ship onto a rock
because they were too busy gawping at *her* to mind where
they were going?

Is this the face that sank a thousand ships? Under
normal circumstances she could believe it; also the face
that smashed a thousand mirrors, cracked a thousand
lenses, soured a thousand gallons of milk – she'd heard
'em all, over the years. But beguiling sailors into running
their ships aground; not me, pal, you're thinking of someone else. Surely.

Maybe I'm imagining it. Probably. After all, picture
the scene, where she's telling it how it was to the police.
Well, officer, they were all standing on deck whistling at
me and saying nice things, and then they hit this rock.
Yes, at me. Yes, I was wearing clothes at the time. No, I
don't think they were all stoned out of their brains . . .

The sun, she muttered to herself, must be hotter than I thought. It's curdling my brains. Me? Nah.

She stood up and tramped painfully over a low rise, from the top of which she could see a pleasant sight: a road of sorts, more of a dirt track really but flat, regular and, best of all, human-made. The logic being; people don't make roads that lead nowhere. Follow this track and you'll end up someplace people are. Goody.

She walked down to the track and was following it in what she hoped was an easterly direction when she heard an even more hopeful sound: the rumble of an engine. Better still; because right then she'd had enough of walking to last her a very long time. The noise was coming from in front of her, where the track disappeared into the trees.

Not one engine. Lots of engines. One hell of a lot of engines.

And then they appeared; twenty or so big, garish black-and-silver motorcycles, all daddy-long-legs forks and spider-bodies a few inches above the ground, straight out of *Easy Rider* genre ripoffs but without the class. On the motorcycles rode vaguely humanoid shapes – huge, burly, hairy men with enormous black beards and arms as thick as legs. She stopped where she could, trying to still the instinctive panic as the bikes surged forward and seemed to flow all round her, their engines deep and growling as the voices of great bears.

Oh *cringe*, she thought.

The ursine nature of their appearance was probably intentional, for they were all wearing black leather cut-offs, on the backs of which were embroidered fancy stitching; somebody's girlfriend? Somebody's mother? Or did they sit round in the evenings beside the campfire threading needles and borrowing each others' silks?

IOWA GRIZZLIES M.C.
OSKALOOSA, IO.

– and a stylised picture of a bear's head, open-mouthed and roaring. One of them even had an *actual* bear's head, and the rest of its skin, wrapped round him like a towelling-robe, or Hercules as depicted in antiquity. Actually, it looked decidedly seedy and moulted, and Janice felt it had probably come from the back room of a pawn-shop, a long time ago.

The bikes stopped, corralling her in. The bikers cut their engines simultaneously, like a platoon of marines coming to attention. That alone was more unnerving than anything else about them.

'Hey, miss. 'Scuse me.'

Janice tensed. Lacking gun, knife, can of mace, electric cattle prod or any other form of weapon, she was going to have to rely on her wits and her heels to get her out of this one. She tried to take a breath, but her lungs were too stiff—

'Only,' the biker was saying, 'we're lost, and we were wondering, is this the right road for Tucseehanna?'

Huh? Janice felt physically unbalanced, the way you do when you step off the escalator without looking down. She wobbled, and pulled herself up straight again. She didn't know quite what she'd been expecting, but a squeaky little tenor voice—

'Only,' the biker went on, 'Maurice reckons we should have taken a left back there on the Fawcett pike, but the map clearly says . . .'

And then Janice noticed the thing that had been staring her in the face, except that she'd been too busy panicking to notice.

They were all wearing dog-collars.

Not leather straps with lots of shiny big studs; clerical collars, as worn by ministers of religion. That, together with the odd tank-sticker that read *Bikin' For Jesus* and *Freeway To Heaven* and *God Rides A Harley*, pointed her in a direction which logic wanted her to follow, although sanity wanted nothing to do with it.

'Excuse me,' she heard herself whisper, 'but are you guys *priests*?'

'Sure are,' replied the biker, beaming. 'I'm Father Armand, this is Father Patrick, Father Maurice, Father Bernard and Father Duane. Pleased to meet you.'

'Very pleased,' murmured Father Patrick.

'You bet,' added Father Duane.

'Excuse me,' Janice croaked. 'It's just a bit—'

Father Armand smiled. 'Yeah, I know,' he said. 'Priests on bikes. People do tend to have a problem with that, to begin with. But basically, you know, we're just guys who're into bikes and into Jesus, and we like to get out of the city once in a while, you know, build a camp fire someplace, open a bottle of wine, sing a few psalms. You know,' he concluded, blinking, 'we kinda figure, if Bishop Odo of Bayeux could ride into the battle of Hastings on a big white horse, then it's probably OK if we ride Harleys.'

'Right on,' agreed Father Bernard. 'It's very, you know, American.'

'Um,' Janice replied. 'Actually, I'm not from these parts myself, so I really don't think I can help . . .'

As she was speaking, she began to feel ever so slightly uncomfortable; not that she'd been wildly comfortable before, when she'd been under the impression that she was about to be raped, murdered and quite probably eaten by a pack of human wolves. But this was a different sort of uncomfortable. The bikers were all *looking* at her.

Looking. More to the point, they were glazing. Yearning, even.

'Priests,' she said aloud. 'Catholic priests, right?'

'You bet,' replied Father Maurice, with a kind of strangled twist in his voice, as if he'd just remembered something he'd forgotten a long time ago. 'That's us,' he added wistfully. 'We're priests, all right.'

'Every one of us,' added a biker behind him. 'You know, like unmarried . . .'

'Celibate . . .'

'Aw gee . . .'

'Hey!' That was Father Armand, calling his people to order. 'Guys! Let's all just bear in mind who we are, OK?'

'Kinda hard to forget sometimes, Armand,' replied Father Patrick, sullenly. If the others were yearning at her, he was double-yearning, in spades. 'Especially when we happen to meet, like, an exceptionally attractive and charming young lady.'

'Guys!' Presumably Armand meant it as a mild rebuke. But since he was yearning at her too, with great big round eyes that'd have looked just fine on a Jersey cow but which were entirely inappropriate for a sworn-celibate man of God, it was hard to see what he intended to achieve. 'OK, so we're only flesh and blood. Still, I feel sure that a couple hours of silent prayer . . .'

'I only became a priest to please my folks,' Patrick was muttering. 'Family tradition, they said. Goddamn stupid Irish pride.'

'Hey!' Father Bernard interrupted him. 'You think that's bad, you should try being Italian. My momma said . . .'

It was, Janice realised, exactly that same *ohshit* feeling she'd had when the ship hit the rock. Inside her mind, the penny gave in to gravity and began its long descent.

'Guys,' she said, 'maybe I should be getting along. Er, go with God.'

'I mean,' Father Bernard went on, fingering the collar at his throat as if it was made of steel and too tight, 'don't you ever ask yourself, *Why'm I doing this? What'm I missing out on?* And sometimes . . .'

'Me too,' whispered Father Armand, nodding. 'Hey, guys, I think we ought to talk about this. What do you think?'

For a time the hills seemed to shake with cries of 'Yo!', 'Right on!' and similar exclamations. One or two of the bikers actually tore off their dog-collars and flung them to the ground. 'Heck,' one of them was saying, 'so what if I have devoted my entire life since I was a little kid to becoming a priest? So what? It's never too late to change.'

Do the individuals who act as catalysts to sudden great events occasionally feel just a trifle apprehensive about what they've started? Did Joan of Arc, on seeing the reaction to her petulant complaint about rich English second-home buyers pricing the locals out of the property market, ever wish she'd kept her trap shut? Does the spirit of Columbus, gazing down from the bar of Heaven at modern San Francisco, ever feel he'd have done better to tell the Spanish king that the whole lot was as flat as a pancake, marvellous site for a hydro-electric plant but a complete non-starter as far as colonisation was concerned? Maybe. Certainly, Janice had her doubts about what she'd started. Thirty outlaw bikers she might just have coped with, assuming that death was something she could take in her stride. Thirty love-struck lapsed priests, on the other hand, wasn't something she wanted on her conscience.

'Excuse me,' she said, and ran.

*

'And what in hell is *that*?' Calvin Dieb asked, pointing. 'Triangulation point? New age TV mast?'

'It's a sword,' replied the lovely girl. 'In a stone.'

Calvin shrugged. 'Ask a dumb question,' he replied. 'And don't tell me what it's doing there, because I don't want to know.'

The girl stopped, and sat down under the sword. 'Sorry,' she said. 'This is what we came here for. If I were you, I'd pay attention.'

'Sure.' Dieb sighed deeply, and sat down on a rock. 'So this is Disneyland.'

'No,' the girl replied. 'It isn't.'

'No? All right then. It's Arthurian Park, and any minute now some guy's gonna come running in saying, *Ah shit, the clones've bust loose again.* That's so passé, you know?'

'Wrong again,' the girl replied, scuffing her toe on the chalky ground. 'Do you always think in clichés, Mr Dieb?'

Calvin thought for a moment. 'Not clichés,' he replied. 'Call it shorthand. Comes of being a lawyer, I guess. We always think in precedents; you know, instinctively try and pigeonhole anything new in with something we've come across before. Saves time and thought, which in our business equals money. At two thousand bucks an hour, you haven't got time to think, you just *do*.'

The girl nodded. 'Valid enough point, I suppose,' she said. 'So presumably, if you were to see a guy in a robe with a tea-towel round his head raising the dead to life, you'd say, *huh, a Lazarus job*. Yes?'

'Yup.' Dieb grinned. 'Hey, wouldn't that be a great trick if you could do it? The tax-planning applications alone would be stupendous.'

'Mr Dieb—'

'Not to mention,' Calvin went on, rubbing his hands together, 'the use you could make of it in insolvency litigation. Your client dies, you call all the creditors together and say, "Sorry, fellas, the guy just died and the whole estate's gone in legal costs, so forget it," and then a week later you can fetch him back and slap in an interim bill. Hell, with that I could run the competition clean out of town.'

'Mr Dieb—'

'Or divorce. In divorce, it'd be huge. Your ex-wife screwing you for two hundred grand a year alimony? So what? You die, and the settlement dies with you. Then up you get and walk away, a free man.'

'Mr Dieb,' said the girl. 'Behind you.'

'What the—? Oh, fuck!'

'Quite.' The girl smiled, tight-lipped. 'A Little Big Horn scenario, don't you think?'

Calvin Dieb started to back away, step for step as the ring of squat, grim bodies advanced towards him. On each leathery, green-tinged face was a look of cold rage. When his back was up against the blade of the sword, Dieb stopped and slotted a feeble grin into the hole in his face.

'Hiya, guys,' he croaked. 'It's been a while. How's things with you?'

The tallest and squattest of the advancing forms snarled at him, revealing sharp, pointed teeth. 'Dieb,' he snarled, 'we want a word with you.'

'You do, huh? Well, that's great, guys, I value new clients over everything else, believe me. It's just that I'm a bit tied up right now, so if you could maybe call in at the office first thing Tuesday, maybe we could . . .'

'Get him!'

Four of the short, squat creatures darted forwards,

fast as big black rats running up the clock, and tied him to the sword. Four or five others came close behind and started stacking billets of firewood round his feet.

'We took a vote on it,' explained their leader. 'In the end it was forty-five per cent for lynching, fifty-five for burning at the stake. Calvin Dieb, prepare to fry!'

'New clients,' murmured the girl, standing back with her arms folded. 'Mr Dieb, I may have got this all wrong but I don't think they want to hire you. Fire, however, would definitely seem to be on the agenda. You upset these people or something?'

'Hey!' Dieb tried to struggle, but the ropes were too tight. 'The case was a big break for me. Here was this major pharmaceuticals company, with this multi-million product liability suit against them. Of course I gave it my best shot, that's what I do. If it had been these guys who'd hired me, I'd have done my best for them too. It's the rules of the game, right?'

'Shut up, you,' snapped the leader. 'You're gonna burn. Hey, guys, anybody got some matches? These goddamn Zippos are supposed to light in any weather, but this one keeps blowing out.'

'Go on,' said the girl. 'You'd got as far as product liability.'

'Don't listen to him, lady,' one of the shapes interrupted. 'Try hearing our side of the story for a change.'

'Very well.' The girl nodded her head politely. 'Fire away, oops, rephrase that. Go ahead. Shoot.'

'What you say?'

'Shoot.'

'Hey!' The creature waved its hands in the air. 'Don't you confuse the issue. We got it down to lynching or burning and now you're saying shoot the bum. We spent long enough deciding as it is.'

'Tell the story,' said the girl.

'Yeah, well,' the leader replied. 'You see, we're all what you might call on the short side—'

'Not short. Altitudinally challenged.'

'Unfairly discriminated against as far as the y axis is concerned.'

The leader frowned. 'Yeah,' he said, 'whatever. Anyhow, along comes this big chemicals company, advertising this miracle enhance-your-height hormone treatment. Of course we go for it. We buy the filthy muck and smear it all over ourselves.'

'Yeah,' shouted a creature at the back. 'Like herrings to the slaughter.'

The girl raised an eyebrow. 'Herrings?' she asked.

'And then,' the leader went on, 'a couple months later, we look in the mirror and hey, we ain't grown none, but we've all gone this funny green colour, and we're sprouting muscles like Arnie's big brother, and we're all starting to grow these teeth . . .'

'You try eating an apple without laying your own face open. It's awful.'

'I see,' the girl said. 'So you sue the pharmaceuticals company, and Mr Dieb here defends them. Am I to understand that you lost?'

'Too darned right we lost,' grunted the leader. 'We end up having to pay this creep's costs, plus damages to the chemicals guys for defamation and God knows what-all else. Man, it was a *disaster*.'

'All his fault,' agreed a spare creature. 'Shoulda been an open and shut case. Instead, this scumbag shuts our mouths and opens our wallets.'

'Cost us so much,' the leader went on, 'we couldn't afford to go into hospital and have the goddamn treatment. We had to live with it.'

'Ah.'

'Which is why,' the leader concluded, 'we're gonna torch you. Here, Jules, make with the kerosene. C'mon, guys, one of youse gotta have some matches. Hey, lady!'

'Sorry.' The girl held up her hands. 'You could always try rubbing sticks together.'

'I've got matches,' Dieb said.

The leader rounded on him. 'Oh yeah?' he said. 'Well, you wasted your bread, pal, 'cos where you're headed you ain't gonna need them. Vernon, find me a couple of dry sticks, will ya?'

'In my jacket pocket,' Dieb continued. 'You're welcome to them, really.'

'Sure.' The leader scowled until his fangs drew blood on his chin. 'But to get to them, we've gotta untie you. And then you make a run for it, and we lose you. No way, buster. If we can't find any matches, then it's back to Plan A and we lynch you.'

'Fair enough,' Dieb said. 'Lucky you've got the rope.'

The creatures started to murmur among themselves. 'He's right, Phil,' one of them said. 'Burning or lynching, we've gotta untie the creep either way.'

'Just a minute,' the leader growled. 'Just a friggin' minute. Didn't somebody say something about shooting him?'

'Nobody's got a gun, Phil.'

Dieb cleared his throat. 'Actually,' he said.

The leader lost his temper. 'Oh yeah,' he cried. 'And it's in a shoulder holster inside your coat, all we gotta do is untie the rope. Gag the son of a bitch, someone, while I find a big rock. Nobody touches the rope, understood? This is a *lawyer* we're dealing with here, remember?'

'Hey,' Dieb said, 'I just thought of something. Why not use the sword?'

'Sword? What sword?'

'This sword I'm tied to,' Calvin said. 'You could cut my head off, slice my guts out, all that kinda stuff.'

The creatures looked at each other. There were cries of 'Neat!' and 'Let's do it.' The leader, however, jumped up and down on the spot, screaming.

'You guys really kill me,' he yelled. 'To use the sword, we gotta untie the rope. When will you ever *learn*?'

It was at this moment that Dieb, who'd been rubbing the ropes up and down against the edges of the sword, finally felt the last strands give way. While the leader was hopping up and down and his companions were shouting at him to calm down, Dieb tugged the ropes free, fell to the ground, rolled to his feet and ran, leaping over the nearest creature like an Olympic hurdler running for a bus and making it to the edge of the clearing before any of them realised what was going on. The leader dropped to his knees, sobbing 'Nooo!' while the others rounded on him, howling curses and kicking him, as if to imply that, in their opinion, he might not have handled the situation as well as he could have, all things being equal.

CHAPTER SEVEN

'Hey, you.'

Captain Hat froze, as if suddenly immersed in liquid nitrogen. He pushed aside the leaf directly above his head, and stared.

'You,' the Big repeated. 'I wonder if you could help me.'

Mother of God, there's a Big talking to me. They're not supposed to be able to see us, for Chrissakes! 'Er,' said Captain Hat, surprising himself with the level of fluency he was able to muster. 'Um,' he added.

'I was wondering,' the Big went on, 'have you seen any submarines around here lately?'

'Submarines?' Hat repeated. 'I mean, no. No, certainly not,' he said defiantly. 'I don't know anything about any submarines. And besides, I was miles away at the time. I have witnesses.'

'Oh.' The Big seemed disappointed, but not for long. 'Australians?'

'Uh?'

'Australians. People from Australia.'

Hat's brow creased. 'You mean, like guys in big hats with corks all round them?'

The Big nodded, her eyes aflame with excitement. 'That's it,' she said. 'Australians. You seen any?'

'No.'

'Oh. You're sure about that?'

Hat nodded. 'Positive,' he said.

The Big bit her lip. 'No disrespect,' she said, 'but how can you be sure they *weren't* Australians? After all, they don't always wear the silly hats or the fluorescent beach shorts, you know. As often as not, they can look just like ordinary people. Especially when they're under cover.'

That one, Hat felt, was so far above his head that you could bounce TV signals off it. 'You may be right,' he said carefully. 'I hadn't thought of it like that. But I can't remember seeing any people who definitely *were* Australians. As in funny hats, psychedelic leisurewear or talking in Australian accents.'

The Big smiled patronisingly. 'That doesn't mean anything,' she said. 'Australia's a culturally diverse country these days. Some of 'em don't sound like Australians at all.'

'Gosh. That must be awfully confusing for the rest of them.'

The Big nodded. 'You bet,' she said, and winked knowingly. 'All right, then, what about high officials of the Vatican? You can always tell them, by their broad-brimmed hats.'

'With corks round them?'

'Don't be stupid. They're red. They call 'em birettas.'

'I thought that was machine guns.'

The Big sighed. 'You're thinking of Lambrettas,' she said patiently. 'Have you seen any guys in red robes and big hats?'

'Sorry,' said Hat. 'Of course, they might have taken them off, if they were pretending to be Australians.'

'Ah.' The Big frowned. Clearly, she hadn't thought of that. 'All right then,' she said, 'what about Australians or high-ranking Papal officers masquerading as perfectly ordinary people? Seen any round here lately?'

Hat considered how he should frame his reply. 'Not to my knowledge,' he said, inadvertently echoing a thousand generations of lawyers. 'But maybe *they* were pretending to be the CIA?'

'Could be,' replied the Big, stroking her chin. 'But that's just conjecture, surely?'

'Maybe,' agreed Hat. 'Maybe not. Things are often not what they seem.'

'True. In fact,' the Big went on, 'in my experience, the more they seem to be something, the more likely they are to be something else.'

'You mean, like the Australians?'

'A case in point.'

'Or the CIA.'

'Perhaps,' the Big said. 'Though they tend to be the exception that proves the rule.'

'Do they? Oh, right. Anyway,' Hat went on, feeling that maybe he'd got the hang of talking to Bigs now, 'the way I see it, anybody I might have seen who was actually wearing a red hat with corks round it and carrying a Lambretta in a shoulder holster, *by that very token*, would probably turn out not to be Australian at all. You see what I mean?'

'I do,' said the Big, her eyes shiny again, 'I do indeed. Naturally, it'd be the CIA, deliberately trying *not* to look like *anybody*. Which'd make a whole lot of sense, of course.'

'It would?'

'Think about it,' said the Big. 'It's all just common sense, really. Hey, you've been very helpful. Can I quote you on that?'

'Well . . .'

The Big shrugged. 'Yeah, OK, I understand. You've got your own back to watch, I can see that. I'll just describe you as "an authoritative source in the upper echelons of the administration". That do you?'

'That'll be fine,' Hat replied. 'And meanwhile,' he added, 'if I do see any submarines . . .' And, having the feeling the Big would like it, he winked conspiratorially.

'You bet!' The Big winked back. Between them, they were beginning to look like a set of indicators. 'And as far as I'm concerned,' the Big went on, 'we never had this conversation, right?'

'What conversation?'

'You've got the idea. Well, stay loose. Be seeing you.'

'Not if I see you first,' Hat replied, with heartfelt sincerity. Then he ducked down under the leaf and crawled like Hell into the undergrowth.

For a minute or so after he'd gone, Linda stood where she was, looking inconspicuous – a skill in which she surpassed several large lighthouses. Then, nonchalantly whistling, she started to walk. And carried on walking, until she suddenly stopped, said, 'Ouch!' and fell over.

The reason being, she'd walked into a large sword in a stone and taken a nasty bump on the head.

She stood up. She waited till the world stopped spinning. She looked at the thing she'd just walked into, and recognised what it was.

And then, inspiration struck.

Linda got these sudden flashes, when things just seemed to appear out of nowhere and dance in front of her eyes, grinning and howling, 'Scoop! Scoop!' It was in just such a flash, for example, that she'd formulated the award-winning theory that it was actually Santa Claus who shot John F. Kennedy – or otherwise, why was there this worldwide conspiracy to convince everybody that he didn't exist? And so, as she stood gawping at the sword in the stone, Linda *knew*.

Arms. Illegal arms shipments. Vaticangate. *They were shipping the stuff out in rocks.* That was why none of the consignments had ever been traced.

It was so beautifully simple. What the government were doing was encasing the arms in huge blocks of concrete, dressing them up to look like Sicilian marble, and then shipping them out on submarines via the Black Sea ports. God, it was so obvious a deranged child's imaginary friend could see it. And now she could, too. This was great!

(Behind her, a goblin crept stealthily forward, muttering something under its breath about third time lucky.)

Oh God, my kingdom for a fax machine! Not being able to get the story out right away was hurting her, physically, like a dagger in her heart or an ingrowing toenail. The biggest news story of the century, bigger even than her exposé of covert US involvement in the Trojan War, and here she was in the middle of the wilderness, unable to communicate with the office. Oh, life can be so *rotten*. Bewildered by the senseless cruelty of it all, she slumped down on a curiously shaped rock and buried her head in her hands.

'This one,' hissed Goblin Corporal Snargh to Goblin Sergeant Gnazhgz, 'is going to be a piece of duff. You watch. Dizzy bitch isn't even *looking*.'

'Bit of meat on 'er, too,' Gnazhgz grunted back. 'Left-overs'll do cold for Monday. I got the in-laws comin' over, it's her mum's malachite weddin'.'

Snargh's craggy, looming brow furrowed. 'How many's malachite?' he asked.

'Two hundred an' ninety-six. Y'know, whenever I think I got it rough, I look at her dad and I think, two hundred an' ninety-six years of *that*, I'd rather be boiled in lead. Still, wouldn't do if we were all the same.'

'Yeah.' Tiny tumblers clicked into place inside Snargh's fallout-shelter-thick skull. 'Jussa minute,' he whispered. 'Granted she's a bit on the buxom side, but there's never going to be enough for all of us *and* your missus's family on Monday. Not even if you was to do a sort of pasta thing and grate the meat up small, like a carbonara or somethin'.'

Gnazhgz grinned, revealing a collection of teeth that would inspire passionate interest in a research dentist and blind terror in anyone else. 'Sarge's perks,' he replied. 'You lot can have the next one.'

'Hey!'

'Shurrup,' the sergeant hissed, clamping a betaloned paw over Snargh's mouth. 'She'll hear you.'

Snargh pulled the paw aside. 'Now just a minute, Sarge, that's not bloody well fair.'

'Who said anything about fair? This is the army, son.'

'Yeah, but.' Snargh's face contorted into an even more horrific expression than usual. 'You said that the last time,' he growled. 'All we got was a load of giblets and bits of pipe and stuff. I'm not standing for it, you hear?'

'Keep your voice down, or the whole bloody world will.'

'Don't care. Fair shares for all this time, OK? Or . . .' The tip of Snargh's noise began to quiver, a sure sign of high passion. 'Or,' he said icily, 'we'll damn well help ourselves and you don't get any.'

'Huh! You and whose army?'

'Yours. Hey, lads! Sarge is gonna rip us off again!'

Goblin heads turned. Goblin eyes filled with rage. If Linda hadn't been so completely submerged in self-pity that a bomb could have gone off in her shoe without her noticing it, let alone think of phoning through the exclusive story to the newsroom, she'd have had an unrivalled view of nine goblin warriors all whispering angrily at once.

'Shove it, you 'orrible little goblins,' Gnazhgz rasped, in a voice like a cheese-grater on living flesh. 'Any more of it an' I'll friggin' well eat *you*. Got that?'

Lance-corporal Zhlaghpf, five foot one at the shoulder and squat as a troll who's been caught in a junkyard car compressor, stood up, breathing hard through his snout. 'You want me to take you up on that, Sarge?' he rumbled.

'Any time, Zhlaghpf. Any time you like.'

'Right.'

'Right.'

'Right.'

A moment later, instead of two goblins standing up and hissing at each other, there was a sort of goblin-rich cyclone-come-snowball rolling and whirling about among the rocks, into which the rest of the goblins were drawn one by one. Of the ten members of the squad, seven of them (namely Corporal Snargh, Lance-corporal Zhlaghpf and General Infantrygoblins Groghdng, Fluraghzd, Twlurgh, Shdlnog and Urghmpf) were trying their best to dismember Sergeant Gnazhgz and the Loyalist tendency, comprising General Infantrygoblins Brzhgnazh and Glarpfgh. Because the enthusiasm and sheer bulk of the mutineers exactly cancelled out the skill, experience and unspeakably dirty fighting habits of the loyalists, it was a completely even contest; and, since goblins invariably fight to the death, there could only be one outcome.

A quarter of an hour later, Linda pulled herself out of her self-induced slough of misery with the thought that if all else failed, she could scribble a note, shove it in a bottle and sling it in the Squash River, and rose to her feet for the long walk back up to the road. She'd taken about twelve steps when she realised she'd just trodden on something squishy. She looked down.

'Urgh!' said the body at her feet.

'Sorry,' Linda said. 'Hey, you all right?'

'I'm dying,' croaked the goblin painfully. 'I got a hole in my lung, my head's caved in an' I think the buggers got half me liver.'

'Good God,' Linda replied. 'Ought I to call a doctor?'

The goblin shook his head feebly. ''Sall right,' he sighed, air wheezing through his punctured lung. 'I'll be right as rain in the morning. They rebuild us, you know.'

'Do they?'

'Clever bleeders. Take it out of our pay, of course, but that's the army for you. Might even get promoted this rebuild, if I can make 'em think it was in the line of duty.'

'Oh,' said Linda, reassured. 'In that case, maybe you could help me. Submarines.'

'You what?'

'Submarines,' Linda repeated. 'Nuclear submarines laden with huge blocks of marble. Have you seen any lately?'

'No,' groaned the goblin. 'Sorry. Why?'

'All right, then,' Linda persevered. 'How about Australians? Probably wearing hats with corks,' she added. 'Maybe even open-toed plastic beach sandals.'

'What you on about?' the goblin whimpered. 'I'm a Sergeant of goblin fusiliers, not a friggin' mind-reader.'

'Hats,' Linda repeated impatiently. 'You know, like Australians wear. Only, the chances are that anybody wearing a hat with corks is likely to be the CIA in disguise. You see, I have conclusive proof that . . .'

'Oh, tell it to the submarines,' snarled the goblin, and died.

Linda shrugged, stood up and looked around. There were other goblins lying about the place, she noticed, but they were apparently dead too. Very dead. She had no way of knowing just how clever the clever little buggers were, but as far as she could judge, the job facing them would have all the king's horses and all the king's men throwing up their hands in horror and sending for a plumber. A pity, but there it was. Even the most dedicated and imaginative journalists run into setbacks occasionally. By all accounts, Woodward and Bernstein thrived on them. She'd just have to keep plugging away. And in the meantime, she could always use the message-in-a-bottle idea, assuming she could find a bottle, a piece of paper, a cork and a pen.

She carried on up the hill.

'This here,' said the tiresome old man, leaning back in his rocking chair and grinning a toothy grin, 'is Lake Chicopee. They do say . . .'

'Save it for the customers,' replied the stranger irritably. 'I'm on a tight schedule. Now, what I'm basically interested in is productivity levels, turnaround times, cost-effectiveness ratios and any areas where costs can be cut without significantly reducing overall efficiency. So, if we can start with last year's budget outline and work forwards from that.'

Slowly the tiresome old man prised his pipe-stem off his lower lip and widened his eyes. 'You're an inspector,' he said.

'Didn't I mention that? I'm sorry.' The stranger pulled

a sheet of paper from the file in his hand and fluttered it under the old man's nose. 'You'll need to see this, I suppose. General requisition from the Area Manager's office, notifying you of a routine spot efficiency check. You're just about to tell me you never got a copy, right?'

'We sure didn't, mister.'

The inspector sighed through his nose. 'Marvellous, isn't it? Five hundred and seventy-four permanent administrative staff, and between them they can't manage to send a simple letter. Makes me look a complete fool, of course, but there you are. Anyway,' he added, cheering up slightly, 'just because they're pathetic at head office doesn't mean you lot out here can afford to let things slip. Right then, those budget figures . . .'

With a shudder, the tiresome old man metamorphosed into a beautiful young girl. The inspector didn't even notice. 'Ah,' she said, 'the figures. Now if we'd only known you were coming . . .'

'Not you as well,' replied the inspector, frowning. 'Why is it that nobody seems capable of keeping a few bits of paper in order? You know, I think it's high time we had a bit of a blitz on filing systems generally. The regulations clearly state—'

'Just a minute,' the girl interrupted hastily. 'I'll just run indoors and fetch the shoebox.'

As she ran, she distinctly heard the inspector wailing, 'Shoebox!' in a distressed voice, but she pretended she hadn't. Of all the lousy timing! Four customers roaming round the place needing looking after, and she had to have a goddamn inspector descend on her.

It was looking as if it was going to be a very long day.

She opened the door of the log cabin, rummaged around under a table and pulled a tatty old shoebox out from under a pile of dirty laundry and vintage washing-up. She opened it. It was empty.

'Hat!' she shrieked. 'Hat, you thieving little bastard! What have you done with my paperwork?'

Inside the cabin, there was a deathly hush and complete stillness; so deathly, in fact, and so complete that any fool would have known there was someone in the room, hiding and holding his breath. The girl counted slowly to ten.

'Hat,' she said quietly. 'One last chance, and then I set the cat on you.'

Slowly, the lid of the cookie-jar lifted. Under it was the head of Captain Hat, wearing a rather sheepish grin.

'Look,' he said, 'I can explain.'

With a movement that was both lightning fast and lissomly graceful, the girl reached over and grabbed Hat round the throat before he could dodge back down out of sight. 'So can I,' she growled. 'You're a thief and a smuggler, and I ought to pull your lousy head off right now. Am I warm?'

Being unable to speak, Hat nodded. The girl slackened her grip a trifle.

'OK,' she said. 'Give me my files back and we'll say no more about it. Of course, I reserve the right to break both your arms about it, but I won't *say* anything. Otherwise . . .'

'Um,' Hat whispered, turning puce, 'there may be a slight problem. You see . . .'

'Hat, I'm warning you.'

'I really am terribly sorry,' the smuggler gurgled. 'Wouldn't inconvenience you for the world. It's just that on the Other Side, your accounts represent a form of higher pure mathematics beyond their wildest dreams, and some of the big West Coast universities have research budgets that'd fry your brain. So . . .'

'Hat . . .'

'So obviously,' Hat went on, choking a little, 'I kept copies. Now, if you'll just let me go for five minutes . . .'

'I'm gonna *kill* you, Hat. I'm gonna squeeze you like a tube of toothpaste till your guts come out your ears. And that's just my version of friendly persuasion. Now, where's this copy?'

'In the crystal cave under the southern waterfall in a black tin box marked SWAG, oh Jesus, you're strangling me,' Hat replied. 'The key to the box is in the right-hand drawer of the old roll-top desk in Grendel's mother's office, please let go, oh *shit*!'

'Crystal cave?'

'Aargh!'

'Southern waterfall?'

'Nggh.'

'Black tin box marked SWAG?'

'Ggggh . . .'

'Key in right-hand desk drawer?'

'G.'

'Thank you,' said the girl, letting go. Hat fell back into the cookie jar, and she replaced the lid. Then she slammed out of the cabin and began to run.

'I suppose,' said the lovely girl, 'you could say that we've now completed Phase One.'

The sun, peering round a cloud, winked in the lake. A few ducks hopscotched on the reflected mountains, meeting themselves coming up as they crashed ripples into the face of the mirror. *What the hell do they wish for?* Wesley asked himself.

'To carry on being ducks, of course,' the girl replied. 'You just wouldn't believe how easy ducks have it.'

Wesley looked up. 'Really?' he asked.

The girl nodded. 'Masses to eat. No need to take thought for the morrow, what they shall wear and all that palaver. If they get right out into the middle of the lake, they're safe from every kind of predator, with the improbable exceptions of very large pike and –' the girl sniggered, though Wesley couldn't see why '– sub- marines. And so, every time they land on the water, they wish to carry on being ducks. These days I just leave them alone and let them get on with it. They know far more about being ducks than I do, so there's not a great deal they need me for.'

'Well, bloody good luck to them,' Wesley sighed. 'I'm glad somebody gets something out of this ghastly busi- ness. What were you saying about Phase One?'

The girl lay back on a flat rock, her arms behind her head, her hair trailing down and just brushing the meniscus of the water without disturbing it. 'The first part of the procedure,' she replied, gazing at the sky. 'The easy bit.'

'The easy . . .'

'You bet. The first three experiences are really only to get you in the mood, accustom you to the environment, give you an idea of the sort of thing that goes on here. The actual character-forming, problem-solving part comes later; that's when we start addressing your deep- seated personal shortcomings and inadequacies. In your case . . .'

Wesley stood up. 'Hang on,' he said. 'I thought this was where all my dreams come true. All that stuff about deeply seated—'

'Dreams,' the girl reiterated firmly. 'Admittedly, some of the dreams that are about to come true tend to be the ones you get after a late-night cheese salad, but what the hell, a dream's a dream.'

Wesley frowned. 'Usually I dream of playing the violin naked in front of packed concert halls. Or running away down corridors chased by big dogs and women with knives. There's also this really weird one where—'

'All that sort of dream,' the girl said calmly, 'comes out of your deep-seated personal shortcomings and inadequacies.' She propped herself up on one elbow, swept a curtain of hair away from her dark, cool eyes and added, 'You're not going to tell me you haven't got any? Personal shortcomings and inadequacies, I mean. Because if you are . . .'

'Look.' Wesley turned round twice and kicked a pebble savagely. 'Of course I have. Heaps of them. But I don't see how being attacked by goblins and watching Vikings drown is going to help me grow as a person. I thought it was more about sitting round in a circle in a school hall every Tuesday night talking about it with a lot of other – I mean, in the company of other people in the same position.'

'That's encounter groups,' the girl replied. 'Quite different. Not that I'm saying they don't work, up to a point. As I understand it, everybody goes away from them with the firm belief that they may be sad and pathetic, but at least there's twenty-nine other people in the same town who're even sadder and more pathetic than they are. Very useful stepping-stone on the path to self-reconstruction.' She smiled and slid off the rock. 'But this way's more fun.'

'Is it? I was the one the goblins wanted to eat, remember.'

'I said more fun. I didn't say who for. You ready?'

Wesley took a couple of steps backwards. 'What for?' he demanded.

The girl grinned; you might say 'playfully', if you'd

ever seen a cat playing with a dying bird. 'Let's put it this way,' she said. 'Nobody's going to expect you to play the violin.'

Wesley was just about to demand an explanation, coupled with a few explicit assurances about not having to take his clothes off, when the air was suddenly full of wingbeats, and a savage gust of air pushed him off his feet into the mud, face down. When he'd prised himself out of the mud and cleared a couple of gaps in the face-pack to see through, he saw a huge black, white-headed eagle, easily fifteen feet from wingtip to wingtip, lifting itself up into the air. Clasped in its talons, and struggling wildly, was the girl.

'Help!' she screamed. 'Don't just stand there, *do* something! This is not a drill!'

'Huh?'

'*Heelp!*' The girl's voice seemed to be ripped away from her by the slipstream from the eagle's wings. As he stared, he saw that its round cruel eye was fixed on him. There's an eloquence in eagles' eyes that beats verbal communication into a cocked hat.

'Hey!' Wesley shouted. 'What's happening?'

But the eagle and the girl were already small, receding dots against the sky. Wesley ran down to the water's edge, and stopped. There was nothing he could do anyway, except watch and see where it went.

First it climbed, soaring on the thermals that rose from the lake until it was nothing but a speck, a memory of its own outline. Then, just as Wesley was convincing himself that he'd lost sight of it and it was long gone, it started to descend, sweeping long, slow circles over the middle of the lake. Now it was directly between Wesley and the sun, but he kept track of it (rather cleverly, he couldn't help feeling) by watching its reflection in the water. Finally it spread its enormous wings and sailed lazily across the lake and up into the high mountain that stood at the lake's southernmost end. It climbed, put its wings back and glided in, pitching somewhere high among the rocks.

'Christ!' Wesley said, and sat down again. Except at job interviews, in exams and on his first and only date with Stephanie Northrop from Vouchers, he'd never felt so helpless or so bewildered in all his life.

Just then, someone shot him in the back.

'Hey,' said a voice behind him. 'You felt that!'

Slowly, Wesley turned round. 'Who the hell are you?' he asked.

'My name's Talks With Squirrels,' the Indian warrior replied. 'If you don't mind my asking, what exactly did you feel?'

'Like somebody just poked me in the back with a stick,' Wesley answered. 'Why?'

'Not agonising pain or your whole life flashing in front of your eyes?'

'Not really, no. Look, who are you?'

'And you can see me all right? I mean, I'm not blurry at the edges or anything? You can't look straight through me at the trees behind?'

'No. What was it you did just then?'

'Shot you,' the Indian replied, indicating the bow in his left hand. 'Right between the shoulder blades. Only this time, you noticed.'

'*This time?*'

The Indian nodded. 'I've been shooting you ever since you got off the bus,' he said casually. 'Direct hit every time. By rights, if you were to drink a glass of water, you'd make somebody a first-class watering can.'

'Hey!' Wesley wasn't quite sure how to react. On the

one hand, he had this overwhelming urge to be very frightened indeed. On the other hand, by his own admission this lunatic had been using him as a dartboard for some time now, and he was apparently none the worse for it, so what was there to be frightened of? 'Who *are* you?' he repeated.

Talks To Squirrels propped his bow against a tree and advanced, hand outstretched. 'I'm a war leader of the now extinct Shashkehanna nation,' he said, not without a certain audible pride. 'Prior to my death in 1703, I was the most feared and respected warrior this side of the Mississippi. Actually, since I died my average with the bow's gone up from 96.28 to 98.3, while with the tomahawk, at fifty yards . . .'

Instinctively, Wesley grasped the proffered hand. His fingers closed upon themselves, enfolding nothing.

'You're dead,' he said.

'In a sense,' the Indian replied. 'Look, it's a bit hard to explain really. Try this. You've heard of negative equity?'

Wesley nodded. He had friends who talked about little else.

'It's when you want to sell the house but you can't, because it's worth less than what's still outstanding on the mortgage, right?' The Indian shrugged. 'Well, that's basically how it is with me and Life.'

'I don't understand,' Wesley said.

'You don't?' The Indian sighed. 'It's not that difficult, for pity's sake. Look. In life, I made certain undertakings, right? I swore this really heavy oath by sun, moon and stars that I'd never rest till I'd killed every paleface between here and the Cedar River.' The Indian shrugged. 'I underperformed, I admit it. Due, in no small part, to misleading information and a serious underestimate of the number of palefaces I was up against. You see, my sources led me to believe there were only thirty-four of them.'

'Ah.'

The Indian nodded. 'But I made the undertaking, nevertheless, and now I'm a bit like a kiddie who's getting his plate of cold shepherd's pie put in front of him every meal till he eats it all up. And since there's even more palefaces around now than there were back in the early seventeen-hundreds, I guess I'm fairly comprehensively stuck. Like I said; negative equity.'

'Gosh.'

Talks To Squirrels shrugged, sat down on the rock and lit a pipe. 'I'm allowed to smoke, it's one of the advantages of being dead,' he explained. 'I'm intrigued, though. You see, there's no way you should be able to see me, let alone feel my arrows. Seems to imply that – nah, can't be that. Forget I spoke.'

'Seems to imply what?'

The Indian waved his hand dismissively. 'Please,' he said, 'don't ask. Too silly for words. Don't want you thinking Death's addled my brains.'

'Seems to imply what?'

'Well,' the Indian said, 'if you insist, and you promise not to laugh, it might be that you're becoming more real on this side than you ever were back where you came from.' He frowned, and blew a smoke ring. 'But that's just plain dumb, because for that to work, you can hardly have existed at all back where you belong. Now, how could that be?'

Wesley rubbed his chin. To his surprise, he felt a slight texture of bristles; curious, since usually a shave lasted him three days. 'Actually,' he said, 'it's not quite as daft as it sounds. You might say I didn't really exist all that much, back home in Brierley Hill. Then again, in Brierley Hill, who does?'

The Indian looked at him. 'Now you're the one talking gibberish,' he said. 'I guess it means you're more than usually perceptive. Psychic or something. Tell me, when you hold them do teaspoons curl and try and climb up your wrist?'

'No.'

'No? Oh well. Anyway, it was good talking to you. Have a nice day, now.'

'Just a minute.' Wesley leaned forward. 'I don't know if you can help me, but . . .'

The Indian raised an eyebrow. 'Look,' he said, standing up, 'no offence, but if you want me to try and make contact for you with someone who's Passed Beyond, then forget it. I may be dead, but all that ouija-board stuff gives me the creeps.'

'Listen,' Wesley said sharply. The Indian sat down again. 'It's nothing like that. A moment ago, I was standing here talking to a girl . . .'

'Nor,' said the Indian quickly, 'am I in a position to help you review your personal relationships. Being dead, you lose touch.'

'And an eagle abducted her,' Wesley continued severely. 'Just picked her up and carried her off to that mountain over there. The pointy one. I think I'm supposed to rescue her or something.'

'You are? Good Lord, how old-fashioned. I thought men these days weren't supposed to do that sort of thing any more. I thought it was all doing your fair share of the housework and not being afraid to cry.'

'Look . . .'

'You're sure she was being abducted? Maybe she just wanted her own space for a while, you know, to find herself or something.'

'Shut up,' Wesley said. 'Come to think of it, I'd

probably be better off trying to handle this myself. Sorry to have troubled you.'

'Don't be like that,' the Indian replied. 'Just trying to be on your wavelength, that's all. Rescuing abducted maidens is bread and butter to me. It's all part of what being a warrior's all about. That's why they call us Braves.'

'Yes?'

'To our faces, anyhow.' The Indian leaned forward. 'That mountain over there?'

'Yup. The tall one with five trees near the top.'

The Indian nodded. 'Lots of eyries up there,' he confirmed. 'I can show you the secret path known only to the now extinct Shashkehanna nation, though actually it's quicker to follow the forestry trail. They've put in little finger-posts so you don't get lost.'

'Whatever,' Wesley replied. 'Can we start now, please, because—?'

'And when it comes to sorting out large, aggressive birds of prey.' The Indian smirked. 'Well, I was about to say "I'm your man," but "I *was* your man, once" would be rather more accurate. Still, with my skill and experience and your strength and courage—'

'We're stuffed,' Wesley said, sinking his chin in his hands. 'Marvellous, isn't it? Unless I rescue that bloody woman, I'm liable to be stuck here indefinitely. And what have I got to work with? Me, and a dead Indian.'

'The best kind, according to General Custer,' replied Talks To Squirrels cheerfully. 'And he should know, damnit. Hey, kid, what are we waiting for? Let's go show those eagles what we're made of.'

Wesley frowned. 'Oh yes, that reminds me. What *are* you made of?'

'Ectoplasm,' the Indian replied promptly. 'Marvellous

stuff, except it's dry clean only. Come *on*, will you? I thought you were the guy who daydreams of adventure and glorious deeds.'

'Yeah,' Wesley answered wretchedly, 'that's me, isn't it? Hey, you. If I get killed in this ghastly place, will I have to hang around here for ever being a ghost, like you?'

'I'm not sure, but it's a very real possibility.'

'In that case,' said Wesley firmly, 'you go first.'

'Go *away*,' said Janice, irritably. 'And you, the whole lot of you. Go on, shoo!'

The goblins didn't move. Instead, they just crouched where they were, simpering at her. Bashfully, one of them reached out and offered her a flower.

'Get outa here!' Janice yelled, stamping her foot. 'Jesus, don't you freaks understand English?'

'Wie bitte, wunderschön Fräulein?'

'Oh . . . !' With painful effort, Janice closed her eyes and counted to ten. They were still there when she opened them again; ten lovesick goblins, grinning at her like something out of a Mills & Boon version of *Nightmare On Elm Street*. She decided to give sweet reason one last go before resorting to screaming and kicking.

'Guys,' she said, trying to sound friendly, 'no offence, but it's a non-starter, really. I mean, look at me, will you? I said look, damnit,' she added, as ten pairs of round red eyes gazed yearningly into hers, 'not gawp. Come on, let's keep some hold on reality here. You – are . . .' She swallowed hard before saying the word. 'Goblins. Orcs. Little short guys who eat people. Really neat, hunky goblins, I feel sure, and if I was a lady goblin I'd be tattooing your phone numbers on the back of my hand right this minute, you bet. But I'm *not* a lady goblin, now am I? I mean, do I look like a lady goblin? No, forget I said that. Just, um, take it from me. Like, you know, no fangs. Not quite up to speed in the talons department. I . . .'

She tailed off. It was hopeless. Whatever she did just seemed to make it all infinitely worse.

She would, she acknowledged, pay good money to anybody who could prevent the big scaly one at the back from playing the mandolin.

'All right,' she growled, 'you asked for it.' She stalked forward and kicked the nearest goblin on the point of the shoulder, as hard as she could.

The goblin grinned soppily at her, and blushed khaki.

'Heeelp!' she screamed, pulling half-heartedly at the hem of her windcheater. 'Help, anybody! Rape! Rape!'

She stopped yelling, and looked round defiantly. None of the goblins seemed to have moved an inch. If anything, they'd moved a bit closer. To protect her, probably.

'Oh, for Christ's sake!' she panted. 'Don't you guys ever—?'

That was as far as she got before an eagle suddenly swooped down and carried her away.

Calvin Dieb stopped running, looked round, saw no goblins and sank, exhausted, onto a tree stump. A moment later, a butterfly fluttered up and perched on his shoulder.

'That's you, right?' Dieb gasped.

'You got it,' the butterfly replied. 'Quick, aren't you?'

'Goes with the territory,' Dieb said, his eyes shut. 'God, I haven't run like that since, gee, the early eighties, maybe even since Jimmy Carter was President.' He opened his eyes and grinned. 'I remember that also seemed like a bad dream, at the time. Did I lose them?'

'The goblins? Sure. Happen to you a lot, that sort of thing?'

Dieb shook his head. 'Scarcely ever,' he replied. 'Which is odd, come to think of it. I mean, I guess I piss off more people in an average week than most people do in a lifetime, but for some reason none of them ever seems to want to get even. I mean, not with me personally, using the medium of physical violence.' Dieb shrugged. 'I'm not complaining. Just odd, that's all. I mean, if I did to me some of the things I do to other people, I guess I'd want to rip my lungs out.'

The butterfly fluttered its wings. 'Perhaps other people aren't as vindictive as you, Mr Dieb. Perhaps they're . . .' The butterfly was silent for a moment, while it searched for the right word. 'Nicer,' it said. 'You ever considered that?'

'Listen,' Dieb replied. 'Nobody ever made money in the legal profession being nice. It's like you don't make good ice cream with a blowtorch. It's just not the right technique.'

The butterfly didn't reply; instead, it spread its wings and flitted away.

'Hey,' Dieb called after it, 'what did I say? Come back!'

But the butterfly kept on flying, until it was nothing but a speck against the sky, and then just a remembered place where a speck was last clearly discernible. Dieb stood up, and then sat down again. 'Hey!' he said quietly.

And then the speck was visible again. It grew. And it grew. When it was larger than a butterfly, Calvin Dieb looked at it and saw that it wasn't a butterfly. It was something bigger, a long way away, closing in fast.

'Hey!' he said.

As it approached, coming in low across the lake, the underside of its huge wings and body were reflected sharply in the water; black and white wing feathers, white belly feathers, red feet, black talons. Its eyes were round and yellow, and it shrieked.

'Look,' Dieb said, backing away, 'I didn't mean anything against nice guys in general. I got a lot of respect for nice guys. Some of my best friends—' He checked himself; his instincts suggested that this was no time for playing origami with the truth. 'Some of my best friends,' he therefore said, 'have a lot of respect for nice guys. Well, not friends as such, more like business acquaintances . . .'

The eagle towered, put its wings back and dropped out of the sky towards him, talons outstretched. There was no point in trying to run, Dieb knew; another thing that goes with the territory is the sure and certain knowledge that there's no defence against things that drop on you from a great height. In Calvin's experience, that usually meant writs, but he had a shrewd idea that it probably applied to huge birds as well.

'Now you understand,' said the bird, halting its onslaught six inches or so from Calvin's head and hovering, 'where the expression *legal eagle* comes from. What's it feel like, being underneath for a change?'

Calvin lowered his arms from above his head and looked up. He could see the points of the talons; amazing how anything not made in a precision engineering workshop could be so sharp. 'Subtlety,' he said, in a rather wobbly voice, 'doesn't come easily to you, I can tell.'

'Lay it on with a trowel, that's my motto,' the eagle replied. 'I mean to say, where's the point in being subtle when you're trying to get a point across to a pig-ignorant jury? Chances are half of them are blacks and Hispanics anyway. That sort wouldn't understand subtlety if you smashed their teeth in with it.'

'Hey!' Calvin said. 'I may be a lot of unpleasant things, but nobody can say I'm a racist. I'm Jewish, for God's sake. We know all about that stuff.'

The eagle continued to hover, although its wings didn't move; it was as if the frame had frozen. 'So,' it said, 'finally there's something nice we can say about you, congratulations. You think that's a good reason why I shouldn't scarf you up in my nice sharp talons and rip your chest open?'

Calvin blinked. 'Is there any reason why you should?' he said.

'Yeah, sure,' the eagle replied, still motionless. 'I'm bigger than you are. I'm stronger and faster and smarter and I can afford the very best legal advice money can buy. That's what gives me wings, man, that's how come I can fly.' The eagle flexed its claws, lazily, with confidence. 'The law is my shepherd, Mr Dieb, wherefore shall I lack nothing. It maketh me to lie fluently in green pastures.'

'Hey,' Calvin said, benighted under the vast shadow of the bird's wings, 'cut it out, will you? I guess you made your point some time ago.'

The eagle opened its hooked beak wide. 'Objection overruled,' it said. 'I'm bigger than you, and I've got wings. Unless you've got a gun, or a better lawyer, you're mine.'

But Calvin stepped back and folded his arms. 'But that's not the way it is,' he replied, 'and you know it. I fight for the little guy, too. I sue the big corporations for the little kid who's been scarred for life by some firebug toy they couldn't be bothered to test properly. I take on the big hospitals when they've crippled some guy when they've cut corners to save a buck. Where there's some poor dumb broad whose old man's beating the shit out of her, I get her the injunction and the divorce. You get the hell off my back, bird, or I'll have the law on you.'

But the eagle flapped its wings, and they cracked in

the air like a whip. Dieb felt the talons hook in the collar of his five-thousand-dollar coat, and suddenly his feet lifted off the ground. All the air was bumped out of his lungs, and the coat was strangling him where it pressed up under his arms. He felt as if he was being crucified.

'Legal eagle, huh?' said the bird, as they hung in the air, so high up that their reflection in the lake below was nothing but a tiny speck. 'So make your own way home from here.'

'Hey!' Calvin shouted. The eagle let go, and flew away, back to its eyrie in the southern mountains.

Although he instinctively knew it was inadvisable, Calvin looked down. And what a lot of down there was to look at, all of a sudden. Vast, unfathomable expanses of down, to be followed in short order by all the splat! he could possibly wish for. *No thanks*, he muttered to himself, and he spread his wings.

Now where in hell did they come from?

Not that I'm complaining. No way. I like them so much I think I'll buy the company.

He concentrated until he could feel the air tingling in the feathers of his wingtips, as his mind hunted feverishly through the manual for something about how to manoeuvre. But all it could find was the long legal note disclaiming liability, and a load of guff about use of non-standard spares invalidating the warranty. Legal eagle, he said to himself. Well, yes. Seventy-five per cent of being a lawyer involves being stuck in precarious situations and not knowing what the hell you're supposed to do next. The trick is not to let anybody else see that you don't know.

In this case, gravity. One false move, one slight hint that he didn't actually know how to fly this thing, and gravity would be up at him like a ton of bricks.

And what did he always tell himself, in these situations? *Hey, relax. We'll just wing it from here and see what happens.*

He relaxed, and spread his wings. And the sky rushed down at him like a falling roof.

CHAPTER EIGHT

'T his it?' Wesley spluttered, hauling himself over a ledge of rock.

'Yes.'

'Oh, *good*.' His hands hurt; there was rather less skin on his knuckles than there ought to be, according to the specification, and he had cramp in his tendons running right up into his elbow. For a man who, twenty-four hours previously, had he thought about it, wouldn't have been entirely sure he *had* tendons, it was a sudden and not entirely pleasant reversal of circumstances.

'Ouch,' he observed. 'Ow.' He huddled on the ledge and hugged his arm ostentatiously, waiting for the Indian to sympathise.

'The eyrie's up there,' whispered Talks To Squirrels, nodding his head towards an opening in the cliff wall facing them. 'Chances are, your eagle's one of the ones that live there.'

'*One* of the . . .'

'Of course,' the Indian went on, his voice so low as to

be scarcely audible, 'scaling the cliff'll be relatively straightforward. Presumably you've got a plan for what we do after that.'

Wesley looked at the cliff – forty-odd feet of smooth, slightly concave rock – and thought, *relatively straightforward.* 'Tell you what,' he said. 'You tell me how you'd set about it, and then I'll sort of chip in with my comments and observations. I'd hate for you to get the idea I was muscling in.'

'If you're happy with that,' the Indian replied. 'Well, if it was me, as soon as I'd scaled the cliff—'

'Uh.'

'Sorry?'

'No,' Wesley said, 'go on, please. Don't let me interrupt you.'

The Indian nodded. 'All I was going to say was, once I'd scaled the cliff I'd be thinking in terms of a direct frontal assault – you know, take out as many of them as I could, wave a torch around, set light to a few eagles, let them spook the rest, and hope I'd be able to find the girl and get clear before they knew what was happening.'

'Ah,' said Wesley. 'I see. And you think that'd work?'

'No,' the Indian replied brightly. 'How d'you think I got to be a ghost in the first place?'

'Oh.'

'And that was just normal-sized eagles,' Talks To Squirrels went on. 'One minute I was standing on this ledge fitting an arrow to my bowstring and thinking, This is easier than I thought, and the next minute I was tumbling back down the cliff, banging my head on stuff and saying *Eeeeee.* Of course, when *you* do it, maybe it'll all work out OK. After all, I'd never done anything like this before.'

'You hadn't?'

'I led kind of a sheltered life,' Talks admitted. 'Was I

dumb, or what? I mean, only a complete idiot would imagine you could work something like this out from first principles.'

'Well, quite,' Wesley said.

'So,' the Indian persisted, 'what's your plan? I'm telling you, I can't wait to hear. You know, ever since that day I've been turning it over in my mind, asking myself, what'd I do different if I had my time all over again, and all these hundreds of years I haven't been able to figure it out.'

'You haven't?'

The Indian grinned self-deprecatingly. 'Pretty dumb of me, I guess. So, you gonna tell me now or do you want it to be a surprise?'

'Oh, a surprise,' Wesley said. 'Definitely a surprise.'

Calvin Dieb landed.

For a moment or so he wobbled, rocking backwards and forwards on his talons like an expensive china ornament on a high mantelpiece; then it occurred to him that he'd probably do better just by holding still. It worked.

'Help!' said a female voice.

He peered into the darkness of the cave behind him. His eagle eyes cut the gloom in a way that astounded him, and he made out a human shape huddled in a fissure of the rock. It was a girl, damnit –

– Well, a girl in a sense. A youngish, thirty-something woman, with big thick-lensed glasses, rather on the stocky side; maybe damsel would be pushing it. But in distress, definitely.

'It's all right,' he said.

'Huh?'

'It's all right,' he repeated. 'Just keep calm and everything'll be just fine.'

'Help! Help!'

Dieb cringed. In the confined space of the cave, her yowling sounded horribly loud. Whoever or whatever it was that she was afraid of (with good reason, presumably) would have to be deaf as a post not to hear. He made a shushing noise and edged towards her.

'You OK?' he whispered.

'*Heeeelp!*'

'Look.' He came closer; she shrank back. 'What's going on?' he asked. 'Who's keeping you here?'

The girl stopped caterwauling and stared at him. 'You are,' she said.

Calvin must have swallowed his breath the wrong way or something. He choked. 'What?' he spluttered.

'You are, you disgusting bird,' the girl repeated. 'You brought me here, damnit.'

'Did I?'

'Oh for fuck's sake. Yes, of course you did.'

'But . . .'

'*Heeeeeelp!*'

Calvin took a step backwards, and felt himself wobble again. He looked down and saw something under his savagely hooked claw. It was a human skull.

'*Shit!*' He jumped about a foot in the air, nearly stunning himself on the roof of the cave. As he landed and regained his precarious balance, a thought struck him—

Eagle.

Cave.

Skull.

Oh Jesus, he cursed inside his mind. *Of all the eagles in all the mountains in all the world, why did I have to change into this one?*

'Hey,' he said aloud. 'Just a minute, pipe down. Did I really bring you here?'

'Yes,' replied the girl, offended. 'You tend to notice these things.'

'Are you sure?' Dieb queried. 'I mean, are you certain it wasn't some other eagle? Dunno about you, but I can't tell 'em apart.'

'It was you,' the girl said unpleasantly. 'White diamond on the breast, split claw on the left foot, slight upward twist to the hook of the upper jaw. It was definitely you.'

'But it can't have been. No, really. You see, I'm not an eagle, I'm a lawyer.'

'HEEEELP!'

Oh for Christ's sake, what's this thing people have about lawyers? 'I'm a human being,' he said. 'I don't know if you're caught up in this crazy weirdness too, but I'm a perfectly normal lawyer who's been turned into this goddamn eagle thing, and I'm not going to eat you. Or anybody. Trust me.'

The girl scowled at him. 'You're just saying that,' she growled. 'Trying to lull me into a false sense of security.'

Suddenly, Dieb felt annoyed. 'Yeah, sure,' he replied. 'Well-known hunting technique of the larger raptors. Soon as they see a jackrabbit or a woodchuck or whatever down there on the prairie floor, they swoop down, call out, *It's OK, really I'm just a lawyer*, and the moment the rabbit comes back out of his hole, they nail him. Look, what've I got to do to convince you, file a suit or something?'

'You don't sound like a lawyer,' the girl said, after a pause.

'Given your attitude, I'll take that as a compliment. Hey, you think I'm threatening, maybe you should see my partner. Man, if I was a rabbit I'd far rather take my chances with the eagle.'

At least the girl had stopped screaming and quivering. 'All right,' she said, 'so really you're a lawyer. Still doesn't explain why you grabbed me and brought me here.'

'I didn't. No, please, just listen up, will you? Maybe it was an eagle grabbed you, and maybe, God help me, I'm that eagle now; but I wasn't that eagle *then*.'

'No?'

'Nah. That was the eagle. The *real* eagle,' he added quickly, as the girl started yowling again. 'The eagle whose fucking horrible body I've somehow gotten myself into. Look . . .'

'It's OK,' the girl said. 'I believe you. It's OK.'

'You do?'

'Yes. It's what you said. Anybody who can come out with all that bullshit and really expect anybody to believe it has got to be a—'

'Yeah,' Dieb snarled, shutting his eyes, 'right. The point is, I'm not gonna hurt you, I'm just as confused as you are, and the sooner it cuts it out and we can get back to real life, the happier I'll be. So if we can both stop acting crazy and just think for a minute . . .'

The girl nodded. 'I guess so,' she said. 'What happened to you, then?' She stopped, and stared at him, as coinage tinkled on impact in her mind. 'Just a second, though,' she went on. 'You haven't fallen in love with me, right?'

'Look,' Dieb said, recovering rather faster than he'd imagined he would, 'don't get me wrong, but . . .'

'Everybody I meet,' said the girl defiantly, 'falls in love with me. Vikings. Priests. Goblins . . .'

'Did you say Vikings? And goblins?'

The girl nodded. 'And just don't make any remarks, OK? Because really, this isn't the time.'

'I've had Vikings,' Dieb said excitedly. 'And goblins

too, I guess. How about bears?'

The girl shook her head. 'No bears. How about you? Any priests?'

'No. But don't let's get sidetracked. We both had the Vikings and the goblins, right? So whatever this garbage is, it's happening to both of us.'

'Maybe. Did you fall in the lake? I did. That's when everything started to go weird.' She scowled. 'Like, men started falling in love with me.'

'Ah.'

'Except you.'

'Um.'

'Which is great,' the girl went on, 'really. And I've been thinking; you know, about the weirdness. You see, all my life I've had this stupid notion about how nice it'd be to be one of those girls who have it really easy because they're attractive, and men just fall over backwards and jump through hoops the moment they see them.'

'You mean, like a bimbo?'

'That's the word I was looking for, yes. All I wanted to be was a genuine, twenty-two-carat peroxide bimbo. Well, that's what's happening to me, almost like someone's teaching me a lesson.' She paused for breath. 'Is that what's happening to you? Not being a bimbo,' she added quickly. 'Punishment by wish-fulfilment, or whatever.'

Dieb shook his head. 'Can't say it is,' he replied. 'I keep meeting these chatty birds and animals who try and psychoanalyse me, but all I really want to do is find my car keys.'

'Car keys?'

'Yeah, my keys. I dropped them. If I could only get into my car . . .'

The girl rummaged in her windcheater pocket, and produced a small, glittering bundle of metal. 'These keys?' she asked. 'I picked them up beside the—'

'*My keys!*' Calvin stared for a fraction of a second, roughly the amount of time it takes for light to travel a quarter of an inch, and then extended a taloned foot and grabbed.

But before he could touch them—

'Sssh!'

'Oh, shut up,' Wesley hissed back over his shoulder. 'It's all right for you, you're a ghost. You don't weigh anything, and if you fall off it won't actually matter. In my case—'

'Look!'

Wesley craned his neck over the lip of the ledge, and peered as far as he could into the cave. 'Oh, *shit*,' he whispered.

'You found him!'

'Yes,' replied Wesley, thoughtfully. 'So I have.'

'And he's about to eat the girl.'

'Could be. Could be. However, let's not jump to—'

The ghost hopped up onto the ledge, drew his bow and shot three arrows in the time it takes to blow one's nose. 'Look at that grouping,' he sighed. 'You could cover all three with a quarter. Pity.'

'Yes,' Wesley agreed. 'Quite.'

The Indian flattened himself against the rock. 'OK,' he said, 'your turn. All you've gotta do is sneak up behind him with that chunk of rock and flatten him.'

'That's all, huh?'

'Sure. Ain't life just full of anticlimaxes?'

Wesley reached out and wrapped his hand around the chunk of rock indicated. 'I'm not sure about this,' he muttered, 'ecologically speaking, I mean. I'm sure I read somewhere that eagles are protected.'

'Not this kind. I refer you to the Protection of Birds Act 1977, section 42, subsection 4(b). Go get the fucker.'

'Right,' sighed Wesley. 'Here goes.'

Rock in hand, he crawled forward.

'My keys *aaaagh*!'

The eagle slumped forward, and its beak hit the ground with a chunky crack, like a coconut falling on a rock.

'Hey!'

Wesley, who had shut his eyes a moment before swinging the rock, opened them again, and saw what he had done. He stood rooted to the spot, while many different reactions and emotions coursed through his mind like cars in an overcrowded multi-storey car park.

'What the hell did you do that for?' demanded the girl.

Wesley looked up, and saw, and said nothing. Instead he goggled.

'And who the hell are you, anyway?' the girl continued.

Despite the sleeting blizzard of pink hearts and fat cabbage roses swirling in front of his eyes and obscuring his vision, he could see that this wasn't the gorgeous female he'd been trudging round after all this time. This was a different creature entirely; squatter, more compactly built, probably much better suited to life on a planet with much higher gravity, with a face that reminded him curiously of a warthog in spectacles. Somewhere in the back of his mind, a thousand violins began to play.

'Er,' he said.

'What?'

It was, insisted the skeleton staff still on duty inside his head, time to explain. 'I . . .' he said.

'You what?'

'Um.'

The girl looked at him, and her glance struck him like a napalm attack on a tribe of snowmen. He stepped back, walking clean through Talks With Squirrels as he did so. The Indian, who had been only one arrow away from ten consecutive hits in the girl's forehead before Wesley jogged his arm, instinctively tried to reach out and catch him; but his fingers passed through Wesley's wrist, a fraction of a second before he stepped backwards over the lip of the cave and into thin air.

'Aaaaaagh!' he observed.

As the cry dopplered away, the girl scurried forward, yelling, 'Hey, wait!' – the sort of damn silly thing girls do say, under such circumstances. Talks To Squirrels sighed, looked down at the drop separating the cave mouth from the ground, sank his tomahawk into the back of the girl's neck and sat down in a corner, sulking.

'Hell!' said Janice.

For want of anything better to do, she tried to find the car keys, which she distinctly remembered dropping just after the funny man had nutted the eagle. Needless to say, they were nowhere to be seen.

Captain Hat, scampering down the mountainside with his latest trophy, was surprised and a little bit put out when a falling human body hit him on the head, squashing him flat. Quite apart from the inconvenience of having every bone in his body broken by the force of the impact, he dropped the car keys he'd just made away with; and, being pinned down under a human body, could only watch helplessly as they rolled down the hill, bounced off a projecting rock and went *plop!* into the lake.

'Urgh,' groaned the human body.

'Excuse me.'

Hat peered up from under the body's armpit. There was a Big peering down at him 'You again,' he said.

'What? Oh, yes. Hi.' Linda Lachuk crouched down on her knees and moved aside the body's arm. 'We've met already, haven't we?'

Hat nodded. 'You're the submarine spotter,' he said. 'Find any yet?'

'One,' Linda replied. 'But it sank. Hey, I found out they're smuggling the stuff out in rocks.'

'Is that so?'

Linda nodded. 'I don't know why I didn't think of it earlier, it's so obvious,' she said.

Hat shrugged. 'Often it's the obvious things that never occur to you,' he said. 'Ain't that the way, huh?'

'You're right. Anyway, I thought it might be a good idea to get up high, so I can see everything that's going on. Is that a cave up there?'

'Could be,' Hat replied cautiously. 'There's an eagle in there, mind.'

'Really? Hey, that's great. All the story needs to make it truly cosmic is a threatened-habitat angle.'

Hat nodded. 'I see,' he said, wriggling out past Wesley's elbow and picking up his hat. 'In that case, I guess I'd better leave you to it.'

'OK,' Linda said. 'And remember, if you see any submarines . . .'

'Sure,' Hat replied. Then he clamped his hat onto his head as firmly as it would go, tucked his shattered arms and legs tight into his body, deliberately fell over and rolled all the way down the hill to get his bones set.

Linda watched him go, shrugged, and set off up the slope, cursing the thoughtlessness of whoever was responsible for the terrain. Some people. No respect. She was just beginning to feel nicely cross when—

Goddamnit!

Heedless of the uneven ground she ran, sliding and staggering, to the foot of the cliff, which she immediately began to swarm up, totally without science but with boundless enthusiasm. No way a piffling sheer rock face was going to get between her and her story!

Above her head was the mouth of the cave. She waited until gravity was looking the other way, and jumped.

The very tips of her fingers hooked over the rocky ledge. Engaging her adrenalin drive and whacking the throttle wide open, she swung herself up, dropping her knee over the cavemouth's lintel just as the strength in her fingertips gave way. A few chunks of rock, dislodged by her entrance, rattled and bounced away down the cliff, taking their own sweet time before hitting the ground. She didn't notice. What she was seeing and hearing in the studio of her mind was far too enthralling for her to bother about crumbling ledges, vertiginous drops or the risk of a horrible death. As far as she was concerned, if a horrible death wanted to meet her, she might just be able to spare it five minutes a fortnight Tuesday, but it would be well advised to phone nearer the time and confirm if it wanted to avoid a wasted journey.

She hauled herself into the cave and lay on her stomach, panting, only an inch or so away from the object of her fascination. It was a hat.

It was round. And broad-brimmed. It had lots of corks hanging from it, attached to the brim by little bits of string. In other words, it was an Australian hat.

'*Yes!*' Linda gasped, reaching out to touch it. Her fingertips were just about to make contact with the outermost fibres of its fabric when, agonisingly, it was snatched away.

'Hey!' said a female voice.

Linda looked up. There was some sort of female attached to the hat by means of a podgy-fingered hand and sixteen inches of arm. Linda blinked. Dear God, she prayed, sweet Lord in Heaven, don't let her be CBS News or the *Boston Globe*.

'What d'you think you're doing with my hat?' she demanded.

Linda stared at her, feeling as if she'd just found the Holy Grail only to find the words *Batteries Not Included* engraved on the rim. 'Your h-h-?' she stuttered.

'Yeah,' replied the female. 'My hat. Lay off it, will you?'

Linda fought back the panic. 'But I *need* that hat,' she gasped. 'Really, I do.'

The girl shrugged. 'So go buy yourself one,' she replied. 'They're only $12.99 from the big Government surplus store in Oskaloosa.'

Linda stared. 'You *bought* that hat?' she whimpered.

'Yes. So what?'

'But – but you're not *Australian*.'

'True.' The girl nodded. 'I'm two-fifths Irish, one fifth Polish, one fifth Italian and one fifth Swede, not that it's any damn business of yours.'

Linda swallowed hard. 'You just *bought* it? In a *shop*? You're certain about that?'

'Yes.'

'In Oskaloosa?'

'Yes.'

'Ah, *damn*!' Linda flopped down on the ground and lay still, while the bailiffs came for her remaining adrenalin. Then a thought occurred to her, and she looked up. 'Did you say one-fifth Italian?' she asked.

'Yes. Do you happen to know how to revive a stunned eagle?'

'No. And Polish, was that?'

'That's right.'

Linda chewed her lower lip thoughtfully. You had to be careful nowadays, but with a little careful scripting and some subliminal camera angles, Polish and Italian could be made to translate as *Vatican Secret Agent*. 'You don't,' she enquired tentatively, 'work for the Pope at all, do you?'

'What?'

'The Pope. No? Oh, never mind. Can I just *borrow* your hat, for a second or two. I just want to look at it.'

The girl shrugged. 'Be my guest,' she said. 'Here.'

Linda took it gingerly and examined it for telltale clues; a smear of submarine oil here, a few flakes of chipped marble there. She didn't find any; instead she saw, inside the lining, a label which read:

COUNTRY CLUB™
SIZE 60 CM
100% NYLON
MADE IN TAIWAN

Slowly she passed the hat back. She couldn't have felt more let down if she'd managed to get to see God, and God had made a pass at her. 'Oh well,' she said. 'One fifth Italian?'

'I think the eagle's about to come round.'

'Eagle?'

The girl pointed. 'Over there. About eighteen inches to your left.'

Linda looked round. 'Oh,' she said, 'that eagle. My endangered habitat angle.'

'Huh?'

It suddenly occurred to Linda that a word of

explanation might be in order. 'I'm a journalist,' she said, and smiled reassuringly.

'You are, huh?'

'That's right.'

'Figures. Did you get the Vikings and the goblins too?'

Linda furrowed her brow. 'No,' she replied. 'What Vikings?'

'Oh.' The girl looked disappointed. 'Then bang goes that theory. Shucks.' The girl shrugged. 'Then it's back to the drawing board, I guess. What are you going to do now?'

'Go back outside and watch for submarines,' Linda replied, puzzled that anybody should need to ask. 'Oh, that reminds me. Have you seen any?'

'Any what?'

'Submarines.'

'No.'

'Oh.' Linda thought for a moment. 'How about tanks and missiles and rockets and things? Probably encased in concrete blocks,' she added.

'Nope. Sorry.'

'Hell. I think your eagle's just woken up, by the way. He just tried to bite my ankle.'

'Actually,' said the girl, 'he's a lawyer.'

'A lawyer?'

'That's what he told me.'

Linda mused for a moment, wondering whether lawyers disguised as enormous eagles could somehow be worked in as background. 'Nah,' she said aloud, 'that's no use, they'd only say I was faking the pictures. If you see any submarines, you will let me know?'

'If you like. You haven't seen a set of car keys lying about, have you?'

'Car keys? No, sorry. Can you remember where you had them last?'

'Yes.'

'Well, there you are, then. Try and remember about the submarines.' She sighed, lowered herself carefully over the ledge and started to climb down the cliff, pre-occupied.

Strange woman, said Janice to herself, as she knelt down beside the eagle. Almost at once, it raised its head and stared at her.

'My keys,' it said. 'My keys!'

'Ah yes,' Janice mumbled. 'Your keys. I'm afraid there's been a bit of an accident. You see . . .'

'My *keys*!!'

'They were here a short time ago,' Janice said. 'But first there was the lunatic with the rock, and then that crazy journalist, and I've looked everywhere, and they've gone.'

The eagle lowered its head and made a high, thin keening noise. Exhausted, Janice leaned back against the cave wall and closed her eyes. 'Do you have to make that horrible noise?' she snapped.

'Yes.'

'I thought you said you were a lawyer. Lawyers don't make high-pitched screaming noises.'

'How would you know?'

'They don't on *LA Law*,' Janice replied firmly. 'And they don't in Cleveland, either. My cousin's sister-in-law—'

'Look.' Calvin Dieb sat up, or as near to sitting up as his shape would allow. 'Somebody's playing games with us, it's obvious. Whoever it is who changed me into an eagle and did whatever's been happening to you has also stolen my goddamn keys. Agreed?'

Janice nodded. 'I hear you,' she said. 'So what do you reckon?'

'Right.' Dieb pulled his mind together, and tried to concentrate. 'I think you and I are just regular people. What about the other two?'

'The rock fiend and the reporter? Hard to tell. On balance, I think the reporter was, 'cos she seemed to be acting the way they usually do.'

'Oh? Like what?'

'Like she was only interested in what she wanted for her story, not what was actually going on.'

Dieb shook his head. 'Unless we're certain, let's assume she wasn't; safer that way. OK, so we know we're both all right. Obviously,' he went on, 'the most important thing is for us to stick together, not let them split us up. Agreed?'

'Agreed.'

'Fine. Now, th—'

He vanished.

'Ugh,' said Wesley.

'Feeling better?'

Wesley looked up. 'Oh Christ, it's you again. Why can't you just—?'

The beautiful girl raised a perfect eyebrow. 'Don't tell me,' she said. 'At your school you could either do tact or woodwork, and you're reasonably good at woodwork. Am I right?'

'No, actually. I always hit my thumb with the hammer. What's woodwork got to do with anything?'

The girl reached out a hand and pulled him to his feet. 'That was Phase Two,' she said. 'You failed.'

'I did?'

The girl nodded. 'You were meant to,' she added. 'In fact, it'd spoil the whole thing if you didn't.'

Wesley scowled, and looked up at the cliff face. 'Who

was – I mean, who were those people? The eagle, I mean, and the . . .'

'The short, fat, pig-faced girl?'

'She's not . . .'

The beautiful girl snickered and turned away to hide her grin. *Yes*, muttered Wesley under his breath. Bet you could make a pretty neat chest of drawers, at that. 'It's all right,' she said. 'Don't worry about it.'

'The hell with you.' Wesley tried to push past, but the beautiful girl tripped him up and he went sprawling.

'She's gone now,' she said. 'There's no point climbing all that way up there again.'

'Where's she gone to?' Wesley gasped, scrambling to his feet.

'Somewhere you can't follow,' she replied, with a soupçon of grated harshness. 'I said, forget it. You had your chance to rescue a damsel in distress and win your only true love, and you blew it. Now we go on to Phase Three. You do still want to get out of here, don't you?'

'Of course I do.' Wesley hesitated, looking up at the cave. 'Of course I do,' he repeated, but with rather less conviction.

'Well then.' The girl grabbed him by the collar and spun him round; she made it look easy. 'And don't worry, you'll forget about her eventually. Give it fifty years or so and you'll hardly give her a second thought.'

Wesley considered saying something, but decided against it. Fury, heartbreak, despair and the like tended to muck up his vocabulary, leaving him with as much chance of hitting on the right word as finding a pint of fresh milk in a supermarket at ten to eight on a Saturday night. Instead, he tightened his fists until they hurt and relaxed them again.

'I see,' he said. 'Fine. Can we get on with Phase Three

now, please? I'm getting rather sick of this game, and I'd like to go home as soon as possible.'

The girl giggled. 'I'd lay off trying to be angry with dignity if I were you,' she said. 'It makes you go all pink, like tinned salmon. Actually, I think you might rather like Phase Three, in the mood you're in. It involves quite a bit of . . .' She paused, flicking through her mental card-index. 'Hooliganism,' she said. 'Don't suppose you ever went in for that when you were a kid. Too scared of getting caught.'

Despite the bad reviews of his angry dignity, Wesley persevered with it. 'If you mean throwing stones through windows and spraying things on walls, you're right, I never did. Not because I was frightened—'

'*Look out!*'

Without even thinking, Wesley hurled himself to the ground, grazing the palms of his hands and bumping his chin, so that his teeth jarred together. 'Agh!' he said.

'Sorry,' said the girl, looking down at him. 'Didn't want you to get hit by the low-flying pigs.'

'Oh, very funny.'

The girl shrugged. 'It wasn't bad,' she said, 'but I don't suppose they'll be leaving out whole chunks of Groucho Marx and Noël Coward just to make room for it in the new edition of the *Dictionary of Quotations*. Are you going to get up, or would you rather crawl all the way to the next location? You can if you like, but it's rather a long way.'

When Calvin Dieb came to, he found himself tied to a stake.

Another thing he noticed was that it had suddenly gone dark, leading him to the conclusion that wherever he'd been while he hadn't been inside the body of Calvin

Dieb, he'd been there for quite some time. The only light, in fact, came from the huge bonfire, around which a large number of people were apparently dancing. Fortunately, the light reflected well off the surface of the lake, so he could clearly make out the curious Native American folk costumes the dancers were wearing, and the strange multi-coloured pigments they'd applied to their bodies and faces. They were also singing, but Calvin had an ear for music the way a snake has a leg to stand on; so they could have been singing Country standards or *La Traviata* for all he knew. He couldn't make out any of the words, but that didn't mean anything either. He had an idea it wasn't the 'Star-Spangled Banner', but that was as far as he got.

'Hello,' he called out. 'Excuse me.'

Nobody seemed to hear; not surprising, given the volume of the singing. He tried to wave to get someone's attention, but the ropes prevented him.

'You haven't got it yet, have you?' whispered a voice in his ear.

'What?'

'I said, you haven't got it yet. What's going on, I mean.'

'Sorry, you'll have to speak up. The music . . .'

'YOU HAVEN'T GOT IT YET, HAVE YOU?'

'That's better. Got what?'

'Oh, for crying out loud. Stay there.'

A second or so later, a bat flittered out of the darkness into his face, making him flinch. It dropped out of flight and hung from the lapel of his coat, like a huge black inverted carnation. 'Can you hear me better now?' it asked.

'You? Oh, *you*. Yes, that's much better. Hey, you got any idea what's going on?'

'You bet,' replied the bat.

'Well?'

'You're going to enjoy this,' the bat chuckled. 'Right up your street, this is.'

Calvin raised both eyebrows. 'You reckon so? Maybe you don't know me as well as you thought.'

'Get outa here, will you?'

'Love to.'

'I mean, on the contrary. I *know* you'll enjoy this, because it's what you do best.'

'Being tied to things? Sorry, lady, wrong guy. It's my associate Mr Piranha who's into chains and whips and things.'

'Litigation,' said the bat, patiently. 'That *is* what you do best, isn't it?'

Dieb nodded, insofar as he could with a thick coil of rawhide rope tightened under his chin. 'But this doesn't look much like a lawsuit to me,' he added. 'The big fire, for a start. And the dancing.'

'Ah.' The bat shook its wings, reminding Dieb of someone shaking out an umbrella after coming in off the street. 'But this is a different kind of litigation.'

'Well?'

'This is litigation,' the bat went on, 'Cherokee style. Though I think they used to have something similar in Europe a long time ago. Actually, it was only abolished in England in the early nineteenth century, by George the Third. The guy must have been nuts, if you ask me.'

'Excuse me?' Calvin enquired. 'Are we talking about canon law or the Star Chamber or something? We didn't do legal history where I went, or at least you could do it but it meant missing Advanced Fee Augmentation, so I didn't bother.'

'Something like that,' replied the bat. 'Like I said, it's an old-fashioned form of litigation, but generally speaking it's quicker, cheaper, fairer and a hell of a lot less traumatic than what you guys do nowadays. So I thought you might find it interesting.'

'Cheaper?'

'Oh, much.'

'Ah. Well, thanks all the same, but . . .'

The bat opened its claws, spread its wings and dropped-cum-flew away, leaving Calvin puzzled and not entirely happy. An obsolete form of legal procedure common to both Europe and Native America. Actions on the case? Ejectment? Oyer and terminer? Tricky.

Two authentic-looking Native Americans with feathers on their heads and rather forbidding expressions left the dance and stalked over to him. They were holding what he assumed were authentic tomahawks and had presumably authentic whacking great knives stuck through their belts. Without a word they cut the ropes, hauled him to his feet and dragged him towards the fire. Amazing, how some of these re-enactment society guys really live the role.

As they came inside the circle of firelight, Calvin was just about to start protesting when, to his great surprise, he saw someone he recognised.

'Leonard?' he said.

'Calvin,' replied the tall, ambassador-like man in the three-piece dark blue suit. 'It's been a long time.'

'Sure thing,' Calvin replied, as the two authentic people let him go. 'I thought you were . . . I mean yes, it really has been a long time. How're you doing? How's retirement suiting you? Hey, you look years younger than when you were at Schadling & Blutsauger.'

'Thanks.' Leonard nodded politely, and the firelight glinted on his almost Presidential grey hair. 'I've been a new man since I quit the profession, Cal. All sorts of new interests, things I'd never have gotten into if I'd stayed behind that desk. So,' he added with a smile, 'as it turns out, you did me a favour when you turned the rest of the partnership against me and squeezed me out.'

Calvin grinned uncomfortably. True, he'd spent five years of round-the-clock intriguing and politicking to dispose of dear old Len, the last remaining barrier between him and the purple; but it was a bit tactless to bring the subject up almost immediately, after so long. 'These new interests,' he said, trying to lighten things up. 'Historical re-enactments, huh? Never thought that was your scene, Leonard.'

The older man stopped smiling. 'It isn't,' he said. 'Though, as a matter of fact, I truly am half Cherokee. You didn't know that, did you?'

'No, Len, I didn't. Gee, it only goes to show, you think you know a guy, and . . .'

'Yes.' Leonard made a small, economical gesture to someone standing just outside the firelight. 'It only does. Well now, Cal, you ready?'

'Huh?'

'For the trial. Actually it's a purely Western tradition that the defendant gets first choice of weapons, but since you're a guest here among my people I guess it's only polite to extend you the courtesy.'

Before Calvin could put into words the question marks and exclamation marks that were clogging the passages of his brain, a totally authentic Native American with a bear's skull on his head stepped forward holding two identical spears. Ah, thought Calvin.

'Among my people,' Leonard went on, 'this is how we do litigation. Apart from it doesn't make any money for anybody, I reckon it's got the other way licked on all counts.'

'Trial by *combat*?'

Leonard nodded. 'Dontcha just love it? Now by rights, being over sixty years old I could name a champion to fight for me.' He peeled off his coat, tie and shirt, to reveal rippling pectorals and bulging biceps. 'But I thought, what the hell, this is something I want to see to *personally*. And if it means I give you the advantage, then so what?'

'Hey,' Calvin muttered. He tried to step backwards, but there was something large and authentic right behind him, prodding him in the back with a knife. 'Just a minute . . .'

Leonard held up his hand. 'You're right,' he said. 'I was forgetting. You have the option of wearing the spirit armour. You wanna go for that, or shall we forget about it? Up to you.'

Calvin heard the word 'armour' and nodded. Immediately a man like a substantial rock formation loomed forward, slapped a thick hairy paintbrush three times across his chest and once across his face, and stepped back. Slowly, feeling very much like Oliver Hardy, Calvin wiped paint out of his eyes.

'Suits you,' Leonard remarked. 'Me, I guess I'll make do without and risk the consequences. You try getting that stuff off again, you'll see why. Pumice-stone'll do it sometimes, but usually you gotta use caustic. Now then, you ready to choose?'

Calvin looked at the spears. They were very long and heavy, and the blades looked revoltingly sharp. 'Say, Leonard,' he whimpered, 'I never imagined you'd be sore about leaving the firm, honest. If only you'd said something . . .'

Leonard gave him a look that made the spearhead seem like a pat of butter. 'You got an injunction, remember? If I so much as showed my face at the office, you were going to get me carted off to jail. And that was three days before I even got the letter suggesting I should retire.'

'Really?' Calvin felt his heart shrivel. 'Guess it must have gotten held up in the Christmas mail, Len. I didn't mean it to be that way. I always had the utmost respect for you. Always.'

'And I always thought you were an evil little shit, Cal. Now, are you gonna choose, or shall I just stick you where you stand?'

There was a lump in Calvin's throat. He tried to swallow it. 'Hey, Len,' he said. 'Let's just toss a coin or something, huh?'

'No way. I want this done *legal*. I mean, if you haven't got law and order, what've you got?'

Calvin stared at the spears. They were both big and horrible and he wanted no part of either of them. The only difference between them was –

– The one on the left had a set of car keys dangling from its shaft, about an inch below the blade socket. The one on the right had a bat hanging from it. It lifted its head a little, and winked at him. He pointed to the one on the left, and said, 'That one, please.'

'Sucker,' said the bat.

CHAPTER NINE

'Hooliganism,' said Wesley, thoughtfully. 'I don't suppose you'd care to amplify, would you? Only it's not a very precise description.'

The girl sighed. 'You want it all handed to you on a plate, don't you?'

'Talking of things on plates . . .'

'Whereas,' the girl continued, binding up her hair in a pretty red silk scarf, 'really, you should be working it all out for yourself. If you want to pass Phase Three and get out of here, I mean. Think about it. *Proper* heroes don't have it handed to them on plates. You don't catch Indiana Jones swinging into action with his bullwhip in one hand and an envelope with detailed instructions jotted down on the back in the other. He's got to make it up as he goes along. And so must you.'

'Nuts,' Wesley replied. 'Indiana Jones's got the full support of the studio behind him. Hundreds of script-writers. Thousands of technicians. Mr Spielberg, with a microphone and an eyeshade. And what have I got? You.'

'If you'd rather I left you to it . . .'

'You think I think that's a really terrifying threat, don't you?'

'Yes.'

Wesley shrugged. 'I could seriously fancy a hamburger,' he said.

'What?'

'A hamburger,' Wesley replied. 'With large fries and a thick shake, vanilla, if you've got any.' He sat down on an ivy-covered tree stump and took his left shoe off.

'Tough,' the girl replied impatiently. 'And we haven't got time for you to adjust your footwear, either. I'm not waiting for you.'

' 'Bye, then.'

The girl turned, strode on four paces, turned back and scowled at him. 'I'm serious,' she said. 'Lag behind and I'll leave you for the wolves.'

'I expect I'll cope.'

'You reckon?'

Wesley shrugged. 'Why not? There won't be any wolves. At least, not unless there's supposed to be wolves. All these Phases and so forth, it stands to reason. You've got your program to run, or whatever you call it, you can't afford to have me randomly eaten by wolves. Bet my life on it.'

'Don't joke about it,' the girl hissed menacingly. But Wesley didn't look up. Instead, he fished a small lump of rock out of his sock and discarded it.

'You need me,' he went on. 'Probably rather more than I need you. I know a bit about large organisations, working for a building society. Things have to be accounted for. Targets have to be met. My guess is, unless you deliver me to a certain place at a certain time, all neatly processed and enlightened or whatever, that's your quarterly quota figures up the spout and you'll have some explaining to do to whoever it is you're answerable to. Am I warm?'

'Drivel,' replied the girl.

(But, in another part of the forest, she could see herself trying to explain a shortfall to the Inspector, who was peering at her over the rims of his spectacles and pursing his lips. *Lost a customer? Mislaid him, you mean? This is very serious. I'm afraid I'm going to have to mention this in my report, and . . .*)

'Fair enough,' Wesley said. 'So I called your bluff and I was wrong. Well, on my own head be it. I'm still not moving from this spot till I get something to eat.'

'But . . .'

'All I've had since breakfast,' he went on, 'is two peppermints and a gnat I swallowed by mistake just before I fell in the lake. I'm hungry. And don't tell me I can't be hungry because this isn't real time, because I know when I'm hungry, and I'm hungry. OK?'

'You're making a big mistake.'

'Am I? Oh well.'

'You'll be sorry for this.'

'Not half as sorry as you'll be when they hand you your cards and tell you to clear your desk by lunchtime. I imagine career opportunities for sacked fairies are few and far between. Perching on top of a Christmas tree, perhaps, but that's purely seasonal work.'

'I am not,' the girl growled, 'a fairy.'

Wesley nodded. 'Whatever,' he said. 'Hamburger. Fries. Shake. I shall count up to ten, and then I'm going back the way I came.'

'You'll get lost in the forest and the coyotes will eat you.'

'One. Two. Three. Four.'

'This is *fatuous*. Here I am making your most deep-seated fantasies come true, fulfilling your secret desires, turning you from a snivelling feckless little runt into a fully rounded, self-confident, quasi-heroic man of action, master of your fate and captain of your soul, and you've got the nerve to go on strike.'

'Five. Six. Seven. Looks like you succeeded with the self-confidence bit, doesn't it? Eight. Nine.'

'Did you say large fries?'

'Mphm.'

'Corn relish and dill pickle on the burger?'

'Sounds all right to me.'

'Have a nice day,' snarled the girl, as a paper bag fell in Wesley's lap. 'Enjoy your meal.'

'You see,' said Wesley with his mouth full, some time later. 'That wasn't too difficult, was it?'

'Huh.' The girl glowered at him and stole a chip. 'The sooner you start taking this thing seriously . . .'

Wesley sucked up the last inch of his milk shake; the solid lump of gritty ice cream that always makes your teeth ache. 'That's better,' he said. 'Now then, what's next?'

'I told you, you've got to try and figure—'

'One. Two. Three. Four.'

'Aaagh!' The girl screamed furiously, grabbed the paper bag and screwed it up into a ball. 'All right,' she said, 'it's like this. You'd better listen good, because if you miss anything . . .'

'I'm listening. Try and stay calm.'

'Over there,' the girl said, pointing, 'is a Cherokee village, some time in the last third of the nineteenth century. Your job is to rescue the prisoner . . .'

'Oh come on,' Wesley groaned. 'Not again.'

'. . . before he's burned at the stake by Chief Talks To

Squirrels' war party. They outnumber you thirty-five to one, but you do have your trusty Spencer rifle, capacity seven shots, maximum effective range two hundred yards, and your equally trusty forty-five six-shooter, and this stick of dynamite. All you have to do is crawl up to the fire, evading or silently killing the guards, throw the dynamite into the fire, untie the prisoner under cover of the explosion and ensuing confusion, steal a couple of horses and ride away. Now, do you think you can manage that?'

'No.'

'Rifle,' said the girl grimly. 'Revolver. Dynamite. Penknife for cutting ropes with. Lump of sugar for the horse. Once you've escaped, ride up the other side of the valley and follow the big Dayglo orange signs saying *This Way*. Don't fall off the horse and don't rescue any Indians by mistake. You get bonus points for élan and flair, and an automatic fail if you get killed. *Ciao*.'

She vanished.

For nearly three minutes Wesley sat where he was, not moving and counting up to ten, over and over again. Then, slowly and with infinite misgivings, he picked up the rifle, making sure the end with the hole in it was pointing away from him, and tried to figure out how it worked.

There was a very loud noise.

'That leaves you six shots,' said a disembodied voice. 'You reload by cocking the hammer and pulling down the lever under the trigger. Shoot up any more of my trees and you'll be getting a bill. Oh, and by the way, the prisoner's a lawyer, but try and bring him back alive nonetheless.'

Wesley nodded. He'd just remembered something. 'Excuse me,' he said. 'What did you say that Indian was called?'

'Talks To Squirrels,' the girl replied. 'Why?'

Wesley grinned. 'Oh, nothing,' he said. 'Well, be seeing you.'

'You sound cheerful. I don't like that. Why are you sounding cheerful?'

'No reason. Cheerio, then.'

He stood up and began to saunter over towards the brow of the hill.

'Ah *shit*,' Leonard groaned.

Calvin Dieb let go of the spear, and Leonard fell over with a crash. Everything had gone quiet, all of a sudden.

'Sorry,' Calvin said.

'Shit,' Leonard repeated. He tried to pull the spear out of his side, but it had gone in too far. He coughed up a little blood, and fell back. 'This is *crazy*,' he said bitterly. 'Ever since I left the firm, I been practising spear-fighting. Twelve, sometimes eighteen hours a day. I'm so good, there's nobody in the whole world as good as me.'

'Sucks, doesn't it?' said Calvin, sympathetically.

'You're goddamn right it does,' Leonard agreed. 'And what happens? First pass, you trip over a tree-root, fall over and your spear goes right through me. It ain't fair, and that's the truth.'

He shook his head, pulled a wry face, and died. With a sigh, Calvin turned away; at which point he became aware of thirty-odd authentic warriors, all looking at him.

They thought it sucked, too.

'Hey,' Calvin objected, as they grabbed him and dragged him back to the wooden stake, 'I won, didn't I? It was a trial, and I won. OK, by rights he *should* have won, but he didn't, and I did. So what's the . . . ?'

'We going to appeal,' grunted the Chief. 'We

implement ancient Cherokee appeal procedure. Four Calling Birds, where kerosene?'

'Hey!' Calvin said again. 'But that's not fair!'

'All fair,' replied the Chief smugly, 'in love and litigation. You lawyer, you figure it out for yourself. Five Gold Rings, you fetch matches.'

Calvin thought quickly, as the kerosene glugged over his head. 'Can't I counter-appeal?' he said. 'There must be some way . . .'

'Easy.' The Chief nodded, and the feathers of his headdress bobbed in the orange light. 'You go before judge sitting in chambers, obtain writ of habeas corpus and injunction, we let you go. Simple as that.'

'OK,' Calvin said eagerly. 'Just untie me and I'll do just that.'

'We no untie.' The Chief grinned. 'Figure we got you on a technicality,' he said.

Before Calvin could object further, someone shoved a kerosene-soaked rag in his mouth and blindfolded him. He heard a match rasp on a matchbox.

'Excuse me.'

The Chief turned round.

'Remember me?' said Wesley. 'We met earlier. You know, when we were chasing after that eagle?'

Talks To Squirrels' face melted into a grin. 'Hello there,' he said. 'How did you get on? Last time I saw you, you were falling to your death.'

Wesley shrugged. 'Annoying, wasn't it? Anyway, I'm here now. Thought as I was passing I'd just call in, say thanks for all your help.'

'Don't mention it,' Talks replied. 'My pleasure. Anything to pass the time. Hey, take a seat, make yourself at home. I've just got a bit of legal business to see to, and—'

'Actually,' Wesley interrupted, 'something you said set

me thinking. And I might be able to help.'

'Really?'

Wesley nodded. 'It was what you were saying about how you're forever shooting people with your bow and arrow and they never take a blind bit of notice. I was really, you know, moved. I felt for you.'

Talks shrugged. 'You get used to it,' he said. 'After a century or so, you learn to take it in your stride.'

'Sure. But I was thinking, maybe if you stopped using a bow and tried something else instead. Say, a Spencer rifle, for instance.'

'Maybe.' Talks To Squirrels shrugged. 'Worth a try, I suppose. But I haven't got—'

'I have. Look. Also this very fine forty-five six-shooter. Or, if all else fails, what about a stick of dynamite? Just light the fuse, stand well back, fizz, *boom*! It's got to be better than bows and arrows, surely.'

'You bet,' Talks replied. 'If only we'd had this kind of gear back in 1703, maybe I'd never have gotten into this mess in the first place.'

'Quite possibly,' Wesley replied. 'Anyway, I knew you'd be interested, so I thought I'd give you first refusal.'

'That's mighty kind of you.'

'You're welcome. Go on, then, make me an offer.'

The Indian's brow furrowed. 'I don't know,' he said. 'Trouble is, we don't use cash here. We got beaver skins. You want any beaver skins?'

Wesley shook his head. 'Fur trade's gone to hell since your time, I'm afraid,' he said. 'What about gold? You got any of that?'

'You mean the soft yellow metal that comes out of rivers?'

'That's the stuff.'

'No. Used to have a whole load of it, but we slung it

out. Pity. What about authentic Amerindian artefacts? We got heaps of them.'

Wesley considered, frowning. 'Tempting,' he said, 'but I think I'll pass on that one, thanks. I mean, if it was up to me I'd say yes, like a shot, but my accountant . . .'

Talks groaned sympathetically. 'Say no more,' he replied. 'Sometimes I ask myself, whose side are those guys on? Trouble is, I dunno what else we got that you might want.'

'Tricky, isn't it?' Wesley rubbed his chin for a moment; and then, apparently, inspiration struck. 'I know,' he said. 'How about a lawyer? You got any of those?'

Talks To Squirrels grinned. 'Mister,' he said, 'this is your lucky day, because it just so happens that we do.'

'Great! Can I see him?'

'There.'

'Where?'

'There. Tied to the stake.'

'Oh, *him*. You sure that's a lawyer? Doesn't look much like a lawyer to me.'

'Just a second.' Talks To Squirrels turned, drew a knife and prodded Calvin in the ribs with it. 'You. Talk some legal stuff, quick.'

'Sure thing. Whereas by a conveyance dated the fifth February one thousand nine hundred and seventy-two and made between the Ideal Tool Corporation of Oskaloosa Iowa a corporation established under the laws of the state of Iowa and having its office at Oskaloosa in the said state of the first part and Henry Carter Zizbaum also of Oskaloosa aforesaid of the second part all that real estate comprising some forty-two acres known as . . .'

'That'll do. Shuttup. Well, what d'you think?'

'Sounds like a lawyer to me,' Wesley admitted. 'Ask him his charges.'

'You.' Prod. 'Tell the man.'

'You bet. Two thousand dollars an hour plus disbursements plus local and national taxes, plus twenty per cent care and control plus an additional seven hundred fifty dollars an hour for matters of unusual complexity by prior agreement with the client.'

'Yup, he's a lawyer all right.' Wesley extended a hand. 'Deal?'

'Deal. Excuse me asking, but what the hell do you want him *for*? I mean, not trying to be funny or anything, but his best friends wouldn't call him ornamental, and as for useful . . .'

Wesley contorted his face into his best approximation at a knowing smile. 'Well,' he said, 'you'd be amazed.'

'Yes. Quite frankly, I would. He's a *lawyer*, for God's sake. I suppose you could cut him up small and feed him to your pet rat, but rats can be fussy devils . . .'

'You want the rifle? Or not?'

Talks To Squirrels shrugged. 'Your business, I suppose. Here you go, and don't blame me. No refunds, no part exchanges, and absolutely no liability accepted for loss, damage or insolvency, whether directly or indirectly caused. Goddamnit, he's got me talking like one now. Get him out of my sight, before I go all frothy at the mouth.'

He gave Dieb a powerful shove. Quickly, Wesley collected him by the arm and started to walk away. They were almost at the edge of the firelight circle when Dieb stopped dead, like a mule.

'Just a moment,' he said. 'My car keys.'

'*What?*'

'My car keys,' Dieb repeated. 'They're still back there, tied to one of those spears. I'm not leaving without them.'

'Something up?' Talks To Squirrels called out behind

them. 'If he's stopped moving, I'm told a kick up the ass works wonders.'

'Sounds good to me,' Wesley called back. 'Look, you,' he whispered to the lawyer, who was still doing Gibraltar impressions, 'keeping moving or I'll leave you here. Understood?'

'I want my keys,' Dieb replied. 'Without them, I'm stuck here for ever. I *need* them, OK?'

'They were going to burn you alive, for God's sake,' Wesley hissed. As he spoke, he heard a noise in the background; not a grating noise exactly, because well-oiled metal components sliding smoothly together don't grate, unless you've been careless and got sand in the works. More a sort of metallic whisper. 'I know these people, they're utter loons. So get moving, or . . .'

'Not without my keys. I'd rather die now. Sorry.'

So Wesley just stood there, like a rabbit in oncoming headlights, thinking *Oh God!* Behind him, he could hear Talks To Squirrels saying, 'I pulled the little lever thing, why doesn't it go bang?' and one of his cohorts suggesting that it would help if he cocked the hammer first. In the split second between Talks To Squirrels saying, 'God, yes, I forgot,' and the very loud bang, he made a mental calculation of the distance separating them from the trees and the time it would take to cross it, even at a mad sprint, and came to the conclusion that it was too late to worry now. He spent the rest of the nanosecond relaxing his muscles and wondering what getting shot really feels like.

'Bugger,' said Talks To Squirrels, thirty yards behind. 'Why's he still standing up? I was sure I'd got him.'

'Can't have done. Here, try again.'

The second bang followed; and still Wesley couldn't feel anything. The lawyer, too, was still resolutely on his feet, though he'd started to go green in the face.

'This sonofabitch thing ain't working. Here, Two Turtledoves, can you see what I'm doing wrong?'

'Sorry, Chief. At this range, they should both be stone dead by now.'

Wesley nudged the lawyer in the ribs. 'Ready to try running away yet?'

'I'm coming round to the idea, certainly.'

'Fuck it,' the Indian was saying, 'it's because I'm a ghost, isn't it? It's just the same with guns as it is with bows and arrows. All right, pass me the dynamite, some-one. We'll soon see about that.'

'My keys,' Dieb whimpered.

BOOM! The ground shook, and the soundwave hit them before the explosion came anywhere near. As it was; well, you know that gust of hot air you get when you open the door of a fan-assisted oven after it's been going for an hour or so? Well, it was like that. Only rather more so.

'Gosh.' Wesley, still face down on the ground, could hear the lawyer's voice somewhere over his head.

'Hey, he was right.'

'Was he?' Wesley asked, without moving.

'You bet,' Dieb replied. 'About the dynamite working even though the gun didn't. They've blown themselves up.'

'You don't say.'

'See for yourself. Little bits of them hanging off the trees, like slices of pastrami. Wonder why we weren't incinerated too?'

'Because,' Wesley was about to suggest; but then it started raining morsels of barbecued Indian, and he didn't feel like saying anything for a while. 'Can we go now?'

'I'd still like to have a look for my keys.'

'Be my guest. I think I'll just stay here for a while.'

A few long, rather horrible minutes passed; and then Dieb came back. 'No sign of any keys,' he said sadly. 'The only chance is that they were thrown clear by the blast. In which case, they could be anywhere.'

'How terribly sad,' Wesley muttered. 'Were there any survivors?'

'Huh? Oh, you mean the Indians? No, we're OK on that score. You might just find enough bits to make up a whole one, but only if you weren't too bothered about the colours matching.'

'I see.' Wesley got up slowly, being very careful where he put his hands and knees. 'I rather liked him,' he said.

'Who?'

'That Chief bloke. He helped me out earlier on, when I had to stalk an eagle.'

Dieb blinked. 'This eagle,' he said. 'Did you happen to crack it over the head with a big lump of rock?'

'I believe so. Why?'

'That was me.'

'Oh.'

'You nearly smashed my skull in,' said Dieb. 'And I was just about to get my keys back, too. A second later, and I'd have had them.'

'Is that so?'

Dieb nodded. 'That girl was handing them to me, and then you came out of nowhere and nearly brained me.'

'Well I never. Small world, isn't it?'

They stood looking at each other for a moment, neither of them liking terribly much what he saw. 'Calvin Dieb,' said the lawyer at last, extending a blackened, blood-streaked hand. 'Pleased to meet you.'

'Wesley Higgins. Are you having all kinds of weird experiences, too?'

Dieb nodded. 'I fell in the lake,' he said. 'I guess that seems to be what causes it.'

'It is.' They started to walk away. 'It's because the lake's enchanted.'

'You don't say.'

'By an Indian deity called Okeewana,' Wesley said. 'If you fall in the lake, she makes your dreams come true, or that's what she told me, anyway. Would you believe it, I came all the way from Brierley Hill just to meet her. Took all my money out of the Post Office, used up a whole year's holiday, just to be blown up by a ghost.'

'I just lost my keys. My car's parked up beside the road, see, and if only I could find them . . .'

Wesley stopped in his tracks. 'The girl,' he said. 'You saw her too?'

'The chubby broad? Yeah, I saw her. Like I said, she'd found my keys, and if you hadn't bashed me over the head . . .'

'She's not chubby.'

'The girl I was talking to was. She looked like the Before picture in a slimming advert.'

'You thought so, did you?'

'Nice enough kid,' the lawyer went on, apparently not noticing the thin film of ice forming over the other man's voice, 'but definitely well insulated. The kind that gets real value for money out of a train ticket.'

Wesley made an effort and put aside his annoyance. After all, he reasoned, jerk or no jerk, this extremely unpleasant person was a fellow victim. Working together, pooling their resources, maybe they'd both stand a better chance of—

'You're no beanpole yourself, Mr Dieb,' he heard

himself reply. 'In fact, if there's anybody round here with an excessive weight problem, it's you. So where do you get off, making cheap cracks about people being fat?'

'Hey!' Calvin Dieb restrained himself. True, he didn't like people making remarks about the large proportion of him that just hung about round his middle waiting for a hard winter; least of all toffee-nosed Brits who went around beating up on harmless birds with lumps of masonry. On the other hand, here was another guy in the same jam as he was. Maybe if they stuck together, worked as a team ... 'Who are you calling fat, you goddamn Limey punk? First you club me half to death, then you get me shot at by a bunch of crazy Indians—'

'*Me* got *you* shot at? Who was it who wouldn't run away because of his stupid keys?'

'I wouldn't have needed to run away if you hadn't attacked me, just when I was about to ...'

In the darkness ahead of them, two horses stood, tethered and patiently waiting. The two men ignored them.

'May I remind you,' Wesley was saying, 'that you'd just abducted an innocent girl ...'

'I did not. That was that goddamn eagle.'

Wesley sneered. 'I see. A different eagle, was it? Another huge mutant bird that just happened to be passing? Oh yes, I'm convinced, I really am.'

'You calling me a liar?'

'I am now, yes.'

'Why, you—'

And then, just when Dieb's fist should have connected with Wesley's jaw and Wesley's fist should have landed squarely in Dieb's eye, they both vanished.

The moment Linda heard the explosion, she turned and ran.

The scene of the blast wasn't hard to find. There are certain tell-tale signs you look for when you're an experienced newshound, such as huge gaping craters, scraps of smouldering cloth, rashers of roasted flesh; that's the sort of clue your dedicated investigative journalist can read like a book. As soon as Linda scrambled over the rise, her heart stopped still.

One hell of a blast, it must have been; chance of finding anybody even remotely photogenic still alive correspondingly remote. Still, she had to look.

After a lot of grubbing about under fallen trees and scrabbling round in the dirt, she found one survivor, trapped under a large stone dislodged by the explosion. With a display of strength that surprised her, Linda managed to heave the rock out of the way.

'Hello,' she said. 'I'm a journalist. What happened?'

'Explosion,' the survivor croaked. 'All – killed – except – me.' His face contorted with pain, and he started to cough up blood.

'Yes, I can see there was an explosion,' Linda replied impatiently. 'I'm not blind, for God's sake. What was it that blew? One of the Rapier missiles? A reactor core off one of the subs?'

'Dynamite,' the Indian gasped. 'Chief threw dynamite into fire. Big explosion . . .'

'The chief engineer threw dynamite into the fire?' Linda's brow creased. 'Why the hell did he do that? Wait a bit – was it some kind of internal power struggle between the Cardinals? Tribal infighting between the Queenslanders and the New South Welsh? Or . . . ?'

'He wanted to see,' groaned the survivor, 'if it would work.'

'I got you,' Linda said, her eyes shining. 'Unauthorised testing of a revolutionary new secret weapon. We could get a worldwide embargo on all US goods if we play our cards right. But then—'

'No – secret. We – all – knew . . .'

'And so they had to silence you!' Linda gasped, and sparks crackled up and down her spine like arc-welding ants. 'A cover-up! They had you terminated so you wouldn't blow the gaff on the illicit arms shipments!'

The Indian moaned softly, and tried to prop himself up on one elbow. 'No,' he whispered, 'not that way at all. You got – wrong end of stick. Just accident, that's all.'

Linda gazed down at him sternly. 'That's what they told you to say, obviously,' she replied, her voice heavy with contempt. 'Don't try and kid me, buster, I'm a reporter. Now, where were the shipments for? Did the President know? Where did the submarines come into it? And exactly what was the Mafia's role in the overall plan?'

'You – crazy,' murmured the Indian, falling back. 'Nothing like that – at all. Only . . .'

Frowning scornfully, Linda straightened up. 'Ah, the hell with you,' she said. 'I'll get to the bottom of this somehow, and if you think for one moment you can palm me off with a load of—'

'Aaagh.'

She looked closely. The Indian appeared to have died; a variant on the old *No comment at this time* routine that even Linda Lachuk found hard to crack. Never mind, she told herself, as she walked on past the crater and the mangled bodies. If they think they can throw me off the scent this easily, they've got a shock coming.

Oh yes.

'Complete dead loss,' sighed Captain Hat, as he slumped into the rabbit-hole where the rest of his company had been waiting for him. 'Waste of bloody time. Absolutely nothing here worth pinching at all.' He snarled and reached for the bottle, which proved to be empty.

'Oh,' said Mr Snedge. 'That's a pity, seeing as how we're stuck here.'

Although he was tempted to refute his first officer's downbeat analysis, on principle, as being bad for morale, Hat decided against it. They'd be bound to ask him why he thought they weren't stuck here; and listening to their commanding officer admitting that he hadn't a clue where they were or how to get home again was likely to be even worse for morale than Snedge's defeatist whimperings. So he ignored them.

'I blame this crop of punters,' he went on. 'Deadbeats, the lot of them. I mean to say, here they are acting out their wildest dreams, and not one decent bit of kit have they come up with, between the four of them. No caskets of uncut diamonds, no chests bursting at the hinges with Spanish gold, nothing. All I got was a set of car keys, and I dropped them.'

Nobody commented; an indication that, contrary to all evidence, they weren't quite as thick as they looked. After he'd sulked for five minutes or so, Hat stood up and began to pace the rabbit-hole, stroking his beard thoughtfully and avoiding the piles of rabbit ordure that would have swallowed up a less observant man of his stature without trace. Something was nagging at the back of his mind.

'I can't help feeling,' he said at last, 'that I'm somewhere else.'

His men looked at each other. Over the past few thousand years they'd developed a non-verbal shorthand, suitable for eye-contact communication. This particular look meant, *Oh God, he's off again.* Accordingly, they stayed quiet.

'And it's because of where I am that we're here,' Hat went on. 'Does that make any sense to anybody?'

'No, Chief.'

Hat shrugged. 'That makes two of us, Snedge, because I'm buggered if I know what's going on. Mind you, that's about par for the course in these parts.' He stopped pacing and peered out through the hole at the daylight beyond. 'On balance, though, I rather think that the me who's somewhere else is hiding from someone and is rather keen not to be found. And that,' he added, closing his eyes, 'is probably why we're lost.'

''Scuse me, Chief?'

'On the principle,' Hat continued, with the air of someone trying very hard not to listen to what he's saying, 'that if we can't find ourselves, then neither can anyone else. Does that sound to you like the sort of thing we'd do? Anybody?'

Mr Twist rubbed his chin; fortunately, the skin of his hands was of the texture of boot leather, otherwise he'd have rasped himself down to the bone. 'Well,' he ventured, 'I heard dafter things in my time, Chief. Anything's possible.'

'True.' Hat nodded in acknowledgement of a valid point. 'We might all get taken rich. You might even shave. Talking of which, Mr Twist, there's something that's been worrying me for five hundred years. How can it possibly be that in all the time I've known you, you've managed to keep the stubble on your chin just precisely the same length? How come I've never seen you clean-shaven, or with a beard?'

'Dunno, Chief,' Twist replied unhappily, for it was something that had often puzzled him as well. 'Though they do say,' he went on, 'as fingernails and hair carry on growing even when you're dead.'

'But you're not dead, Twist. And your hair never grows.'

'Maybe it don't grow *because* I'm not dead, Chief.'

Hat winced. Too much of that sort of logic can rot a man's brain. 'Anyway,' Hat said, as soon as he'd managed to jemmy his brain back into gear, 'we're still stuck here, with nothing to steal and not much hope of getting out of here unless . . .'

'Unless what, Chief?'

'Well, not really unless anything,' Hat conceded despondently. 'If I'm right, the only people who can let us out is us, and we don't seem to know how to go about it.'

Mr Snedge considered this for a moment. 'D'you think we're giving it our best shot, Chief? I mean, we would give it our best shot, wouldn't we?'

'Shut up, Snedge.'

'Yes, Chief.'

Hat stood up again, and resumed his pacing. Being the only sentient life-form among so many pillocks had its positive side as well; in the country of the thick, the half-witted man is king. On the other hand, it made for a certain degree of isolation, not to mention stress. It'd be nice if, just once, they got themselves into some horrible jam and someone else figured out how to get them out again.

''Scuse me, Chief.'

Hat looked round and recognised Mr Flurt, the company's master-at-arms, who also doubled as their quarter-master and, when necessary, a battering-ram. Compared with the prospects of getting a sensible remark out of Mr Flurt, blood spouts out of stones like something out of Sam Peckinpah's nightmares.

'Hm?' Hat said, allowing his mind to idle again.

'Well,' said Flurt, 'if it's us hiding, then if we knew who

we was hiding from, we could go hide somewhere else where they still wouldn't find us.'

Just as Hat's subconscious was pressing the *Delete File* key to get all that gibberish out of his short-term memory, a gleam of sense caught his mind's eye. 'Say that again,' he ordered.

'If it's us hiding,' said Flurt, reciting carefully, 'then if we knew who we was hiding from—'

Hat pounded his fist into his cupped palm excitedly. 'Then,' he shouted, 'we could go and hide somewhere else where they still wouldn't find us! Of course. That's brilliant.'

'What's brilliant, Chief?'

'What you just said, Flurt. Honestly, there are times . . .'

'No, Chief,' said Flurt patiently. 'What's it mean?'

Hat allowed his excitement to subside a little. Other things come out of the mouths of babes and sucklings beside wisdom, as anybody who has to clean up afterwards can testify. 'I'll explain later,' he muttered. 'Right now, I've got to think.'

Indians!

Janice froze. For all that it was the last decade of the twentieth century, and people don't think that way any more, she still had a residual level of sludge at the bottom of her mind in which lurked, secretly nourished by the cowboy movies of her youth, an irrational fear of being overtaken in the middle of nowhere by a Native American war-party on the rampage. What she was afraid of, she didn't know; that's often the way with irrational fears. Maybe they'd say unkind things about her, or accidentally drop tomahawks on her foot.

She looked again. Yes, there were Indians, right enough; but these particular Indians were unlikely to pose a threat to anyone, in the short term at least. If nothing was done about them for several days, it'd be a different matter.

'Hello?' she said.

No reply; under the circumstances all to the good, because the last thing you want if you're of a sensitive disposition is dead people answering you when you say, 'Hello.' It's bad enough when they knock once for yes, two times for no and start playing silly buggers with the table.

'Um,' she went on nonetheless, 'are you guys all right? Can I help anyone?'

But they continued to be dead, and took no notice. Or at least, the ones near to where Janice was standing continued to be dead. Further off, where the briars and undergrowth obscured her view, there was something moving about.

Janice ducked behind a moss-covered rock.

'Bloody hell,' said a voice. 'Just look at this lot, will you?'

'They just don't think,' someone else replied.

Shivering, Janice peered over the top of the rock, and saw two men. They were wearing brown overalls and baseball caps with some sort of logo or crest on them, and they carried big red plastic toolboxes. One of them knelt down and picked up a stray arm.

'Just look, will you?' he said. 'Brand new 36D. Remember the trouble we had getting hold of these?'

The other man nodded as he unfastened his toolbox. 'They're buggers, they are. Bloody old UNF threads, you need a special grommet or they just flop about. Well, he'll have to make do with a 41 metric, 'cos that's the nearest I got. Don't suppose he'll live long enough to notice, the way they're carrying on.'

'That's if we've got a 41 metric,' said his colleague. 'I got a feeling we bunged the last one on one of them Vikings. I ask you, how can you lose a bloody arm when you're drowning?'

'They do it on purpose, if you ask me.' The man was doing something Janice didn't want to think about with a mangled torso and a ratchet screwdriver. 'Just to be awkward. Fifteen holes I counted in one of them goblins. Well, that's this month's body putty gone, and the others'll just have to lump it.'

Whatever it was they were doing, they were certainly quick about it. They worked with the certain, economical movements of men who know what they're doing and have been doing it for a very long time. Janice could hear clicks and clunks and the occasional whirr of a cordless drill.

'I only fixed this bugger dinner time,' growled one of the men. 'Came in with his head on the wrong way round. Only been trying to mend it himself, the daft sod. Here, you got a 97B in heads, twelve mil. by thirty-six?'

'Only in pink.'

The man shrugged. 'Sling it over,' he said. 'Don't suppose anybody'll notice under all that warpaint they wear.' Something round and soccer-ball-sized looped through the air and was caught. The drill whirred. A socket wrench clacked. The man swore.

'Taken all the skin off me knuckles,' he explained. 'Got any?'

'Here.'

'Ta. When's this lot got to be done by, anyway? There's a couple here ought to go back to the works.'

The other one shrugged. 'They didn't say,' he replied. 'They ought to keep a few back as spares, then we wouldn't have all these rush jobs. I've had it up to here with getting the blame when arms fall off, and it's only 'cos I haven't had time to do a proper job.'

'Yeah. They just don't think.'

My God, Janice muttered to herself, they're repairing all those dead guys, this is *amazing*. Or maybe they aren't guys, maybe they're just robots. That'd still be pretty amazing.

'Hey!'

This time, the voice was coming from a few yards away. Janice ducked down again and held her breath.

'Hold yer water, son,' replied one of the men wearily. 'We'll get to you soon as we can. Only got one pair of hands, you know.'

'Here, that's a good one, Phil. Only one pair of hands.'

'What? Oh, yes, right. Go and see what he wants, will you, Dave? I've got this one's liver all in pieces, and you know how those little return springs jump out soon as look at them.'

The man called Dave gathered up his tools and trudged over to where the voice had come from. 'Call out, will you?' he said. 'Can't see bugger all in this long grass.'

'Over here,' the voice replied. 'Look, sorry to hassle you, but I'm due on in a minute and all that's left of me is a couple of toes.'

Dave located the source of the voice and stood for a moment or so, clicking his tongue and making well-I-dunno noises. 'Tell you what,' he said after a while, 'the best I can do for you is bung you in one of them other bodies, just for now. Then, when you've done your bit, I'll have you in down the depot and sort you out properly.'

'Ah shit,' replied the toes, disgustedly. 'Can't you just patch me up with a bit of insulating tape or something? It's only a non-speaking part.'

'I'll pretend I didn't hear that,' Dave replied frostily.

'You know what my boss'd say if he saw one of you buggers walking about all bodged up with sticky tape. Either you can go in someone else, or you'll have to wait till we get back to the works. It's up to you.'

'Bloody prima donnas,' muttered the toes. 'All right, then. But find me a good one, will you? And not that one, he's got rheumatism.'

Dave worked in silence for a while, clicking and clunking his way through a growing pile of small, bloody, oily bits. 'What the hell happened to you lot anyway?' he asked eventually. 'Looks like you got blown up.'

'We did.'

'How'd that happen, then?'

'If you must know, I threw a stick of dynamite on the fire.'

'You did?'

'Yes. It was in the scenario. I don't enjoy getting blasted into catfood, you know.'

'You lot, you just don't know how to look after decent kit. I mean, just look at this leg.'

'All right, you've made your—'

'With a bit of luck I might be able to salvage the universal joint, and that's it. Hold still, will you? Don't want to waste another heart valve, thank you very much. Now then . . .'

'Hey!'

'Shuttup,' hissed Dave. 'And keep still. There's something behind that rock.'

'So?'

'Stay there. Don't move.'

'Haven't really got any choice in the matter, have I?'

Janice contemplated flight, but not for very long; because before she could sweet-talk her limbs into unfreezing, Dave was standing over her, looking very apprehensive and gripping a big spanner tightly in both hands.

'Oh balls,' he said.

'Excuse me?'

Dave scowled at her as if she were a crossed thread. 'You're one of them, aren't you?' he growled. 'A customer.'

Janice nodded.

'You're not supposed to see any of this.'

'No?'

'No.' Dave was looking at her differently now; that slightly bewildered, slightly boiled, slightly stuffed expression she was coming to know so well. 'No,' he repeated, letting the spanner drop. 'Well, er, no. Actually.'

Janice hauled herself back onto her feet, with rather more enthusiasm than dignity. 'I'm terribly sorry,' she mumbled. 'I'd better be going, then.'

'No, don't go,' Dave said, looking even more boiled and stuffed. 'I mean, no harm done, and we, er, don't want to seem unfriendly or anything.'

'But I'm keeping you from your work,' Janice protested feebly. 'I'm sure you've got ever such a lot to get on with, and . . .'

Dave made a dismissive, hang-spring-cleaning gesture. It was about as convincing as a four-dollar note, but he didn't seem to care. 'Let it wait,' he said. 'All rest and no play, eh? Why don't you, er, come and have a look at the, um trees and things. Flowers,' he added hopefully. 'Sure we can find a flower or two around here if we look hard enough.'

'Flowers?'

He nodded like a well-socked punchball. 'Heaps of 'em, probably, unless the blast shrivelled 'em all up. Let's go and take a look, shall we?'

He made a wild grab for her hand, but she whisked it away. *Oh Christ, not again. Why can't everybody just ignore me, like they usually do?* Unfortunately, she knew the answer to that. 'Look,' she said, trying to sound brisk and no-nonsenseish. 'I know what you're thinking, it's been happening a lot lately, and I'm afraid it simply isn't on. It's not real, you see, it's only this dumb wildest-dreams thing, so perhaps I'd better just leave before we both say things we'll regret . . .'

He wasn't listening, needless to say. The look in his eyes was so intense that Janice could almost smell the formaldehyde. It'd be so nice if he'd just go away.

'Excuse me saying this,' he burbled, 'but you've put me in mind of something, let's see, it's on the tip of my tongue, memory like a tea-bag, my wife says. Oh, that's it, a summer's day. You and a summer's day could be sisters, really.'

The word *wife* fizzed in Janice's mind like an aspirin in water. 'Talking of your wife,' she said, 'd'you think she'd take kindly to you comparing strange girls to summer days? I really think you should—'

'Don't care what *she* thinks, rancid old cow,' Dave replied savagely. 'I can think of all sorts of things to compare her to, but they've mostly got four legs and horns. The only day she puts me in mind of was back along last February, that time all the pipes in the roof froze solid and we had water dripping in the soup. Got a temper on her, too.'

'I . . .' Janice shrugged. Why risk getting involved, after all? Although, on balance, her sympathies were probably with Mrs Dave – it couldn't be pleasant washing his work clothes, given his trade, and the dirty marks he must leave on the towels didn't really bear thinking about – the fact that Dave's marriage appeared to have been made in

Hell wasn't her fault, and she'd have nothing to reproach herself for if this particular brief encounter gave the wretched thing its final shove. 'Whatever,' she said. 'In the meantime, unless you get back to work right now, I'll tell your supervisor. You got that, or shall I write it down?'

'Actually,' Dave said, 'I'm the supervisor. Well, there's only two of us in the department, what with the cuts and all, but nominally I'm the supervisor and Phil's the foreman. Daft, really, but you try telling them anything.' He smiled, and the effect was something like a Death's head in a Comic Relief nose. A small, rebellious part of Janice sympathised, for in her time she'd been the unwanted admirer more often than she cared to remember, and she clearly recalled that one of the symptoms was being as unwilling to take a hint, or even a direct command, as a market trader is to take a cheque. Love is deaf as well as blind, and can construe, 'Get stuffed, you prune-faced warthog's arse', as a thinly veiled come-on. Sympathy, however, is all very well.

'Piss off,' she said.

'Sorry?'

'Piss off,' Janice repeated, elocuting. 'Go away, with prejudice. Go play with a dead body. Understand?'

'Oh.'

'I mean it. Given a choice between you and one of your dismembered corpses, I'd choose the corpse every time.' She paused, and grinned unpleasantly. 'Go jump in the lake,' she added.

'Jump in the lake?'

Janice nodded. 'It's over there somewhere. Big wet thing, with upside-down trees all over it.'

'Done that.'

'Huh?'

Dave nodded. 'Done that, what, eighty years ago. Back

in the First World War. That's why I'm here.'

Janice didn't like the sound of that. 'And you're still here?' she asked. 'After all this time?'

'Yeah. Bummer, isn't it? You see, I used to be a doctor. Really keen on doctoring, I used to be. What I really wanted more than anything else was to be able to take people who'd got all smashed up, like the poor bleeders we used to fish out of the trenches and pick off the barbed wire, and put 'em back together again, good as new. So, when I fell in the lake . . .'

A dull, sick feeling slapped itself across Janice's mind. 'But that's crazy,' she said. 'That was a good thing to want, surely.'

'I used to think so, too,' Dave sighed. 'Never could see the harm in it.'

'But they're *punishing* you for it,' Janice said, horrified. 'You wanted to save people's lives, and they kept you here. That's *bad*.'

Dave shrugged. 'Got what I asked for, though, didn't I?' He chuckled bitterly. 'Can't complain on that score. The only difference is, in the trenches we used to get a couple of days off every month. Used to enjoy me days off, I did. Used to go into Armentières and play dominoes with the Canadians.'

Janice took a step or so backwards, ignoring whatever it was that felt soft and squidgy under her foot. Up till now, she'd felt confused and put-upon. Now she was starting to get angry.

'I've had about enough of this,' she said. 'I guess it's OK what they're doing to me, because I asked for it, in a way. But picking on a doctor because he wanted to make people better just isn't right.'

Dave frowned, puzzled. 'So what're you going to do about it?' he said.

'Complain,' Janice answered immediately. 'Demand to see the manager. Write my Congressman. I don't know. I'm going to do something, though, just you wait.'

'How about . . . ?'

'Oh, get lost, I'm busy. I want to talk to someone in authority.'

'But . . .'

Whatever Dave said next, he said it to empty air.

CHAPTER TEN

Wesley fell over.

There was a simple reason for this. At the moment he disappeared, he'd been aiming a punch at a fairly substantial lawyer. When he reappeared, the space the lawyer should have occupied turned out to contain nothing but oxygen, nitrogen and a few trace elements of no great importance. Since there was nothing to stop the momentum of his fist, he accordingly fell over and landed, face down, in what had once been a bison's dinner. Subsequently it had gone clean through the bison and come to rest, in a collapsed pyramid shape, on the ground.

'Ack!' Wesley observed, sitting up and wiping it out of his eyes.

'Serves you right for playing rough games,' said the bison reproachfully. 'Bet you didn't expect to see me again.'

'Where'd he go?'

'The lawyer?' The bison's jaws moved methodically.

'Sorry, but you don't need to know that. Classified.'

Wesley said something succinct under his breath that summed up what he felt about classified information. 'Look,' he went on, 'this game, or ordeal, or whatever it's supposed to be. When's it due to finish?'

'When it's over.'

'Fine. Thank you ever so much. And when will it be over?'

'When it's finished.'

Carefully, trying not to get the former bison food on more of him than he could help, Wesley got to his feet and looked round. There had been a time, he freely admitted, when he looked at the world through rose-tinted glasses. In retrospect, that had been better, surely.

'Do you realise,' he said wearily, 'that not so long ago, I used to feel sad at the thought that the American bison was hunted to the verge of extinction. Now I only wish they'd done a thorough job.'

'So?' The bison turned its head and looked at him through soft, brown, stupid eyes. 'There's no point blaming me,' he said. 'I didn't start this. You came all this way specially, remember, just to meet me. Hey. You're on holiday, lighten up. Isn't this still more fun than being in the office?'

Wesley thought about that for a moment. 'Well,' he said, 'yes. But then again, so would hanging by my feet over a vat of molten lead. That doesn't actually prove anything. More to the point, we don't seem to be *achieving* very much. OK, I've had exciting experiences I'd have missed out on if I'd stayed in Brierley Hill, but they've all been horrible; except for meeting, um, her, but now she's gone again and it doesn't look like I'll get to meet her again.' He sighed. Below where he stood, the lake lay like a newly ironed duvet, lovingly hand-embroidered with a curious motif of upside-down mountains. 'If we've got to do this, can't we at least make it useful?'

'You mean profitable?'

'Well – yes, in the wider sense, I suppose I do. Well, quite. What's in it for me?'

'I see. You'd rather it was like a game show or something?'

'No,' Wesley replied firmly, 'of course not. I only meant—'

But the bison had vanished, and the girl had come back; except that now she'd exchanged her fringed buckskin tunic for something skimpy and sequin-covered. She was also taller, blonde and totally different, though naturally still gorgeous.

'Better?' she said through a rose-rimmed hole in her smile. 'More in keeping with the way you perceive this experience?'

'Oh, don't be like that.'

'What's in it for me, you said,' the girl continued, the savagery of her tone of voice contrasting markedly with the toothpaste-ad smile it came out through. 'I now see that you're one of those people who wouldn't accept a first-class suite in the Kingdom of Heaven unless there was a radio alarm-clock thrown in free as well. All right then, buster, have it your way. This is your chance to win Fabulous Prizes. But don't come whining to me if you don't like this format after all.'

'No, look, really,' Wesley said, but the girl had stomped off in a huff and vanished, leaving only a Cheshire-Cat echo of her smile behind, like the green blobs you see with your eyes shut after you've stared into the sun. Since he had no idea what he was supposed to do now, Wesley sat down on a rock and waited.

But not for long. In fact, he just had time to think, *Oh for pity's sake*, before the sky went red on him.

'Here we are,' said the girl, with synthetic cheerfulness. 'Sorry to have kept you waiting.'

The inspector took the ledgers from her with a grunt. 'Now then,' he said, 'we can get started. I've had instructions to pay particular attention to operating systems, with a view to identifying any possible misapplication of resources, inefficient use of materials or funding, unnecessary duplications . . .'

He broke off, and looked ostentatiously around. He didn't say anything for quite some time.

'Sorry about this,' said the girl, avoiding his eye. 'It happens sometimes. Doesn't mean anything, of course. We're all used to it by now.'

The inspector didn't appear to have heard her. 'Perhaps,' he said, in a voice marginally more aggravating than the one he'd been using before, 'you'd care to explain why we appear to be standing in a theatre.'

The girl grinned. Sheepishly would be an underestimate. Sheep have more sense than to get themselves into messes of this magnitude. 'It's not a theatre,' she whispered, 'not as such. More like a TV studio.'

'Those people . . .'

'The audience.'

'Ah.' The inspector made a note in his notebook. 'I take it they're not full-time employees. I'd hate to think you were incurring regular expenditure . . .'

'Oh no.' The girl shook her head, perhaps a little more vigorously than necessary. 'Well, they are, full-time employees, I mean; but they're not just employed to sit. If you look closely, you'll see they're all Vikings and Indians in disguise.'

'Ah.' The inspector stole a quick look over the rims of his spectacles. 'Apparently they are. You keep a full-time staff of Indians and Vikings, then? Perhaps you'd care to explain . . .'

The girl cringed. 'Sorry to butt in,' she muttered, 'but would you mind awfully, er, saying something to them? A few jokes, just to warm up, get the sound levels right, that sort of thing? You see, you're actually the—'

'The what?'

'The host.'

'I *see*.' An expression of bewildered disgust migrated across the inspector's face. 'Could you perhaps explain the reason for that?'

'Oh, saving costs, of course,' the girl replied, crossing the fingers of both hands behind her back. 'We found that if we were prepared to be, you know, adaptable, turn our hands to different skills, we could save substantially on manning levels without in any way impairing the smooth running of the, um, whatever. Just a few jokes? Why did the chicken, that sort of thing? It's for a good cause.'

But the inspector only turned his head to the left, gave the red velvet backdrop a severe look, and jotted down something in his notebook. While he was doing this, a door in the wings opened and an unseen hand shoved Wesley into the middle of the stage.

'Excuse me,' whispered the girl.

'Hmm?'

'Sorry to interrupt, but the, um, first contestant . . .'

The inspector looked at her, and then at Wesley, and then back at her. 'I'm sorry,' he said, 'but this is going to have to go in my report.'

'OK, fine. Look, could you just, um, read what's on the card, please? Just this once. For me.'

During this exchange, Wesley had looked round, seen the faces of the audience like a great expanse of water lapping at his feet, tried to make a run for it, been retrieved by two of the larger Vikings in evening dress and frogmarched back to where he'd just run from. He now had the aspect of a caged crocodile in a handbag factory, and both arms held firmly up his back. He was being ordered to smile.

'Please,' begged the girl. 'Oh, go on.'

A refusal was just about to jump out of the inspector's mouth and pull the ripcord when a little voice in the back of his mind said, *Well, why not?* He didn't know how it came to be there, or why on earth he should be listening to it; on the other hand – why not indeed? He looked down at the card the girl had given him, cleared his throat and tried to do something he hadn't attempted since he was a mere stripling of four thousand and six. He tried to smile.

'Hello,' he read, 'and welcome to Death Or Glory, the game where you only get the prizes if you're really unlucky.' He stopped, frowned and turned back to the girl, who nodded reassuringly. He went on, 'Now a big hand please for our first contestant, Wesley Higgins.'

For some reason, the Indians and the Vikings and the bears and the goblins and the other parts played by members of the company found this statement tremendously exciting, because they started to cheer and whoop and whistle as if he'd just announced free beer all round. While all that was going on, the girl handed him another card.

'Thank you, thank you,' he recited. 'And Wesley's first task will be, pause for effect – not the bits in brackets? Got you, right – to take all his clothes off and play the violin. Contestant, you have three minutes starting *now*.'

'Hey!' Wesley shrieked, as the Vikings started to con-
fiscate his clothes. 'I thought you said I wasn't going to
have to . . .'

A third Viking shoved a violin into his hands. The
audience was making the sort of noises audiences everywhere make under these conditions. It's probably
fortunate that Charles Darwin never saw a game show
studio audience, or else he might have started to wonder
whether he hadn't got his celebrated theory of evolution
the wrong way round.

As Wesley stood, wearing nothing except what was left
of the bison by-product he'd fallen in, and doing his
inadequate best to hide his embarrassment from a hallful
of Vikings with one small violin, the inspector read out
another card.

'Having the courage to confront our inner anxieties,'
he read, in a voice that would have made the average
Dalek sound like Laurence Olivier hamming it up, 'is a
fundamental stage on the road to personality growth. By
making our nightmares come true, we can confront
whatever it is they really stand for, and resolve the inner
turmoils that cause them. You have ninety seconds. Man,
play that thing!'

Very reluctantly, Wesley lifted the violin to his chin,
drew back the bow and let it glide across the strings. The
result was perhaps the ghastliest noise ever made by
catgut in the absence of the rest of the cat.

'Sixty seconds. And he's going to have to do a bit
better than this if he wants to stand a chance of winning
tonight's grand star prize!'

'But I can't—' Wesley started to say; then it occurred
to him that anything further might lay him open to a
charge of stating the obvious. He gritted his teeth,
clamped his eyes so tightly shut that muscles in his

cheeks started to ache, and tried again.

And succeeded.

Admittedly, it was only *Baa Baa Black Sheep*, and there was little in it to prompt his colleagues at the day job to buy a big card for everybody to write farewell messages on; but considering that the nearest he'd ever come before to playing the violin was when he used to stretch rubber bands along his six-inch ruler at school and scrape them with a pencil, it wasn't bad at all. For the first time in a long while, Wesley felt –

– Proud? Good about himself? Maybe.

'Time's up,' read the inspector. 'And it looks like Wesley's won tonight's grand star prize. Which is—' He turned the card and found his place again. 'Death by – what's that word? Oh, sorry. Electrocution, so let's have a big hand for . . .' He stopped reading, lowered the card, paused as directed, and raised the card again. 'Old Sparky!'

Whereupon the door in the wings opened; and someone dressed in a comic electric-chair costume waddled on, big felt smile stuck to the front of his seat, big white padded hands waving adorably, big live blue sparks arcing across his terminals—

Wesley opened his eyes. Time to wake up.

But he didn't wake up, and his eyes were already open.

When Calvin rematerialised, he found himself standing beside his car, with the keys in his hand.

Before that, he'd been just about to start a fight with someone, and then he *felt* himself disappearing; a very brief but entirely unmistakable experience, equivalent to watching yourself vanish before your very eyes.

'Tonight's star prize . . .'

He spun round on his heel, to find he was being

watched by a theatre full of people. Which meant he was
in a theatre. Which meant that he was indoors. Which
meant, though he wasn't quite sure why, that this wasn't
his car.

Except that it palpably was. In the same way that a
woman can always recognise her own new-born baby's
cry in the middle of a wardful of howling infants, a man
can always recognise his own car. Probably it's the same
basic instinct; the natural and subliminal bonding
between two souls formed from the same piece of stock.
And if all that mystic stuff wasn't sufficient evidence,
there were palpable physical signs; the tiny scratch on the
front fender that nobody but he would ever know to look
for, the minuscule abrasion on the front offside hubcap,
the all but invisible scar in the paintwork under the filler
cap where he'd once slipped with the filler cap key. His
car; flesh of his flesh, chrome of his chrome, vinyl of his
vinyl.

So what the hell was it doing here?

'A big hand, please . . .'

Who cares? He fumbled on the keyring for the
doorkey. If only he could get inside, he'd be safe; he could
triple-lock the doors, turn on the alarm, use his phone to
call a SWAT team. According to the brochure, the
quickest time in which the world's most accomplished
automotive thieves had been able to break into this
model had been twenty minutes. Give the boys in the flak
jackets and baseball hats twenty minutes, and they'd have
this whole lot looking like Monte Cassino on a bad day.
Except for this car, of course; according to the literature,
a direct nuclear strike might bubble off a couple of layers
of paint, but that was about it. A serious car for a serious
world, the brochure said; the picture its well-chosen
phrases conjured up was of an intact, barely scratched

car free-floating in the vacuum of space, while the exploded fragments of Planet Earth sailed harmlessly by on the interstellar winds. Once inside this mother, he'd be *safe*.

He located the key in the lock, pushing away the spring-loaded lock cover. He pushed.

The key wouldn't go.

'. . . For our second contestant, Calvin Dieb!'

The theatre exploded into pandemonium; howling, whistling, rebel yells and so on. Two large men in tuxedos materialised behind Calvin's shoulders. And still the key wouldn't go.

'Excuse me, sir,' muttered one of the men. 'Auto club.'

Whereupon he took the keys from Calvin's hand and put them in his pocket. As Calvin straightened up to punch him (although, without a stepladder, he'd have been hard put to it to do any significant damage), two huge hands pushed down on his shoulders, sitting him efficiently and with minimum dignity on the floor.

'Hey,' he whined, 'gimme my keys, will you?'

A giant hand reached down, gathered a fistful of lapels and lifted Calvin up by them. He found himself looking into the unfriendliest pair of eyes he'd seen in a long time; ever since, in fact, he'd been cross-examining a rape victim in the witness box and caught sight of his own reflection in a window.

'No keys,' said the proprietor of the unfriendly eyes. 'First you gotta play the game.'

The hand let go of his lapels and he slid back downwards, until he came to rest against the passenger door of the car. It was then that he noticed another man, this time wearing a spangly white tuxedo and reading aloud from a card.

'Your chosen subject,' the man said, 'is Law. You have

two minutes in which to answer one question – just one – correctly. If you do, then tonight's wonderful grand star prize, a complete set of keys specially custom-crafted to fit *your* car, will be yours to take home. If you don't, then you get to sit in . . .' The man lowered the card and counted under his breath before speaking again; when he did, his words were drowned out by the unison chant from the audience.

'Old SPARKY!'

Old Sparky? The electric chair? Calvin looked round quickly, to see if he had a chance of rolling under the car before the two tuxedoed monsters could stop him. Then he thought, Just a minute, one correct answer in two minutes? On Law? And they give me my keys?

He didn't exactly relax, in the same way as the polar ice never actually melts; but a different kind of tension thrilled down to his nerve-endings. If there was one thing he knew, it was Law. This was a gamble he'd be prepared to take.

'Your two minutes,' the man said, 'starting . . .'

And then he recognised him.

Strange, how quickly the mind can work when there's absolutely nothing that can be done in time to avert disaster. IBM never built anything with a better response time than the mind of a man who notices through the windscreen of his speeding car that the tall object five yards dead ahead is a tree. All that long interim, between the moment of initial recognition and waking up to find your arm full of plastic tubes, is filled with an almost infinite number of thoughts, suggestions and referrals from the self-preservation sub-committee and strong recommendations from the theology department; all marvellously good stuff, but there's no time to act on the advice.

The man smiled, and said, 'Now.'

'Hi, Dad.'

'In *State of Colorado v Stein*,' the man read out, 'was the third party's collateral warranty held to bind the defendant regardless of the terms of the original agreement?'

Dieb swallowed hard. 'Look,' he said, 'I really did mean to come to the hospital, it was just a bad day for me—'

'Incorrect. In actions for defamation, is slander actionable per se or must the plaintiff prove special damage?'

'I was all set,' Dieb went on, 'and then just as I was about to leave the phone rang, and it was this really important client—'

'Incorrect. In *Sharps v Rowan*, was the defendant's inability to fulfil the contract owing to intervening factors beyond his control sufficient to relieve him of his obligations to the plaintiff?'

'And about the funeral, I really did mean to go, but my dumb secretary'd booked me lunch with the board of Freemans', and you just don't call up old man Freeman and say, Sorry, can you do Tuesday instead? So . . .'

'Incorrect. Thirty seconds remaining. Briefly explain the maxim *res ipsa loquitur*.'

'Anyhow,' said Calvin desperately, 'I hope you liked the flowers. Sorry about the mix-up, I told my secretary you always liked carnations, but she must have gotten carnations and chrysanthemums mixed up. Besides, you wouldn't actually have seen them, would you? Not from where you . . .'

'Incorrect.' Calvin Dieb senior gave his son a big, friendly smile. 'Time's up, and gee, son, you've blown it! Which means—'

'Old SPARKY!'

As the cuddly, padded, smiling electric chair waddled in from the wings, and the two gorillas dragged Calvin towards it, his father waved to him, not unaffectionately. 'Son,' he said, 'you should have listened to Mom and me. Didn't we say if you threw in your job with the circus and ran away to law school, one day you'd be sorry? So long, son.'

'So long, Dad.'

Calvin Dieb senior turned to the audience and smiled. 'A big hand for Calvin Dieb junior, folks. Serves the little bugger right.'

He turned. Flashing blue light was reflected in his silver hair as he left the stage, a handkerchief pressed to his nose because of the smell.

In the chair, Calvin was just getting to the interesting bit when he vanished.

The Proprietor was dreaming.

It was a curious dream. It seemed to involve four blind mice, scampering round the shores of His lake, pursued by the farmer's wife, Sabatier XL stainless carver in her hand and a great big silly grin on her face. There were other ingredients to the dream – Indians and Vikings and goblins and talking bears and a thing like a walking armchair that fizzed blue, and a few others He couldn't yet see clearly. Everyone except the mice seemed to be enjoying themselves enormously; but this was wrong, because the dream was supposed to be for the mice's benefit.

It then occurred to the Proprietor that things which are good for you – medicines and cabbage and cold baths and quitting smoking and good healthy exercise and going to bed early – do seem, as often as not, to be horrible at the time. It's only afterwards that you appreciate their virtue; usually when you've grown up and have children of your own on whom you can inflict the torments of your youth.

The Proprietor wondered about that. He wondered why bad things taste nice, and good things taste nasty. He wondered why it was good to waste the golden sunlit afternoons of childhood doing piano practice so that, when you turn forty, you'd be able to play the piano indifferent-badly if only you had the time. He wondered why Youth must learn how to do long division so that Middle Age can tap a few buttons on a calculator. He tried to remember the things He'd been at pains to learn when He was young, but couldn't.

And He resolved; learning is to punish the ignorant for offences they would have committed if they hadn't known better. Having sorted out the point, definitely for ever, He slid back into full sleep.

The mice were still running; they ran through the briars and they ran through the brambles and they ran through the thickets where the rabbits wouldn't go, and still the farmer's wife followed them, and the sun flashed off the broad blade of her knife, in which were reflected many tall trees and mountains. This implied that He had missed the point, something He never liked to do.

So He wondered about the blind mice. He had already Resolved that learning is punishment; and when He came to look at them He could see that all four mice did indeed deserve to be chased, and that their tails had been forfeit for most of their adult lives. They needed to be taught a lesson. Well.

But they hadn't come to learn; they'd come to dream. One of them had capital-D Dreams like the New York sewers have alligators; one dreamed greed and selfishness and a callous disregard for everything beautiful and good that stood between him and a dollar; one lived in a dream so complete and so unreal that it wouldn't have mattered, except that she wanted to make other people believe it too; and one dreamed of being an unmitigated pest, which was antisocial behaviour by anybody's standards. Very well, then; let them have their dreams, and learn that their dreams are nightmares.

He tried to Resolve accordingly, but found that He couldn't.

Janice felt herself reappearing.

It wasn't anything like she'd imagined. As far as she'd always been concerned, you reappeared in a shower of tinselly glitter, to the accompaniment of a melodious electronic twang, and the first thing you saw was the face of Mr Scott, peering at you over the top of his instrument panel. Then, if you were lucky, deferential security guards escorted you to the recreation room, where you could have a refreshing pink milk shake and a recycled currant bun.

The reality was rather different; a bit like the feeling you get when your leg, having gone to sleep, wakes up again. One of the things you don't readily do is move.

So, rooted to the spot, she looked round to find out where she was. She didn't like what she saw.

She was in an auditorium. High up, on scaffolding towers, there were TV cameras. White lights as bright as the Second Coming blazed at her, and beyond them was a sea of pink and red faces, some of them worryingly familiar. They appeared to be an audience, looking at her. She was on the stage.

She was also, she discovered, wearing a costume, or part of one. It was hard looking down, but she seemed to be wearing a sparkly sort of swimsuit; either that, or the parts of her that had to be at least vestigially covered had been smeared in glue and dusted down with sequins. There was glittery stuff in her hair, and enough paint on her face to do the outside of a block of flats.

And the audience was staring at her.

Sharing the stage with her was a tall, silver-haired type in a glittery white tuxedo and a smile that made the studio lights seem unnecessary, and also a stunningly attractive girl with golden hair and eyes as blue as the mould on decomposing bread. They looked as if they were supposed to be the centre of attention. They weren't. She was.

By now, she knew the signs as instinctively as seaweed knows the weather. The whole goddamn audience was in love with her.

Vaguely remembering something she'd once heard about someone being a lion in a den of Daniels, she looked round for an escape route: but there didn't seem to be one. The MC and the dreamboat stood directly between her and the doorway in the wings. The only other visible way out was down off the stage and through the audience; an option as attractive to her as a short cut through a minefield would be to a thirty-foot-long centipede.

The beautiful girl; didn't she know her from somewhere? The eagle's cave? Something about submarines? She concentrated, and tried to hear what the MC was saying to her.

'Now then, Lindsey,' she heard, 'perhaps you'd like to explain your theory about the Vaticangate affair to our studio audience.'

'Right,' said the lovely girl. 'First, it's not Lindsey, it's Linda; or, to you, Ms Lachuk. Second, well, it's basically fairly simple. The beef is, they're bringing the stuff in somehow; I'm not sure of the details yet, but it seems to involve midnight airlifts using Mafia-owned Sea King helicopters. Then they encase it in blocks of— Hey!'

'Hm?' The silver-haired man, who'd been ogling Janice's legs, made an effort and turned back to the lovely girl. 'Sorry?' he said.

'The cameras,' she complained, 'why are they all on her and not me? I'm the one doing the story.'

'What? Sorry about that. I was miles away.'

'The cameras,' the angelically gorgeous female repeated angrily. 'And the mikes, too. I know about these things; they aren't picking up a single word I'm saying.'

'Huh? What did you say about the cameras?'

'Oh for crying out— Look, do you want me to give you my world exclusive scoop, implicating the US government and the Pope in illicit undercover arms shipments? Or would you rather all just gawp at the goddamn chubby bitch over there?'

The MC glowered at her. 'Not chubby,' he said sharply. 'Voluptuous.'

'Hey!'

'Or even,' he continued dreamily, 'Rubensesque. By God, there's enough meat on that to feed a family of five for Thanksgiving and still have enough for sandwiches clean through to New Year.'

Whereupon the audience burst out into an explosion of cheering, yowling and wolf-whistling that must have been plainly audible in Pennsylvania, and left Janice feeling torn between a desperate longing never to have been born, and a ferocious desire to scalp each and every one of them with a blunt putty knife. In the event, however, she did neither of these: instead, she carried on standing there, sweating through the makeup and looking like a cross between the Statue of Liberty and one of the young ladies who spend their days sitting in shop windows in Amsterdam. Probably the only person in the whole world who was more furious than her was the lovely girl; and that was a laugh, because she had all her clothes on.

'Hey!' she was howling. 'If this is your idea of a serious in-depth current affairs programme, you can . . .'

'Sorry? Oh hell, yes. I'd clean forgotten about you. Right then, Laura, er—' The MC glanced down at the card in his hand. 'Lachik, right? Laura Lachik, ladies and gentlemen, special current affairs correspondent for the *New York Globe*, who's going to give us the low-down on the latest . . . what was it again?'

'Oh for God's sake!' The dreamboat was scrabbling at her cleavage for the little concealed microphone. 'I've had enough of this. Here I am with the most significant news story in history, and all you creeps are interested in is that cow's legs. And they aren't even nice legs, damnit, they look like pink elephants' trunks.'

'Not just her legs,' replied the MC equably.

'Oh . . . !' The lovely girl was having difficulty tracing the course of the microphone lead, which had apparently been threaded through her underwear and out through a hole in her left shoe. 'The hell with you! I'm not standing for this. I'm . . .'

The MC was staring at her with baffled concern. 'But Ms Lachuk,' he was saying, calmly and quietly, 'I thought this was what you wanted. Peak air time, ten minutes all to yourself, your own script—'

'Stuff it!' With a yelp of pain as the flex bit into her hand, she yanked the mike off the end of the wire, pulled it free and stomped off into the wings, while the cameras followed her every step and the studio audience threw empty styrofoam cups. She was just about to slam out of the door when the length of wire she was trailing behind her snaked into the coils of spaghetti hanging out of the sound desk. There was a sudden cracking noise, a puff of smoke and a big fat blue spark, which travelled along the wire and, catastrophically, up her skirt.

'Hey,' said the MC, pulling out his handkerchief and holding it over his nose. 'A big hand, people, please for Old . . .'

CHAPTER ELEVEN

Not long after his death, Wesley woke up.

He was lying on the grass. A very faint breeze was blowing, just enough to be noticed. Above him, a pine tree rose straight towards the sky, its branches scattering the sunlight. He tried to turn his head, and found he couldn't.

Panic.

Finally, when he'd found that none of him would move, and despair had taken possession of his mind and was measuring the insides of his eyes for new curtains, he stared down his nose and saw why.

Mostly, it was the ivy. For example, it was so hopelessly intertwined with the enormously long, straggly white beard he appeared to have grown at some stage that it anchored his head as effectively as a nail driven through his forehead. Other parts of the same ivy had overgrown his arms and legs, so that he lay under a sort of woven harness of the stuff like Daddy on the beach, buried in sand by his offspring while he slept. Some enterprising bird or animal had used his hair as nest-lining material without first severing it from his head, with the result that there was a substantial build-up of twigs and leaves round his ears. Although he couldn't see them, he was prepared to bet he had fingernails and toe-nails like the quintessential wicked witch, all long and curled and brittle. There was a beetle strolling up and down his nose, and there was nothing he could do about it.

Hair, beard and nails grow after death, they say; a curious fact which explains why the hairdressers of the great kings and pharaohs of the heroic age were buried side by side with their masters. Wesley ran a quick mental status check: unable to move, plus substantial hair growth, ditto nails suspected. But he was too well pre-served in other respects to be dead; and besides, he was still breathing. There was also something else—

Ah yes, the noise. By his ear, something was buzzing with quiet persistence. It was a nondescript sound, but vaguely familiar. He concentrated on it, and had just worked out a hypothesis when the noise changed, prov-ing his theory correct.

It wasn't going ᵇzzzzzzzz any more; it was going *gloop-gloop-gloop-aargh*. It was a Teasmaid.

'Hello,' said the beetle on his nose. 'Sleep well?'

Wesley managed to bump-start the muscles he needed to talk with. 'Huh?' he said.

'Sleep well? Actually, that's a pretty dumb question. Still, you'll feel a bit more lively after you've had a nice hot cup of tea. That's one of your nice English customs, a cup of tea first thing after you wake up.'

'Asleep?' Wesley grunted. 'How long?'

'A hundred and sixteen years,' the beetle replied. 'I'm afraid you missed the whole of the twenty-first century.

Still, it was very popular, so I expect they'll repeat it again soon. I'm assuming you've got cable?'

'A hundred and sixteen . . . ?'

The beetle waggled its mandibles, presumably by way of confirmation. 'Rather longer than originally scheduled,' it said. 'You see, the idea is that by the time you wake up, everybody you could possibly have known will be long dead. Thanks to the wonders of twenty-first-century medicine, though, everybody lived much longer than ever before, so you've had to have a bit of a lie-in.'

'Just a minute,' Wesley croaked. His vocal cords, unlubricated for over a century, were scarcely functional, so that he sounded like Lee Marvin singing 'Wandering Star' with a sore throat. '*Every*body dead?'

'As nail in door,' the beetle replied cheerfully. 'But that's not going to worry you, is it? I mean, you always reckoned you never liked any of them anyway.'

Wesley's mind was moving sluggishly, but even so the big triangular warning sign that read *Rip Van Winkle* was rushing up towards him at one hell of a rate. 'What's happening?' he rasped, 'Who—?'

'At any rate,' continued the beetle, 'you missed the war; and anyway, it wasn't too bad here. Far enough away from a major city for there not to be much fall-out. Actually, the war was something of an anticlimax. Twenty-five per cent survival rate, as it turned out. Well, not here in America, of course, more like fifteen. But in Australia they got away with twenty-nine per cent, and Iceland scarcely copped it at all. I expect you'd like to try moving about now.' The beetle peered about, lifting its two front legs into the air. 'What we really need is a goat, they'll eat *anything*. A nice patch of brambles like that'd be like smoked salmon and caviare to a goat these days.'

'The war? What war?'

'What *war*?' The beetle scrabbled furiously with its front legs, then dropped down again. 'Of course, you don't know, do you? *The* war. The *big* war. World War – now let me see,' it added, counting. 'You know, it's at times like these you realise how useful it is having six feet. World War Five.'

'Five?' Wesley's jaw dropped as far as its beard-and-ivy cradle would allow. 'What about Three and Four, then?'

'Huh? Oh, right. Three and Four. Well, Three was something and nothing, really, except of course that your place, funny L-shaped island with a frilly top, it's on the tip of my – Britain, that's it. Doubleyou-doubleyou-three was more or less the end of the road as far as Britain went. And that other place. Um . . .'

'Ireland?'

'Europe. Still, no great loss, it was all worn out anyway. Doubleyou-doubleyou-four was when Japan and China and all those places got broken; and really, that was what ushered in the Forty Golden Years of Prosperity for the US of A, because with no Europe and no Far East to get under our feet and keep asking us for favours, we could really get on with our lives, you know? All told, it was a pity it had to end. I suppose—'

'Yes?'

'I suppose,' said the beetle, thoughtfully, 'if we can't find a goat, a sheep would do. One of the new sheep. That's if you're feeling brave.'

In spite of the heavy traffic through the still heavily coned highways of his mind, Wesley was still able to spare a few million brain cells to pick up on that one. 'Why would I have to be feeling brave about sheep?' he said. 'Goats, yes, up to a point. But sheep—?'

'Ah,' said the beetle smugly, 'these are different sheep. You see, they inherited the earth.'

'I beg your pardon?'

'Well, it was promised them. I'm not saying they wanted it; I expect they'd have been happier with some furniture or a few pictures or a clock or something. But it said in the book of words, the meek shall inherit the earth. And they did.'

'Ah.'

'But I've got to admit, it didn't make them nicer people, I mean animals.' The beetle opened its wing-case and closed it again. 'Isn't that always the way, when people inherit things? Never makes them happy. No, they changed.'

'They did?'

'Oh yes.' The beetle see-sawed backwards and forwards on its middle legs, as if nodding. 'They grew, for a start. Ten feet high at the shoulder they are now, fifteen some of them. And of course there was precious little grass left for them to eat, so they had to turn carnivorous.'

'Car—? You mean, they eat *meat*?'

'Most definitely,' replied the beetle, repeating the middle-legs manoeuvre. 'That's why there's no humans at all left in New Zealand. Plus, all their hair fell out, so they took to wearing human skins to keep themselves warm.'

'Dear God!'

'Very good at it, mind,' added the beetle. 'They make lovely thick coats and warm fleecy gloves and manskin-lined boots and everything. In fact,' the beetle went on, waving its mandibles at Wesley's abundant hair, 'I don't really think you'd want to meet a sheep right now. You know what they say, temptation beyond endurance. First thing you know, they'd make a three-piece suit out of you. Jesus, they're almost as bad as the lemmings.' The beetle rubbed its back legs together in an agitated manner. 'Believe me,' it said. 'You *don't* want to meet the lemmings.'

A surge of horror coursed through Wesley's nerves, like a bolt of lightning shinning up a strip of copper. A nanosecond behind it, taking its time and refusing to get excited, came a small detachment of cynicism. *Just a minute*, it was saying, *it's sheep we're talking about, right? Piano-stool-sized woolly nitwits who make town hall clerks seem intelligent, and the electorate look like they have a mind of their own. Come on, now, think about it.*

Wesley thought about it.

'This is one of those alternative futures, right?' he suggested cautiously. 'It hasn't happened yet, but it might *if*. Any minute now, Dr Sam Beckett will appear in a cloud of blue sparks, looking confused.'

The beetle vanished, and was replaced by a girl. Wesley was starting to feel fed up at the sight of her.

'Well done,' she said. 'That's more or less it, though I don't quite get the Beckett reference. Didn't he write gloomy plays about men in dustbins?'

Wesley shrugged. 'I don't think they showed that one in the UK. Anyhow, the point is that I *haven't* been asleep for a hundred and something years, and the world *isn't* terrorised by giant mutant killer sheep. Or at least,' he added, before the girl could speak, 'not in my universe it isn't. Please tell me I've got it right.'

The girl nodded. 'But,' she said, 'this is what *will* happen, unless something's done about it. You might say this future hasn't actually gone into production yet, but they've commissioned the script and started auditioning for the leading roles.'

Wesley mused on this for a moment. 'When you say something's got to be done about it, I have this awful feeling that what you really mean is that *I've* got to do something.'

'Not just you,' replied the girl, cheerfully. 'There's the others too. Well, two of them.'

'Ah yes.' Wesley frowned thoughtfully. 'I've been meaning to ask about that. Who are these others I keep bumping into? There's that lawyer I nearly had the fight with—'

'Calvin Dieb.'

'Right, yes. And the, um, girl.'

'Janice DeWeese.'

'Thank you. And the mad woman with the submarines, and the Indian, Talks To Squirrels . . .'

'The submarines lady is Linda Lachuk, and she's the fourth. Talks is, like, staff. So are all the others. It's just the four of you that's customers.'

'I see.' Wesley chewed his lower lip. 'And we're all sharing this horrible game, are we?'

'Not quite,' the girl said. 'You each get a set of experiences custom-fitted to your own problems and inadequacies. But we use the same sets and the same cast, is all.'

'Bit cheapskate, that, isn't it? Touch of the B-movie syndrome there, I'd have said.'

'Not at all,' the girl replied severely. 'Let's just say we're economical with fiction. And all that's beside the point. The point is, Phase Four involves saving the world, otherwise you don't get your grades.'

'I love your sense of perspective,' Wesley muttered. 'You're saying that unless we save civilisation as we know it, you'll send us to bed without any pudding. Anyway, what've we got to do? And I might as well warn you, if it involves dogs or spiders, you can count me out. Let the lawyer do it.'

'No dogs,' sighed the girl, 'and no spiders. Look, do you want me to explain, or would you rather we spent the last few hours before the point of no return finding fault with each other? It's all the same to me, because I can be a sheep just as easily as a human.'

'Explain,' Wesley said. 'Please.'

The girl shrugged. 'I was trying to,' she said. 'But you kept talking. The point is, doubleyou-doubleyou Five was a direct result of doubleyou-doubleyou Four, and doubleyou-doubleyou Four was the inevitable consequence of doubleyou-doubleyou Three. And doubleyou-doubleyou Three is due to be caused in about nine hours. Here, in Iowa.' She smiled, and added, 'Oh, and in case you were wondering, this is for real. Not a drill. OK?'

Wesley closed his eyes, trying to get his mind round it all. It was a bit like trying to fit a grand piano in a sock, but he did his best. 'All right,' he said. 'And what's going to happen in nine hours?'

'Quite simple,' said the girl. 'A top-flight attack journalist, writing for a leading schlock-horror New York tabloid, will put out this beautifully crafted, absolutely convincing story about global conspiracies and illicit arms shipments and Papal Armageddon and organised crime infiltration of Government and Lord knows what else. And, because the sheep and the lemmings actually inherited the Earth a long time ago but keep getting mistaken for people, the story goes over big. Networks all over the world pick it up. It gets splashed all over everywhere; which is a pity, because there's a lot in it you could take offence to if you happen to be, say, a small but well-armed non-aligned nation. Next thing you know, governments in all continents are issuing categorical denials, which is like having an affidavit from God that it's all true, as far as the media's concerned. In a frighteningly short time there's the usual media-induced hysteria – did you know it was that bunch of criminal psychotics who actually decide what happens on this planet, by the way? Not so much a democracy as a mediocracy. Then there'll be diplomatic incidents, and trigger-happy border patrols coming to blows all round the edges of four continents. After that it's only a matter of time before buttons get pressed, and, hey presto, the thing that just whizzed by in a puff of black smoke was the Third World War. Very short war, that was. Forty minutes after it had started, there wasn't much left to blow up.'

Wesley sat still for a long twenty seconds. 'I see,' he said. 'And this pillock journalist, the one we've got to stop; that wouldn't be the submarine fancier – what was her name again?'

'Linda Lachuk.'

'Fine. And how are we supposed to stop her sending in her copy?'

The girl grinned. 'That's easy,' she said. 'You kill her.'

Calvin Dieb opened his eyes.

For a moment, he was confused; but, active as ever, his brain was ready with two alternative explanations, both of which fitted the available data like a Florentine glove, almost before his eyelids were fully up.

Explanation One was that he'd died and gone to Heaven.

Explanation Two was that – finally – he'd woken up, and normality had been restored, we apologise for any inconvenience.

He looked again. Both explanations were wrong. Damn.

It had seemed promising at first, because the first thing he'd seen had been a judge's table on a raised dais under the good ol' Stars and Stripes. He was, in other words, in a courtroom; and yes, there was the jury hutch, there was the witness box, there were the cops and there were the cameras.

And there, unfortunately, was where the comforting illusion of reality faded; because he was sitting at the defendant's table and the man he was sitting next to was also, apparently, Calvin Dieb. Likewise the prosecutor. As far as he could see, he was the one on trial here. The good news was, he had Calvin Dieb to defend him. And the bad news was, Calvin Dieb was the prosecutor.

He tugged the sleeve of the Calvin Dieb next to him; the one who was lolling back in his chair doing the crossword. 'Hey,' he whispered urgently, 'what's—?'

'Shh.' He looked back at himself. 'Like I told you, stay cool. I got everything under control.' That smile; the one he'd practised in the mirror, all those years ago. 'Trust me,' he heard himself say. 'I'm your attorney.'

'Yes, but—'

Before he could complete the sentence, the usher called out, 'All stand,' and an automatic reflex operated the muscles of his knees.

Enter the judge.

In a way, he was relieved to find that the judge, unlike virtually everyone else in this nightmare, wasn't Calvin Dieb. Nor was he particularly surprised to see that the judge was, in fact, an otter. He wasn't even mildly perturbed when the otter, having taken its seat and found it couldn't see over the desk, shook itself and became a beautiful brown-haired girl.

The usher cleared her throat. 'In the matter of the Universe versus Calvin Dieb, Ms Justice Okeewana presiding.' Cameras started to whir. The judge leaned forward, and smiled.

'Mr Dieb,' she said, 'maybe it strikes you as odd that you've been executed first and tried afterwards. Let's just say I'm on a schedule, and this is the only way I could fit you in.' She turned her head, and nodded to the prosecutor. 'OK, Mr Dieb, you may begin.'

'Thank you.' The version of him on the other end of the table rose; and yes, damnit, it *was* Calvin Dieb; same smoothly oiled manner, same tactically perfect mannerisms. A stray thought, parked illegally in the back lots of his mind, wanted to know whether, since he was prosecutor, defendant and defence attorney, he'd be getting three fees, and if so, was there more of this kind of work available? A moment later, the stray thought was grabbed by the rest of the contents of Calvin's brain, and lynched. The prosecutor cleared his throat, as if he'd been conscious of the stray thought and had been waiting for it to subside, and placed his hands on the table, palms downwards. Do I do that? Yes, come to think of it, I do.

'Your honour,' the prosecutor said, 'the People's case against this man is exceptionally strong. We've all seen the evidence; from his business partner Hernan Piranha, who described him as, I quote, "a coyote". From his former wife, who referred to him as "pathetic" and told this court that he'd "always be nothing". From the victims of his ruthless ambition; the pharmaceuticals victims he cheated out of the compensation they so desperately needed, and his early guide and mentor, Leonard Threetrees, whom he callously ousted and, indeed, cold-bloodedly killed in front of this very court. We even have the testimony of Calvin Dieb senior, who cheerfully sent his own son to the electric chair.'

At Calvin's side, the defence attorney sprang to his feet. 'Objection,' he called out. 'In sentencing my client, witness was merely abiding by the rules of the game.

There is no evidence to suggest that he did so cheerfully.'

Way to go, Cal, Calvin thought; but he didn't like the look on the prosecutor's face. It was his own malicious grin. Ah shit!

'Indeed,' the prosecutor said. 'As I recall, Mr Dieb senior's last words were, "Serve the little bugger right." ' Oh Christ, Calvin thought, there's my very own triumphant smirk at the jury when I've just scored a really telling below-belt hit. 'Coming from the man's own father, members of the jury, don't you find that just a bit significant? Just a tad?'

Calvin looked round. The jury-box was, in fact, empty; but he felt he knew why without having to ask. It was because, no matter how weird the laws of physics might be in this lousy place, there's still no way you'd fit the entire population of the Universe into that little thing.

'But,' the prosecutor went on, 'the testimony I intend to rely on is that of the defendant himself. We've all seen and heard it, members of the jury. It speaks for itself.' He paused, like a lazy but skilful lion about to spring. 'That's what really makes this guy so much worse than all the other creeps and low-lifes we get in this court, because basically, even after everything he's been through, everything he's put everybody else through – and let's not forget those Vikings, members of the jury, for whose deaths he's solely responsible – he hasn't changed a bit. He's been scared, but he ain't sorry. The only thing that's been on his mind all along is to get his keys back and get the hell out of here, fast, before he wastes any more valuable, chargeable time. Even now, right this minute, there's a part of his evil little brain that's working out how he's gonna stick the last seven hours on Mr Lustmord's bill.'

Hey, how did he know that? Calvin wondered, and in so doing, knew the answer. Oh, but it was *depressing*. He glanced sideways at his defence attorney, who grinned back.

'I know,' his image whispered. 'But it's worse for me, 'cos I'm on a contingency fee.'

He was about to reply when he realised the prosecutor was looking straight at him. 'You heard that, members of the jury?' he said, with savage delight. 'Doesn't that just say it all? He hires himself to defend him, but he'll only get paid if he wins. I know he's a lawyer, sure, but what kind of guy sinks so low that he goes around ripping *himself* off? I don't think I really need to answer that one, folks. Just take a look and see for yourselves. The Universe rests.'

There was a moment of embarrassed silence; then the defence attorney stood up and addressed the bench. 'Your honour,' he said, 'if I can just confer with my colleague for a moment? Thank you.'

The two Calvin Diebs stood up and went off into a huddle over by the witness box; then the prosecutor sat down again, while the defence approached the bench. Although he was whispering to the judge, Calvin could hear every word.

'It's like this, your honour,' he was saying. 'It seems my colleague's on a contingency basis too, so we've agreed to split the fee between us and I'll throw the trial. I trust that meets with your approval? In the interests of justice, I mean.'

The judge nodded. 'Sure thing,' she said. 'Last thing anybody wants is for the scumbag to walk.'

Calvin – the Calvin Calvin hoped was the real Calvin – jumped to his feet and started to protest, whereupon the court cop leaned over and dealt him a horrendous blow on the head with his nightstick. The last thing he remembered seeing in this life was the jury-box, crammed to bursting with the entire population of the Universe (Hey! Get a load of those guys from Ursa Minor! Count those prehensile ears!) and they were all waving and cheering like mad.

The defence attorney gathered up his papers, nodded to his colleague and left the court.

The prosecutor stood for a moment, looking down at the file open before him, and then across at the body slumped over the table, dead as a manifesto promise in mid-term. Then he felt something in his left hand, and unclenched his fist.

It was a set of keys.

He looked up at the judge, who nodded. 'You'll have to split them with the rest of you,' she said. 'That's the part of you that was prepared to sell the rest of you down the river, remember, so I guess your problems aren't entirely over. Still, it's an improvement. How about if you keep the ignition key and give him the filler cap key and the mascot?'

'He can have the mascot,' Calvin Dieb replied solemnly. 'We'll negotiate for the rest.'

'So long, Calvin.'

Calvin inclined his head. 'So long,' he said. 'And thanks, I guess. If ever there's anything I can—'

'You'll be sorry you said that,' answered the judge.

'Hey, it was just a figure of—'

Calvin vanished.

When Janice rematerialised, she found herself back in the forest. Having looked round carefully to make sure there were no Vikings, motorcyclists, eagles, doctors, game-show hosts or other pests anywhere to be seen, she sat down on the trunk of a fallen tree, crossed her arms and waited to see what would happen next.

She didn't have long to wait. About twenty seconds later, she heard a soft hissing noise down by her ankle, looked down and saw a hat.

'Pst!' it was saying.

She frowned. There was something in the hat's demeanour – the angle of its brim, perhaps, or the slight droop in its feather – that suggested that it was about to try and sell her life insurance.

'Well?' she said.

'Wanna buy a map?'

Janice started. 'What kind of map?' she asked cautiously. 'If it's one where X marks the spot, and there's dead men's chests and so on, I really don't want to know.'

The hat rotated half a turn clockwise, then swung back again. 'Nothing like that,' it said. 'Listen, it's a map of how to get out of here. Only five hundred bucks. Guaranteed. No quibble warranty. This does not affect your statutory . . .'

'*Really* out of here?' Janice demanded. 'You mean, back into real life, where I don't have to hide in the bushes every time a male squirrel runs along a tree, just in case it falls in love with me and follows me about?'

The hat tilted backwards and forwards. 'User-friendly,' it urged. 'Easy to read, guaranteed not to crease or tear if used in accordance with manufacturer's directions.'

The frown on Janice's face thickened into a scowl, as if cornflour had been added. 'I don't care if it glows in the dark and hums Scott Joplin so long as it shows me the way out,' she replied irritably. 'Here, let's have a look.'

'Oh no you don't,' said the hat, moving back a pace or

two. 'If you look at the map, you see the way out and you don't buy.'

'Forget it, then,' Janice said, forcing herself to sound indifferent. 'You see, unless I actually look at the map, I won't know if it's what you say it is. It's not that I'm calling you a liar,' she added quickly, as the hat started to vibrate. 'But you're a hat, for Chrissakes. How'd you know it's really real? For all I know, hat, you could be talking through yourself.'

'No money,' said the hat sadly, 'no deal.'

'Tell you what. I'll give you fifty bucks. How does that sound?'

'Insulting,' replied the hat sulkily. 'Hey, lady, what d'you do in your spare time when you aren't pulling gift horses' lips apart and sticking little mirrors in their mouths?'

Janice yawned. 'All right,' she said, 'seventy-five. But that's my last offer, 'cos that's all I got.'

'Seventy-five lousy bucks for your dream come true?' The hat slowly rotated. 'Lady, I *know* you're gonna be sorry. This is a once-only offer, remember, so . . .'

'What did you say?'

'Once-only offer,' the hat repeated. 'You're gonna be sorry.'

'No, before that.'

'Seventy-five lousy bucks for your dream come true?'

'That's the bit,' Janice said. 'Look, I can do seventy-five bucks cash, and the rest by card . . .'

The hat sniggered. 'Sorry, lady,' it said. 'Strictly cash. So long.'

'No, wait—'

The hat wasn't there any more. Janice looked for it under the repulsive-looking yellow fungus it had been leaning against, but there was no sign. She swore quietly and stood up, reasoning that if nobody was going to come and collect her, she might as well go and find somebody. With luck, whoever she found might be neither malevolent nor crazy. You never knew.

'Excuse me.'

She whirled round, overbalanced, and slipped, ending up in an undignified stack directly on top of the repulsive fungus. She looked up, and saw a man—

The hell with it; a *dazzlingly handsome, incredibly gorgeous* man in – she hated to have to admit it, but they were princely robes. He had a small gold crown nestling in the equally golden curls of his hair, and he was flanked on both sides by footmen in fancy dress and powdered wigs. And one of them was carrying a cushion.

And on the cushion—

'Excuse me,' the prince repeated, adorably, 'but would you mind awfully just, um, putting your foot in this, how shall I put it, slipper? That's if you don't mind, of course. I'd hate to think I was imposing, or anything.'

Janice stared at what was on the cushion as if it had been her head rather than a glass slipper. Not that it was what she'd call a slipper; where she came from, slippers had no backs and soft pink fur, and you kicked them under your bed when friends dropped by because you'd die of shame if they saw them. This object had a three-inch heel.

'Is that what I think it is?' she asked quietly.

The prince looked at her curiously. 'I don't know,' he said. 'That depends on what you think it is, surely.'

'I think it's the glass slipper left behind by the beautiful but mysterious maiden you danced with last night,' Janice muttered. 'Am I warm?'

'I don't know. If I had a thermometer we could take your temperature, I suppose.'

Janice frowned ever so slightly. 'No,' she said, 'what I meant was, am I sort of right about the shoe? And the beautiful but mysterious maiden and all that.'

The prince nodded. 'I expect you heard the pronouncement,' he said, and his voice was like that soft rustling as you pull out the thin bit of corrugated cardboard they put into boxes of chocolates to stop the coffee creams getting squished in transit. 'I had it pronounced all over the kingdom, you see. I imagine you heard it somewhere, sort of out of the corner of your ear. Subliminally, I think they call it.'

Janice nodded. The footman advanced, bearing the cushion. Janice unlaced her left sensible walking shoe. The footman lifted the slipper off the cushion.

'Actually,' Janice said, as the footman slid the slipper over her toes, 'there's something that puzzles me. Mind if I ask you to explain it to me?'

'By all means,' replied the prince, smiling stunningly.

'Well,' Janice said, as the back of the slipper nestled up against her heel like a cat after the tinned salmon you're just easing out of the can, 'it's like this. You danced with this girl all night, and you thought she was so gorgeous you couldn't live without her, so you're searching the kingdom till you find her, yes?'

'That's right.'

'Your Majesty,' hissed the footman with respectful urgency. 'The slipper, your Maj—'

'OK,' Janice said. 'If she made this amazingly deep impression on you, how come the only way you can recognise this person is by whether or not a shoe fits her foot? I mean, wouldn't you be better off looking at girls' faces and seeing if maybe something goes *ching!* in the old memory banks? Quite apart from the fact that this slipper's a standard 5C fitting, which means that in the

USA alone there's upwards of a million and a half girls it'd fit like a glove. Had you considered either of those points, by any chance?'

'Your Majesty,' the footman persevered, maybe just a little louder, 'the slipper. It fi—'

'Gosh,' said the prince, biting his lip. 'I hadn't thought of that. Had you, Murdoch?'

'No, Your Majesty,' replied the other footman.

'How about you, Skellidge?'

The footman with the slipper didn't sigh; footmen, like Mr Spock, don't show emotion. But there was just the faintest hint in the way he didn't say anything, move or make a sound that implied the words, *Oh shit, here we go.* 'No, Your Majesty,' he said. 'If Your Majesty would care to look, Your Majesty might observe that the slipper fits.'

The prince started. 'It does?'

'Perfectly, Your Majesty.'

'Then – oh.' The Prince hesitated, and his divinely beautiful forehead crinkled. 'But, as the young lady just explained, that's not really conclusive evidence, is it?'

'No, Your Majesty.'

'All it does is whittle it down to a million and a half possible candidates.'

'Quite so, Your Majesty.'

'Just a moment,' Janice objected.

'Whereas,' the Prince went on, 'I really ought to be able to recognise the girl of my dreams when I see her, oughtn't I?'

'Yes, Your Majesty.'

'And,' the Prince went on, peering carefully at Janice's face, 'I'm afraid I can't remember ever having seen this young lady in my life before.' He sighed, and straightened up. 'Well anyway,' he said, 'it's not her, so we can eliminate her from our enquiries. So that leaves just—'

'One million, four hundred and ninety-nine thousand, nine hundred and ninety-nine to go, Your Majesty. In North America, that is. Elsewhere in the world . . .'

'Quite.' The Prince nodded gravely. 'Miss,' he said, turning to Janice, 'I'm most dreadfully obliged to you. You see, I was all set to marry the first girl this thing fitted, and then love her devotedly for ever. Thanks to you, though . . .'

Janice thought about that, and was left with the feeling you sometimes get when you've just turned the ignition key, and the key snaps cleanly off in your hand. 'On reflection,' she said feebly, 'I can see a few obvious flaws in my logic, so perhaps you shouldn't pay any attention to a word I say. In fact, if I were you I'd wipe it from my mind completely.'

The Prince smiled again; so warm a smile, you could dry socks over it. 'You're far too modest, Miss,' he said. 'It's only your clear thinking and exceptional insight that's saved me from making a truly, truly horrible mistake. I really am most awfully grateful.'

'Yes, but . . .'

With a grunt so soft that only a bat with a hearing aid could have heard it, the footman removed the slipper, wiped it out with a lace kerchief, and laid it carefully back on the cushion. 'And as a small gesture of appreciation,' the Prince went on, 'on behalf of the Kingdom as well as myself?'

'Yes?' Janice demanded breathlessly.

'I'd like you to accept this ten-dollar book token, with my compliments.' He snapped his fingers, whereupon the second footman stepped forward, put a white envelope in Janice's hand, bowed at an angle of precisely twenty-one degrees, and stepped back again.

'Gee,' Janice said, in a low, thin monotone. 'I don't know what to say.'

The Prince beamed at her. 'Think nothing of it,' he said. 'All right, Murdoch, back the way we came. There's an old chateau about three miles along the top road we haven't tried yet.' He was about to walk off, but turned and gave Janice a long, thrilling look. 'And don't worry,' he added, with a flash of his sparkling eyes. 'I feel sure that one day *your* prince will come. Just you wait and see.'

'You reckon?'

The Prince shrugged. 'Who knows? Don't give up the day job, though. Skellidge, the route map.'

The little procession departed, leaving Janice standing there doing active volcano impressions. It wasn't so much that she'd just trodden on the happy ending, she decided, as the fact that she'd been right, and they'd punished her for it. That made her think about the doctor, the one who'd been here since World War One just because he wanted to make people better. Then she remembered that she'd also turned down the offer of a ridiculously cheap escape out of all of this, and began to whimper.

She was snuffling away like a chain-smoking baby seal when a soft cough behind her made her turn. There, damnit, were Murdoch, Skellidge and the Prince.

'Excuse me,' said the Prince.

She looked at him warily. She knew what was coming; he had that dreadful pink-hearts-and-plastic-flowers look in his eyes that she had come, in a relatively short space of time, to know rather well.

'Um,' she said.

'I hope you don't mind me asking,' he said, 'but, um, what are you doing for dinner this evening?'

Janice took a deep breath. Oh, she reflected, it would

be so easy. After all, he was unspeakably attractive and his voice was like a violet-scented breeze humming in the neck of an empty milk bottle and all the cloudless skies of summer were reflected in his deep blue eyes—

'Huh?' she asked.

'Only,' he went on, 'if you're not frightfully busy I happen to know this really rather nice Sumatran restaurant where they do this really authentic . . .'

And not only the Prince. Skellidge was gazing at her like a lovesick traffic bollard, and Murdoch was respectfully pining away before her very eyes. Aaagh! she thought.

'Sorry,' she replied quickly. 'I'm, um, busy. I'm meeting someone. My, er, boyfriend. Well, when I say boyfriend, really I mean to say husband. He's a prince too, you know; or rather, more like a king. An emperor, actually. Sorry about that. Another time, perhaps.'

The Prince gave her a smouldering look down the side of his perfect nose. 'An emperor, huh?'

'That's right.'

'Anybody I'd have heard of? I know most of the emperors in these parts.'

Janice swallowed. 'Oh, he's not from round here,' she said, as casually as she could. 'Actually, our empire's ever such a long way away, in, um, Australia, but we're on a state visit, and there's this dreary old diplomatic function we've got to go to, so . . .'

'I see,' replied the Prince. 'In that case, I shall make a point of seeking out this emperor, putting him to the edge of the sword and claiming you for my own. Murdoch, mobilise the army. Skellidge, declare war on Australia. In fact,' he added, brightly, 'we could all save a lot of time, if I abducted you now and we did the fighting later. Would that be all right with you? It's just as well,' he added, 'that we've just finished upgrading our first strike capability, because that means my FT62s will have taken out Melbourne and Brisbane before we've finished our prawn cocktails. You do like prawn cocktails, I hope, only I've taken the liberty of ordering . . .'

'Hold it,' Janice said. 'Are you seriously telling me you'd bomb Australia and kill thousands of people just to get me?'

The Prince nodded. 'It's traditional,' he added. 'That's how a Prince shows he really cares. A declaration of war says more than flowers ever can.'

'Ah.'

'That's what all girls really want, you see. Well-known fact. Is this the face that launched a thousand bombs and burned the topless towers of Adelaide? That's psychology, you see. You need to know that sort of stuff when you hold the lives of millions in the palm of your hand.'

'I see.' Janice nodded slowly. 'You don't feel that killing thousands of people, as against the more usual bunch of flowers and box of chocolates, isn't maybe a bit . . . ?'

The Prince shook his head slowly. 'For beauty such as yours,' he said softly, 'what other tribute could there possibly be? You were born to be fought for—'

'You mean, like the Gaza Strip, sort of thing?'

'No,' snapped the Prince. 'Like Helen of Troy, except that you outshine Helen as the sun outshines the furthest star. And we've got to make sure that the body-count reflects that.'

'Right,' Janice said, walking slowly backwards. 'I hear what you say, but—'

'In fact,' whispered the Prince dreamily, 'on reflection I can't see that anything short of an all-out nuclear holocaust wouldn't be a positive insult. Murdoch, the smart missiles, quickly!'

As Murdoch bowed and produced an attaché case that opened to reveal a miniature control console with a shiny red button in the middle of it, Janice couldn't help wondering why the sheep on the hillside opposite were looking at her and rubbing their front hooves together.

CHAPTER TWELVE

Linda Lachuk opened her eyes.

So much, she reflected bitterly, for the ultimate scoop. At the precise moment when she connected with the live wire and felt a billion or so volts start to pump through her body, the thought uppermost in her mind had been that she was on the verge of getting the inside story on the biggest feature of them all; namely Death. *Hell*, she'd said to herself as she felt her heart stop beating, *if only there was some way to get my copy in, I'd die happy—*

And here she was, alive and apparently none the worse for wear, and she couldn't remember a thing about it. What, she wondered, had happened to her during that unquantified lost time? Had she died and gone to Heaven? Had she been chucked out of Heaven back down to Earth for pushing her way through the crowd of angels gathered round the celestial throne and demanding that God admit to his complicity in the Vaticangate scandal?

Hmmm—

Nah. Not without something like corroborative evidence. She'd probably be able to sell it to the California papers, but it wouldn't cut any ice in New York.

She sat up and looked about her; nothing but trees, rocks and the lake, lying flat on its back like a giant mirror.

Query; if you fall into a giant mirror, does that mean seven years' bad luck? If so, it would explain the rotten day she was having. So close, so very close to a story that'd guarantee her the Pulitzer Prize, and yet there was something she couldn't quite . . .

She stood up. Overhead, a thick wedge of ducks circled, watching her. A stream of bubbles a few yards from the shore showed the passage of an otter like a vapour trail. For a fleeting, treacherous moment, Linda wondered whether she mightn't have been better off right from the start if she'd gone into nature features instead of current affairs. From where she stood she could see yards, literally yards of potentially award-winning copy: waterfowl clowning adorably, small mammals furrily fornicating, butterflies doing whatever the hell it is butterflies do. Goddamnit, Linda thought bitterly, people get up and make cups of tea while a man stands talking into a lonely lens in the middle of some East European battle; but let someone go creeping up on a bunch of gorillas and the nation holds its breath. So what? Where the hell's the *story* in wildlife?

And then she noticed something.

The ducks weren't circling because she was there; it was the small party of men in faded green cotton shorts, wearing wide-brimmed hats with corks dangling from them, that had flushed them off the lake. And the string of bubbles wasn't an otter. It was a periscope.

Instinctively, Linda dropped to her knees, grinding her shin against a pointy rock as she did so. She didn't feel the pain; all Pain got was her answering machine, because she was far too preoccupied to take any notice. As carefully as she could, she crawled downhill towards the water's edge.

'G'day.'

Linda froze. Even the blood in her veins stood still.

'I said, G'day, miss. Where d'you want it?'

Slowly as a lazy glacier on its way to the dentist's, Linda turned her head. She was looking at a pair of plastic open-toed beach sandals. Raising her head a trifle, she could see a pair of brown hairy knees.

'Sorry?' she said.

'This flamin' block of stone,' the man said patiently. 'Where d'you want us to put it?'

'I . . . I'm not sure,' Linda stuttered. 'H-haven't made up my mm—'

The man gave her a long look, such as you'd use on a particularly stupid log. 'Tell you what,' he said. 'You just sign for it, here.' A clipboard moved down until it was on a level with her nose. 'Then we can be on our way, and you can put the ruddy thing wherever you want, soon as you've made your mind up. Got a pen?'

'Pen,' Linda repeated, trying to remember what a pen was. 'Oh, right, yes. Thank you, I have got a pen, yes.'

The man sighed. 'Then why don't you get it out and sign me flamin' chit? That's it, you got it. OK darlin', it's all yours. Careful with it, mind, it's all bombs and rockets and things inside.'

'What?' Linda shrieked; but the man wasn't there any more. In his place stood a huge concrete block, out of which were sticking nosecaps and tailfins and small areas of side panel with DANGER stencilled on them. As Linda crawled over to it, she noticed an envelope Sellotaped to the side; she ripped it open, unfolded the paper inside and read –

> *Delivery Note*
> *Express delivery FOB to St Peters, Rome*
> *Tractor spares*
> *For the personal attention of His Holiness Shane III*
> *Do not bend, drop or expose to naked flame*

– all underneath an official-looking crest with an eagle and E PLURIBUS UNUM involved in it. Linda folded the note carefully, as if it were God's signed confession, and tucked it away in her top pocket.

Tractor spares! Hah! That's what they always say!

Well now, she said to herself, running a hand down the side of the block just to make sure it was really real, you wanted hard evidence, here it is. Now there's just the problem of how the hell to get it back home and in front of a camera. Piece of cake? Well, not quite.

Indiana Jones, she mused, never seems to worry about this sort of thing; and neither does James Bond, or the guys in Westerns who discover wagonloads of Confederate gold buried in the heart of the desert. The camera fades out, and the next shot is either THE END or our hero snogging the girl in a gondola floating down the Canal Grande. There's a cinematic convention that allows you to assume that somehow or other the heavy lifting gets done, the treasure is all neatly packed up in tea-chests and shipped back home, without even a squeak out of the customs men. Getting back to civilisation from here *without* a twenty-ton concrete block was probably going to turn out to be a bigger adventure than anything Mister Bond ever did in his life; and even if she somehow succeeded in getting this infernal megalith out to the airport and onto the plane, the baggage handlers at New York would probably manage to send it to Fort Worth along with the rest of her luggage, the way they usually did.

Which was something of a nuisance, all told, bearing in mind that she was the only person standing between civilisation as we know it and global Armageddon.

A bit over the top? Not likely; because unless she could somehow get this evidence away, break the story and stop the shipments, there could only be one outcome. Because whatever His Holiness wanted with all this hardware, it wasn't to turbo-charge his Massey-Ferguson, and it wasn't to hang on the Vatican wall. So; newshound to the rescue. It crossed her mind that, for most of the time at least, Superman was also a journalist. Must sort of go with the territory.

She gazed up at the block. Portable it wasn't. Rather, it was the sort of thing the Pharaohs used to build pyramids with. Even in the centre of Queens you could leave it lying about in the street for ten minutes and be pretty sure it'd still be there when you got back.

This was going to call for some imaginative thinking.

She thought for a while. Her imagination, quicker than lightning and, as often as not, every bit as destructive, graunched into action. She had an idea.

She stood up and walked down the hill.

The men in hats were still hanging about, muttering among themselves. The periscope was now about eighteen inches above water level. The ducks had slung their collective hook, but a couple of whitetail deer were standing tentatively on the opposite side of the lake, watching and looking as if they were making up their minds to write to somebody about it. Enter Linda, walking briskly.

'Hey,' she called out, 'you.'

'*G'day.*'

'You guys,' Linda snapped, fiddling with the large bit of tree-bark she'd managed to make look something like a clipboard. 'Quit loafing about there, and help me get the stuff on to the sub.'

Two of the hatted men looked at each other. One of them shrugged, and spat into the water. It was at this point that Linda reached in her pocket and brought out money.

'Where's the stuff you want shifted?'

'Over there,' she replied. 'Careful with it, there's bombs and all sorts.' The money vanished from her hand as quickly and completely as the ham from your sandwich when the pub cat's taken a fancy to it, and a moment later the submarine had surfaced and the block was being winched aboard on a derrick. Although her face remained a mask of polite disinterest, deep in her heart Linda allowed herself a huge, smug grin. True, the money was everything she'd had; until she could get to a bank, she was as broke as a child's toy on Boxing Day. It was worth the risk, though; and besides, fairly soon, sums like that would be too small for her to comprehend.

'Is that the lot?' demanded one of the men in hats.

'That's it,' Linda replied. 'OK, then, I'll just—'

Before the words had cleared the gate of her teeth, the conning tower hatch slammed shut, and the submarine slid under the water with the speed and grace of a diving otter, until only a string of sparkling silver bubbles remained to suggest that it had ever been there.

'Hang on,' Linda shouted, bewildered. 'Wait for me!'

The cork-hats looked at each other. 'You wanted to go too, huh?' they said.

'Yes, of course I do,' Linda snarled, jumping up and

down on the spot. 'That's my evidence they've got in there.'

'You should have mentioned it,' observed the first cork-hat, reaching into a plastic coolbox and pulling out a can of beer. 'What a pity, eh?'

Linda stopped jumping for a moment and turned to him. 'Well, don't just sit there, you moron,' she yelled. 'Get on the radio and call them back.'

'Can't do that. Sorry. Against regulations.'

'The hell with – look, nobody'll know, couldn't you just—?'

The beer-drinker scratched the tip of his nose thoughtfully. 'Tell you what,' he said, 'for another three thousand—'

'I haven't got any more money, damnit,' Linda growled. 'I gave you every last penny—'

'Bloody cheapskate,' observed the cork-hat to his colleague sadly.

The colleague nodded, and stroked his beard. 'You wouldn't read about it,' he replied solemnly, as he retrieved a small yellow knob of chewing gum from the lining of his hat and began to chomp.

'Hey!'

The cork-hats stared at her blankly, shrugged and turned away. When Linda made further attempts to communicate they shooed her off with hand gestures and threw beer cans at her, a hint that even Linda felt she couldn't really ignore. Accordingly, she left, trailing her dreams like a bird with a broken wing.

Once she was safely out of earshot, the first Australian nudged his mate in the ribs with his elbow. 'Hey,' he said, 'how are we off for time? Actually, I got my Indian outfit on under this coat, so that's an extra minute or two.'

'So've I. Quick game of Goblins' Teeth?'

'Why not? Right then, nearest the nose to start.'

Linda meanwhile had reached the tree-line and carried on walking into the wood. She wasn't looking where she was going; understandably, because not only had she lost her evidence, she'd also arranged for the loading and despatch of enough thermo-nuclear weaponry to blow up the world three times over. It's times like these, she told herself, I almost wish I'd stayed on the fashion page.

And, because she wasn't looking where she was going, she didn't see the cunningly disguised tripwire that released the bent-over sapling to which was attached the length of wire, the looped end of which Linda had just put her foot in. There was a twang, and a moment later she was hanging three feet off the ground, upside down, with reporter's accessories falling out of her pockets like heavy snow.

Any suggestions?

No?

Very well, she told her brain, in the manner of a teacher announcing that unless someone owned up she'd keep the whole class in after school, I'll just have to hang here till someone lets me go. She dangled, therefore, with the blood pumping through her head, like a solitary spider caught in a web put up secretly by the local flies' co-operative. One good thing, though; it gave her time to think before scampering off after that goddamned submarine.

There was a war in there; all neatly done up and packaged like sandwiches in a Tupperware box, but a war nonetheless. And it was thanks to her it was on its way, rather than just sitting beside the lake minding its own business.

She had to stop it. It wasn't just that the human race was only a matter of hours away from Armageddon.

More to the point, that was her *story* in there.

First things first, however; there was the small matter of getting down out of this rope.

She considered her options and the resources available to her; which were? Difficult one, that. But, above all, she was a communicator, communicating was what she was good at. If she wanted out of here, it'd have to be a communication.

'*Help!*' she communicated.

'Hi,' said a voice below her. 'What're you doing up there?'

Linda opened her eyes. She'd been calling for so long that her voice had been sandpapered away, and most of the rest of her was so full of pins and needles that if only she could get down she'd be able to put all the haberdashery stores in the US out of business in a week.

'*Help*,' she whispered.

'Hey,' chimed the voice. 'Pleased to meet you, my name's Calvin Dieb.' Linda looked down and saw that Mr Dieb had stuck out a hand for a handshake.

'Can't move,' she moaned. 'Numb. Get me down.'

'Sure,' replied Mr Dieb. 'I'll need a ladder and maybe a knife or a pair of scissors. Haven't we met already?'

'Get me *down*.'

Mr Dieb nodded. 'No problem,' he said. 'A chair'll do if there's no ladder. You see, I just turned over a new leaf. Yessir, a whole new chapter's about to open in my life. From now on, I'm gonna change my attitude towards other people, especially people less fortunate than myself.'

'No chair. Please hurry. Going to—'

'No chair, huh? Pardon me asking, but how in blazes did you get yourself up there, anyhow?' Mr Dieb jumped a couple of times, reminding Linda of a small, yapping dog. 'Hey,' he said enthusiastically, 'maybe if I pull on this rope I could bend the tree down so you could – no, that's no good. I'd need someone else to hold the rope while I untie you, otherwise you'd just go *boing!* up in the air again. Still,' Mr Dieb continued, smiling cheerfully, 'there's gotta be a way, so if you'll just bear with me—'

Linda tried to move the pincushion that had once been her right arm; it was now so empty of blood, it would have served a vampire well as part of a rigorous calorie-controlled diet. 'Pull – rope,' she groaned, 'tie – to – tree.'

'Hah!' Mr Dieb tried to smother a giggle. 'Sorry, miss, I'm not laughing at you, don't do that kind of stuff anymore. You just reminded me of some red— Native Americans I ran into, is all. You sounded just like them, the way you were talking. Now, what was that you said? Pull on the rope and tie it to this tree here – hey, that's neat! Did I happen to mention I can see right up your skirt from here?'

Eventually, Linda hit the ground with a thump you could have felt through thick boots. Calvin Dieb got a substantial smack between the eyes from a branch of the sapling as it sprang back upright, but it didn't have much effect on his rate of speech or his born-again benevolence. Far from being annoyed, he blamed himself for being clumsy, and then helped Linda to her feet, nearly dislocating her shoulder in the process.

'Thanks,' she said, thereby proving that force of habit is the most durable thing on earth. 'Who are you, anyway?'

'Me? My name's Cal Dieb, I'm a lawyer.' The phrase, so automatic as to be faster than any conscious thought, seemed to jar on Calvin. He frowned. 'Well,' he said, 'up till now I've been a lawyer, but right at this moment I'm considering a change of direction in my life. You see, just lately – well, I won't bore you with all the pesky details, but I died, and now I'm just beginning to see how little I've really achieved in my life, you know, vis-à-vis making the world a better place. Actually, as far as I can see, not actively making the world a lousier place would probably be a giant leap forward for me in terms of personality development and realising my true potential as a human being, which I guess is why as of now I'm giving serious thought to doing something else, you know, feeding the poor and the sick and all. What do *you* think?'

'What do you know about the submarines?' Linda asked. As the words left her mouth, she wished she'd been really subtle and said it in an Australian accent, or Latin, just in case the guy replied in kind before he realised the implications. 'Are you with the Vatican?'

'Sorry?'

'The submarines,' Linda repeated. 'The big blocks of cement full of rockets. The Vatican.'

'The Vatican?'

She scrutinised Dieb's face closely, as if looking for secret microphones hidden among the hairs in his nose. 'You haven't seen any submarines?' she hazarded.

'Sorry.'

'Illegal arms shipments? Men in funny hats? Cool-boxes full of cans of beer?'

Dieb sighed. Here he was trying to help people, and his first effort was turning out to be a complete failure. 'I really wish I could be more help,' he said, with heartbreaking sincerity, 'but I guess the last thing you need is guys pretending to have seen submarines when they haven't, just because they think that's what you want to hear. Lawyers do that a lot, of course; you know, like, "Oh yeah, I think you've got some helluva case there," or, "No, I don't think it'll be all that expensive." Well, I'm through with all that from now on. When there's an unpalatable truth to be told, I'm just going to darned well out with it and tell it how it is. Like, really, what else is there in this life if to your own self you can't be true, huh? Don't you think so? Which is why, if I *do* decide to stay in the legal profession, I reckon I'm gonna start doing all that civil rights stuff, you know, oppressed minority groups and all? Take Native Americans, for example. You tell me, how many Native American judges are there in the whole of the City of New York?'

'Seventy-two,' Linda replied, remembering the figure from a feature she'd been working on. 'Sorry, how come we're talking about judges all of a sudden?'

Dieb hung his head. 'My fault,' he said. 'Sorry. There's me getting sidetracked when you're trying to ask me important questions. So I'll just shut up for a moment,' he said, settling himself comfortably against the trunk of a small rowan tree. 'Do please carry on with what you were saying.'

'What? Oh, er, right.' Linda wrinkled her nose, trying to remember. 'Illegal arms shipments,' she said. 'There was one here just a minute ago, but it went away. On a submarine.'

'I see.'

'I sent it, as a matter of fact.'

Dieb raised his eyebrows. 'Oh, I *see*,' he said, enlightened. 'You work for the Government.'

'No!' Linda replied angrily, 'I do *not* work for the Government, I just sort of accidentally got the arms loaded aboard the submarine.'

'By accident?'

'That's right.'

'Sort of an involuntary reflex action? Like Pavlov's dogs or something?'

Linda shook her head impatiently. 'I wanted to get the arms out of here so I could use them.'

'Really.' Dieb pursed his lips. 'How interesting.'

'As *evidence*,' Linda replied in exasperation. 'For the report I'm doing for the paper back home. You see, I'm a journalist.'

'Right,' Dieb said. 'So shipping arms is just a weekend job, then.'

'No, of course not. Like I told you, that was an accident. A mistake.'

Dieb smiled. It was an I-don't-believe-you-but-I-like-you-anyway smile, the sort you see a lot around mental hospitals. Rather a lot of Calvin Dieb's clients were familiar with that smile; the category of his clients whom you wouldn't believe if they told you the time while standing under the town clock. 'Ah well,' he said, 'don't suppose there's any harm done, so I wouldn't worry yourself about it if I were you.'

'Not *worry* about it!' Linda started to wave her arms about, as if she'd secretly always wanted to be a windmill but had never actually seen one. 'Jesus Christ, you fool, they're going to start *World War Three* with those weapons, and you say there's no harm done! We've got to stop them.'

'We've?'

'Well, who the hell else is there?' Linda stopped waving and flumped down on an anthill, her chin moodily cupped in her hands. 'Only, I don't see how we can. That submarine's probably halfway up Lake Erie by now.'

'Not unless it's really a salmon in disguise,' Calvin replied. 'For a start, there's an awful lot of waterfalls between here and the Lakes. Can't say as I can see how it's gonna get round them.'

'Waterfalls?'

Calvin nodded. 'That's places where the river kinda falls off a cliff, you know? Don't reckon as how the crew's going to be able to get out and carry a submarine down one of them. Can't see how you'd manage it even if you had a fleet of helicopters.'

Linda's face collapsed. It was as if she'd looked up at the sky and had it fall in her face. 'But that can't be right,' she said, 'or how did the damn thing get this far in the first place?'

'Don't know.' Dieb shrugged. 'Maybe they built the thing here on the lake. I seem to remember the Germans built ships on site to sail up and down big lakes in Africa.'

'But . . .' Linda watched as, in her mind's perfectly focused eye, little charred fragments of her theory rained down all around her, like the scene in a Western where the bank robbers have used too much dynamite to blow the safe, and suddenly it's snowing banknotes. 'But I *saw* the sonofabitch thing, here, not five minutes ago. With my own eyes. There's got to have been a submarine, really.'

'I believe you,' Calvin replied. 'All I'm saying is, it can't have got far.'

Linda nodded; as if, in the Western scenario cited above, she'd just managed to catch one ten-dollar bill. 'You mean,' she said, 'the submarine's just for getting the weapons as far as the first waterfall?'

'Could be. You never know, with the government and all.'

'And then,' Linda whispered hopefully, 'they transfer the actual arms to a helicopter or something for the rest of the journey.'

'It's possible,' Dieb replied. 'Hell, anything's *possible*.'

'There, you see?' Linda smote her fist into the palm of

her hand. 'So all we've got to do is find the first waterfall and there we are. We can intercept the shipment, capture it, and—'

'Yes?'

'I'm not sure,' Linda confessed. 'Still, we'll think of something.'

'You bet.'

'I mean,' she continued, 'we can cross that bridge when we come to it.'

'Of course.'

'And we mustn't count our chickens before they're hatched.'

'Goes without saying.'

'There's many a slip between cup and lip.'

'You said it.'

'Right, then,' Linda said, and she set her jaw in a determined line. 'Let's go, then.'

'With you all the way, honey.'

'Great.' Linda paused, and frowned. 'Er, which way?'

Calvin closed his eyes and pointed at random. 'How about over there?' he suggested.

'You positive about that?'

'If you want me to be, I am.'

'OK, then. That way it is.'

Grimly determined, icily calm, every fibre of his being dedicated to the mission he had embarked upon, Wesley stood on the top of a low rise and looked round.

'Um,' he said.

It was all very well setting out to kill a journalist. Nobody could find fault with the general principle. The mathematics are simple in the extreme: to find the optimum number of journalists that there ought to be in a perfect world, divide the actual number of journalists there are at the present time by itself, and subtract one. But Wesley's task was slightly harder, because he had to single out one particular journalist, and that of necessity involved finding her.

Not as easy as it sounds. Not, at least, in the environs of Lake Chicopee, where topography isn't a precise science. It's hard to do a systematic search of somewhere that keeps rearranging itself with every step you take. To put it another way: there's not enough timber in all the rain forests of South America to make enough paper for a 1:2500 scale map of the seven square miles immediately surrounding the lake.

When you're looking for someone in unfamiliar territory, the sensible course of action is, of course, to ask a local. That's what Wesley decided to do. And fortuitously, there was a party of locals just appearing over the skyline to his left.

'Excuse me,' Wesley said.

'Hello?'

'Sorry to bother you,' Wesley called out, 'but have you seen a journalist?'

The party came closer. It consisted of a man in exotic ermine-trimmed robes, two footmen in powdered wigs and—

Her!

'A journalist, did you say?' said the Prince. 'Might have done. Truth is, I wouldn't recognise one if I saw one. What's this feller look like?'

'Um,' Wesley replied. 'Actually, it's a she. Sort of—'

'Yes?'

'Um.' Wesley shrugged, made a vague gesture with his hands. 'Sort of, er, gorgeous. Well, gorgeousish,' he added, trying not to look at the girl. 'If you like 'em tall and blonde and . . .'

'Ah.' The Prince rubbed his chin thoughtfully. 'Murdoch,' he said to one of the footmen, 'have we seen anyone like that around here lately?'

'No, sir.'

'You sure about that, Murdoch?'

The footman inclined his head gravely. 'Entirely, sir. Your Majesty will recall that, since Your Majesty's subjects are all exceptionally comely and tall, such a person would scarcely be conspicuous. However, we have been checking all the female subjects we encounter with the slipper.'

'Yes, of course. Silly me. How about you, Skellidge?'

'I regret to have to inform His Majesty, no.'

The Prince clicked his tongue. 'Sorry,' he said. 'Was it important?'

Wesley shrugged. 'Not really. Well, quite important, actually. Rather a matter of life and death, in fact.'

'Oh.' The Prince half turned and addressed her. 'How about you, my dear?'

'Mm. Mmmmm. Mmmm mm mmm mmm.'

'I beg your—? Oh, quite. Skellidge, the gag.'

Wesley hadn't noticed the gag, or the ropes, or the handcuffs. Now he did; and it occurred to him that maybe she wasn't too happy about accompanying the party. He took an advance on next year's courage ration and cleared his throat. 'Excuse me,' he said.

'Yes?'

'Um, why's she all tied up?'

'To stop her escaping,' the Prince replied. 'When you say a matter of life and death . . .'

'Would you mind—?' Wesley took a deep breath, aware as he did so that he was doing something really rather brave and quite remarkably stupid. 'Would you mind letting her go, please? If it's no trouble, of course.'

'But my dear fellow.' The Prince gazed at him, utterly bemused. 'If I do that she might escape. I can't fight a war for her sake if she's not there, it'd rob the whole thing of any significance whatsoever.'

'A *war*?'

The Prince nodded. 'The finest gift a man can give,' he replied proudly. 'Like they always say, carnage is a girl's best friend. And think what an anticlimax it'd be without her.'

Wesley thought for a moment. Hitherto, his experience of dealing with dangerous lunatics had been extremely limited; one of those things he'd always suspected he'd been missing out on, no doubt. However, where there's a loon there's a way. 'But surely,' he said, 'you've missed the point. With all due respect,' he added quickly, as Skellidge took a step forward. 'I don't mean to be rude, but don't you think you've got it the wrong way round?'

The Prince began to look worried. 'Whatever can you mean?' he asked anxiously. 'This is very important. Murdoch, the tablets of stone, quickly.'

'Well,' Wesley said, as Murdoch produced a slab of granite and a cold chisel from the pockets of his tailcoat, 'take Helen of Troy, for instance.'

'Always a good place to start,' the Prince agreed. 'So?'

'Well then,' Wesley said. 'Just ask yourself; in the end, who won? Who got the girl? Was it the kidnappers, or the people she was kidnapped from?'

'I see what you mean,' the Prince said slowly. 'Do go on, this is probably very relevant.'

'Think about it,' Wesley urged. 'Which lot was it that launched the thousand ships? And which side would you rather be, more importantly? Remember, it's the side who wins that gets the glory.'

For a while there was silence, except for the sound of

steel on stone and a polite enquiry as to how you spell *importantly*. 'What you're saying is,' the Prince replied eventually, 'is that I'd do far better to let someone carry her off, and then fight the war to get her back. Is that it?'

'In a nutcase, sorry, nutshell, yes.' Wesley could feel moisture ooozing out of his pores, but decided it would be a tactical error to do anything about it. 'That way, you'd be right as well as romantic. You do see that, don't you?'

The Prince nodded. 'That only leaves the problem,' he added, 'of who's going to be mug enough to carry her off. Bearing in mind that he'd have to fight this amazingly destructive thermo-nuclear war shortly afterwards, I mean.'

'Thermo—'

'Absolutely,' the Prince said, his head bobbing like something hanging from a car mirror. 'Murdoch here's got seventy-five Pershing missiles trained on the major population centres right now, haven't you, Murdoch?'

'Of course, Your Majesty.'

'Oh.' Wesley hesitated. 'I see. And as soon as someone abducts the girl, you'll, um, press the—?'

'That's it,' said the Prince, smiling benignly. 'Our response time's really rather impressive, though I say it myself. Seventeen minutes and thirty-two seconds, and we could have most of Europe and the United States glowing so bright you could see them from Alpha Centauri. And that's just Phase One.'

'Gosh,' Wesley said. He looked at the girl out of the corner of his eye. True, she was ravishingly gorgeous, in a substantial sort of way. True, all he really wanted to do for the rest of his life was stand on one leg at a distance of twenty yards or so gazing adoringly at her. On the other hand; most of Europe and the United States . . . 'Well,' he said, 'I'm glad we've got that sorted out. And if I happen to bump into anybody who might be interested in abducting girls, I'll be sure to let them know.'

'Oh.' The Prince's face fell a little. 'Oh, I see. I'm dreadfully sorry, I'd sort of got the impression that you—'

'Me?' Wesley's nose twitched. 'Gosh, no, not *me*. I mean, usually I'd be only too happy, but I've got this journalist to find, matter of life and death, so . . .'

'Of course,' the Prince sighed. 'I quite understand. I'd better not keep you any longer, in that case. Much obliged to you, by the way, for clarifying that point about the war. Skellidge, make this chap a viscount or something.'

'Very good, Your Majesty.' Skellidge straightened his back a little and cleared his throat. 'You're a viscount,' he said. 'All hail.'

'Thank you,' Wesley said, walking backwards. 'Thank you ever so much. Well, must fly, 'Bye for now.'

The girl, who'd been painstakingly chewing through the gag all this time, chomped out the last few strands, spat and yelled out, 'Hey, come back!' just as Wesley disappeared over the rise and into the trees. However, since he didn't return, he couldn't have heard her.

CHAPTER THIRTEEN

The Proprietor began to stir.

He was, of course, fast asleep; but the images reflected on the still mirror of His mind were unquiet, and tiny ripples from the top side clouded His enormous dreams. He grunted, muttered, and stirred ever so slightly.

Then an image moved in His mind that really had no place being there; something which could never have got in there and certainly couldn't get out again. It was long and black and vaguely cigar-shaped, and it left a stream of bubbles behind as it slipped upwards out of existence.

The Proprietor didn't like it; not one bit. Having checked His memory, just to make sure He hadn't eaten a huge chunk of cheese shortly before He fell asleep, He came to a decision.

Damn, He thought.

'You sure it was this way?' Calvin Dieb enquired cheerfully. 'Only, it's at least an hour since we set off, and I'll swear I've passed that rock four times already. I remembered it particularly because it reminds me so much of my ex-wife's brother.'

Linda didn't reply. She was not, in truth, in the best of moods, and Calvin's blithe, carefree chatter was beginning to annoy her. She stopped, shaded her eyes with the palm of her hand and looked out over the lake.

'Hey!' she yelled. 'Over there!'

'Yes?'

'Look!' She jumped up and down five times. 'It's the submarine. Look, you can see its periscope, just breaking the . . .'

'Where? I can't see . . .'

'Where I'm pointing. Oh, come on, you dimwit, it's as plain as the nose on your face. Just there, where those ducks are swimming round.'

'What?' Dieb squinted. 'Oh yes. Well, I can see *something*, anyway. You sure it's not the Loch Ness Monster? I mean, you're always hearing reports of people seeing what they think are remarkable things, such as submarines, and they turn out just to be something mundane and ordinary, like sea-monsters.'

In spite of her excitement, Linda frowned. 'Mundane and ordinary? The Loch Ness Monster?'

'I reckon so,' Calvin replied. 'At any rate, it's a sight more mundane and ordinary than submarines that can shin up waterfalls. Which is probably just as well, don't you think?'

Linda left that remark well alone, and resumed her excited staring. She was so preoccupied, in fact, that it was quite a while before she noticed that there was someone standing beside her.

Four people, in fact; a man in peculiar clothes, something like a fur-trimmed dressing gown, two other men with powdered wigs on their heads, and the ugly girl she'd bumped into earlier.

Something about legs like pink elephant's trunks . . . No, she couldn't quite remember. Nevertheless, she had the feeling she didn't like the ugly girl. Call it a hunch; and hunches don't just materialise, you pay for them with hard-earned experience. No such thing as a free hunch.

'Excuse me,' said the man in the dressing-gown, 'but are you by any chance a journeyman?'

'Journalist, Your Majesty.'

'Sorry, a journalist? Only I gather there's one running around loose in these parts, and . . .'

Linda looked at him. 'Yes,' she said, 'I'm Linda Lachuk, current affairs correspondent of the *New York Globe*. Tell me, does that thing over there look like a submarine to you?'

The Prince nodded. 'I should say,' he replied, with a hint of pride. 'As a matter of fact, I know darned well it's a submarine.'

'You do?'

The Prince inclined his head. 'I should do,' he said, 'it's one of mine. Murdoch, the Aldis lamp.'

Linda's jaw fell like a drawbridge. 'One of *yours*?' she gasped. 'But that's crazy. I mean, you're not the President of the United States.'

'Very true. Actually, that's probably the nicest thing anybody's ever said about me. Thank you.'

'And you're not the Pope, either.'

The Prince's brow clouded slightly. 'True,' he replied. 'And, no disrespect for my Brother in Christ intended, but I can't really see what His Holiness'd be wanting with a submarine, what with his dominions being some way inland and all. He's got the Tiber, I suppose, but that's so polluted these days, the average nuclear submarine'd probably dissolve in it like an aspirin.'

'Right,' Linda replied, taking another good look at the Prince out of the corner of her eye. 'In that case, who the hell are you?'

'Me?' the Prince grinned pleasantly. 'I'm Prince Charming, of course. Why, didn't you recognise me?'

'Prince . . .'

The Prince nodded. 'Actually,' he said, 'don't be misled by the Prince bit, I'm actually the head of state. And yes, that's one of my submarines. The *Bloodspite*, actually, ex-Soviet navy, picked it up for a song at the liquidators' auction. One of the reactors is a bit dicky, but it's fine for just pottering about in. By the way, would you mind awfully if I were to ask you your shoe size?'

While he was saying this, the footman called Murdoch was flashing merrily away with the signalling lamp, and a succession of rapid blips of light appeared on the surface of the distant waters, presumably by way of reply. The Prince, meanwhile, had strolled over to where Calvin Dieb was sitting on a rock.

'Hello,' he said.

For a moment the new Calvin Dieb, friend to all humankind, flickered like a flame in a breeze. Basic survival instincts whispered things in his mind's ear about strange men in peculiar fur-trimmed outfits who sidle up to you and say, 'Hello.' The moment of apprehension passed, however, as soon as the Prince spoke again.

''Scuse my asking,' he said, in a pleasant sort of chummy drawl, 'but you wouldn't by any chance be interested in abducting women, would you?'

Calvin looked at him. An entirely different set of survival instincts took their places on the bridge of his mind, kicked their shoes off and switched on their work-stations. 'Pardon me?' he said.

'You *are* an American, aren't you?' the Prince went on, as if checking on an important detail he'd forgotten to clarify at the start.

'Why, yes,' Calvin replied. 'Though I should point out that abducting women isn't really part of the American heritage. Perhaps you were thinking of the Romans, or Vikings, maybe. We generally find we have more than enough of our own without stealing other people's.'

The Prince nodded. 'Fair enough,' he said. 'Only, you see, I need a whatchamacallit, *casus belli*. That's what diplomats say when they mean something to declare war about.'

Calvin looked at the Prince long and hard; and the old Calvin Dieb peered longingly through the bars of his cage and thought what a wonderful client this guy would have made – obviously rich, obviously deranged, obviously not too bright into the bargain. Legal dynasties have been built on such clients.

'You see,' the Prince went on, 'I've got this girl, you see, and she's so utterly, utterly gorgeous I feel I've got to fight the biggest and best war ever for her sake, just to tell the world how absolutely smashing she is, you know, but I can't do that unless someone abducts her, now can I? And so I thought, you being an American and America being such a big, powerful country . . .'

Calvin swallowed something that had suddenly appeared in his throat. 'You want to declare war on the USA?' he said.

'Well, it's a start,' said the Prince. 'It's always been my dream, you see, ever since I was just a kid; you know, to meet this wonderful, wonderful girl and fight for her sake, like the knights of old. And now, suddenly, here she is, and nobody to fight with. So darned frustrating, don't you know?'

'Excuse me,' Calvin asked quietly. 'Did you happen to, um, fall in a lake recently?'

The Prince frowned. 'Why, yes, as it happens I did. How did you know that?'

'Oh, blind guess.' Calvin thought for a moment; and the refrain was, in spite of his very best endeavours, *Well, why not?* After all, what possible harm could there be in turning his special skill, hitherto only practised to the detriment of his fellow creatures, to the service of the human race? To save them, in fact, from the prospect of universal extinction? And maybe make a buck along the way, no harm in that, the labourer is worthy of his hire. 'Excuse me,' he said, 'but let me put a suggestion to you and see if this makes any kinda sense. When you say war—'

'Yes?'

'Well,' Calvin went on, taking a deep breath, 'I know you say you've got your heart set on an actual shooting war, but has it perhaps occurred to you that a really prolonged and destructive lawsuit might not have the same effect, in the long run? You know, in terms of grand-scale expenditure of resources, pain, suffering and trauma inflicted, lives torn apart, national economies bankrupted, all the things you tend to associate with wars, but in a rather more controlled and civilised framework? Think about it,' he urged, observing the Prince's brow furrow. 'Maybe you remember a few years back there was all that hype about a new bomb that wipes out human life but leaves the real estate unscathed? Well, it's here and it's now and we call it litigation; and as Head of State, don't you owe it to your realm to have the very best? Huh? Am I right or am I right?'

The Prince's lips moved silently for a moment. 'You're saying,' he said slowly, 'instead of having a war over the girl, why not go to law about her instead?' His face clouded. 'All due respect, old thing, I'm not so sure about that. I mean, going to court, it's all a bit middle-class, isn't it?'

'Middle-class?' Calvin's face reflected the magnitude of the blasphemy. 'Going to law *middle-class*? Excuse me, Your Majesty, but have you any idea how much going to law costs these days? I mean, forget your yachts and your palaces and your private jets and all. If you want to talk about the ultimate status symbol, the kinda thing only the huge corporations and the divinely wealthy individuals can even dream of affording, look no further, 'cos what *you* need is a lawsuit. Damnit,' he went on, warming to the theme, 'any miserable little country can have a *war*. Bosnia can have a *war*. Only the serious players can afford serious lawfare. In fact,' he added, seeing in his mind's eye the twitch on the float that suggests that the fish is nibbling, 'before I'd agree to act for you I'd need to see some serious credentials from your banks.'

The Prince looked at him. 'You would?'

Calvin nodded. 'Definitely. And the audited gross national product figures for the last ten years. Sorry, but these days you gotta be businesslike.'

'Oh, quite.' The Prince nodded. 'I take your point entirely. Murdoch, the bank statements.'

Which is how, alone and unaided, Calvin Dieb very nearly saved the world. Unfortunately, while he'd been chatting up the Prince, Linda had been asking Janice whether she'd happened to notice any men in funny hats; and she'd replied that although she hadn't seen any men in funny hats, this was probably because she'd been captured and tied up and blindfolded at the time when the men in funny hats may well have been in evidence; whereupon Linda had asked whether, when she said tied up and held captive, she'd meant held captive like, say, a hostage; and she'd said, Well, yes, she supposed so; and Linda had suddenly realised that single-handedly rescuing the hostages and getting them home for Christmas would not only prevent the War but make the best possible finale to her story; and so she'd said, 'Skellidge, the sharp knife,' and Skellidge had handed her a sharp knife, and she'd cut the ropes and grabbed Janice by the wrist and said 'This way!'; and the Prince, observing all this, had asked Calvin which country Linda came from; and Calvin had replied that he was fairly sure she was American; and the Prince had smiled and said, 'Splendid, splendid. Murdoch, the button—'

And Murdoch had said 'Yes, Your Maj—' and then fallen silent and gone red.

'Murdoch?'

'I regret to say,' Murdoch replied painfully, 'that someone would appear to have stolen the button.'

'What?'

'The fire control button, Your Majesty. Colloquially referred to as the Doomsday—'

'Yes, I know all that,' replied the Prince impatiently. 'How do you mean, *stolen*—?'

'What is it, Hat?' Talks to Squirrels demanded, as the small and secret entrepreneur scratched his head and stared at his latest prize. 'Looks like some sort of briefcase.'

Hat shrugged his shoulders. 'Haven't the faintest idea,' he replied. 'Don't know why I bothered pinching it, to be honest with you.'

Talks considered for a moment. 'Because it wasn't

spot-welded to the ground, Hat?' he hazarded.

'Ah yes, that was the reason.' Hat prodded the catches tentatively, recalling the time he'd swiped a similar case from someone who daydreamed of being Agent 006. Occasionally, in the cold weather, he felt it still. 'One of these damned combination locks,' he observed mournfully. 'Last one of these I got took us twenty years of trying different combinations before we got it open. And you know what was inside? Sandwiches. Or rather,' he added, 'a place where sandwiches had once been, a long time previously. Still, we might get lucky this time.'

Talks shrugged. 'Why not just bust it open?' he suggested. 'All it'd take would be a tomahawk spike behind the hinges there, and . . .'

Hat scowled. 'True,' he said, 'but that might just shave a few cents off the resale value, don't you think? No,' he went on, 'I guess I'll just have to be patient and keep plugging and plugging away . . .'

He pressed both catches at once, and the lid flew open. 'Hell,' he said disgustedly, 'it's empty.'

'No it's not,' Talks pointed out. 'There's things built into it. What're they, Hat? That red thing, and all the flashing lights?'

'I'm not sure,' Hat replied, fiddling. 'Could be a portable fax, or a laptop PC, or a photocopier. I guess this red button's the on/off switch.'

'Only one way to find out, Hat.'

'True.' Hat peered more closely. 'Only it does say DANGER in big stencilled letters. Do you think—?'

'Nah, that's just public liability stuff, their lawyers make them put that in just in case it gets hit by lightning while you're using it. You don't want to worry about things that say DANGER.'

'You don't?'

'Well, I don't. Mind you, I'm dead already, so I worry about very little.'

Hat nodded. 'All right, then,' he said. 'You press it.'

With a sad smile Talks With Squirrels put his ghostly hand right through the keyboard. 'Love to,' he said wistfully. 'But I can't. Sorry.'

'Fair enough. You're sure it'll be all right?'

'Of course. Trust me.'

'Trust me, I'm a dead Indian?'

Talks wrinkled his nose. 'Be like that,' he said. 'Would you trust me any better if I was alive?'

'Well, no. Less, actually.'

'There you are, then. Press the button.'

'I'm not sure . . .'

'Could be a CD player,' Talks said, his nose an inch or so from the button. 'Worth a buck or two, they are.'

Hat inclined his head. It looked safe enough; no wires, no leads, it must just run on batteries. Even if he did get an electric shock, the chances were it'd be so slight he'd hardly even notice it. 'The hell with it,' he said. 'Why not?'

'Go on, then.'

'You're *sure* it's safe?'

'How the hell could just pressing a button be dangerous? Gee, but you have one hell of a vivid imagination.'

Captain Hat bowed his head. 'Sorry,' he said. 'I was being silly. All right, then, here goes.'

He pressed the button.

And—

Beside His bed, the Proprietor's alarm clock started to scream.

★

And Wesley, who'd been running as fast as he could down the slope in the vague hope of getting to Hat before he pressed the button, put his foot behind a tangle of bramble, landed on his nose, said 'Ung!', scrambled to his feet, launched himself again, slipped athletically in a patch of mud and did the rest of the distance, quickly but with a minimum of dignity, tobogganing on his backside. He arrived just in time to slither straight through Talks to Squirrels (who nearly jumped out of his skin, but still recovered his composure in time to put three consecutive arrows in the back of his head in the space of four seconds; not bad for offhand shooting at a moving target) and land on top of Captain Hat, sending the briefcase flying.

A second and a half earlier, and he'd have been in time.

He was just propping himself up on his elbows and wondering (a) where the little bloke with the button had got to and (b) what the small, squishy, squirming thing he was lying on might be, when a fast-moving procession appeared over the skyline. It was led by Linda and Janice, running with more enthusiasm than wisdom straight for the bramble-patch. Seventy yards or so behind them came Calvin Dieb and the Prince, anybody's race with a hundred yards still to go, and Murdoch and Skellidge making quite reasonable time at a sort of stately canter.

All a bit pointless now, Wesley reflected; unless, of course, the Prince had some way of stopping the bombs his button had presumably launched. But he wouldn't *want* to, would he, any more than a bullet would suddenly decide to change course and go round rather than through you. Pity, that.

Even though he wasn't feeling at his blithest and best, he couldn't help smiling just a bit when Linda and Janice caught their feet in exactly the same brambles, did exactly the same little dance and arrived beside him in exactly the same way. He'd remembered thinking while he'd been bum-sliding down that self-same slope, 'I bet this'd be very funny to watch,' and this time he had the satisfaction of being the audience.

He'd been right. It was hilarious; more so, he guessed, with two of them doing it. Ah, well; last orders for humour at the bar, please, ladies and gentlemen.

'Hello,' he said. 'It's too late.'

'Huh?' Janice, who'd come to an abrupt halt on and around his legs, raised her head and looked at him as if he'd just turned himself into a strawberry flapjack. 'Too late for what?'

'Everything,' Wesley replied sadly, as the rest of the cast (who'd managed to avoid the brambles and the mud; spoilsports, the lot of 'em) came panting up. 'This little pillock I'm lying on pressed the button.'

'What button?'

'Never mind. Doesn't matter. Forget I spoke.' Wesley stood up, apologised politely to Captain Hat, smiled politely at everybody else present and wandered away to throw stones in the lake. Or at it, rather, since he had a shrewd notion that everything was somehow the lake's fault anyway.

'Who was that?' Linda demanded, and although she didn't actually add out loud that the public had a right to know, her tone of voice implied it. 'And what's this button?'

Calvin Dieb cleared his throat. 'Something you obviously didn't know about,' he said. 'A shame, really. You see, His Royal Whatever here wants to blow up the world, all in the name of pure, true love of course, so it's OK really, or at any rate it makes a refreshing change

from politics; and the deal was, if he could find someone
to kidnap the, um, I'm sorry, I didn't quite catch the
name, Ms—?'

'DeWeese,' Janice said. 'Janice DeWeese.'

'Very pleased to know you, if only temporarily. Anyhow, you kidnapped Ms Deweese—'

'I did not,' Linda objected. 'I rescued her. Didn't I?'

'Arguably,' Janice said.

Calvin held up a hand for silence. 'The way His
Majesty saw it, you kidnapped her. And so his buddy in
the wig and the fancy dress produced the good old
doomsday button – that's it there, on the ground. And it
seems like this small person here—'

'Hat,' said Hat.

'Gesundheit. This small guy appears to have walked
off with it and, um, pressed it. Which means, I guess,
we're all going to—'

'*Hey!*' Janice objected. 'Don't talk crazy, Mister
whoever-you-are.' She stopped, and squinted. 'Just a
minute, aren't you that goddamn bird?'

Calvin nodded. 'I was,' he admitted, 'but I guess I
grew out of it.'

Janice decided not to pursue that. 'Whatever,' she
said. 'Still doesn't mean that button's actually going to
blow up the world. It's not like any of this is *real*, for
Chrissakes.'

'Who is this broad?' Talks to Squirrels demanded
loudly, shooting Janice in the ear. 'And where does she
get off saying we're not real?'

'But you're not,' Janice replied. 'And please have the
good manners not to shoot people when they're talking
to you.'

Talks shrugged. 'Does it matter?' he replied. 'After all,
any minute now you're all just gonna be black outlines

and puffs of smoke, which'll make shooting you even more pointless than it already is. I figure I might as well enjoy myself while I can.'

'But it's all just an illusion,' Janice protested loudly. 'Nothing really *happens* here. Even the people who get blown up get put back together again. It's just symbolism and stuff. Nobody's actually gonna *die*, are they?'

Calvin raised both eyebrows. 'One thing's for sure,' he said pleasantly. 'In about ten minutes or so from now, we'll all know the definite answer. And in the meantime,' he added, 'I don't see as there's a hell of a lot we can do about it. I suggest we all stop fussing about it and relax. You know, go with it. Be as one with the holocaust.'

There was a brief silence, broken only by Skellidge discreetly tapping Talks To Squirrels on the shoulder, clearing his throat head-waiter style and murmuring, 'Excuse me, sir, but do you have a reservation?'

'Just a moment.' This time it was Linda; and shortly afterwards there was a fine old debate going on, with Janice proposing the motion that it was all some kind of dream, Calvin being aggravatingly well adjusted about everything, Linda writing things down on her shirt-cuff to be used in evidence, the Prince nodding agreement with everyone in the intervals of looking up at the sky and then down at his watch, Talks to Squirrels shooting people and Captain Hat quietly examining the contents of their pockets for items of value. For his part, Wesley carried on throwing stones until he hadn't got any more stones to throw; at which point, he turned to the nearer of the two footmen and coughed.

''Scuse me.'

'Sir?'

'Which one are you?'

The footman thought for a moment. 'I, sir, am Murdoch.'

'Fine.' Wesley smiled pleasantly. 'Murdoch, the stones.'

'Certainly, sir. The sandstone or the flint?'

'Oh, let's make it the flint, shall we? It isn't every day the world gets blown up.'

Murdoch raised an eyebrow. 'Blown up, sir?' he enquired.

Wesley nodded. 'That's what that button thing was for, wasn't it?'

'No, sir,' Murdoch replied, bending at the waist as he produced a large, satin-lined box full of the finest selected Brandon flints. 'Certainly not, sir. That would be most injudicious, if I might say so.'

'Ah.' Wesley reached out for a flint, and paused. 'Which one's the coffee cream, then?'

'Sir?'

'A joke. Forget it.' He frowned. 'So the world *isn't* going to get blown up, then?'

'No, sir. You should be so lucky, sir.'

'Ah.' There was one particularly fine flat-bottomed flint near the left-hand edge, and Wesley picked it out. 'You mean, something worse?'

'Something bigger, sir. Will that be all?'

Wesley nodded; then he drew back his arm and let fly. The stone spun from his hand, hit the surface of the lake and bounced, the way flat stones do unless they happen to have politicians living under them. It seemed to bounce for ever such a long time, and Wesley (who'd never managed to get a stone to skip more than twice before) watched it until it was nearly out of sight; at which point, it changed into a mallard drake and made a perfect landing out near the middle of the lake. Then he saw something else.

'Murdoch.'

'Sir?'

'What's that funny-looking greyish brown splodge?'

'Sir?'

Wesley pointed. 'On the hillside there, between the trees. It looks like someone's just poured gravy over the top of the hill.'

'No, sir. That would be the lemmings.'

'Ah.' Wesley double-checked his mental file, just in case there was something obvious he hadn't taken on board. 'Lemmings,' he repeated.

'Indeed, sir. The Doomsday lemmings, to be precise.'

'Right,' said Wesley, 'got you. Thanks a lot.'

'Sir.'

'Murdoch.'

'Sir?'

Wesley rubbed his chin, and said, 'Excuse me if this sounds a bit feeble, but I'm from England, and we don't actually have Doomsday lemmings there. Could you just sort of explain? A bit?'

Murdoch's lips twitched into a thin smile. 'Certainly, sir,' he said. 'You are aware, I take it, of the tradition that holds that all lemmings have a death wish, in pursuance of which they leap off cliffs into the waters below?'

Wesley nodded. 'There's a computer game, in fact, where you have to . . . Sorry, please go on.'

'And,' Murdoch continued austerely, 'you will be aware by now that to jump into this lake is to have your wish come true?'

'Yup.'

Murdoch turned and pointed at the grey tide washing over the bluffs into the lake, like beans in sauce slopping out of the tin. 'Their wish is about to come universally true, sir. Hence the expression, Doomsday lemmings.'

'Ah. Right. Sorry I asked.'

'My pleasure, sir.'

Wesley propped his chin on his hands and decided to sulk. After all; buttons to blow up the world; Doomsday lemmings; all these people who'd been cropping up all over the place, sometimes real and sometimes not.

It was time, he said to himself, that someone sorted it all out.

Yeah, well. When, looking back over the history of the planet, wasn't it? But nothing ever was, not in real life. Confusion and chaos crash down from the high points of the past, spitting foam and spray; but they hit the surface of the present, and everything evens out into one flat, calm mirror. Nothing is solved or explained, but after long enough none of it matters. The worst part was that he'd come here deliberately.

He studied the lake, and the ridge of the mountains encircling it like someone curled up on his side, asleep under an eiderdown of trees. He'd long since given up trying to find his bearings; it was never the same twice, although he hadn't actually seen the mountains move or the trees being herded like sheep to another position. By way of experiment, he closed his eyes and opened them again; sure enough, the whole landscape was different when you looked closely. Where there had been a cliff – the one the lemmings had been jumping over – there was now a sparsely wooded incline running right down to the lake's edge. Where a rocky outcrop had stood a moment ago, there was now a low knoll crowned by a clump of thin, straggly fir trees. This is all a picture, he realised, in the mind of someone with an unreliable memory or a slapdash attitude towards continuity. Someone who doesn't think backgrounds really matter very much. Like me, for example.

Figures.

306 • Tom Holt

'Pretty, isn't it?' He looked round to see Calvin Dieb sitting beside him. 'Hey, you can just see my car from here.'

Wesley looked hard. 'You can?'

Dieb nodded. 'Well, not the actual car. You can just see the sun glinting on the windshield.'

'A reflection, you mean?'

'Yeah, a reflection. And don't bother saying it,' Dieb added with a grin, '''cos I'm way ahead of you. I realised. There is no car, only a reflection.'

Wesley didn't reply. The duck that had been his stone was still there, but it wasn't doing anything of note, even though it was now an otter. 'What do you think is going to happen?' he asked.

'Happen?' Dieb shrugged. 'Search me, pal. Does it matter?'

'Well, yes.' Wesley found a stone that hadn't been there a moment ago, a round pebble shaped like a duck's egg, and lobbed it smoothly into the water. It hit the surface and skimmed away out of sight. 'Even if it is all imagination, like whatsername says. I mean, if I believe it's happening, then surely it is. To me, I mean.'

'Maybe.' Calvin's shoulders rose and fell. 'I used to believe my life was happening to me, so what do I know? I used to think I was the big lawyer all American mothers want their kids to be. I used to think I had money and power and a superior intellect, which made it all right for me to do the things I did. I used to think my ex-wife didn't understand me. I used to think my Dad understood why I never called home. I even used to think I had a set of keys for my car. Only goes to show, huh?'

'But you did.'

Calvin nodded. 'That's the worst kind of fantasy,' he said, 'the kind that's true. And before you ask, yes, I missed the Sixties too.'

'Um.' Wesley shifted an inch or so away, trying not to be too obvious about it. 'So you're going to chuck in the lawyering, are you? When you get back, I mean?'

Dieb looked at him as if he'd just offered him a dollar fifty for his soul. 'Chuck in the law?' he repeated. 'Hell, no. Why the hell would I want to do that, for God's sake?'

'But I thought . . .' Wesley groped for words in the lining of his mind's pocket. 'All this revelation and seeing the light stuff. I thought you meant you'd, oh, I don't know, decided to turn over a new leaf, live a nobler and more fulfilling life, that sort of—'

'Kid.' Dieb looked at him as if from a long way away. 'Just because I've finally realised what a shitty person I've been all these years doesn't make me want to stop being *me*. It just means I can stop feeling guilty, is all. I mean, if I'd discovered that deep down I was a really nice guy, caring and considerate and concerned about people, then I'd be worried sick. No way would you get me back in that office, not even if you called out the National Guard with firehoses.' He smiled. 'But I ain't. I'm a jerk. But now I can feel *good* about being a jerk. That's why I feel – well, kind of at peace, I guess. And you know, I suppose that's all I ever wanted. Deep down, I mean. How about you?'

Wesley shrugged. 'Oh, that's easy,' he said. 'I always wanted it to be like this. You know, magic and adventure and nothing really being what it seems. Which proves that you can be a really substantial idiot for a quarter of a century and never even know it.'

'Ah,' Dieb nodded. 'But do you feel at peace now you know you're an idiot?'

'No.'

'Oh, well. Whatever's right, I guess.' Calvin glanced down at his watch. 'A quarter of an hour, the prince guy said. If it's gonna happen, it ought to be roughly now.'

'Ah. That's . . .'

'Yes, isn't it?'

And it was.

It began with a slight nodding of the heads of the tall trees that stood on the crest of the hills at the north end of the lake. They nodded reluctantly and with an ill grace, as if they'd just lost an argument and were being forced to agree with their opponents' views. As they swayed, birds left them in prodigious quantities, until the sky seemed full of them.

Next, the shape of the hills themselves began to change. Earlier, those same hills had reminded Wesley strongly of a sleeping man lying on his side; the long, low slope to the west being the line gradually ascending from the feet to the rounded prominence of the hip; a valley where the line falls from the hip-bone to the slimmest part of the waist; another long, steadily climbing gradient to the highest point at the shoulder; another valley falling away to the level of the neck; another, steeper increment to the summit of the head on the far eastern side of the lake, and finally a sharp drop almost to the level of the water. Now, as the two men stared at the skyline, the mountains seemed to –

– Swivel, as the peaks of hip and shoulder dropped down –

– And rise, as shoulder and head lifted up, propped on one arm –

– And the knees bend, bringing the feet round –

– And then He lifts His torso from the waist and sits up, stretches His arms up until they're lost to the elbow in the clouds too high to disturb the uniform blue of the sky. And He yawns –

– Filling the amphitheatre of the lake with sound, and rubs His hands into the sockets of his eyes, grinding away undergrowth and scrub and topsoil. He blinks, and yawns again, and stretches out His hands towards the surface of the lake, groping, as if He can't see –

– Without His spectacles. He's bigger now, of course; every moment He seems to become larger and larger, although He doesn't actually grow. He stays the same size, but where you're standing looking at Him becomes steadily further and further away. So; now He's big enough for the perspective to make sense, He picks up the surface of the lake and screws it into His eye, like Bertie Wooster's monocle.

'Grrnghzhgr,' He says, and yawns again.

He peers round, looking for His slippers. He sees them, brushes snow and cloud off the high points of the uppers, and jams His feet into them, treading down the backs.

The mountain has woken up, and wants His coffee.

CHAPTER FOURTEEN

'Yup,' said the squirrel, her cheeks full of part-masticated nut, 'that's him. The boss. Be careful how you talk to him, he can be a bit grumpy when he's just woken up.'

'The boss,' Wesley repeated, as his mind tried to make sense of the sheer size of what he was looking at. 'You mean like – well, God or somebody?'

'God?' The squirrel nearly choked on its chewed nut. 'Hell, no. He's just the boss, is all. The Proprietor. The guy who owns this valley.'

'Ah.'

The Proprietor was standing upright now, and where the lake had been was an irrelevant emptiness filled with His shadow. The mountains were gone too, presumably; except that you couldn't see the space where they'd been because the Proprietor was in the way. He filled all available space, in the way light and air and water tend to do.

'You sure he's not God?' Wesley hazarded. 'There's a

sort of family likeness, maybe something in the line of the jaw . . .'

'Nah,' the squirrel replied cheerfully, dropping nut-shell crumbs on Wesley's head. 'He's just – tall.'

'Bet he has trouble buying shoes,' Calvin muttered.

'He can afford to have them specially made,' the squirrel replied. 'Believe me.'

Wesley looked down; he was feeling dizzy. 'What's he doing now?' he asked.

'Not much,' the squirrel said. 'Trying to remember what century this is, probably. Like I said, he's not at his best first thing.'

'Just a moment,' said Janice, shading her eyes with the palm of her hand. 'If he's the guy who owns all this, who're you?'

'Me?' The squirrel lifted her head, ran round the bole of the tree three times and came to a halt, standing at ninety degrees to the ground with her nose pointed downwards. 'I just run this place for him.'

'You're the manager?'

'That's right,' the squirrel said. 'He finds it easier that way. You see, it can be awkward when you're a giant, relating to people and all. They tend to feel a tad over-awed, you know? But I can be anybody or anything I choose to be, so it's not a problem for me. Nowadays, he stays out of things right up till the end.'

'The end?' Calvin looked at her. 'Excuse me for nit-picking, but that's an ambiguous phrase. Is that end as in goodbye, world or end as in school's out?'

The squirrel shrugged, sending a ripple running from her shoulders to the tip of her bushy tail. 'You disappoint me,' she said wearily. 'Sorry, but you do. I thought you'd understand about perspective and scale by now, specially since you've seen the giant. Most people get the hang of perspective after they've been looking at him for a minute or so.'

'Pardon me for breathing,' Calvin muttered. The squirrel ignored him.

'The point is,' she said, 'what it's the end of depends on where you're looking from. Don't you see? If you were standing on the edge of the lake looking into it, what'd you see?'

'Water,' Calvin said. 'Pondweed. Maybe ducks. Sorry, was that the wrong answer?'

'You'd see,' the squirrel said, her tail twitching, 'your reflection. OK so far? Very good. You'd see this guy standing beside the lake, and behind him lots of trees and mountains and stuff, but they'd all be very small and far away. They'd look like they were all much smaller than the guy – that's you, of course; or else they'd be the normal size for trees and mountains, but the guy would be huge. Like a giant. You follow?'

Wesley nodded but Calvin shook his head. 'Sorry,' he said, 'but I don't reckon it'd stand up in court. I'd know the scenery was really bigger than me, 'cos it'd just be an optical effect. A trick; you know, like a figure of speech or something, like you use to make things seem other than they are. I know about these things, I'm a lawyer.'

The squirrel rubbed her nose with her paws and spat out a piece of walnut shrapnel. 'Yes,' she said, 'you probably are, at that. Still, we don't claim to succeed in every case. Fortunately, it's not us that have to live with the consequences.' She twitched her whiskers, changed into a beautiful girl and landed beside Wesley. 'Ow,' she said, 'my ankle.'

'Hey.' It was Linda this time, emerging from some reverie of her own, admittance by ticket only. 'That's no damn use. How'm I supposed to get that into a camera lens?'

'You could try standing back,' the girl said. 'But I wouldn't bother if I were you. Nobody'd believe it wasn't faked.'

Linda scowled horribly. 'Then where's the fuckin' *point*? What earthly good to me is something like this if nobody's going to believe it? I'd be the laughing stock of the profession.'

'That's interesting,' the giant said; and the force of His voice hitting them was like the great wind that blew Dorothy clean out of Kansas. 'The journalist believes it herself, doesn't she?'

'Sure,' Linda replied, hands on hips. 'But nobody else will.'

The giant laughed, like His counterpart in the sweet-corn commercials, except that He wasn't green or notice-ably jolly. 'I like it,' he said. 'The journalist thinks that it doesn't matter if she believes something; unless she can make someone else believe it, it can't be true.'

'I didn't say that,' Linda replied irritably. Remarkable, the others thought, she isn't a bit afraid or overawed. 'What I said was, it's no use. Doesn't matter a toss if it's true or not. What good is something only I believe in?'

'This is wonderful,' the giant said. 'And I suppose that if she can make other people believe in something, whether it's true or not, is equally unimportant. This one's been wasting my time. That's two of them.' He sighed, and His breath made ripples in the air that broke up vision. 'Is that damned inspector still hanging around? We're going to be in trouble at this rate.'

Okeewana shrugged. 'Can't be helped,' she said. 'And I think the other two are going to be all right.'

'I'll come to them in a moment,' the giant replied.

'Don't confuse me, for God's sake, or I'll miss something. Let's deal with the lawyer and the journalist first.
Ready?'

Okeewana nodded and produced notepad and pencil.
'Shoot,' she said.

'Right.' The giant thought for a moment. 'The journalist is easy,' He said. 'Obviously she's a dangerous pest
and can't be allowed out again, but she'll be happy
enough here. Find her something she'll enjoy, clear up
the loose ends Flipside, put her on the staff. You can let
one of the others go in exchange.'

The girl nodded, and turned a page in the book. 'What
about the lawyer?' she said.

'His wish is granted,' the giant replied, 'and let it be a
lesson to him. All his life, ever since he was a kid, he
wanted to be the big lawyer, the guy who could make the
right seem wrong and the wrong seem right. But all the
time, while he was hacking and slashing his way, like
psychotic Jack scrambling up the beanstalk, there were
always these niggling feelings of guilt holding him back,
making him doubt whether it was all OK, whether he'd
be able to get away with it. Very good; his wish was that
those aggravating doubts should stop. Let it be.' The
giant paused, while the girl tapped some keys on a pocket
calculator. 'What's the result?'

Okeewana nodded. 'It's fine,' she said. 'Happy
ending.'

(She didn't say out loud what she saw; which was that
seventy-two days later Calvin Dieb squeezed his partner
Hernan Piranha out of the firm and almost immediately
afterwards landed three new corporate clients of such
staggering magnitude that even he was happy, for a while;
and that three years to the day after that, he died, at his
desk, of a massive coronary, aged forty-nine.)

'That's all right, then,' said the giant. 'Let's do the boot-faced girl next, shall we? Nice, easy job. She wanted to have men fall in love with her. Does she still want that?'

The girl looked at Janice, who made a peculiar noise. 'I guess not,' she said. 'Can she go?'

The giant nodded. 'From now on, she'll wake up every morning, look in the mirror and thank heaven she was born lucky.' He grinned. 'That just leaves the wetslap, yes?'

The girl nodded. Wesley was just about to ask Hey, what about him, when he realised—

'Difficult,' the giant said. 'After all, his wish was so peculiar. Do you think it's done him any good?'

'Hard to tell,' the girl replied. 'We've squeezed some of the godawfulness out of him, so I don't think he'd be too much of a nuisance if we let him go back. On the other hand . . .'

'Hey,' Wesley objected, but his voice was completely inaudible against the giant's soft tongue-click.

'I know,' the giant said. 'Yes, got it, I know what we'll do to him. All right, that about covers it for now. Any more?'

The girl shook her head. 'And next time there's going to be four at once,' she added, 'I'd appreciate a bit more notice, if that's no problem.'

'That's fair enough. Actually, you didn't do too badly, all things considered. What about that sonofabitch inspector, by the way?'

'Leave him to me,' the girl replied with a smile. 'Oh, and one last thing. You said I could lose one of the permanents now we've taken on the journalist. Any preferences?'

The giant shook his head. 'I'll leave that one to you,'

he said. 'You know about these things.'

'Fine. Actually,' she added with a wicked grin, 'that'll help me deal with the inspector. Ciao, then.'

'Whatever.' The giant waved vaguely, took out His monocle, breathed on it, polished it on His sleeve and walked through it, leaving only a few concentric circles of ripples behind, and a duck sitting on water.

The girl put away her notepad and stood up. Wesley, Calvin, Janice and Linda weren't there any more; even their reflections were almost completely faded off the face of the lake. 'OK, guys,' she said, 'show's over.'

'Good,' Talks to Squirrels replied. 'That was a hard day's work. Can't remember the last time I got killed so many times in one day.'

'You did good, Talks,' the girl replied. 'You all did,' she added, with a big smile. 'You too, Prince. You really had 'em going with that bomb stuff.'

Prince Charming bowed. 'My pleasure,' he replied. 'They're all on their way now, then?'

'At last.' The girl stood up, shook herself like a wet dog and became an otter. 'And before you ask . . .'

'Yes?'

'I haven't decided yet who gets to go home,' the otter said. 'But don't give me a hard time, OK? I'm thinking about it.'

She yawned and stretched; and as her arms rose above her head they became wings, and the dove flew away towards the mountains, which were back where they belonged and trying to get some sleep.

Linda emerged from the water like a bobbing cork, and felt for the bottom with her feet. The mud was only just deep enough to pull off one of her shoes. She stuck her arm in the water, grubbed around in the ooze until she struck footwear, pulled it out with an effort and squelched to shore.

She was sitting beside the road, wringing out her socks and wondering how long it took to get pneumonia, when a car drew up beside her. The window whirred down and a head poked through. On top of it was a round, broad-brimmed hat. From the brim dangled little bits of cotton. From the little bits of cotton hung corks.

'G'day, love,' said a voice from under the hat, 'but am I right for the submarine base?'

Linda froze, one half-wrung sock in her hand. She decided to adopt an experimental attitude towards the truth.

'Yup,' she said.

'Thank Gawd for that,' replied the funny hat. 'I was sure this was the right road, but Rocco here keeps insisting we should have hung a left at the secret nuclear testing site.'

'All right, Bruce, you made-a your point,' said the man in the passenger seat, who was wearing a scarlet dressing-gown, a rosary, one of those Lambretta hats, red gloves and a ring the size of a walnut. 'Hey, you seen a couple of cement lorries pass this way?'

Linda held her breath. 'You mean,' she said, as casually as she could manage, 'the lorries fetching the cement they use to make the concrete blocks they conceal the unauthorised arms shipments in?'

'That'll be right,' the funny hat confirmed.

'They went, um, that way,' Linda said, pointing at random. 'About a quarter of an hour ago.'

'Huh!' The passenger snorted derisively. 'Late as usual. I told the President, "Boss," I said, "you no use that firm, not reliable. My brother-in-law, he very reliable, do you special deal." The President, he no listen.

Pfui!' the passenger added. 'Come on, Bruce, time we go. Ciao.'

As the car drove off, Linda counted up to ten and pinched herself. Shit, she thought, if only I'd got that on tape . . .

Then she noticed the faint whirring noise.

She ripped back the zipper on her haversack. There, nestling among the socks and the underwear, was her pocket dictating machine. It was running, and on Record. Something must have jarred it – maybe the bump when she fell in the lake – and it had been recording away all this time . . .

She wound the tape back, and forwarded, and rewound, and backwards and forwards until she heard it. 'G'day, miss, but am I right for the submarine base?'

Reverently, she closed her eyes. There was, after all, a providence that looks after newshounds; one that shapes our ends, rough-hew them how we will. She started to grin –

And looked down at the lake, and saw the submarine.

A few moments later, she was scrambling back down the hillside. By the time she reached the shores of the lake it was fully emerged; and there, standing on the conning tower, were four women. They were all indescribably beautiful, in an otherworldly sort of way, and they wore robes of white samite; which turned out not to be a sort of cheesecloth, as Linda had always assumed.

'Hail,' they said in chorus.

'Sorry?'

'Hail,' they repeated. 'Are you Linda Lachuk?'

Linda nodded. 'Yes,' she said.

'Linda Lachuk the *journalist*?'

She nodded again. 'That's me,' she said, not without a certain pride.

'Then you must come with us.'

'I beg your—?'

'To Avalon,' the fair ladies said, 'which lies in the Blessed Realms beyond the sundering seas. To cover the story of a lifetime,' they added.

'Huh?'

'The truth,' said the four ladies, as the wind billowed their sleeves like sails. 'The truth about the Kennedy assassination. Come with us, and we shall show you.'

Linda paused, still holding one wet sock. 'Just a minute,' she said. 'Is this some sort of a wind-up, because . . . ?'

The ladies frowned, all at the same time. 'Certainly not,' they said. 'We thought you wanted to know the truth about that fateful day in Dallas, Texas, is all. But if you're too busy . . .'

'No!' Linda moved to spring forward and stubbed her toe on a rock. She didn't feel anything. 'Wait, please. Tell me, what did . . . ?'

'Ah!' The ladies smiled enigmatically. 'You always thought, didn't you, that Kennedy was *shot*, that fateful day outside the Texas Book Repository.'

Linda nodded; and as she did so, she thought, *But he wasn't, was he? How could I have been so blind?*

'Whereas in fact,' the ladies said, 'what actually happened was that, using the staged assassination attempt as a diversion, we caught up JFK in a cloud of fire and carried him, still living, into Avalon, where he lives yet, along with King Arthur and Sir Francis Drake and Elvis Presley and Princess Di and all the rest of 'em. But we expect you'd already half guessed. Now hadn't you?'

Linda couldn't help herself. She nodded. 'There were some strong indications,' she murmured, 'if you knew what to look for.'

'Of course,' said the ladies, nodding sagely. 'And we

guess you know he'll stay in Avalon, timeless and unchanging, until such time as the peace of the Earth is once again balanced on the razor's edge; whereupon he will come again into the world of men, riding in his manifest glory on the wings of the storm, and . . .'

'Yes?' Linda whispered.

'Start World War Three,' said the ladies. 'Come, time is short and we have far to go. How are you off for video-tape, by the way? We have plenty, should you require it.'

'Thanks,' Linda said.

'Batteries?'

'What? Hell, I knew I'd forgotten—'

'We have many batteries,' said the ladies. 'Come. Your destiny awaits you. Only you can cover the story.'

'Yes,' Linda breathed, as if in a dream. 'Only me . . .'

'The public has a right to know. Come! Away! Away!'

And so Linda Lachuk, flower of all earthly journalism, took submarine for the fair isle of Avalon, that lies beyond the threshold of the dawn; and there she dwells yet, ageless and untiring, along with all the other anti-social pests they keep locked up there.

And all the headlines sounded for her on the other side.

As Calvin Dieb squelched his way out of the lake, his feet making wet-kiss noises at every step as the mud tried to steal his thousand-dollar gumboots, he noticed something small and shiny hanging on a bramble-branch that trailed down into the water. His car keys.

Hell, he muttered to himself, just as well I didn't lose them or I'd have been in real trouble.

After a short but knackering climb back up the hill he unlocked his car, which shrieked its alarm at him in friendly welcome, sat down heavily in the driver's seat and pressed the message button of his telephone.

– *Hello, Mr Dieb, this is Cindi from the office. Your ex-wife called, can you call her back? She sounded – um, well, strange. Kinda, I don't know how to put this, friendly. She didn't yell. Well, not much. To start with. 'Bye, now.*

– *Hi, kid, this is Hernan. When can I have that goddamn Pedretti Brothers file back, and Dan Vleek says lunch Thursday is OK. Who the hell is Dan Vleek, and when he says lunch, does he mean lunch, or just lunch? Call back immediately. Ciao.*

– *Helloewe, Mister Deeb, this here is from Norway Olaf Bjornssen calling, me you not are knowing, a line of shipping I ern, you I am anxious to instruct a maritime insurance claim for to be pursuing. My nermber is . . .*

– *Hello, Calvin, this is Leonard. Been a long time, hasn't it? Maybe we could have lunch some day when you're free, there's a few things I'd like to talk over. Be seeing you.*

– *Hi, son, this is your dad here. I love you, son. I guess that's all. See you sometime, maybe. 'Bye.*

The last message gave Calvin quite a start, since his father had been dead these five years. In the end he figured it must be an old tape, not thoroughly wiped. He wiped it. Then he called Frank Lustmord.

'Frank? Hi, pal. Look, this Lake Chicopee thing. I'm at the lake now, and . . . You bet, guy, no substitute for seeing with your own eyes. And it's just as well I did, Frank, 'cos believe me, you got a serious problem here. Serious problem. Huh? Well, Frank, it's otters. Yeah, otters are a serious problem. Yes, Frank, like in serious *environmental* problem. Well yes, I guess you could, if you wanted to get blasted into mush by every TV station and newspaper from here to Seattle. You wouldn't be able to *give* the goddamn plots away free with gasoline, Frank, those green freaks'd have you looking like Hitler's elder brother, the one the family was too ashamed to talk about . . . Well, think about it, Frank, it's better you know these things *before* you spend twenty-seven million dollars . . . Yeah, well, you know, it's what we're here for, buddy. That's why you pay me, to think of these things. No, that's fine. That's great, Frank. What, *all* your corporate business? Why yes, sure, I'd be only too happy – sure thing, pal. See you around. Yeah, bye.'

Calvin put down the phone with a dazed grin smeared all over his face like a comedian's custard pie. He had no idea what had possessed him to tell Frank Lustmord that the otters were going to be a problem; because they *weren't*, goddamnit, he'd checked on that very point. But whatever the reason, it had worked, and now he had the Lustmord Corporation's business tied up and in the bag. It was as if he'd taken a shotgun to shoot his own foot off, missed and blown a hole in the ground that exposed a seam of gold-bearing quartz.

Or was it . . . ? Nah. Been out in the sun too long without a hat. There is no patron god of lawyers, and if there was one He'd be so expensive that not even lawyers could afford to go to Him. There's Kali Ma, of course, and the Father of Lies and Mercury, god of thieves; but they're retained occasionally on a sort of consultancy basis, not to be construed as implying any ongoing contractual relationship. The lawyer stands alone in the cosmos, or at least he clings to its back, inserts his proboscis and sucks. If he, Calvin Dieb, had managed to ensnare the Lustmord corporation, it was through his own unaided efforts, or the random workings of Luck, or because Frank Lustmord had offended his own personal corps of gods badly enough to let himself in for a level of punishment on which locusts, boils and frogs are too cissy even to be considered.

He shrugged, switched on the engine and engaged drive. Just before he pulled away, however, he caught sight of someone on the road ahead of him, waving. Normally, he'd have driven straight on past; but hell, it was his day for acting out of character. He put the car in neutral and wound down the window.

'What's the matter?' he asked.

'Are you Calvin Dieb?' the stranger asked. A strange stranger, by all appearances; wearing a sort of black dufflecoat thing with the hood up, and carrying a long bundle wrapped up in black cloth that might have been fishing-rods but probably wasn't.

'That depends,' Calvin replied. 'Who wants to know?'

'My card.' The stranger thrust a rectangle of black and red pasteboard through the window.

'Pleased to meet you, M—' Calvin broke off as he read the one word on the card. He looked at it again, and then back at the stranger, or as much of the stranger as he could see past the dufflecoat hood. 'Hi,' he croaked.

'I've been looking for you all over,' the stranger said. 'Your office said you might be here, so I came over.'

'Ah,' said Calvin, making a mental note to sack everybody when – if – he got back. 'Great,' he added. 'You found me.'

'Yup.' The stranger nodded. 'And in case you don't believe what it says on that card,' he added, throwing back the hood, 'these might go some way to confirming it. Yes?'

Calvin nodded. 'Say,' he asked, curious in spite of everything, 'don't mind my asking, but don't those things rip up the pillows when you sleep?'

'They would, if I ever did,' the stranger replied, combing a stray lock of jet-black hair back into place behind the right-hand horn. 'But I don't. Kinda goes with the territory.'

'That figures,' Calvin muttered. 'And what about the, uh, feet? What do you do about them?'

'Nothing. That's the joy of hooves, they don't wear out. Look, why I wanted to see you was, for some time now I've been thinking it was time I got myself a really good lawyer.'

Calvin frowned. 'I thought you got 'em all,' he replied. 'Eventually, I mean.'

'A good *living* lawyer,' Satan replied. 'Someone with expertise in contract work particularly.'

'Contract?'

'Sales and purchases.' Satan grinned disconcertingly. 'I need someone who can make an agreement that's *completely* watertight. For which,' he added, 'I'm prepared to pay top dollar. Interested?'

Calvin couldn't speak, but he could nod. He nodded.

'The package I had in mind,' Satan continued, 'was basically a three-year fixed term. During that time, of course, you can have anything you want.'

'Anything?'

'Anything. Your dearest wish. Your heart's desire. You name it, you can have it.'

'For three years?'

'Three years.'

'And after three years?' Calvin said, feeling as he did so that this was rather like shoving a mirror on a stick into a gift horse's mouth and asking it to say 'Aaah'. 'And after that?'

Satan shrugged. 'Then,' he said, 'we might consider a more permanent arrangement. What do you say?'

Calvin opened his mouth.

There's a word in the English language that could

have been specially custom-coined to encapsulate Calvin's response. It's short, only three letters; it begins with Y and ends with S, and there's an E in it somewhere.

'Yes,' Calvin said.

Janice DeWeese scrambled out of the shallow water at the lake's edge, cursed her own clumsiness, sat down and took off her boots. By the look of it, there was enough water in her left boot alone to irrigate the Nevada desert. Marvellous, she thought; just wonderful. I've got a nine-hour hike to look forward to, in wet boots. This is probably going to turn out to be my best holiday ever.

She was emptying an equivalent quantity of water out of her right boot, and wondering how come the lake seemed to be as full as ever when so much of its contents had found its way into her footwear, when she became aware that someone was watching her.

Maybe under other circumstances she'd have been intimidated; not, however, under these. The prospect of a twenty-two-mile squelch in sopping wet clothes had made her quite possibly the most dangerous life-form in Iowa.

'Creep,' she called out imperiously. 'Yoo-hoo, creep, come on out of there, where I can throttle you. I'm gonna count to three and—'

'All right, all right.' The undergrowth to her right rustled a little. 'There's no need to get all snotty about it.'

The vegetation parted, and a very small anthropoid shape under an enormous hat waddled towards her. It looked like a mushroom; at least, it looked like the sort of weird mushroom you might see after eating too many weird mushrooms. In any event, it looked about as threatening as a bottle of ketchup, and not much bigger.

'Fine,' Janice said, with a yawn. 'Now piss off, before I cut you up and fry you.'

The rim of the hat tilted upwards, giving Janice a dim, overshadowed glimpse of a pointed nose-tip and two shining pink eyes. 'Very droll,' it said. 'All I need after the day I've had is amateur humour. I don't think I'll even bother with you now.'

The hat rotated through a hundred and eighty degrees and was about to disappear back into the bushes when Janice snapped, 'Hoy!' in a tone of voice that'd have got her slung out of any army training camp for being too brusque. The hat stopped and swivelled back, like the turret of a floppy felt tank.

'Well?' it said.

'Just a minute, you,' Janice growled, stooping down to try and see under the brim. 'Just why were you looking at me, anyway?'

'Market research,' the hat replied.

'Market what?'

'Research. I thought you might be interested in buying something, that's all. But I can see I'm wasting my time.'

'How can you see anything, underneath that thing?'

'Ah,' the hat sighed, 'humour again. What is it with you people, anyway? With you it's nothing but humour, humour, humour all the damn time.'

'Sell me what?'

'Oh, you wouldn't be—'

'Sell me what, goddamnit?'

The hat wobbled, as if shrugging its brim. 'Oh, just some old stuff. Gold, diamonds, that sort of thing. Nothing that's any use for—'

'What did you say?'

This time the brim lifted at the front, until the long, droopy feather stuck in its band dipped in the mud. 'Gold,' it said. 'A dollar fifty a kilo. Diamonds. Ten dollars a kilo. Platinum. Ninety-five cents a kilo, or buy ten kilos of diamonds, get a kilo of platinum absolutely free. Can I go now, please?'

For a split second, Janice gawped, her mouth opening and closing again like a goldfish who's just been told it's won the Lottery. Then a bored expression took possession of her face and changed all the locks. 'Get outa here,' she said. 'Listen, shortass, I may be stupid but I'm not that stupid. An all-powerful supreme being couldn't create anybody *that* stupid, even if you gave him a pattern to work from. Go on, get lost.'

The hat bristled; that is, the pile of its felt seemed to stand on end. 'Are you calling me a liar?' it demanded. 'Well? Are you?'

'Yup.'

'Well, you're wrong, see? Because this is the genuine stuff. You want to see it?'

'No.'

'Tough, 'cos you're going to.' A tiny hand appeared from under the hat, clutching a fair-sized sports bag in defiance of all the laws of physics. 'Go on, open it.'

Janice shrugged, and pulled back the zip—

'Oh,' she said.

How she knew it was all good stuff, the genuine article, ninety-nine-point nine per cent pure, she didn't actually know; but she did. The gold had that dull shine that no brass can ever quite match. The diamonds had that cold, blue sparkle that glass has never quite got the hang of. As for the white stuff, she didn't actually know what platinum looked like but she was prepared to bet this was platinum. There was enough wealth in the bag to elect four presidents, assuming you could find anybody idiotic enough to want to do such a thing.

'Satisfied?' asked the hat, coldly. 'Right, then. Do the zip up and give it back, and I can be on my way.'

Janice shook her head. 'No way,' she said. 'Sorry, pal, but this lot goes with me. How much did you say you wanted for it?'

'The whole lot?'

'Yeah,' Janice said, her voice slightly wobbly, 'why not? The whole lot.'

'Well.' The front of the brim oscillated as the life-form under it made some calculations. 'I couldn't take less than forty dollars,' it said. 'For that, I'd throw in the bag as well.'

'Forty dollars.'

'OK, thirty-five. Damnit, the diamonds alone are worth that.'

'Deal.'

'All right, if you insist, thirty-two fifty. Jesus, but you know how to – what did you just say?'

'I said Deal,' said Janice.

'Cash?'

'Sure.'

'I'd need at least ten per cent up front, and the rest by—'

'Here,' Janice pulled out three tens and a five from her top pocket and stuffed them under the hatband. 'Paid in full.'

'Really?'

'Really.'

'Wow.' The hand reappeared, grabbed the notes and pulled them in under the brim. 'Thanks. Hey, that's really – thanks.'

'Don't mention it,' Janice replied, gripping the bag firmly in both hands. 'Can I ask you a question, mister?'

'Sure thing. Shoot.'

'You won't take this the wrong way?'

'Guaranteed.'

'Then how come,' Janice asked, as calmly and rationally as she could, 'you've just sold me millions of bucks' worth of diamonds and stuff for thirty-five dollars? Not,' she added quickly, 'that I'm complaining. And you can't have it back, either.'

The hat rotated backwards and forwards through a hundred and eighty degrees. 'Don't want it back, lady. Thirty-five dollars in hard currency may not be all that much to you, but where I come from . . . Hell, you could buy where I come from for thirty-five dollars in US Treasury bills. In fact,' it added, after a moment's reflection, 'I might just do that.'

'Where's that, then?'

'In there.' The hat nodded towards the lake. 'And before you ask how can I live in a lake, please don't. I have this feeling that a serious credibility shortfall at this juncture might endanger our future trading relationship.'

'How can you live in a lake?'

'How can you live outside of one?'

Janice wrinkled her nose. 'You're a fish? Actually, I've seen those jellyfish, the ones with the big—'

'I am not a fish,' replied the hat austerely. 'If you must know, my name is Captain Hat, of the Lake Chicopee Free Traders Association. And where I live,' he added, 'we use that sparkly stuff for pebble-dashing houses.'

'Diamonds?'

'Sure. Whereas thirty-five dollars American—'

'I see,' Janice said, inaccurately. 'You've got a lot of, ah, unexploited mineral resources, then?'

'You could say that. It's props.'

'Props?'

'From the scenarios.' The hat tilted a few degrees. 'You know, the scenarios. The little shows they put on for the customers.'

'Customers?' Janice raised an eyebrow. 'You mean, this lake's some kind of holiday resort? Like a summer camp or something?'

'You could say that,' the hat replied. 'Better still, call it a theme park. But of course you . . . No, wait, of course, you don't remember a thing, do you?'

'Remember what?'

'About what happened to you, when you were in the lake.'

Janice rubbed her chin. 'Let's see,' she said. 'I fell in, I got wet, I splashed about a bit and then I got out again. Can't say there's any significant gaps in that.'

Although Janice couldn't see it, because of the brim of the hat, she could sense that somewhere in the shadows there was a big grin, generated at her expense. 'Right. Now then. Did your entire life flash in front of your eyes, all in one split second? Probably happened in the moment between your head going under the water and coming back up again.'

'No, I don't—' Janice paused. 'Hey, now you mention it, maybe it did. Or at least there was *something*. More like a dream, I guess. I can't remember anything about it, but . . .'

The hat repeated its nodding manoeuvre. 'That's it, then. I don't suppose you're going to believe this, but I'll tell you anyway. During that very short time, you went through this series of really weird adventures, courtesy of the ole Indian spirit that haunts the lake. She's called Okinawa, something like that.'

'Okinawa's a city in Japan.'

'Okeewana, then. Whatever. The way it works is,' the hat continued, 'if you fall in the lake and make a wish, the wish comes true. Doesn't have to be a *conscious* wish, either. It works just as well if there's something you're secretly daydreaming about, like in your subconscious mind. That can be very hairy, believe me. You had a pretty strange time of it yourself, come to that. I'd tell you about it, but you don't want to know.'

'Yeah?' Janice yawned. 'You're right, I don't. But what's all this about props and scenarios? If this is some roundabout way of telling me this stuff's all stolen—'

The hat quivered a little. 'Of course it's *stolen*,' it said. 'Who the hell do you think I am, Montezuma's rich brother-in-law? The scenarios are what happen on the other side of the lake.'

Janice turned her head towards the tall, round hill with trees on it that stood on the other side of the water. 'What, you mean over by that clump of fir trees? I can't see—'

'On the flipside,' the hat said patiently. 'The obverse.' A finger emerged from under the brim and pointed at the middle of the water. 'Under that.'

'Under the lake?'

'Not under,' said the hat, exasperated. 'On the other side. Come on, it's not a difficult concept, surely. Anyhow, when they do these scenarios, sometimes they get careless with the props, leave them lying about and all, and my boys and me – well, we help keep the place tidy. We have very strong views about ecology and stuff.'

'Tidy as in free of waste gold?'

The hat nodded. 'You bet. Gold's a good example; I mean, it's one hundred per cent non biodegradable, gold. Leave damn great chunks of gold lying around the place, it's there for ever.'

'And diamonds?'

'Diamonds are forever, too. Well-known fact. So we, er, recycle them.'

'I see.' Janice looked at the hat, and then down at the

sports bag. On the one hand, she knew all about stealing and how wrong it was; but on the other hand, stealing from a fiction of the hallucinating imagination probably wasn't nearly so bad. On a par, perhaps, with murdering the imaginary friend you had when you were six. 'Well,' she said, 'you may be telling the truth or you may just have escaped from the home for deranged millinery, but to be honest with you, I don't give a damn. I think I'll go home now.'

'Good idea,' said the hat. 'I think I'll do the same. Call me superstitious if you like, but this place gives me the creeps.'

'This hillside?'

'This side of the lake. So long, Janice DeWeese.'

'Hey, how do you know my—?'

The hat started to scuttle, like some experimental model of soft-shell crab that got shelved when the funding ran out. 'I know all about you,' it said. 'Sister, what I don't know about you ain't worth knowing. You and those priests! Wow!'

'Hey!' Janice looked again, and realised that she was shouting at an empty landscape. She noticed something else, too.

'Neat,' she said.

It was a rainbow; a huge, scintillating, warm, humming rainbow, and one end of it was coming out of the sports bag. The other end, needless to say, was in the middle of the lake, and its reflection looked just like a big, friendly grin. It vanished as abruptly as it had appeared, and then it began to rain.

Janice looked down at the sports bag as she pulled her collar round her ears. All that gold, all those diamonds; she checked, and they were still there. With that much money, you could buy one hell of a lot of cosmetic surgery. Alternatively, with that much money you wouldn't need to, because with that much money you'd automatically become irresistibly attractive no matter what the hell you looked like; and the beauty that comes with obscene wealth never fades or tarnishes, and you can eat whatever you like, and there's no need to sit around for hours with grey slime on your face and slices of cucumber over your eyes. From now on for the rest of her life, Janice realised, she need never be alone or unadored again.

Nice thought . . .

Fairly nice thought . . .

Something to think about . . .

CHAPTER FIFTEEN

'So,' demanded Talks To Squirrels, 'who's it going to be?'

Lake Chicopee; the round blue centre of the round blue Earth. From the hilltop with the trees it looked like a small Earth, blue and green, white and brown patches where the trees and clouds and mountains were reflected in it. From higher still, on the other side of the sky, the big Earth looks very much the same; another world, a place to go away from and come back to, but made separate by an elemental barrier that only the mind can cross.

'I've decided,' Okeewana said, looking closely at her shoes.

'Yeah, right,' said the Chief Goblin impatiently. 'So share. Who is it?'

An otter waddled down the slope and slid into the water, leaving behind it a trail of bubbles, like a submarine. Like submarines and (to a certain extent) ducks, otters can make themselves at home on either side of the

334

water, at least for a while, just as squirrels divide their time between the ground and the treetops. Whether they're different submarines, otters, ducks and squirrels when they're on the other side, nobody really knows. Only Man, the measure of all things, knows when he's truly in his element.

'I just want you to know,' the girl continued, 'I've given this a lot of thought. And my decision's final, so there's no point making a fuss.'

'OK, OK,' sighed a Viking. 'Understanding you all we are. The person name, so kind if you will be.'

The girl stooped, picked up a stone and threw it as far as she could. It hit the water with a tremendous splash.

'Me,' she said.

Everybody spoke at once; it was, in fact, what the writers of communiqués call a free and frank exchange of views, to the point of almost total unintelligibility. The gist of it, however, wasn't hard to grasp.

'You want to know why?' the girl said quietly.

Immediately, the babbling stopped.

'No,' said Mummy Bear.

'Tough,' the girl replied, 'because I'm gonna tell you anyway. I'm sick to the teeth of this place, is why. And I'm sick to the teeth of this lousy job, and I've had it up to here with you. I want to travel. I want to see the world. I want to *live* a little.'

'I tried that once,' said the doctor. 'Overrated. A bit like Japanese food.'

The girl shrugged. 'Anyhow,' she said, 'that's it, and it's final. I've got a job to go to, all lined up, even a body to do it in, so . . .'

'A body?' demanded the Goblin, his tongue involuntarily flicking round his lips, like the mortuary cat when they're scrubbing up for an autopsy. 'Lucky you.'

'Where'd you get that from?' asked Talks to Squirrels. 'You mean that crazy journalist bitch?'

The girl smiled. 'Not her,' she said. 'The Inspector. Captain Hat stole him for me, and now I'm going to be him. My replacement starts tomorrow, so I suggest you do a stocktake and get the place tidied up.'

'Replacement,' the doctor echoed. 'Hey, just a . . .'

But before he could say anything else, the girl jumped up, shook herself and leaped into the air. Her wings opened, and with a joyful quack she shot up above the trees, circled the lake three times and planed down, at full speed, right into the middle of the water, like a torpedo. Ripples welled out of the gash she made in the reflected sky, and faded away.

'It's a ruddy fix,' growled Prince Charming, his aristocratic drawl slipping. 'They ain't 'eard the last of this, not by a long way. I got a good mind to tell the giant.'

'Cut it out, will you?' sighed Talks To Squirrels. 'I reckon it's only fair, at that. I mean, she's been here ever since the lake was a boggy patch on a flat plain. If she's had enough, she's had enough. Let's go eat.'

He stood up, bent his bow, shot one arrow into the water at the point where Okeewana had dived in, three more into Daddy Bear and another two into Prince Charming's ear, and trudged away down the hill.

The rest of the redcoats watched him go in silence. Something he'd said had woken an old, submerged memory in all of them. They looked at each other.

'Eat?' said the Prince.

'That's food,' explained Baby Bear. 'We have food in our act, only it's not real, only pretend. Wax fruit and plaster bread and stuff.'

'Real food,' murmured one of the Russians.

'Smorgasbord,' whispered a Viking.

'Honey sandwiches,' breathed Daddy Bear.

'Children,' sighed the Chief Goblin. 'With sage and parsley and just a soupçon of turmeric.'

'I'd be quite happy with ham and eggs,' said the doctor, staring wistfully at the lake. 'And a couple of waffles with maple syrup, naturally.'

'And coffee,' the Prince interrupted. 'Dear God, real coffee. Made with genuine atoms and molecules, not like that 'orrible imaginary stuff you get in the canteen.'

The goblin nodded. 'What I wouldn't give,' he said, 'for a cup of real Blue Mountain coffee, with cream and lots of brown sugar; you know, the crunchy stuff that looks like bits of ground-up whisky bottle.'

'Quite,' agreed the Prince, looking at him sideways. 'My dearest wish, you could say.'

The doctor lifted his head, like a warhorse at the sound of the trumpet. 'Your heart's desire, even?'

'You're way ahead of me, Doc, I can see that.' The Prince grinned. 'Well, why not? In fact, we should get a staff discount or something.'

'Let's do it.'

'Yeah.'

The rest of the company looked at them. 'What are you two gibbering about?' Mummy Bear demanded. 'How do you mean, staff rates?'

'He means,' Daddy Bear said, his face split by a grin like a scale model of the Grand Canyon, 'staff rates. Wait up, you guys, I'm coming too.'

As the three of them began to run down the hill, straight towards the lake, there was a general tumbling of pennies from a great height. 'Oh, I *see*,' muttered Murdoch the footman. 'Heart's desire, right.' He shrugged. 'It might work, at that.'

'What might—?' Mummy Bear began to ask; then she

understood too, and a moment later she was running after them, folding her pinny as she ran. By the time she reached the water's edge, the doctor and the Prince had already jumped in. She wasn't all that far behind; and, with a loud rebel yell and a cry of: 'Madeira cake!' she closed her eyes, crossed her claws and jumped.

Wesley climbed out of the water and looked around.

'Oh,' he said.

Life can be very cruel, but it's scarcely if ever unusual; which is why it's legal as a form of punishment in the USA. The term 'life sentence', seen in that light, becomes rather frightening.

'Oh well,' Wesley said, and he waded ashore. Might have known, he muttered to himself. Must have been soft in the head, coming all this way and jumping in a lake, and really and truly expecting that the wish would come true. If he'd whispered, 'Double pneumonia,' under his breath as he jumped, he might just conceivably not have been disappointed. But he hadn't; so he was.

He looked round again, and then up at the sun, though he didn't actually know how to use it as an aid to navigating his way back to Brierley Hill. All this way, and for nothing. At times, life can be very, very usual.

Just as he'd made up his mind to try north, he heard a splashing noise coming from behind him and looked round, in time to see –

- A man in bedraggled ermine robes, eating a hamburger –
- A man in a white hospital coat with a stethoscope round his neck, eating a club sandwich –
- Three bears, eating muffins –
- Sundry Cherokee braves, in warpaint and clutching feathered spears, on which were impaled

    appetising-looking bits of chicken tikka –
– Sundry Vikings, in armour and winged helmets,
    gnawing on whole chickens –
– Sundry Goblins, gnawing on something that looked
    sort of vaguely familiar –
– and some others he couldn't even begin to identify,
all walking up out of the lake, grinning, laughing and
talking with their mouths full. As soon as they saw Wesley
they stopped dead in their tracks and saluted. One of
them, apparently a Viking warrior with a chicken leg
poking out through his beard, giggled.

'Er, hello,' Wesley said, out of a combination of nerves,
embarrassment and force of habit. 'Can you tell me the
way to Oskaloosa, please?'

None of the strange-looking people spoke. A goblin
shook his head. A man in what Wesley guessed was a
butler's outfit started peeling a banana.

'Oskaloosa,' Wesley repeated, wishing very much that
he'd kept his mouth shut and kept on going. 'Do I go
back up to the main road and bear east, or . . . ?'

'You can't,' mumbled a bear through a mouthful of
honey. 'Not allowed. Thought you'd have known that,
Chief.'

Wesley began to get *that* feeling: the unmistakable
one that starts in your throat and dribbles down like
splodged-on gloss paint until it fills you right up. Rabbits
and hedgehogs get it when they look up from the patch of
hard, black, grassless ground they've just shuffled on to
and see two very bright white lights coming straight at
them.

''Scuse me?' he croaked.

'Are you going to do roll-call, then?' asked the man in
the white coat. 'Because I've got a workshop full of
Vikings with their heads in pieces, and once you lose one

of those little eyelid return springs, you've got to tear the place apart to find it.'

'Roll-call,' Wesley parrotted. 'Sorry, I don't quite—'

The man in the wet ermine tutted. 'Sorry, Chief, we forgot. The routine is, roll-call followed by kit inspection followed by the day's assignments and 'anding out the luncheon vouchers, followed by sick parade and ten minutes when we can see you if there's anything we want to talk about, but we never do. You 'ave got the register, 'aven't you?'

'Register.' Wesley's mind filled with images of school (he always stood at the back and could never see a thing over the heads of the boys in front; he only knew what the Headmaster looked like because he'd seen a picture of him in a giveaway newspaper, and even then it was only a hazy mental image, because the vinegar had made the paper all transparent). 'Look, I'm not a hundred per cent sure I know what you mean. Are you sure it's me you—?'

'Wesley Higgins,' said a goblin, chewing a fingernail, not his own. 'You're the new manager, right?'

'Uh?'

The goblin glanced back at the rest of the crowd. 'She didn't tell him,' it hissed. 'Goddamn sneaky daughter-ofabitch didn't tell him. That's *bad*.'

'Tell me *what*?'

'Typical,' sniffed Skellidge the footman. 'Suppose she didn't want to give him the chance to refuse.'

'You can see her point,' whispered a bear. 'I mean, I'd have refused. Wouldn't you?'

'Refused what?'

'That the point is not. The point is after being to have told him common courtesy. Administrative smoothly the likewise.'

''Scuse me,' Wesley said; and he said it in a voice that

faintly surprised him. 'Please tell me if I've got this wrong, but am I meant to be, you know, in charge?'

The strange-looking people nodded in unison, like a Hollywood script conference. 'You're the new manager,' the ermined bloke said. 'Congratulations and all that. Now, while I'm talking to you, do you possibly think I could put in for a new robe? Only water does tend to play 'avoc with me trimmings, I'll never get it quite right ever again.'

The doctor frowned. 'If he's having a new robe, then I really ought to get that impact screwdriver I put in for last month. I mean, it is actually a tool of my trade, and the time I waste having to drill out neck axis pins that've rusted in solid. I mean, fair's fair—'

'Yeah, but what about my new wrist?' whined a goblin. 'I've been waiting weeks, and if he's getting a screw-driver—'

''Scuse me—'

'Or,' the goblin went on, suddenly smiling, 'if it's easier, I could go on the sick until the delivery arrives. I expect it'd make the paperwork easier, too.'

'A new battleaxe four months I waiting have been. Fair fair's, as he the man said.'

'Quiet!' Once again, Wesley's voice surprised him, and he found himself automatically standing up straight and trying to shove an imaginary conker through where he remembered the hole in the lining of his jacket used to be. 'Now then,' the voice that was coming out of Wesley went on, 'let's get this straight, shall we? I'm supposed to be your new boss, right?'

'You got it, Chief.'

'So it would seem,' Wesley said irritably. 'Apparently from a great height, too. Would this be anything to do with me falling in the lake?'

'You go— I mean, yes, Chief. Your heart's desire.'

'Was it?' Wesley demanded, shocked. 'Can't have been. And anyway, it didn't work.' He looked up at the row of attentive, profoundly weird faces and mentally revised the last statement. 'I assume it didn't work. Did it work?'

'You bet, Chief.'

'And I wished to be in charge of you lot, did I? Seriously.'

The bear shrugged. 'You must have done,' he said.

'He did,' Skellidge broke in. 'I seem to remember it was something vague about wishing he lived in a magical fairy-tale land and how he wished he could be a noble or a baron or some such. According to the old saying, there's one thousand, four hundred and forty just like him born every day, in which case God help us all.'

Wesley hesitated. Someone had dumped a whole load of gubbins in his windpipe, making it hard for him to breathe, and his vocal cords had been repossessed by the finance company. Apart from that, he felt just fine. And he understood. In a sense. Up to a point.

'So it did come true,' he said. 'Gosh.'

'Bit slow, isn't he?' whispered a goblin. 'Mind you, I'm not saying that's a bad thing in a boss. Probably the reverse.'

'Yes, but there's slow and there's half-witted,' replied the doctor. 'And when you think about it, who's going to get the blame when everything goes wrong? Give you three guesses.'

So it had come true, Wesley repeated to himself. Amazing; but there it was. And now, presumably, his whole life would change for ever and he'd be . . .

His whole life. For ever.

Um . . .

Maybe what he was thinking seeped through on to his face, because one of the bears stepped forward and gave him a friendly pat on the back. 'Look,' said the bear, 'I know what you're thinking. And you're right.'

'I am?' Wesley replied, once his head had stopped reverberating. 'But . . .'

'What you've got to do,' said the bear, 'is look on the bright side. Be positive. After all, it's not as if you're leaving anything particularly wonderful behind, is it?'

'True,' Wesley conceded, as his memory put together a quick montage of all the things that were nice about his daily routine back in Brierley Hill. It didn't take long.

'You see?' said the bear. 'Look at it this way. Whatever it turns out to be like running this place, it can't possibly be worse than what you're leaving behind, surely.'

Wesley frowned. 'Actually,' he said, 'it could. I might get killed, or horribly maimed, or I might get a hideous disease or even just toothache, which'd be bad enough without dentists or antibiotics. And what about food and somewhere to live and, er, toilet facilities, and a pension plan so I can make sensible provision for my old age? Or there could be wars and violence and stuff. Or mosquitoes, and I haven't got one of those net things you sleep under, so what'd happen if I got malaria? And I don't suppose there's central heating anywhere, and it's supposed to be very difficult to light a fire if you don't know how, and I haven't got any matches or anything, and what am I supposed to do about clothes, or are they provided? Or . . .'

'Boss,' sighed the bear, 'shut up. Just take it from me, will you? It's better here. For someone like you, with an untrammelled imagination that can never find rest in the mundane, everyday . . .' The bear stopped talking and sucked its lower lip. 'Mind you,' it said, 'you do have a point. Hadn't you considered that before you made the wish?'

'Well, no,' Wesley replied. 'I just sort of assumed, you know. That there'd be food and proper toilets and somewhere you could have a bath without fish nibbling at you.' He stared at the bear with frightened, unsettling eyes. 'I don't think I want my heart's desire, after all,' he whispered. 'Especially not if I've got to be in charge of anything. I've never been in charge of anything in my whole life before.'

'You'll manage,' the bear replied, with at least forty-five per cent sincerity. 'Just you wait and see. And besides,' it went on, looking away, 'you haven't got a choice. You've got to be in charge. Goes with the territory.'

'Ah,' Wesley said. 'I see.'

'Should've been more careful what you wished for, huh?'

'I suppose I should,' Wesley said. 'And I'm very grateful to you and everyone else, it's really nice of you to go to all this trouble. But—'

'No buts, Chief,' said the bear. 'And you can't just jump back in the lake and wish for it all to go back exactly the way it was. Which is odd, when you think about it,' it added. 'Inconsistent, really.'

'Yes.'

'Like Life, in fact; which, of course, this is. You going to do roll-call now, then?'

Wesley shrugged. Projected against the backs of his eyelids he could see exactly what it was going to be like from now on; his future life flashing before his eyes, in fact, which was a subtle variation on the old drowning routine. It was endless, and boring, and there wasn't even death to look forward to, let alone lunchtimes and weekends and evenings and two weeks holiday a year. And no money, either; not that there'd be anything to spend it on, except for the pitifully few black-market goodies Captain Hat might be able to come up with – a new pair of socks once every ten years, a half-empty tube of toothpaste, three peppermints at the end of a ragged paper roll.

'It's like this,' said the bear, compassionately. 'You only get out of the lake what you put into it to begin with. And what you put into it is always you. Which means you always get you out of it, ultimately.'

'Great,' Wesley said, bitterly but with resignation. 'You've no idea how cheered up that doesn't make me. All right, where's the register? S'pose I'd better get on with it.'

'That's the spirit,' said the bear. 'Wish fulfilment's a bitch and then you die. She always used to keep the register under that rock there.' The bear walked back to join the rest of the redcoats, who were dwelling lovingly on the last few crumbs of their food. 'Some of them find it helps to have a hobby,' it said. 'Talks To Squirrels shoots people, for instance. The Vikings play Monopoly every Tuesday fortnight. They made the set themselves out of stones and bits of tree bark. I expect if you ask them nicely they'll let you be the little racing car.'

To begin with, they tell you there's magic. Elves live in woods, there are witches under the stairs and trolls in the airing cupboard. Father Christmas brings you presents if you're good, and the horrible green slimy thing that lives in the toilet cistern will get you if you aren't. There's magic, and there's justice, and you know where you stand.

Later on, they tell you there's no magic; but there's

electricity and physics and computers and all sorts of machines for flying and killing and making you better, which do the same things as magic used to do, only cheaper and better and without the need for skilled labour. But there's no justice, there's not even any logic, and you know that if you stand there, chances are something's going to fall on you and make you go *splat*!

In the end you come to realise that there are still witches under the stairs and trolls in the airing cupboard, and the green slimy thing can take many forms and live in many places besides the cistern; and yes, jolly fat men do come down the chimney from time to time, but in reality they turn the place over and take your video and your CD player with them when they go. You do have the option of resisting, of fighting back with everything you've got; but don't let them catch you doing it, or you'll go to prison. Most of all, you come to realise that you've got nothing except what you stand up in, and that's somehow never enough.

Lake Chicopee exists all right; and the magic does work. The fact remains that the most anybody's ever got out of jumping into it is a bad cold.

The lake is quiet now. A few ducks chug up and down, steering with their feet. An otter ploughs a V-shaped wake through the reflected mountains. They have the sense not to be under the surface of the water, and to have no wishes whatsoever.

You only get out of it what you put into it, and what you put into it is never enough.